What the reviewers are saying ...

'Well-drawn, believable characters combined with a storyline to keep you turning the page'
Woman

'The latest instalment in the Shipyard saga is a pleasure to read. 4 Stars'
The Sun

'Our favourite author, Nancy Revell . . . Heart-warming, emotional and gripping as ever'
Take A Break

'A riveting read in more ways than one. Nancy Revell knows how to stir the passions and soothe the heart!'
Northern Echo

'The usual warmth from Revell, featuring lovable characters and heart-warming storylines'
MyWeekly

'Researched within an inch of its life; the novel is enjoyably entertaining. A perfect way to spend hours, wrapped up in the characters' lives'
Frost

'Nancy Revell has created a fantastic saga that could literally have fallen from the TV. As a reader you feel like you are right there watching all the action take place'
Chellsandbooks

'Heart-warming . . . powerful story telling from a great saga author.'
Choice

'Another superb read from Nancy Revell. Full of all the hope, humour and heart that have become her hallmarks'
Bookish Jottings

'You can always rely on Nancy Revell to offer up a story that is full of hopes, struggles and valuable friendships'
A Novel Thought

Shipyard Girls
Under the Mistletoe

Nancy Revell

PENGUIN BOOKS

PENGUIN BOOKS

UK | USA | Canada | Ireland | Australia
India | New Zealand | South Africa

Penguin Books is part of the Penguin Random House group
of companies whose addresses can be found at
global.penguinrandomhouse.com

Published by Penguin Books in 2021
001

Copyright © Nancy Revell, 2021

The moral right of the author has been asserted

Typeset in 10.75/13.5 pt Palatino LT Pro
by Integra Software Services Pvt. Ltd, Pondicherry

Printed and bound in Great Britain by Clays Ltd, Elcograf S.p.A.

The authorised representative in the EEA is Penguin Random House
Ireland, Morrison Chambers, 32 Nassau Street, Dublin D02 YH68

A CIP catalogue record for this book is available from the
British Library

ISBN: 978-1-787-46429-2

www.greenpenguin.co.uk

To 'Team Nancy' at Arrow,
You all work so hard and with such
expertise and professionalism on every
one of *The Shipyard Girls* series.
Thank you! x

Acknowledgements

Thank you to all those readers who write to me and tell me how much they are enjoying *The Shipyard Girls* series. Your comments and love of the characters fire me on more than you will ever realise. So many of you also take the time to write to me and tell me your own stories, or those of relatives long since gone. I read every one and always learn something from every message, email or letter.

A special thank you to Joy Jefferson for writing a wonderful description of what it was like to work in the drawing offices at Thompson's, and to Sheila Miller about growing up just a stone's throw away from the Wearside shipyards.

Thank you also to all the lovely staff at Fulwell Post Office, postmaster John Wilson, Liz Skelton, Richard Jewitt and Olivia Blyth, to Waterstones in Sunderland, the Sunderland Antiquarian Society, especially Linda King, Norm Kirtlan and Philip Curtis, researcher Meg Hartford, Jackie Caffrey, of Nostalgic Memories of Sunderland in Writing, Beverley Ann Hopper, of The Book Lovers, journalist Katy Wheeler at the *Sunderland Echo*, Simon Grundy at Sun FM, Julie Pendleton from Nova Radio (North East), Pauline Martin at The Word, the National Centre for the Written Word, and to the late Lisa Shaw and producer Jane Downs at BBC Newcastle.

To artist Rosanne Robertson, Soroptimist International of Sunderland, Kevin Johnson, and Sunderland City Council for their continuing work to make the commemoration to the real shipyard women a reality.

To Ian Mole for bringing the series to life with his *Shipyard Girls Walking Tour*.

To Gina Wilson for her guidance and encouragement.

To my lovely editor and publishing director Emily Griffin and copy editor Caroline Johnson.

To my mum Audrey Walton (née Revell), for allowing me to keep dragging her back to her childhood in Tatham Street.

To my sister, Jane Elias, and her lovely family, and my husband, Paul Simmonds, for listening to me, encouraging me, and for the love they give.

Thank you all.

'But for those who love, time is eternal.'
William Shakespeare

Prologue

The Havelock Residence, Glen Path, Sunderland

Christmas Day 1919

A huge, beautifully decorated Christmas tree dominated the grand hallway of the Havelock residence. The air was warm and infused with the smells of Yuletide – pine and cinnamon, and a touch of nutmeg. A mouth-watering waft of roasting goose escaped from the kitchen whenever one of the staff answered the pull of the servants' bell. A fire had been lit in just about every room in the house, making the place feel cosy and warm.

Everywhere, that was, apart from the master's study, where the air might have been warm, but the atmosphere was cold. Ice-cold.

'I know what you've done!' Henrietta rounded on Charles. Her cobalt blue eyes were blazing with anger. Her whole being was filled with disgust. She put her hand on her stomach as though she were about to vomit up the knowledge she had just been fed.

Charles Havelock regarded his wife, but didn't say a word. Instead, he walked to his desk and sloshed brandy from the decanter into a cut-crystal tumbler.

Taking a large mouthful, he grimaced as he swallowed. Then he smiled.

A wide, thin-lipped smile, devoid of joy, but full of pure malice.

'Pray tell me, darling, what am I supposed to have done?'

Henrietta held a lace handkerchief to her mouth, her other hand clutching the side of her long, hooped taffeta skirt, the alabaster white of her skin contrasting with the deep purple-coloured fabric.

'How stupid I've been, not to have realised it before,' Henrietta said, as she gazed through the large sash window that looked out onto the gravelled driveway. The woman who had just told her of her husband's evil was crunching through the snow, away from the house. Henrietta watched as the mother of one of her favourite maids wrapped her shawl tightly around herself – as much, Henrietta thought, to combat the after-chill of being under the same roof as the man who had destroyed her young daughter's life as to keep herself warm.

'You violated poor little Gracie – ' Henrietta spat out the words ' – and now she's dead!' Her stare burrowed into her husband's black eyes.

'What do you mean? Dead?' Mr Havelock asked.

Henrietta was clutching her skirt so tightly that her long, manicured nails were digging into her palms through the thick taffeta. If there had been the slightest hope that what Henrietta had just been told by Gracie's mother was the fabrication of a grief-stricken mind, the fact that her husband didn't bat an eyelid after being accused of raping her maid put paid to it.

'Yes, Charles. Little Gracie is dead because you defiled her in the worst possible way.'

Mr Havelock sighed impatiently. 'You're not making any sense.' Another sigh of irritation. 'Being *defiled*, as you put it, does not equate to a loss of life.'

Henrietta swallowed, fighting hard not to retch. Not only was he not denying such a heinous act, he clearly saw no wrong in it.

'You impregnated her!' Henrietta managed to push the words out despite her heart hammering and making her breathing sharp and shallow. She looked at the man she had married and for whom she had borne two children and did not think it was possible to hate a person more.

Mr Havelock shook his head as though confused. 'Am I to guess that she died in childbirth?'

Henrietta took a step towards her husband.

'No, the baby – a boy – was given up for adoption.' Henrietta hissed the words. 'A few months later her mother found little Gracie hanging from the bannisters. *Dead*.' Henrietta took another step across the Turkey-red Persian carpet towards her husband. She was so angry. Angry and disgusted with this man now inches from her. Angry with herself for being so blind. So naïve. So caught up in her own world, her books, her drinking and her pill-taking, that she had been oblivious to what had gone on in this very house.

Charles struck Henrietta hard across the face with his open palm. 'Calm down!' He looked at the woman he had married – not for love or for money, but because he knew she would be easy to manipulate. *How dare she challenge him now.*

'Who's dead?' Miriam asked.

They both turned on hearing the door to the office creak open.

'Miriam! Margaret! What are you doing here?' Henrietta looked at her two grown-up daughters, shocked by their sudden appearance. They were not expected until later in the afternoon. They were both holding large, boxed-up presents, beautifully wrapped and tied with gold bows.

'We thought we'd come a little earlier. Give you both your presents before Nanny brings the baby,' Miriam said, looking from her father to her mother.

3

'Who's dead?' Margaret asked. She could see the red print of her father's hand on her mother's cheek.

'No one's dead, darling. No one you know, anyway,' Henrietta lied. Both her daughters had known Gracie and both had been fond of her.

'Mother, are you all right?' Miriam asked.

'Yes, darling, I'm fine. Your father and I are just talking.'

The two sisters looked anxiously at their parents.

'Why don't you both go into the front parlour? I'll come and see you in a little while,' Henrietta said, putting her cool hand to her burning-hot cheek.

The two sisters didn't move.

'Leave us!' Mr Havelock bellowed.

Startled, the two women quickly turned and left. They had just reached the sitting room when the door to their father's study slammed shut. The whole house shuddered.

That would be the last Christmas they would ever spend with their mother. And one of the last times they would see her for many, many years.

Chapter One

When Bobby walked through the main gates of J.L. Thompson & Sons, Shipbuilders, he saluted Davey, the timekeeper. Returning the gesture, the young lad beamed back at the tall, burly riveter who, everyone knew, had once manned ships like those he now helped to build.

Bobby glimpsed a list of vessels, scrawled in large, child-like writing, pinned up on the inside wall of the cabin, and smiled. Each name represented a ship commissioned by the Ministry of War Transport and built in this very yard – the second largest in town. The other day, *Empire Haldane* had been christened and the sense of pride and camaraderie a ship's launch always brought still pervaded.

As he stepped over the threshold into the yard, Bobby automatically did what was fast becoming a habit as he walked into his workplace – he sought out the woman he loved. The woman he had fallen for, hook, line and sinker, the moment he'd clapped eyes on her. The woman who loved him back with equal fervour – only she hadn't realised it yet. Or if she had, she wouldn't admit it.

Dodging an unmanned crane, then jogging past a huge mound of metal sheets waiting to be taken over to a cargo vessel taking shape in the dry dock, Bobby headed over to the quayside. This was where his squad of riveters would be, and where the women welders would be eating their packed lunches – where the woman he was determined

5

to make his wife would be sitting. Dorothy. Dorothy Williams. Hopefully, one day, Dorothy Armstrong.

'Afternoon, all!' he shouted out.

Rosie, head of the women welders, his mam, Gloria, and the rest of the workers, Polly, Martha, Angie and Hannah, all turned their heads and smiled. All except Dorothy, who kept her focus firmly on the grey-green waters of the Wear.

'Hey, Rosie!' Bobby said as he approached the women, all sitting on randomly stacked wooden pallets.

'Hi, Bobby, what's up?' Rosie asked.

'I think one of your squad might need to go for a check-up.' He cocked his head in the direction of Dorothy, who was still staring out at the congested waters.

'Why's that?' Rosie asked, taking a bite of her sandwich.

Bobby chuckled. 'She seems to be having problems with her hearing.'

The women looked at Dorothy, who slowly turned her head to look at Bobby, a dark scowl on her face.

'It's called selective hearing,' she said, tucking her long dark hair behind her ears. 'Something *you* know all about.'

Bobby pulled a puzzled face and touched his ear. 'Pardon?'

The women all laughed. Bobby had lost the hearing in his left ear during the Battle of the North Cape. His partial deafness was something he liked to play on.

Dorothy rolled her eyes.

Bobby smiled and winked at her, before heading over to his own squad.

'Come on, Dor,' Hannah said. 'Tell us what's really going on with you and Bobby.'

'And Toby,' Polly chipped in. 'Why are you suddenly not sure about marrying him?'

'Yeah,' said Martha, the group's gentle giant. 'For months now you've been wanting Toby to propose, and then when

6

he does, you say you need time to think it over. Why the sudden change of heart?'

Dorothy's stomach tightened on recalling Toby's crest-fallen face when she'd told him that she needed time before committing herself to marriage. He'd tried hard to hide the fact that he was totally gutted and had tentatively said he'd thought she loved him as much as he loved her. She'd told him that she *did* love him – which was true – but she was undecided about the whole idea of marriage – which wasn't entirely true. She'd only become undecided after Bobby had kissed her – and she'd kissed him right back.

'Something's obviously happened that you haven't told us,' Hannah said gently. The slight inflection in her accent due to her Czech roots was now barely noticeable.

'Which means it must be really serious, because you always tell us everything, even if we don't want to hear it,' Polly said, yawning. Her son Artie might be almost ten months old now, but he was still a bad sleeper.

Rosie smiled at her gang. She hadn't really stopped smiling this past week since she had been reunited with her husband, Peter Miller, after his return from France, where he had been working alongside the French Resistance as part of Churchill's Special Operations Executive. Her happiness had soared higher still when Peter and her sister, Charlotte, who had just turned sixteen, hit it off straight away.

Dorothy looked at her workmates. *She* was not smiling. She had not been smiling much this past week since she had let down her guard and kissed Bobby and then, within hours, had been proposed to by Toby. Her dashing officer and gentleman. The man she loved, or thought she loved.

Gloria and Angie glanced at each other.

It was a look Martha caught. 'What is it you two know that we don't?'

7

'It's time yer spilled the beans, Dor,' Angie said, staring at her best friend.

'Agreed,' the women chorused.

Dorothy shuffled herself around so that she was sitting cross-legged, facing the women.

'There's no beans to be spilled,' she said.

'Oh, fer heaven's sake, Dor!' Angie said, exasperated. 'Of course there are! If yer dinnit say anything, I will.'

'About what?' Dorothy faked ignorance.

Angie looked daggers at Dorothy.

'I saw yer!'

Dorothy pretended to be confused, but she was blushing.

'I saw yer,' Angie repeated. She looked around at the women. She paused for a moment, shoving a stray strand of strawberry-blonde hair back under her headscarf, before declaring: *'I saw Dorothy and Bobby kissing!'*

There was a collective intake of air.

'Really?' Hannah said, shocked. 'But I thought you loved Toby?'

'I do,' Dorothy said in exasperation.

'Yeah, and I thought you hated Bobby?' Martha said, genuinely confused.

'I do,' Dorothy repeated through clenched teeth.

Polly was staring at Dorothy. 'Blimey, I've never seen you go so red, Dor. Did you really kiss him?'

'She did!' Angie said, eyes wide. 'I came back from the shops the day Rosie found out that Peter was alive, and when I walked into the flat, yer could've knocked me out with a feather – there were Dor 'n Bobby, *kissing*.' Angie's eyes widened even more as she looked at all the women. 'They were kissing so much they didn't even hear me come into the flat – or my jaw hit the floor in shock.'

Everyone chuckled.

'Why didn't you tell me you'd seen us?' Dorothy said. 'It's been almost a week and you've not said a dicky bird.'

'I was waiting fer yer to tell me, but yer never. Every day, yer've just been gannin on as if nowt's the matter.' Angie looked at the women. 'My shock at seeing yer both kissing was actually surpassed by yer not telling *me – yer best mate.*'

'I'll bet you blabbed to Quentin?' Dorothy demanded. Quentin Foxton-Clarke was Angie's sweetheart.

Angie's guilty look answered her question. The two spoke regularly on the phone as Quentin worked in London for the War Office.

'Honestly, what about *friends for ever* and keeping each other's secrets – friends first, boyfriends second?'

'Exactly!' Angie gasped. 'Friends for ever tell each other everything. And you didn't say owt about Bobby. Yer should have told me. If yer had, I wouldn't have needed to confide in Quentin.'

'Well, at least it's now all out in the open,' Gloria said, trying to defuse the situation.

Dorothy looked at Gloria. 'Did *you* know? Did Bobby tell you?'

'He did,' Gloria admitted. She had talked a lot to her son this past week since they'd sorted out their differences.

Dorothy made a gasping, strangled sound.

'So, what are you going to do about Toby?' Polly asked.

Dorothy let out a long, weary sigh.

'I don't know. I don't know what I think or feel or want to do any more.'

She looked round at her friends' faces.

'I seem to have got myself into a bit of a pickle, if I'm honest.'

Her words were punctuated by the klaxon proclaiming the end of the lunch hour. The sound of the shipyard

9

starting up ended the chance of any more chatter. It would have to wait until going-home time.

As Dorothy dusted crumbs off her overalls and packed up her haversack, she couldn't help glancing over to Bobby. He was chatting to Jimmy, the head riveter, and rubbing his hand over the top of his buzz cut. She looked away, but not quickly enough.

Bobby caught her looking and his heart soared.

Chapter Two

Mr Havelock was sitting alone in the large dining room of his very grandiose home in Glen Path, a wide, tree-lined avenue in one of the most affluent parts of the town. His mood had plummeted after he'd perused the headlines over breakfast. There was no denying the success of the Normandy landings and the opening up of the Second Front. You didn't need to have a crystal ball to see that an Allied victory was on the horizon – it was just a matter of when. The photographs and illustrations in the *Sunday Pictorial* said it all. WE'RE SQUEEZING IN – NOTHING CAN SAVE HITLER NOW! screamed the banner at the top of the page in bold, black ink.

Reading the piece, Mr Havelock's appetite left him, and he pushed his plate of bacon and egg away. Lighting up a Woodbine, he alternately smoked and drank his tea, flicking ash onto his untouched food before stubbing out the half-smoked cigarette in the middle of the perfectly fried egg. He knew it would hurt his housekeeper, Agatha, to see food spoiled and wasted during these times of rationing. It gave him a smidgen of sadistic joy.

Scraping back his chair, he made his way across the large oak-panelled room, banging his walking stick on the polished parquet flooring as he headed out of the door, making a beeline for his study. Stepping into the room, its size condensed by the walls lined with shelves stacked with books, Mr Havelock slammed the door shut and went straight to the safe situated behind his mahogany desk. Unlocking it and letting the small, heavy door swing back, he started foraging around. Finally, under the thick parchment of his Last Will and Testament and other important wax-sealed documents, he found what he was looking for – his membership of Oswald Mosley's now defunct political party, the British Union of Fascists. He had kept it in the hope that Hitler would win the war. It would have been proof of his political leanings and alliances. Had the Nazis successfully invaded the British Isles, Mosley would have been installed as head, albeit a puppet head, of a pro-German government.

Mr Havelock muttered blasphemies under his breath as he took the souvenir of a future that would never be over to the fireplace. Pulling out a silver lighter from his trouser pocket, he clicked it open and held the flame under the thick card, on which the letters B.U.F. had been heavily embossed in black. It slowly caught light. Leaning one hand on the mantelpiece, he watched the card burn, letting go of it only at the last minute.

He had to accept that there really was no chance of Hitler making any kind of a comeback. Why the British were so against the man, he did not know. His policies made good sense. His own people had certainly thought so, otherwise why would they have voted him in?

Mr Havelock turned and sat down at his desk. His mind wandered, as it often tended to of late, to his wife, Henrietta. A wife who, on paper, had died of a terrible tropical disease in India, but who, in reality, was very much alive and well. If only she really had died, he would not be in his current predicament.

For Henrietta was the only one who could legitimately bear witness to his past misdeeds – the only one who could speak with any credibility about his past life. Without her, Pearl and her daughter – *his* daughter – Bel Elliot had nothing on him. Nothing that would stand up in a court of law, anyway. If it wasn't for Henrietta, he would be able to do exactly what he wanted – starting with showing Pearl, Bel and that mishmash of women welders that Charles Havelock was not someone to be crossed.

But he couldn't, could he? Because of Henrietta. Without knowing it, she had control of him. And *no one* had ever controlled him in his entire life.

Mr Havelock sat forward, his elbows pressing into the embossed leather top of his desk, his hands clasped as though in prayer. He thought again about Mosley. And Hitler. And the hoped-for future that now had no chance of becoming a reality.

He thought of Hitler's policies. He thought about Henrietta. Insane. Or at least she was deemed to be on paper. He thought of the controversial T4 euthanasia programme adopted by the Führer at the start of the war, sanctioning the killing of the incurably ill, the elderly, the physically disabled – and the mentally ill.

The mentally ill.

Those housed in lunatic asylums.

Like the one in Ryhope.

Mr Havelock turned and looked out of the large sash window of his study, still covered in anti-blast tape even though there hadn't been a single air raid in well over a year. He sat quite still and thought. And thought some more. And slowly the skeleton of an idea started to take shape in his head. It took a while as he put flesh on its bones, but once he had, he knew what he had to do.

It was as clear as the day outside.

And with that knowledge came a sudden wave of impatience.

Sitting up in his chair, he snatched up the receiver of his black Bakelite phone and dialled a familiar number.

'Good morning, the Campbell residence.' His eldest daughter's soft voice sounded down the line.

'Margaret!' Mr Havelock shouted.

'Well, hello there, Father.' The tone was no longer soft. 'You do realise that most people start their telephone conversations with "Hello, how are you?" rather than simply bawling their name down the line?'

Mr Havelock ignored the reprimand. 'When's Miriam coming back?'

'She's not,' Margaret said simply.

There was silence down the phone.

'Again, I have to inform you, Father, that it is customary in civilised society to ask how someone is if they have been unwell. Especially if that person is your daughter.'

'In my book, being a drunk does not constitute being unwell … Lacking in willpower, more like!' Mr Havelock sniped.

He waited for a reply, but instead heard his daughter sigh with irritation down the phone.

'For God's sake, Margaret.' Mr Havelock forced the words out. 'How's she doing?'

'*She's* doing just fine, Father.' Margaret tried hard to remain civil.

'Well, if she's doing *just fine*, then why hasn't she been discharged from that sanatorium she's been holed up in for God knows how long? She should be here – back home, where she belongs. She's got a divorce to sort out if nothing else!'

'Miriam's on the mend, but she's not well enough to return home just yet,' Margaret said. She would have liked to ask why it was her father wanted his daughter home, but knew it was unlikely she'd get either a straight or an honest answer. Her father, she had learnt over the years, was a pathological liar.

'Bloody hell, how long does it take to squeeze someone dry?' Mr Havelock yelled down the phone in exasperation. *He needed her home. And sooner rather than later.*

There was a click as his daughter hung up. Then dead air. He banged down the receiver, fighting the urge to pick it up again and smash it back onto the cradle. Repeatedly. Even as a child, Margaret had always defied him. She was only eighteen months older than Miriam, but the pair were like chalk and cheese. Miriam had always been desperate to be a 'Daddy's girl'. Not Margaret, though. She was as stubborn as a mule. Always answering back. Never doing what he wanted. It had been a relief when he'd got shot of her and she'd moved over the border to marry that husband of hers.

'Eddy!' Mr Havelock bellowed. It felt good to shout. Flicking open his box of cigars, he took one out, clipped the end and lit it impatiently, puffing on it so hard he was soon surrounded by a fog of smoke.

'Yes, Mr Havelock!' Eddy's voice could be heard before he appeared through the half-opened doorway.

'I need a drink – and quick!'

Eddy gave a curt nod, disappearing as quickly as he had arrived, and returned a few minutes later with a silver tray on which there was a bottle of his master's favourite brandy and a large balloon glass.

Seeing the bottle, Mr Havelock started to calm down. Shooing Eddy away, he took the Rémy and poured himself a good measure. He'd just have to be patient, remind himself of one of his long-held beliefs.

Slowly, slowly, catchy monkey.

He'd have to hold his horses until Miriam got back.

Then he could put into play his plan of action.

Chapter Three

July

Heading up the long driveway to the Sunderland Borough Lunatic Asylum, Helen sighed to herself. It had been over a fortnight since her 'chat' with Dr Claire Eris, when she'd told Helen to stay clear of Dr Parker or else she'd let the cat out of the bag about Henrietta, about her real identity and how she'd been incarcerated under false pretences.

Helen wished she'd been able to tell Claire to go ahead and do it. She would revel in seeing her grandfather brought to some kind of justice. But of course, she couldn't. Claire had no idea that should she tell the world the truth about Henrietta, it would not be just Helen's grandfather who would suffer, but others too. For Charles Havelock would make sure he wreaked his revenge before he went down with the sinking ship. He would expose all the women welders' secrets: Dorothy's mother's bigamy, Angie's mam's adultery, and the truth about who Martha's birth mother was – a child killer whose crimes were folklore in these parts. He would destroy the lives of all those he perceived to have done him an injustice, starting with his former scullery maid Pearl Hardwick, now Mrs Pearl Lawson, joint licensee of the Tatham Arms, and her daughters, Bel and Maisie. He had already threatened to expose Maisie as a working girl, along with the bordello where she worked.

Pulling up on the gravelled driveway, Helen didn't bother checking herself in her little compact as she would normally. There didn't seem much point. She wasn't seeing John. Wasn't sure when she would see him again. Wasn't sure what she was going to do about John. Every day, she woke up hoping that an answer would come to her. But it hadn't.

Henrietta, though, was a different matter. Helen knew exactly what she wanted for her grandmother. So much so that she had devised a plan. And it was a plan she was going to start putting into action today.

Getting out of her beloved green sports car, Helen slung her handbag over her shoulder and grabbed a copy of *The Times* she'd brought with her. Walking up the stone steps of the Gothic red-brick building and through the main front doors, she spotted the elderly receptionist, Genevieve. Helen wondered if she ever left the asylum. John had told her that Genevieve not only worked at the town's mental institution, she lived there as well. There were staff quarters towards the back of the hospital. The entire place was more or less self-sufficient, with its own bakery, kitchens and two large farms. John had described it as being more of a hamlet than a hospital.

God, she missed him. It might only have been a couple of weeks since she'd last seen him – not so unusual, as their work schedules often meant they went without seeing each other for weeks at a time – but the knowledge that she could not love him in the way she knew they could love each other made their time apart seem so much longer. So much more painful.

Helen smiled at Genevieve, sitting behind the large receptionist's desk, and followed the now familiar route to her grandmother's room. The place had felt like a maze when she'd first started coming here seven months ago, but now she could probably find her way blindfold.

Knocking on the heavy oak door, which had been left ajar, Helen heard the familiar tinkle of her grandmother's voice, alongside a song playing on the wireless.

'Come in, come in!' Henrietta trilled.

'Hello, Grandmama.' Helen stepped into the room and smiled on seeing Henrietta. She guessed she'd been bored today as she had piled on her make-up. Blue eyeshadow, rouged cheeks, white-powdered face, thickly drawn eyebrows, and a deep crimson on her lips. Her hair looked a slightly darker red than normal.

'You look like you're ready to hit the town, Grandmama?' Helen smiled, giving her a gentle hug. She was always careful not to squeeze her too hard for fear she might break. Henrietta reminded her of a china doll. Very beautiful, very colourful, but also very fragile.

'Do I really?' Henrietta put her hands on her ankle-length silk skirt, under which there was layer upon layer of tulle. She turned slowly, like the little ballerina figurine in a musical box.

'Any reason why you are looking so splendid today?' Helen asked as she sat down at the round table in the middle of the high-ceilinged room.

'I have just taken receipt of some new make-up,' Henrietta said, bringing the jug of water over and pouring them both a glass of what they pretended was Russian vodka.

'Well, aren't you the lucky one,' Helen said. 'I know some women would give their right arm for some new make-up. Any make-up, come to think of it.'

Henrietta looked confused. Helen had tried to tell her grandmother about rationing and what was happening in the world outside the asylum, but she didn't think she really understood.

'And I've had my hair dyed with henna,' Henrietta informed her.

'Well, it looks lovely,' said Helen.

'So, tell me ...' Henrietta took a sip of water and grimaced a little as if it really was neat vodka '... why do you not have that sparkle about you today?' She put up her hand to stop Helen speaking. 'No, let me guess ... No rendezvous with your doctor friend?'

Helen sighed. 'Grandmama, you are very perceptive ... You're right. I haven't seen John today.' She paused, unsure how much to say. 'Actually, I probably won't be seeing much of him at all from now on.'

'Oh, my dear.' Henrietta put her hand on top of Helen's. 'Why ever not? Have you two had a lovers' tiff?'

Helen gave a sad smile. Her grandmother was of the belief that Helen and John were courting, or at least having some kind of illicit romantic affair. *If only.*

'Tell me, tell me everything,' Henrietta coaxed. 'We have an entire hour. I want to hear.'

The song playing on the wireless changed and the unmistakable voice of Bing Crosby filled the room.

The sad, forlorn vocals swirled from the wireless and over the barriers she had tried to erect around her heart. It was as though the lyrics had been written for her.

The voice and the beautiful orchestral music caused a well of tears.

'Darling!' Henrietta reached up and wiped away a tear that had escaped and was starting to make its way down her granddaughter's cheek. 'Tell me what has happened.'

Helen blinked back more tears, took a deep breath and told her grandmother of her heartbreak: how she and John had been good friends, how he had helped her through some bad times, and they had become close. But she had not thought that John's feelings for her went beyond the brotherly kind and had learnt too late that she'd been wrong.

'But there's nothing I can do about it now,' Helen said. 'He's in a relationship with another woman.' She purposely left out that the other woman was Dr Eris, Henrietta's psychologist.

'But I don't understand why you can't still tell John that you love him. If he's not engaged or married to this other woman?' Henrietta asked.

Helen smiled. 'That's where it all gets a little complicated, Grandmama. You see, John's sweetheart has something on me – something that's stopping me from telling John how I feel.'

'Oh, dear me,' Henrietta said, taking another sip of her drink and putting it back on the coaster. 'It sounds as if you've been boxed into a corner.'

Helen nodded. 'I have. And worst of all, if I let John know how I feel, it won't be me that gets hurt, but others. Innocent people who don't deserve it.'

'Well, we must do something!' Henrietta said, alarmed. She shifted around on her seat, as though getting ready to take action. 'What is it this woman has on you?'

Helen took her grandmother's pale, sinewy hand. She could never know the truth that it was she who was being used to blackmail Helen.

'There's nothing we can do. There's certainly nothing *you* can do.' Helen smiled sadly. 'But what you *have* done and what *has* helped me – *a lot* – is that you've *listened* to me, and I've been able to confide in you.' Again, Helen felt the sting of tears. She looked at her grandmother and thought how different things might have been had Henrietta been a part of her life growing up.

'No more about my wretched love life,' Helen said determinedly, sitting up straight and putting a smile on her face. 'I thought it might be a good idea for us to swap our book-reading for a browse of the newspapers.' Helen looked at her grandmother, who was eyeing up the paper as though it were the enemy. She wondered if she'd been purposely shielded from life beyond the asylum.

'I've been thinking I need to know more about what's happening in the world,' Helen went on. This was a white lie. Every day, she had a quick glance at *The Times* and the *Sunderland Echo*, and in the evening she tried to catch the news on the BBC Home Service.

'All right,' Henrietta agreed. 'If it'll help you.'

Helen moved their glasses and the jug off the table so as to be able to spread out the paper. They looked at the main headlines about the V-1s, Hitler's jet-powered flying bombs, which were presently decimating parts of London as well as other areas of the south-east.

When they started reading an article about Minsk being liberated by Soviet forces, Henrietta's eyes glazed over a little, although she perked up when they flicked through the rest of the paper and came across a feature on new Make Do and Mend tips and Utility fashions.

As they continued to chat, Helen's mind kept wandering to thoughts of her mother, Miriam. She wondered when she would be back. She'd have thought she'd want to return to sort out her divorce.

As Helen watched her grandmother read out an article that had taken her interest, she thought how strange it was that Henrietta was Miriam's mother. You couldn't get two more different women.

Miriam was most definitely her father's daughter.

Chapter Four

The women welders had been doing touch-up work all day over in the Manor Quay at the far end of the North Sands yard. It was where most of the fitting out and the repair work was done. They'd been set to work on *Empire Dynasty*, which they had seen go down the ways in May and which was due to leave soon on her maiden voyage. It had been a long day and they were tired, but they were determined not to renege on their arranged get-together at the Admiral after work. They'd all agreed it was well overdue. They had not been out en masse for an age.

Hurrying across the yard to the main gates, they got caught in the bottleneck of workers all lining up to hand in their time boards.

'Helen not coming?' Rosie asked Gloria as they shuffled forwards.

'She said she was leaving work early – ' Gloria dropped her voice ' – to go 'n see her *relative* over in Ryhope. She said she probably wouldn't be back in time.'

The crush of workers inched forwards.

'Actually, there's something I need to tell everyone about Helen and Dr Parker.' Gloria glanced round at her workmates, who were squashed up next to her. '*And* Dr Eris.'

'Sounds intriguing,' said Dorothy.

'What is it?' Polly asked, letting her long chestnut hair free from the confines of her headscarf.

'Well, in a nutshell, Dr Eris knows about Henrietta,' Gloria said with a grim face.

'She *knows*?' Dorothy hissed.

'How come?' Martha asked.

Gloria took a deep breath. 'To cut a long story short, Helen was gonna tell Dr Parker how she felt about him the day Rosie found out that Peter wasn't dead. She drove to the Ryhope after ringing to tell him she wanted to see him 'n that it was urgent.'

'Sounds romantic,' Dorothy said.

'Yes,' Gloria agreed, 'and it would've been if Dr Eris hadn't beaten her to it 'n told her to stay away from Dr Parker otherwise she'd blow the whistle on Henrietta – about her being *you-know-who's wife*.'

'So, she's found out?' Hannah said sadly.

'She has,' Gloria said.

They all inched forward.

'Obviously, she just thinks Helen's worried about the Havelock name – she doesn't know about *everything else*.'

The women huddled nearer as Gloria lowered her voice.

'So, Helen agreed?' Angie said, getting out her clocking-off card, ready to hand it over.

'She did,' Gloria said. 'She didn't really have any choice.'

'We'd have been done for if she hadn't,' Dorothy said, digging around in her haversack.

'Poor Helen,' said Hannah. Her feelings for Helen had grown considerably, as had all the women's, after Helen had put her life on the line and saved Gloria and her daughter, Hope, on the day of the Tatham Street bombing

'Yeah, 'n poor Dr Parker – being with such a horrible, conniving cow,' said Angie.

They had now reached the timekeeper's cabin and took it in turns to hand their white boards over to Davey.

'That makes me so angry,' Dorothy said through pursed lips.

'Me too,' said Polly. She had a particular soft spot for Dr Parker and Helen after they had helped to deliver Artie; it was why she had asked them both to be godparents.

The rest of the women muttered that they, too, felt the same as they made a beeline for the Admiral, the yard's main watering hole.

'Is there anything we can do?' Rosie asked.

Gloria shook her head. She had thought long and hard about a possible solution.

'I really don't think there is.'

Pulling open the door, they were hit by the overriding smell of spilled beer and wafts of cigarette smoke. Hannah suppressed a cough.

'There's a seat!' Dorothy said, pointing over to the table by the window.

'I'll grab it,' said Hannah. As the smallest in their group, she was the best at weaving her way quickly through a thick sea of overall-clad shipyard workers.

'I'll get the first round in,' Dorothy said. She didn't need to ask what they all wanted.

'Give us a shout if yer need a hand,' said Angie, before following the rest of the women over to the table that Hannah had just commandeered.

Dorothy eased her way to the bar, which was full to heaving.

Feeling someone nudge up behind her, she looked round. It was Bobby.

'I just wanted to grab a quick word,' he said.

Seeing Pat, the barman, heading towards her, Dorothy shouted out her order.

Turning her attention back to Bobby, she glared at him. 'You've got until the drinks arrive.'

Suddenly, there was a burst of raucous laughter behind her. A group of platers were well on their way and getting rowdier by the minute. One of them staggered back, pushing Dorothy against Bobby. For a moment their bodies were pressed together. Dorothy could feel herself wanting just to melt into his arms and stay there. She watched as Bobby put his arm over her shoulder. For a moment she thought he was going to pull her close and kiss her.

But he didn't.

'Watch yourself, mate!' Bobby shouted out, giving the bloke who had pushed Dorothy a quick, sharp shove. The man turned round. His expression instantly snapped from lairy to angry.

'There's ladies present!' Bobby looked at Dorothy to prove the point.

'*Pfft!* Ladies!' The man looked Dorothy up and down, taking in her dirty overalls, her hair still tied up in a faded green headscarf, her face smeared with dirt, and guffawed.

'Call that a lady?' The man laughed loudly.

Bobby's face had gone like thunder. He gave the plater another robust shove, causing him to stagger back.

'Enough!' Dorothy said, grabbing Bobby's arm.

Bobby looked at Dorothy's worried expression and took a deep breath.

'Apologise!' Bobby glared at the bloke, who was now rubbing his shoulder.

'Sorry, mate, I didn't knar she was yer bit.' He looked at Dorothy and gave her a sheepish smile. 'Sorry, pet, didn't mean to offend.'

'Apology accepted,' Dorothy said, holding back from informing him that she was not Bobby's, or anyone else's, *bit*.

Looking back at Bobby, she saw he was still glaring at the man.

'Leave it,' she said. 'He's said he's sorry.' She tugged his arm so that his focus was back on her. Just then the drinks arrived. She handed over the money.

'I'll take them,' Bobby said, picking up the tray.

The women had seen the exchange between the two men and were watching as Dorothy and Bobby weaved their way through the crowded pub and arrived at their table.

'Everything all right?' Rosie asked, looking over at the gang of platers now singing some kind of football song.

'Aye, beer in, wits out,' said Bobby, putting the tray down.

'Thanks,' Dorothy said. Out of the corner of her eye, she saw the women forcing themselves to turn away and start making conversation amongst themselves. 'For bringing the drinks over – and for defending my honour.'

Bobby laughed out loud.

'Aren't I meant to be the one living in the "Dark Ages"?' he said, quoting Dorothy. He smiled at the woman who he was crazy about – who had been driving him crazy in more ways than one since his medical discharge four months ago.

Dorothy allowed herself a slight chuckle. 'You're right. It does sound like I'm endorsing some medieval code of chivalry.' She looked up and held his gaze. 'Anyway, forgetting that – you said you wanted a quick word?'

Bobby took a deep breath.

'I did.' He paused. 'I wanted to say that I understand you're in an awkward position after what happened the other week.'

Dorothy felt herself blush just thinking about it. She hoped it wasn't obvious.

'I know you've been courting Toby—' Bobby started to say.

'And am *still* courting Toby. Present tense,' Dorothy said, her angry words pushing back her guilt. She'd only spoken

27

to Toby on the phone once since the day of the proposal. She'd tried to sound normal, like her usual self, but it was obvious something was up. *Not jumping up and down with excitement when he'd popped the question was a bit of a giveaway.*

'OK, *are* still courting Toby,' said Bobby. He hesitated. Talking about his feelings was not his forte.

Dorothy widened her eyes to encourage him.

'I guess,' Bobby said, 'what I want to say to you is that you'd be making a big mistake if you said yes to Toby.'

Dorothy had guessed Gloria would have told Bobby that Toby had asked for her hand in marriage.

'So much for keeping secrets,' she said, glancing over at Gloria.

'She *is* my mam. Blood thicker than water and all that.' He let out a burst of incredulous laughter. 'Anyway, it was you who was on at us to talk. *You* who pummelled me into submission.' It was actually something for which he wanted to thank Dorothy. So far, though, he'd not had the chance. Since they'd kissed that day, Dorothy had been avoiding him like the plague.

Dorothy was at a loss for words. She tried to feel angry but couldn't. All she really wanted to do was lean into Bobby and kiss him and have a repeat of their two minutes of passion standing in the middle of her kitchen.

'Why would saying yes to Toby be such a mistake?' she asked, forcing herself back into combative mode. She saw Bobby turn his head slightly to the left and knew he was struggling to hear her. She spoke into his good ear. 'Why would marrying Toby be a mistake? It's not as if you really know me or Toby.'

'Perhaps not.' Although he did feel as though he and Dorothy had got to know each other these past few months. 'But I do think it'd be a mistake, marrying someone else after what happened between us.' Bobby paused. 'Even if you didn't want to marry me.'

'What?' Dorothy let out a mock gasp. 'Am I hearing my second proposal in a matter of weeks?'

Bobby ran his hand over his head self-consciously, aware that Dorothy's squad were near and would undoubtedly be straining to hear what was being said. 'You know what I'm meaning, Dorothy.'

He looked down at her with serious eyes.

Dorothy allowed herself to return his look.

He touched her arm gently. 'You know I want you.'

Dorothy looked into his eyes. He was making no effort to hide his desire.

'I do,' Dorothy said with a sharp laugh. 'You want me for one thing.'

Bobby was just about to say something when Jimmy came over.

'Yer gonna gerrus that round in, mate? We're all dying of thirst over there.' He looked over to the far corner where the riveters had been waiting for Bobby to return from the bar.

Bobby looked at Dorothy.

'Just think about it,' he said, before turning away and heading back to the bar with Jimmy.

'Look, the ferry's in!' Dorothy shouted out as the women bustled out of the Admiral.

They all hurried down to the landing and piled on, paying Stan, the ferry master, the penny fare.

'So, come on, Dor, spit it out,' Angie said as they reached the bow of the old paddle steamer.

'Yeah, we couldn't hear a thing in the pub,' Martha chuckled.

'Try as you might!' Dorothy jibed back.

Dorothy looked at Rosie, Gloria, Polly, Martha, Hannah and Angie. Their faces were expectant. It had been too loud in the pub to talk and they were all aware they could be overheard.

'Well, we did hear Bobby say something like *"You know I want you"*,' Hannah said, dropping her voice as a couple of shipyard workers started chatting and smoking next to them.

'Yeah,' Dorothy laughed a little bitterly. 'He wants *one thing*. And I think we all know what that is.' She looked at Gloria. 'Sorry, no offence, Glor, but I think we all know what Bobby really wants.'

Polly looked at Dorothy. 'Actually,' she said in earnest, 'I think Bobby wants *you*. You know – Dorothy. The person.' Since Bobby had started lodging at the Elliots', Polly had got to know him well. He was brilliant with Artie and he was always keen to chat about Tommy, who he clearly saw as a brother in arms, them both being in the navy.

'Yes, I agree with Polly,' Hannah said. 'I think Bobby wants Dorothy the person.'

'I agree too,' Rosie said. She was leaning against the metal railing, enjoying the feel of the evening sun on her face. 'There's no doubting Bobby's a red-blooded male, but I don't think that's the only reason he wants you.'

'You all think he wants to court me properly?' Dorothy looked askance at the women.

'*Of course* he wants to court yer properly, yer daft narna,' Gloria said in exasperation. She wanted to add that her son was completely besotted with her, but didn't.

'Why wouldn't he want to court you properly?' Hannah asked, genuinely perplexed.

''Cos she's as nutty as a fruitcake,' Martha chortled.

Dorothy looked at Martha.

'Many a true word's said in jest,' she said with a heavy sigh. 'Martha's got a point. Toby loves me, the whole of me – the nutty me as well as the packaging.' She looked down at her dirty overalls and suddenly felt deflated.

She and Toby had been an item since he had turned up at the bordello and mistaken her for one of Lily's girls. They'd been attracted to each other from the off. She had invited him to Polly and Tommy's wedding and they'd been an item ever since. They might not have seen each other as much as a couple would in normal times, but whenever Toby was given leave, he'd jump into his little grey Austin and drive up north to see her. She loved him. Had wanted nothing more than to be his wife. Everything had been clear-cut – *until Bobby had come on the scene*.

Angie elbowed her best friend. 'What's wrong, Dor? You've got a face like a slapped backside. Yer should be cock-a-hoop yer've got two blokes after yer.'

'But that's just it,' Dorothy said, as the ferry bumped into the landing and they all made their way off. 'I was quite happy with just the one – Toby – and then Bobby came and put a great big spanner in the works.'

They all started the walk up the embankment to High Street East.

'I know Toby wants me – all of me – wants me as his wife. For life,' Dorothy said, thinking of his soft brown eyes, so soulful, so sincere whenever he spoke of his love for her.

'Whereas Bobby definitely wants me,' she added, thinking of his mischievous eyes, dancing as he enjoyed their verbal sparring, 'but for what, and for how long, I'm not so sure.'

They all walked on in silence.

Seeing her bus, Rosie waved it down.

'Perhaps *you* should decide who it is you want. And *what* it is you really want,' she said, hurrying off.

31

Chapter Five

Stepping out of the first-class carriage of the train, Miriam put a gloved hand out to the young boy dressed in an oversized porter's uniform. Gripping his skinny arm tightly, more tightly than necessary, she stepped out of the brown-and-cream-painted wooden carriage and onto the busy platform. As steam hissed from under the train's metal belly, she curled her nose, the smell of soot and the dry, dusty air making her cough. She'd got used to the clean air of the Scottish Highlands. Releasing her talon-like grip, Miriam cast a look back through the open carriage door to where a leather suitcase waited to be claimed.

'Is that yours?' the young lad asked, unsure of himself. Unsure of the job he'd just started that very same day.

'Of course it's mine!' Miriam snapped. 'I can't see anyone else it might belong to, can you?' She looked around to prove her point. She had been the only person from the first-class compartment to alight.

'Sorry, miss.' The boy hitched up his trousers and climbed on board.

Miriam watched with disdain as he struggled to lift the case, its weight nearly taking him with it as he lowered it onto the platform.

Tutting loudly as a naval officer jostled past her to reach the train just as the stationmaster blew the whistle, Miriam started to make her way towards the stairs that led up to the exit. The throng of fellow travellers and those who had come to meet them caused her progress to be slow. She glanced behind. The prepubescent porter was dragging the suitcase with two hands as though it were a dead body. The sight irritated her. *A boy doing a man's job.*

As the chattering crowd moved like sloths up the two flights of steps at the top, Miriam felt a wave of well-being as she imagined her first sip of a large gin and tonic. She could almost hear the clink of ice and imagined the slight fizz as the bartender dropped in a slice of lemon. Impatience immediately followed. She had waited months for a drink, and now it was imminent it was as though she couldn't wait another second.

Glancing back at the boy, she saw he was banging the suitcase up each step.

'Lift it!' she ordered. 'You're scuffing the leather! It's not a sack of potatoes you're hauling about.'

The young boy looked mortified. Spitting on the sleeve of his uniform, he started trying to rub the dirt off the side of the case, terrified he might have scratched it.

Miriam grimaced, closed her eyes and shook her head. She'd get one of the doormen at the Grand Hotel to give it a good clean and polish.

'Let me give you a hand there.'

Miriam turned as a tall, well-built young man dressed in oil-stained overalls took the suitcase off the young boy and carried it up the rest of the stairs. He ruffled the boy's hair before disappearing through the crowd.

When Miriam finally handed over her ticket and made it out of the train station, she breathed a sigh of relief. She looked down at the skinny young boy who was looking up at her expectantly, pleased that the suitcase looked none the worse for wear.

'You'll get a tip when you earn a tip,' she said. 'When you don't have to get others to do your job for you.'

The boy looked downcast as he hitched up his trousers and walked back into the station.

Miriam felt her spirits rise once again as she thought of the Grand, her first gin and tonic in months and seeing her old friend Amelia. She wondered if any of the Admiralty they'd befriended were still billeted there.

'Taxi!' She raised her hand as a black cab pulled up.

She'd just caught the driver's eye when she felt a presence next to her.

'Welcome back, Mrs Crawford.'

Miriam turned to see Eddy, her father's butler-cum-valet-cum-general-dogsbody, picking up her suitcase.

'Mr Havelock has sent me to collect you. He wants to welcome you back in person.'

Miriam's heart sank. She should have guessed her father would have learnt about her return. No doubt Margaret or Angus would have told him.

Miriam huffed loudly.

'Well, I better get it over with, eh, Eddy? What Father wants, Father gets.'

Eddy didn't respond. Instead, he picked up the suitcase, which weighed a ton, and humped it over to his master's black Jaguar.

'Ah, the prodigal daughter returns!' Mr Havelock was standing in the doorway, rubbing his hands together in glee.

'Hardly *prodigal*,' Miriam said. 'Being locked up in a sanatorium does not make for wanton or excessive behaviour – quite the reverse.'

Walking up the steps to her childhood home, Miriam thought her father looked full of it. Was the old man ever going to pop his clogs? Most men born around the same time as her dear papa had met their Maker at least a decade ago.

'Perhaps not quite prodigal,' Mr Havelock tried to keep his tone light and welcoming, 'but some might say such establishments are extravagant and expensive.'

He stood aside so that Miriam could enter the impressive hallway, which was as large as most people's living rooms. Eddy followed.

'But it has clearly been worth it. You look splendid, my dear.'

Miriam patted her short blonde hair, which had been set into curls. She'd been told she looked the spit of Betty Grable, which had pleased her no end.

'A compliment from Father, no less,' Miriam said, eyeing Mr Havelock suspiciously as she shrugged off her coat and held it out for Eddy to take.

Miriam followed her father into his study. Of all the rooms in her childhood home, this was the one she disliked the most.

'As I've been shanghaied within seconds of stepping foot back into my home town, I will have to ring the Grand if I'm to be here long, so they can relay a message to Amelia that I'm going to be delayed.'

Having reached the large oak door, Miriam forced herself to look at the man she now despised. The man accused of raping young girls. Of fathering illegitimate children. Of incarcerating her mother because she was going to report him, expose him for the man he was – and the crimes he had committed.

'Unless the reason I've been brought here will not take long?'

'Not long. Not long at all,' Mr Havelock replied, forcing a smile and ignoring the edge in his daughter's voice.

'Come in. Agatha has kindly made you some sandwiches and a pot of tea.'

At the mention of tea, Miriam felt like screaming. She'd drunk enough tea to sink an armada these past few months. She wanted a proper drink. And she wanted one as soon as possible.

'First of all, Miriam, I want to say how lovely it is to have you back. It's been nearly eight months since I've seen you. Far too long.' Mr Havelock kept his tone warm. He congratulated himself on sounding genuine. He leant forwards, his hands clasped as though in prayer, a balloon glass of brandy to his right. Miriam wondered if the drink was to torment her, or was just her father – oblivious to anything that pertained to anyone but himself.

Miriam looked up at one of the Aboriginal drawings her father had brought back from one of his many trips abroad. She pulled up a seat and sat down.

'Well, I have to say, Papa, my feelings about being back here are mixed, to say the least.' Miriam eyed the brandy and the original flat-bottomed ship's decanter. She took a sip of her tea.

'I'm sure your feelings *are* very mixed,' Mr Havelock sympathised. 'You've had quite a year of it so far. But I have to say that you're looking like your old self. Your time away has done you good.'

Miriam took a bite of her sandwich. She watched her father, unsure of what to make of him. Since she'd heard what Pearl and Bel had disclosed on Christmas Day last year, in her mind her father had morphed into a monster. But now that she was here and he was in front of her – well, he was just like the man she'd always known. Arrogant. Egotistical. But not exactly the Devil incarnate.

'I don't want to beat about the bush,' Mr Havelock said, lifting his hands palms up, working hard to show his daughter that he did not want any kind of confrontation. 'I'll get straight to it. What happened when I saw you last …' He paused, shaking his head sadly. 'I don't think Christmas will ever be the same again.'

'I'll second that,' Miriam agreed. Her recall of that afternoon was a little sketchy. She had drunk a lot that day. More than usual. But she remembered enough: Pearl and Bel turning up at the house, threatening to tell the world that her father was Bel's real father – and that he had also sired a child by Gracie the maid, who had given the child up for adoption before taking her own life. They'd come armed with a report that she vaguely remembered went some way to proving what was being said, with Bel adding that she would make it clear her mother had not been a willing participant in Bel's conception. And if that was not enough of a shock, she'd listened with incredulity as they had exchanged their silence for Jack's return!

She could still feel the all-consuming sense of injustice. She had worked so hard to get Jack banished to the Clyde – had gone as far as hiring a private detective to find out secrets about those close to her husband's mistress, forcing him to abandon both the woman and their bastard and live in exile over the border. Only for her father to agree to Bel's demands and allow Jack to come back home after a two-year hiatus.

She was being punished for the sins of her father.

Miriam took another sip of her tea, forcing back the sense of outrage that had come to the fore.

'On that ghastly day,' Mr Havelock began, 'I wanted to talk to you, but you just upped and left. Then the very next day – on Boxing Day, no less – you headed off to the Highlands.'

Miriam opened her mouth to speak, but her father beat her to it.

'*I know*, it was a shock, and you were worried about Jack coming back. I understand.'

Miriam looked at her father. 'Do you? Do you really understand?' Her voice was getting louder by the second. 'I had managed to banish my cheating husband from my life – had worked my socks off to get the dirt I needed to use against him – only for it all to be undone in the blink of an eye. And then,' she gasped, 'I had to deal with the fact that he would be back within *days*.'

'And you were right in your supposition.' Mr Havelock pressed his hands together. 'Your estranged husband certainly wasted no time in returning. I believe he was back here – with his *other family* – late on Christmas Day.'

Miriam felt herself prickle at the mention of Jack and Gloria and their love child. Again, she looked at her father's brandy.

Mr Havelock watched Miriam's reaction. He had seen her eyes flickering to his drink. He needn't have worried about her returning home a committed teetotaller.

'But let's not talk about your soon-to-be *ex*-husband just yet,' he said, taking a sip of his Rémy and savouring it. 'How's Margaret? Is she all right? She sounded very tense when I spoke to her last.'

'She's fine, Father. Fine. I think she's just been a bit worried about me. I'm her little sister, after all. She's always been a bit protective of me.'

'Well, there's no need for her to worry about you now – not now you're back home.' Mr Havelock shuffled in his seat and straightened his back.

'So, Miriam,' he began. 'We need to address what was said about me on that frightful day.'

Miriam felt her heart start to race. She would have preferred to simply sweep it all under the carpet. Shove the family skeleton back into the cupboard with all the others, lock the door and throw away the key.

'I need you to know,' Mr Havelock gave his daughter a grave look, 'that none of it was true. Not one word.'

Miriam didn't know what to say. Instead, she took another sip of her tea.

'There's a lot you don't know, Miriam. About your mother. What she was really like when she was at home. When you and Margaret were away at school. Her oddities.'

Miriam thought of her mother when she and Margaret were young. There was no denying she was eccentric.

'But I categorically deny – hand on heart – that I ever touched that Pearl woman. That washed-out wreck of a woman. I would never have touched her with a bargepole,' he said, knowing that Miriam would have no idea that the woman who had stood in their dining room last Christmas Day had once been quite stunning. Petite. Blonde. Almost angelic-looking. The way he liked them.

'They were plainly desperate. And her daughter Bel is clearly cut from the same cloth. A fraudster. A con artist. Helen's been taken in hook, line and sinker.'

Miriam was trying to keep her concentration. This was important. She tried to push back thoughts of a cool gin and tonic.

'Anyone in their right mind could see they were desperate. The state they turned up in, with their shabby coats and worn-out shoes.'

Miriam vaguely remembered Bel wearing a black dress. Or was that Helen? She could recall a flash of Pearl and Bel leaving, putting on their damp coats. *Yes, they had looked shabby. Hadn't they?*

'They both obviously realised you share an uncanny resemblance and decided to try and cash in on it. And they very cleverly decided to do it on Christmas Day, knowing we'd all be here, enjoying a family day together.'

Miriam thought her father might be recalling that part of the day, before Pearl and Bel's arrival, with rose-tinted glasses. All she could remember was wishing it was time to leave and go to the Grand. Rather like she was now.

'You were right.' He looked at his daughter with admiration. 'Totally spot on when you told that horrible woman and her child that they were imposters trying to "bleed us dry of our hard-earned cash".'

Miriam felt herself warm a little to her father. It was not often he praised her words or actions.

'In hindsight,' Mr Havelock continued, 'I thought it very conniving but also very astute of Bel to get herself a job at Thompson's. To spend months getting on Helen's good side.' He let out a sharp, mirthless laugh. 'And guess what? As soon as the big shakedown was over and done with, she packed in her job. She's not working there now. The last I heard, she'd adopted twins from the orphanage.'

'But, Father,' Miriam said, thinking of the dossier that purported to back up the claims that Bel was her father's daughter, 'what about the report?'

'Load of old Trollope.' Mr Havelock dismissed it immediately. 'A work of pure fantasy. A very convincing one, it has to be said. But a load of baloney, as the Yanks would say. There's not even any proof that dreadful woman ever worked here.'

Miriam was quiet, desperately trying to recall exactly what the report had said. She couldn't remember there being any concrete proof, but, still, the contents had been convincing. She had believed Bel was her sister. Or rather, half-sister.

'So there was nothing in the report that constituted actual evidence?' Miriam asked.

What a relief it would be to find out this was all some elaborate set-up. That her father was not a monster. Just a man.

Mr Havelock studied his daughter's demeanour and could see that he was doing well.

'Of course there wasn't!' he said. 'Lies. All lies!' Mr Havelock drove the point home.

'But what about Mother?' Miriam asked.

'Ha! It was your dear mama's fault that we're sitting here now having this horrible conversation. Her sickness has continued to contaminate – even after all these years.'

Mr Havelock took a large gulp of his brandy, making a show of needing to ease his faux pain. His lifelong suffering.

'It was your mother who unwittingly started this entire debacle,' he said, wearily. 'I didn't get her put away because she was going to report me to the authorities, like that woman and her daughter tried to make out. I got her put away because she was ill. Mentally ill.' He let out a bitter laugh and looked at his daughter with sadness. 'This is the reason I've wanted you back here. You'll never know the anguish it has caused me, knowing that you left believing such revolting lies about me. *Your own papa.* No wonder you took to the drink.'

Miriam exhaled, relieved that her father understood and empathised.

'It feels wrong to be talking to you about such things as a father, but it is necessary, otherwise I will lose you. And I don't want to. I lost my wife a long time ago and you and Margaret are all I have.' Mr Havelock took a slow drink of his brandy.

'But, Father,' Miriam challenged, 'you were the one to get dear Mama put away in the asylum. You didn't even let us say goodbye to her.'

'There was good reason,' Mr Havelock said with utter conviction. '*Yes*, I had your mother sectioned, but you have to believe me when I say it broke my heart. And it would have broken yours too, had you seen the state of her just before they took her away.'

Mr Havelock sighed.

'I don't think a day goes by that I don't think about that time. But there hasn't been a minute I've regretted my actions.'

Mr Havelock looked at his daughter long and hard.

'I really did not have a choice. Your mother has always been a little *different*. It was partly why I fell in love with her.' Mr Havelock took a sip of his brandy. He was actually quite enjoying the role play. 'But she became ill. Very ill.' He tapped the side of his head. 'Mentally unstable. Of course, you and Margaret were totally unaware. It wasn't as though you were here a lot anyway. Thank goodness. Thank goodness for boarding schools and finishing schools, eh?'

Miriam didn't agree or disagree. She had enjoyed school, but she had missed her father and her mother.

'It was horrible to see and hear your mother that awful, awful day.' Mr Havelock pulled a sour expression, as though he had just eaten something unpalatable. 'In her head, it's the truth, which is why she is so convincing.' He took a deep breath. 'I would never – *ever* – have got her put away against her wishes. The reason I had your mother taken to the asylum that abominable, unforgettable day all those years ago ...' He paused. He had to get this right. 'It was not just because your mother had finally lost her marbles, but because she had started to become delusional. The psychiatrist who persuaded me to section Henrietta said it was as though her mind had taken a step over to the dark side and was unable to come back again. He thought it might have been partly due to all those Gothic novels she liked to read.'

Miriam remembered how her mother always seemed to have her nose in a book when Miriam was a child.

'Henrietta had begun to imagine that I was ...' Mr Havelock paused as though it pained him to say the words '... defiling the young girls who worked as maids. The sickness of her mind had conjured up the most appalling – quite perverted – scenarios in which I was raping and impregnating the poor young girls that came to work as maids here – in this very house.' Mr Havelock waved his hand around the room to demonstrate his point. 'I can only surmise that when that woman Pearl happened upon Henrietta in the asylum, Henrietta filled her head with her putrid imaginings, which in turn gave Pearl the idea to blackmail me.'

Miriam felt a huge relief. Of course, that made sense. She could easily imagine someone like Pearl jumping at the chance of using it as a means for blackmail.

Miriam felt a surge of hope.

She had been wrong.

Her father was not a monster.

God, she needed a drink. She felt the heavy weight that had been pressing down on her these past eight months slowly lifting from her shoulders. If only she hadn't run away to Scotland.

'I so wish I'd been able to tell you all of this before now,' Mr Havelock said, seeing the relief on his daughter's face and reading her mind.

'So, Pearl pretended she'd been a maid here – and that Bel was your offspring?' Miriam said, wanting to hear her father's affirmation – to continue to feel the weight lifting.

'Exactly!' Mr Havelock said. 'Do you really think I would do something like that?' He looked at his daughter with what he hoped were eyes that spoke of both his innocence and his outrage at what he had been accused of.

'But why,' Miriam asked, 'did you cave into their demands if it wasn't true? Why did you let Jack come back here to live – to humiliate me – if it was a set-up?'

There it was – the inevitable question, for which he'd prepared himself.

'That's the point,' Mr Havelock said, sounding defeated. 'The woman had me at her mercy. You saw how convincing she was. She should have been on the stage. And her daughter, too.'

Miriam had indeed seen. They had been so convincing. She'd left the house that day believing their lies – believing that her father was a rapist.

'Well, can you imagine what might have happened if she had carried out her threat and gone to the authorities with her report, with her tales of my purported malevolence, and then taken them to the asylum, where they would have found your mother living under an assumed name. Imagine if they had listened to Henrietta's diabolical accusations – and believed her?'

Miriam was quiet. She had been taken in by their lies – their act – and she was his daughter. If that was the case, there'd be a good chance that others would be too.

Mr Havelock dropped his shoulders as though age had finally caught up with him.

'I'm an old man, Miriam. I didn't want to have to go through any kind of scandal or, worse still, a court case. Mud sticks. The very accusation would tarnish my name – even if it was proved, as it surely would have been, that it was all a fabrication. God only knows, I might have died without having the chance to clear my name.' He gave Miriam a baleful look. 'I'm so sorry, my dear, but allowing Jack back home seemed the lesser of two evils.'

Miriam was quiet. She understood now why her father had acquiesced, but it did not make Jack's return any less painful. Nor any less humiliating.

'And while we are being so plain-spoken ...' Mr Havelock said, straightening his shoulders. 'This might be hard for you to hear.' He tried to give his daughter a look that conveyed care; a sense of having to be cruel to be kind. 'But you were never going to be able to keep Jack away for ever.' Another pause. 'And I honestly don't think anything you do would keep him away from his other woman and their bastard. I'm in no doubt that if I'd been forced to fight the false accusations of that deplorable woman and her daughter, then it would have flung the door wide open for Jack to come back anyway.'

Miriam thought for a moment. Her father was right. He was always right.

'I suppose so,' she said.

They were quiet. Mr Havelock knew when to speak and when not to.

Miriam finished her tea, digesting everything that had been said. She had felt so alone these past months in the sanatorium. Her relationship with her father could often be tumultuous – sometimes she felt as though she hated him as much as she loved him. But when she had thought he had done those terrible things that Pearl and Bel had said he had done, she had felt bereft – as though her father had died. She had felt so alone. But now, thank

45

goodness, it had all been put right. She had her father back. He might be far from perfect, but he was not a sexual deviant.

As Miriam looked out of the window, her thoughts wandered back to the present – to her own life. Her own marriage. Her own problems.

Now that she was relieved of the crisis with her father, she needed to refocus on her own situation.

'Jack being back is a nightmare – totally humiliating,' she said. 'I'm going to be the laughing stock of high society.'

'Well, my dear, if anyone laughs at you, they'll be feeling my wrath – and besides, if they dare to laugh at your misfortune, they are not worth knowing.' The joy he felt at having turned her around – having got her back onside – was great and he tried to keep it from showing.

'Do you want my advice?' he asked, surprised at his capacity to sound so totally sincere. So kind and caring. So fatherly.

Miriam nodded. She was now the daughter and he the all-knowing father.

'I think you should divorce the man and be done with it. Go and see Rupert at Gourley and Sons. He's good at what he does, and discreet, and he'll be able to push it through post-haste. I've already had a chat with him – all confidential, of course – and he says there's ways and means of getting it through with the minimum of exposure.'

They were quiet again.

'The horse has bolted and there's no dragging it back in the stable,' he said. 'Much as you might want to. My advice would be to simply cut your losses, divorce Jack as quickly and quietly as possible and move on. It's not as if you are reliant on him for anything. You certainly don't need him for any kind of financial help. Divorcing Jack would give you a fresh start. And you couldn't do it at a better time, while the whole nation's focus is on the war.' He couldn't bring himself to say, 'And on our impending victory.'

'I won't give him what he wants,' Miriam said, her mouth set in a firm line. 'I want him to suffer.'

Mr Havelock smiled. 'You're a chip off the old block, Miriam. Too much like your dear papa.' He smiled indulgently at her. 'But don't make the mistake of cutting off your nose to spite your face. Think about it.'

'I will, but I won't change my mind,' Miriam said.

'Well, whatever you decide to do, Miriam,' Mr Havelock manufactured a look of deep sincerity, 'I'll support you. Just ask and I'll be there to help in any way I can.'

Miriam looked at her father. How could she have believed those things he'd been accused of? *He wasn't a monster*. Why had she believed people she didn't even know over her own family? Her own flesh and blood?

'Thanks, Father,' she smiled.

'Well, off you go.' Mr Havelock shooed her away. 'I think you've kept your friend waiting long enough.'

Mr Havelock smiled to himself as Miriam left the room. That could not have gone better. Even to his own ears, his lies about Henrietta and her delusions inspired by Gothic novels had sounded totally convincing. He had known that Miriam would not want to see her own father in such an abhorrent light; he'd just needed to give her a believable alternative.

Hearing Eddy's monotonous voice offering Miriam a lift into town, he reached for his brandy glass and took a long drink. He heard the front door bang shut and a few moments later the engine of the Jaguar turn over.

He relaxed back into the leather upholstery of his chair.

Now Miriam was back and on board, he could put into play his plan of action.

He smiled and took out one of his most expensive cigars, held it to his nose and inhaled its aroma.

A knock on the door interrupted his reverie. He looked up to see Agatha walking into the room with a tray under her arm, ready to clear away Miriam's cup and saucer and a half-eaten sandwich.

'I take it Miriam's homecoming was a success, sir?'

Agatha and Eddy had speculated about the reason why the master's daughter had been summoned back to the house as soon as she'd stepped off the train after returning to 'civilisation', but they were still none the wiser.

Mr Havelock clipped the end of his cigar.

'Yes, yes, Agatha. A successful homecoming!' He clicked open his engraved silver lighter. 'Couldn't be better.'

Holding the flickering flame to the end of his cigar, he puffed a few times, creating a swirling grey cloud around him.

'Now that Miriam's back, there's lots to be done. Lots,' he said, with a triumphant smile.

*

As Eddy drove down Ryhope Road, Miriam's mind skittered about – dodging between her need for a drink and the conversation she'd just had with her father.

Looking out the window as they started to make their way down Burdon Road, Miriam saw that Mowbray Park was in full bloom, although the crater caused by one of the town's many air raids was still very much in evidence. She squinted as the sun's reflection off the huge glass panelling of the Winter Gardens dazzled her. Closing her eyes for a moment, she saw a flash of her father's face when Pearl was threatening to expose him.

He had not denied the accusations. She would have thought he would. But then again, that was her father. He rarely did what was expected. He was his own man. An anomaly. That was for sure. Anyway, what did it matter how he'd reacted? He was innocent. She'd got it all wrong. And if that wasn't a reason to celebrate, she didn't know what was. She was going to have a drink come hell or high water, and no matter what she had promised Margaret.

As the car pulled up outside the Grand, she felt a slight twinge of guilt, having promised her sister that she would not drink a drop when she got back. Margaret really did care. She really wanted her younger sister to stop drinking, but they were different – they always had been, even as children. They'd often joked that it was strange they looked so similar yet were polar opposites in nature. Margaret had always been the level-headed one, perhaps because she was the firstborn. Who knew? Anyway, it was all right for Margaret. She had Angus and their big house on a big country estate. They were happy, settled, solid. She, on the other hand, had a husband who was now shacked up with his new family. A husband who could not be sent back to the Clyde – that ship had well and truly sailed. If Margaret was in her shoes, she'd be doing exactly what she was doing at this very moment in time – getting out of the car and walking straight up the steps to the Grand.

The doorman tipped his cap as she walked through the main entrance and into the foyer. Breathing in the familiar smell of the place that had become her second home, Miriam felt herself relax. The thought of having a drink made her feel happy and excited for the first time in seven months.

'Amelia!' she called out on seeing her friend perched on a bar stool, chatting to one of the Admiralty.

Her friend turned around and her face lit up.

'Miriam!' She stood up, a little unsteady on her feet. '*At last*, you're back!'

The pair embraced.

'I thought I was never going to get you back.' She turned and smiled at the bartender.

'A gin and tonic for my friend here. And make it a big one.'

Chapter Six

The women all settled down at their table in the canteen. They were still keeping up their 'lessons' in current affairs, although of late they had dropped to every other day. Now that Peter was back and the liberation of France was fast becoming a reality, they no longer urgently needed to scour the papers for news that might pertain to Rosie's husband's welfare. It was the same with articles about Gibraltar, where Polly's husband, Tommy Watts, was stationed. The success of the North African campaign and the surrender of Italy meant that the Rock's primary role was now as a supply depot for those ships crossing the Mediterranean.

As they started to tuck into their lunches, Hannah read out a piece about the Majdanek concentration camp on the south-eastern outskirts of Lublin. The city, along with several others in Poland, had been liberated by Soviet forces.

'Do you think it might mean that the one your parents are in will also be liberated?' Martha asked.

Everyone knew that Hannah's Jewish parents, who hailed from Prague, had been taken to the Auschwitz camp two-and-a-half-years ago – and that she had no idea if they were alive or dead. The only reason Hannah was not there with them was because they'd sent her over to England to live with her aunty Rina just before the start of the war.

'Let's hope so,' Hannah said.

Angie and Dorothy were paying particular attention. They were also interested in hearing about what was happening in Poland so that they could relay any news back to Mrs Kwiatkowski, whose command of the English language was good, but less so when reading.

When Hannah finished the article and started to eat her sandwiches, the conversation turned to news closer to home: which yards were launching what kinds of vessels, as well as any gossip that was doing the rounds.

'Did you know the women at Doxford's have their own room where they can eat their lunch?' Polly said.

'Really?' said Martha.

'Well, it's a good job we've not got one here,' Angie jibed, "cos then yer wouldn't be able to have Olly here.'

Hannah smiled at Olly, who pushed his thick-framed spectacles up the bridge of his nose. It was a nervous tic of his when he was the focus of attention. Hannah had become close to Olly after she had swapped her welding job for work as an apprentice draughtsman. The two were now inseparable.

As they all munched their packed lunches, they argued the case for and against having a women-only room. Having agreed they were happy with the status quo, Dorothy surveyed the table and cleared her throat. When that didn't stop the women's chatter, she picked up her teaspoon and tapped the edge of her teacup.

Everyone looked up.

'Yer ganna make a toast, Dor?' Angie laughed.

'Not quite,' said Dorothy. 'More an announcement.'

'What's it about this time?' Martha chuckled.

'I have made up my mind!' Dorothy declared, surveying her workmates' faces.

'What? About Bobby and Toby?' asked Polly.

'Indeed,' said Dorothy. 'About Bobby and Toby.'

The women looked at Dorothy with great expectation. Their normally loquacious workmate had been unusually quiet on the topic of the two men vying for her attention since their drinks at the Admiral.

Dorothy looked at Rosie. 'I thought about what you said – you know, about it being *me* who should be the one to decide who or what it is I want.'

Rosie nodded and smiled.

'And?' Gloria asked. Her son was going to be heart-broken if he wasn't the chosen one. He might come across as a bit of a Jack the Lad, always joshing about and joking, but deep down he was a serious soul – and he was most certainly serious about Dorothy.

'Who have you picked?' Hannah asked. She and Olly had agreed that Dorothy's two suitors might well be com-plete opposites in looks, backgrounds and personalities, but they were the same in one regard. They were both dotty about her.

Dorothy cleared her throat.

'Well, it's not so much about me choosing between the two.' She paused. 'If I'm honest, I don't really know *who* I want. But I've been doing a lot of thinking. *A lot of thinking.*'

'Must have been hard,' Martha joked.

Dorothy gave her a mock scowl.

'And what conclusion have you come to?' Olly asked, intrigued.

'I've decided that I'm going to tell Toby that I don't want to marry him.' Dorothy pulled a face. It hurt her to have to say it. Until a few weeks ago, she had been sure that all she wanted was to see Toby drop down on one knee and ask her to be his wife. Her life would be set out before her. Court-ship, marriage – then family. How had it all gone awry?

'Aww,' said Polly.

'What? You don't think I should?' Dorothy panicked. *Perhaps she should just tell herself to get a grip. Forget her kiss with Bobby. Concentrate on a future with Toby.*

53

'No, no, I didn't mean that,' Polly said. 'It's just that I feel a bit sorry for Toby. He's crazy about you. He's going to be heartbroken.' All the women had thought Dorothy and Toby made a perfect couple.

Dorothy's shoulders sagged. 'I know. I feel awful. I'm going to feel worse than awful when I tell him.' She was dreading telling him. The weight of guilt had lain heavily on her since she'd made up her mind. As had the push and pull of indecision. Was she doing the right thing – or not?

'So, why exactly have you decided to turn Toby down?' Rosie asked, taking a sip of her tea.

'Because it just wouldn't be fair on him,' Dorothy said, her mind starting to run through the reasons she'd listed in her head. She'd asked herself the same question countless times. 'I can't say yes to marrying him, knowing that I've just kissed someone else. I mean, it's not right, is it?' She looked at Polly. 'I bet you didn't even *look* at another bloke when you were with Tommy.'

Polly gave a sad smile. *God, she missed Tommy.* 'No, I didn't.'

'I think yer've made the right decision,' Gloria ventured. 'And I'm not speaking as Bobby's mam, but as a friend.' She looked at Dorothy. 'I think yer need to be a hundred per cent about someone if yer gonna agree to marry them – 'n obviously yer not.'

'So, does that mean you're going to end it with Toby?' Martha asked.

All the women looked at Dorothy.

'I don't know,' she said, a look of pure wretchedness on her face. 'I just keep thinking that something's not right if I'm off kissing another bloke, is it?' Again, Dorothy's mind swung back to Bobby. And that kiss. Then back to Toby and all the good times they'd had – the future that could be theirs.

There were a few mutterings of agreement, although none of the women really wanted to commit themselves. They knew that this was a decision Dorothy had to make for herself.

'I mean, I can't see Vivien Leigh off kissing someone else when she's got Laurence Olivier, or Katharine Hepburn when she's with Spencer Tracy … And if it was the other way round, and I knew Toby had been kissing some other woman behind my back, I'd dump him in a flash.'

Another pause.

'Kissing someone who isn't your fiancé does not bode well for a future marriage, does it?' she said. *Nor the way kissing Bobby had made her feel.*

This time there were more robust murmurs of agreement from the women.

'Do you think I'm doing the right thing?' Dorothy asked, looking around at her friends for affirmation.

'It's what feels right for you,' Rosie said.

'Definitely,' agreed Gloria.

Dorothy looked at Angie. 'We've had a good chat about it, haven't we?' she said, smiling at her friend. 'Even though everything we've talked about has probably been repeated verbatim to Quentin.'

Angie shook her head in denial, although it was true. She had indeed told Quentin every cough and spit.

'So, when are you going to tell him?' Polly asked.

Dorothy grimaced.

'Well,' she looked again at Angie, 'we decided it was unfair to drag him all the way up north to tell him my answer's no, only for him to then have to go all the way back down south again.'

'And it's not as if Dor can gan down 'n drop in on Toby – him being all top secret,' Angie said. Like Peter, Toby was also with the SOE, although his war work had kept him on British soil.

'So,' Dorothy said, 'it was a toss-up between a phone call and a letter.'

'She's gonna dee both,' Angie informed them. 'Speak to him on the blower 'n write him a letter.'

'Tell him that I feel it's too early to be talking about marriage. That it's a no for the time being ... and then see what he says about everything,' Dorothy said.

'Sounds to me like yer want him to tell yer what to do,' said Gloria.

No one said anything, but it was clear they agreed with their mother hen's summary of the situation.

'So, when are you going to speak to him?' Rosie asked.

Dorothy pulled a long face.

'Tonight. He's calling me tonight.'

As Dorothy and Angie made their way from the ferry landing back home, they were both in unusually sombre moods.

'Gloria's right, yer knar,' Angie said.

'About what?' asked Dorothy.

'Yer *knar* what,' Angie said. 'Yer wanting Toby to make yer decision for yer – about whether yer both keep courting.'

Dorothy was quiet as they turned down Norfolk Street. A group of shipyard workers walking in front of them turned down one of the backstreets that led to one of the rougher east-end pubs.

'I think,' Angie continued, 'yer really hoping that Toby won't be too happy about having his offer of marriage turned down and he'll suggest calling it a day.'

Dorothy looked at Angie but didn't say anything. They turned right onto Borough Road.

'Oh, Ange,' Dorothy lamented. 'I just don't feel like I know my own mind at the moment. I felt so sure I wanted Toby – wanted to marry him, share my life with him—' She broke off, thinking of all the moments she had enjoyed with Toby, chatting about the end of the war and how wonderful it would be for them to be together all the time. She'd known he was going to propose. She'd been so excited by the prospect. And then bloody Bobby had stomped onto the scene.

'And then Bobby tipped up,' Angie said, reading her thoughts.

Dorothy nodded.

'If I hadn't had that kiss, I wouldn't be in this emotional quagmire.'

'Mmm,' Angie said, 'I dinnit knar about that. What would happen if yer got engaged – or worse still, yer got hitched – and then someone like Bobby came along who yer fancied? Yer'd been in an even worse *emotional quagmire*.'

As they turned into Foyle Street, they slowed down.

'Do yer wanna hear what I really think?' Angie asked.

Dorothy nodded.

'I think yer knew the moment yer kissed Bobby it was all over with Toby.' Angie said what she was sure all the women were secretly thinking. 'I dinnit think yer the type of person who can kiss someone else 'n then just carry on with yer fella as if it never happened. I think the guilt'll eat away at yer – 'n you'll eventually have to confess all. And then it'll be much worse – much more of a betrayal.'

Dorothy stopped outside their front door. She pulled off her headscarf and sighed heavily and with great sadness.

'You're right, Ange. I wish you weren't, but you are.' She sighed again as she rummaged in her bag for the front-door keys.

'I'm gonna have to tell him it's over, aren't I?' She pulled out her keys.

Angie looked at her best mate and thought that she had never seen her look so forlorn.

'I think yer are, Dor.'

At seven o'clock, Dorothy and Angie walked down the stairs to Mrs Kwiatkowski's flat on the ground floor. As usual, her door was open and there was the comforting smell of home-made bread wafting out into the main hallway.

Angie knocked on the door. 'Cooee! Mrs Kwiatkowski, it's only us.'

Their old neighbour came bustling out of the back bedroom.

'Wejdźcie moi drodzy wejdźcie,' she said, waving them in. She shook her head. 'Come in, my dears.'

Dorothy and Angie had noticed that of late their neighbour had seemed to be slipping back into her native language more frequently.

'My, you two look ... how you say it ... *dressed to kill,'* she chuckled. 'But hopefully, not literally.'

'Thanks, Mrs Kwiatkowski,' Dorothy said as they followed the old woman into the kitchen. 'Although I do feel what I am about to do is tantamount to murder.'

'Honestly, Dor, yer are a drama queen.' Angie rolled her eyes at Mrs Kwiatkowski.

They all looked over at the phone. The weapon with which Dorothy was going to commit her murderous act – the killing of a love affair.

Mrs Kwiatkowski looked up at the clock. She knew Toby was due to ring at quarter-past seven.

'Let's have a nice cup of tea,' she said, bustling over to the kettle.

Dorothy and Angie sat down.

'I'm guessing you two are going to the Ritz tonight?' Mrs Kwiatkowski twisted her head round and looked at her two pretty neighbours.

'We are,' Angie said without much enthusiasm. 'Dor has insisted we gan, otherwise she said she'd be pacing around the flat feeling guilt-ridden, down and depressed.'

'And the Ritz will stop her feeling these emotions?' Mrs Kwiatkowski said, putting the teapot on the table.

'Nah,' Angie laughed, 'but a few port and lemons might.'

Dorothy tutted and glanced nervously at the phone.

'I feel more evil than the Wicked Witch of the West when she snatches Toto and threatens to kill him,' she said, forlornly.

Mrs Kwiatkowski looked puzzled. She had never seen *The Wizard of Oz*. Angie shook her head to show it wasn't important. 'Dorothy's just being silly.'

Mrs Kwiatkowski poured out the tea.

Dorothy looked at the clock. It was nearly quarter past. She felt sick with nerves.

'I can't remember what we'd agreed I was going to say ...' She looked to Angie for help.

'That yer really sorry,' Angie reiterated, 'that yer think it's too early to get engaged – or married.' She was now actually feeling guilty by proxy. She had got to know Toby. He was a lovely bloke. Which made him being dumped all the worse. 'That yer might have been seeing each other for a year and a half, but really you've not spent that much time together ... That when you add it all up, it's probably the equivalent of being together just a few months.'

'You don't think that's demeaning what we had?' Dorothy asked.

59

Seeing the confused look on Angie's and Mrs Kwiat-kowski's faces, she added, 'You know ... *belittling* our relationship.'

'Maybe,' Angie conceded.

'Perhaps leave that bit out,' Mrs Kwiatkowski suggested.

They all looked at the phone.

'It's plugged in, isn't it?' Dorothy panicked. She couldn't miss the call. She needed to get this over with.

'And you're not going to tell him about the other young man?' Mrs Kwiatkowski asked. She had seen Dorothy with Bobby. The chemistry between the pair was obvious.

'No, no, definitely not,' Dorothy said, anger towards Bobby sweeping to the fore. All this heartache and the ter-rible feelings of guilt were Bobby's fault. She had really loved Toby. Loved him as a person. Loved being with him. If Bobby hadn't come along, she'd have been more than happy with Toby. *Wouldn't she? Or was it easier to blame Bobby than herself?*

'We think telling Toby about Bobby would be too hurt-ful,' Angie said. She wanted to add that Quentin thought so too, but didn't.

'But it might help him understand *why* Dorothy is reject-ing his proposal of marriage,' Mrs Kwiatkowski said. 'Rather than him thinking it's something to do with him.'

'I think it would be rubbing salt into the wound,' Doro-thy said. In reality, she did not want to be cast into the role of wanton woman.

'Do you think that if I change my mind later and tell him I've made a mistake, he'd have me back?'

'Perhaps, if he didn't get to know about Bobby,' Angie mused.

'And if he did get to know?' Dorothy asked, even though she knew the answer to her own question.

'Toby might be nice, but he's not that nice!' Angie said.

'So, you're not just telling him no to marriage, but no to everything?' Mrs Kwiatkowski asked. 'You're going to end your courtship with him?'

Dorothy looked pitifully glum. 'I am.'

Mrs Kwiatkowski reached out and put her gnarled hand over Dorothy's and squeezed it. 'Well, I think you have made the right decision.'

All of a sudden, there was a loud knock on the main front door. They all jumped.

'Who's that?' Dorothy looked at Mrs Kwiatkowski. 'Are you expecting anyone?'

The old woman shook her head.

Angie got up and hurried over to the window that looked out onto the street.

'Bloody Nora, Dor,' she said, turning to look at her best mate. 'He's here! Toby's here!'

Chapter Seven

'Wow! You look amazing,' Toby said on seeing Dorothy open the main front door to the flats.

He looked puzzled. 'You weren't expecting me, were you?'

Dorothy felt another punch of guilt.

'No ...' She stepped out onto the front step and shut the door behind her.

'The Ritz?' he asked.

Dorothy nodded. She was finding words difficult. She looked at Toby and thought how handsome he was in his officer's uniform. *The first time she'd seen him at Lily's, he'd been in his uniform.* She took his arm and guided him down the steps.

'I hope Angie doesn't mind?' he asked.

'No, no, not at all.' Dorothy forced a laugh. 'She's probably glad. Probably racing upstairs this very moment to put her pyjamas on and then ring Quentin.'

When they reached the end of Foyle Street, they stopped.

'The Palatine?' Toby suggested.

Dorothy had to stop herself from screaming 'No!' After Toby's proposal in the hotel's dining room, she didn't think she wanted to step foot in the place ever again.

'Why don't we just go somewhere more casual,' she said, turning left into Borough Road.

'Suits me,' Toby said, sensing an awkwardness from Dorothy. An awkwardness he had picked up over the phone when they last spoke. Which was why he'd travelled up this evening to see her. To speak to her face-to-face. Find out exactly what was really going on in her head. Did she want to marry him or not? He could normally read Dorothy like a book, but her reaction to his proposal had thrown him.

They walked past Gloria's flat – now Gloria and Jack's flat. Crossing the road, they arrived at the Burton House pub. Toby opened the door and Dorothy stepped inside. She felt her heart hammering with nerves. This was going to be so much harder face-to-face.

Once they'd got their drinks and were sitting at a table by the window in a quiet corner, Toby looked at Dorothy. He had never seen her so subdued. Or was she nervous?

'We've not had a chance to really talk properly after …' Toby hesitated '… after I asked you to marry me.' He took a sip of his beer.

Dorothy didn't say anything. Didn't know what to say. She kept thinking of what she and Angie had agreed would be good to say, but her mind had gone blank. All she kept thinking about was the good times they'd had together, their walks along the promenade, the Valentine's Day when he'd surprised her at the yard and taken her to the Bungalow Café – then told her he loved her. And she had fallen in love with him, hadn't she? Or had she fallen in love with the idea of falling in love? *Oh God, she just didn't know any more.*

'I know you wanted some time to think things over, which I totally understand. But I thought rather than talk on the phone, it would be best for us to see each other.'

Dorothy nodded. Her mind was still racing with a myriad thoughts and feelings – and memories. She took a large gulp of her lemonade. She had ordered a soft drink because she wanted to keep her head clear.

Toby looked at Dorothy. Since she had told him she needed time to think about his proposal he had begun to

63

doubt her feelings for him. He'd have been a fool not to. Something had made her unsure. Something had changed, although he was not sure what that something was. Nor when that change had happened. He had thought it had been on the day of the proposal, but had there been hints of change before then?

'If I said to you,' Toby asked tentatively, 'that I had taken the ring back to the jeweller's, what would you say?'

He watched Dorothy's expression change to one of relief and felt his heart drop.

'I would say,' she said carefully, 'that doing so might have been a good idea.' She took another big glug of her lemonade.

'Should I take that to mean you don't want to marry me?' Toby decided to just come out and say it. There could be no more beating about the bush.

Dorothy could feel tears start to prick her eyes. She had never felt so terrible in her entire life. She almost wished the tables were turned and it was Toby who had done the dirty – not her. At least that was something she was used to.

'I'm so sorry, Toby,' she began. 'I really am.'

'I'll take that as a no, then.'

Dorothy nodded.

They were quiet for a moment. Suddenly, it felt as though there was nothing else left to say.

They supped their drinks in silence for a few minutes.

'I just don't understand,' Toby said. 'I thought we were happy. We've known each other for a year and a half, and I know we've not had a lot of time together, but when we've not been able to see each other we've chatted on the phone – I've even met your parents. I thought we were good together?'

'You're right,' Dorothy said. 'We do know each other. We have been happy. Very happy.'

'And I have to say,' Toby continued, 'I really thought the love I felt for you was reciprocated.'

'It was. *It is*,' Dorothy said, unsure of herself.

'*Was* or *is*?' Toby asked.

Dorothy let out a huge sigh. She couldn't do this any more. Suddenly, Mrs Kwiatkowski's face came to mind and her words about being honest.

'I kissed Bobby,' she said simply.

Toby sat speechless for a moment.

'You kissed Bobby,' he repeated. Still not quite believing his ears.

'I don't know what came over me. He came round and told me he'd sorted things out with his mam and, well, we ended up kissing.'

Dorothy looked at Toby's face. Saw hurt and anger.

'You kissed him the evening I asked you to marry me?'

'Yes, but it was before you asked me.'

Toby let out a bitter laugh.

'Ah, that makes it all right then.'

He shook his head and looked out of the window.

'You kissed Bobby and then sat with me through an entire three-course meal at the Palatine and let me propose to you – all the while having just been with Bobby.'

Dorothy looked at Toby and couldn't think of anything to say that might justify what she'd done.

'You know,' Toby said after a few moments' silence, 'I thought there might be someone else, but I dismissed it. I actually felt guilty for thinking it about you.' He looked at Dorothy as though she were a stranger, which at this moment he felt she was. 'When you didn't say yes, I thought something was up. I've thought about it a lot these past few weeks, but every time I wondered if there was anyone else, I slapped the very thought of it away. Not Dorothy. *Not my Dorothy*.'

He let out a bark of mirthless laughter.

'I should have known,' Toby said, finishing off his beer. 'Ever since Bobby came on the scene it's been *Bobby this, Bobby that* – I should have realised.' He could have kicked himself. *Of course.* There'd been an awkwardness that afternoon when he had arrived at the flat and found them both in the kitchen. *What an idiot he was!*

'But it wasn't like that!' Dorothy tried to justify herself. 'All I really wanted was for Bobby to make it up with Gloria.' She bit her lip. 'And then … well … he did make it up … and … I don't know what happened … It just came out of the blue.'

Even as she was speaking, Dorothy knew she was not being entirely honest. Ever since Bobby had turned up at Gloria's flat that night after being medically discharged from the navy, she had felt a pull towards him. Not just of attraction, but something more. A feeling of simply wanting to be with him.

'I'm sorry, Toby. I really am,' Dorothy said, not knowing what else to say. Everything she and Angie had planned for her to say while they'd been getting ready had gone out the window.

'I'm sorry too, Dorothy!' Toby stood up and put his cap back on. 'I don't think you will ever know how much.'

Dorothy stood up. 'You're going?'

'I don't see much point in sticking around, do you?'

Again, Dorothy found herself at a loss for words.

Toby turned and headed towards the exit. Dorothy followed. They each forced a smile as a worker coming into the pub held the door open for them.

Stepping out onto the pavement, the stony silence between them remained strained.

As they started walking along the street back to the flat, a familiar figure suddenly appeared striding along Borough Road, heading in their direction.

It was Bobby.

Dorothy recognised him first. His tall, muscular physique and rolling gait, which only seemed to accentuate his broad shoulders, were now familiar to her. She guessed he must be heading to Gloria's to see Hope. She hadn't thought about the possibility they might bump into him. But then again, she hadn't expected Toby to turn up. *God! Talk about bad timing!*

It took a few more seconds before Toby saw him and realised who it was. As soon as he did, he came to an abrupt halt. As did Bobby when he looked up and saw it was Toby.

The two men were now facing each other, just yards apart. A standstill followed by a stand-off.

'Hello, Bobby,' Toby said, his voice flat and unfriendly.

And then – quick as lightning – he pulled back his arm and punched Bobby in the face.

Dorothy let out an involuntary scream.

Bobby staggered back a few paces, his hand rubbing his chin. The blow had split his lip and there was blood.

'I'll let you have that one for free,' he said, dabbing his mouth with the back of his overall sleeve. 'I deserved it.' He looked at Dorothy. 'Although I have to admit, it was worth it.' He saw Toby's fists clench, ready to let rip again, provoked by his words. 'The next one's not for free, though,' he said, straightening himself up to his full height.

The words were barely out of his mouth when Toby took another swing. This time, though, Bobby was ready. He ducked, causing Toby's bunched-up fist to glance off the side of his face.

'Stop it!' Dorothy screeched.

Neither man was listening. They were both grappling with one another and throwing the odd punch.

Dorothy saw something small and square drop out of Toby's pocket and fall to the ground. She went to pick it up and saw it was the little velvet box that contained the diamond engagement ring.

Looking up, she saw that a few drinkers had come out of the pub.

Behind Bobby and Toby's brawling bodies, she noticed Jack coming up the steps from the basement flat. He, too, had heard the commotion.

Two of the men from the pub grabbed hold of Toby at the same time that Jack grabbed Bobby from behind.

Toby fought to be free.

Bobby, seeing that it was Jack who was trying to restrain him, didn't. He dropped his fists and Jack let go of his grip.

Toby and Bobby stood panting and glaring at each other. Each man had a trickle of blood coming from the corner of his mouth and what looked like the beginning of a black eye.

Bobby allowed himself to be pulled back by Jack, then guided away from any more confrontation and down to the basement flat.

Dorothy yanked Toby by the sleeve of his uniform, forcing him to walk along the road and turn the corner into Foyle Street.

Pulling out a hanky from her handbag, she gave it to him.

'Come back to mine and let me see to those cuts,' she said. She didn't know whether to feel angry at Toby for having a go at Bobby or to feel sorry that he was hurt – and not just physically.

'No, I don't think that's a good idea. I'm fine,' Toby said, handing her back the handkerchief.

He walked over to his car. Swinging the driver's door open, he glared at Dorothy.

'I hope Bobby makes you happy,' he said, his words devoid of sincerity.

Dorothy wanted to say something – but couldn't think of anything at all.

Suddenly, she realised that she was still holding the small box with the ring in it.

'Oh my God,' she said, holding the box up in the air. 'Toby!' She ran over to the car. 'Your ring!'

Toby was sitting behind the wheel. He wound the window down.

'No,' he said, 'it's *your* ring, Dorothy. Do what you like with it … You can chuck it in the Wear for all I care.'

And with that he wound the window back up, turned the ignition and fired up the engine.

Tears started to form in Dorothy's eyes. She tried to blink them back, but it was no good, they started to drip slowly down her face.

Through a blur she looked on as the man she had loved – the man she had believed she would marry – pulled away.

Watching as the car turned right at the bottom of the street and disappeared from view, she knew Toby was gone for good. She knew she would never see or hear from him again.

When Dorothy came through the main entrance to the flats, she went straight to Mrs Kwiatkowski's. Angie was, as predicted, in her pyjamas, nursing a cup of tea, having just got off the phone to Quentin.

'Dor! Yer back!' Angie said, staring at her friend. 'We thought yer might be longer, didn't we, Mrs Kwiatkowski?'

The old woman nodded.

Seeing the tear stains, Angie jumped out of her seat. 'Are yer all reet, Dor?'

Dorothy took one look at her friend and burst out crying.

Angie guided her towards one of the chairs by the kitchen table.

Dorothy slumped down on it.

'I feel so awful,' Dorothy said between the tears. 'Really, really awful.'

'What's happened?' Angie asked, suddenly noticing that Dorothy was gripping something in her right hand.

Mrs Kwiatkowski poured out a cup of tea.

'I told him ...' She looked up at Mrs Kwiatkowski. 'About Bobby.'

'Oh dear,' said Angie.

'Then we bumped into him on the way back home.'

'What? Bobby?' Angie asked, incredulous.

Dorothy nodded.

'They had a fight.'

Angie's hand went to her mouth.

Mrs Kwiatkowski went over to the cupboard and pulled out a bottle of Polish vodka. She held it up for Angie and Dorothy to see. They nodded vigorously.

Realising she was still holding the ring box, Dorothy suddenly let it go as though it was poison.

'Is that what I think it is?' asked Angie.

'It is,' Dorothy said, glancing across at her elderly neighbour, who was pouring good measures into three small shot glasses. She pushed the box towards Angie, who took it and tentatively opened it.

'Cor!' Angie's eyes almost popped out. 'I've never seen a diamond ring like this.'

Dorothy smiled through the tears. 'It's beautiful, isn't it?'

'It is that,' Angie gasped, entranced. 'But yer have to give him it back.'

'I tried to, but he wouldn't have it. He said I could chuck it in the river for all he cared.'

Angie looked at her neighbour. 'What dee yer think, Mrs Kwiatkowski?'

'I think the ring would just be a reminder of his heart-ache,' she mused. 'And it sounds as though he is not in need of the money. From what I have gathered during your courtship, he is a man of not insubstantial means.'

'Yer reet there, he's loaded,' Angie confirmed, looking back down at the ring in the box she was still holding.

'Well, if that's the case,' Mrs Kwiatkowski surmised, 'you'll have to think about something good you can do with it.'

Chapter Eight

August

The bank holiday weekend was being celebrated in earnest as the beaches had been opened to the public for the first time since war began. The promenades along Roker and Seaburn were chock-a-block with townsfolk who had crammed onto the trams and buses and travelled across the river for a much-needed break. Absenteeism was high in the shipyards, coal mines and other industries, but no one would be reprimanded too harshly for the Allies were well on their way to victory.

D-Day had resulted in the liberation of Western Europe and there was no denying that the 'biggest shipbuilding town in the world' had played its part. Even those still in domestic service in the more well-to-do areas had been granted time off to enjoy the break. All apart from those employed at the Havelock residence, where the master of the house was not in the mood to be gracious to his staff and allow them even a few hours off. His malady had worsened of late as every day it seemed the headlines brought news of yet more Allied successes. The Warsaw Uprising, staged by the Polish Home Army, was being enthusiastically reported on, the Americans and the Chinese were making inroads into northern Burma and had overcome strong Japanese forces to take the city of Myitkyina, and Rennes in north-western France had been taken by American forces.

The only slightly uplifting news, in Mr Havelock's opinion – an opinion he kept firmly to himself – was the trial of those who had tried to assassinate the Führer, and, of course, the massacre of tens of thousands of civilians in the Wola district of Warsaw.

Mr Havelock had also managed to buoy up his spirits by mulling over the plan he had formulated back in June, which was the reason he was now walking from his study, across the hallway and down a short flight of stairs to the back of the house where the kitchen and the staff accommodation were located. Not that there were many servants any more. Since the outbreak of war, he'd lost half his staff – his valet had joined up, his two maids had gone to work in a munitions factory, and the cook, Velma, who had been with the family most of her life, had succumbed to influenza.

Not bothering to knock, Mr Havelock pushed open the door with the end of his walking stick.

'I thought we'd all go for a little walk around the garden!' he announced, stepping into the kitchen. It was warm and smelled of baked salmon. The back door was open as the day was hot. Eddy immediately stubbed out his cigarette and Agatha put down her cup of tea. Both stood up, like army recruits ready for inspection. Eddy flashed Agatha a worried look. They had worked for Mr Havelock long enough to know that this was not simply because the master wanted to enjoy the beauty of the gardens. There was something in the air. There had been since Miriam's return. They had chatted about it and agreed they thought it might have something to do with Henrietta. She was a thorn in Mr Havelock's side – one they knew he'd want removed.

'I've been talking to Sinclair,' Mr Havelock said as he stepped out of the back door and onto the lawn that stretched halfway up the garden to the start of a large vegetable patch and an equally large greenhouse. 'And I thought I'd come and see for myself all his hard work.'

Neither Eddy nor Agatha could remember a time when the master had felt the need to view, or appreciate, the hard graft of others. Especially in the gardens. He'd never been particularly interested in nature of any kind. They also knew that this suited Sinclair down to the ground as he enjoyed working alone and, although he had never said so outright, was not Mr Havelock's greatest fan. His employer did, however, have an amazing plot of land that Sinclair had been able to nurture to his heart's content over the years, as well as some spectacular plants that weren't native to these parts.

'Dig for Victory, eh?' Mr Havelock said, repeating the slogan of the government campaign. He looked up the garden towards the wealth of vegetation growing in the perfectly cultivated allotment. 'Well, old Sinclair has certainly achieved victory in his little part of the world, hasn't he?'

Eddy and Agatha mumbled their agreement, their unease increasing with each step they took towards the vegetable plot and the greenhouse.

'I thought we might go and have a look at some of the wonderful foreign flora I brought back from my travels all those years ago.'

Eddy shot Agatha another anxious look. Whenever the master had returned home from his trips abroad as a negotiator for one of the major shipbuilders, he would always bring with him something from the countries he had visited. Sometimes it would be food, other times a rug or some silk, and they would all stand and admire it before it was taken away. Of course, the tokens he brought back from other countries and cultures were never gifted to his servants. Their treat was in the looking. View what you can never have, hold, touch or taste. Occasionally, he would

74

bring back some seeds or a plant, which he would give to Sinclair to nurture. He would often make a show of gifting some to the town's Winter Gardens, which would entail a small ceremony with a handful of local bigwigs and the unveiling of yet another small brass plaque with his name on it.

'Here we are!' Mr Havelock said, pulling the wood-framed glass door of the greenhouse to one side and stepping in.

'It's a true saying ...' Mr Havelock turned his head slightly to speak to the two minions following him into the warm, rather stifling atmosphere. 'All good things come to those who wait.' He continued walking along the wooden slats that had been put down as a walkway. 'And these particular beauties have taken a while to grow and come into blossom, but I am reliably informed by Sinclair that they are now in their prime.' He stopped in front of a lush green shrub and caressed its flat-topped clusters of pretty white flowers.

'White snakeroot, or as it is known by its Latin name, *Ageratina altissima*. When I brought these over from North America, they were just seedlings. I was amazed they survived the journey.'

He turned his attention to his two servants, talking to them as though they were his students.

'But against the odds, they did. I gave a few to the Borough for the Winter Gardens and kept the rest. I knew they would come in handy one day. And lo and behold, that day has come.'

He smiled and looked at the two people who were going to help him put his plan into action, whether they wanted to or not.

*

Half an hour later, Agatha and Eddy were on their own back in the kitchen, the master having just left.

'He's got us over a barrel,' Eddy said, fishing his half-smoked cigarette out of the ashtray.

Agatha looked grey. She was staring at the plant lying on the kitchen table as though it were roadkill.

'I know,' she said gravely, 'but this is a step too far.'

She looked at Eddy with fearful eyes.

'This,' she said darkly, 'would make us accessories.'

Eddy inhaled deeply on his cigarette.

'No more than in all the other misdemeanours he's committed during our time here.' Smoke billowed out of his mouth as he spoke. He took another drag. 'During our *lifetime* here,' he added, his tone heavy with resentment.

They looked at each other and then back at the plant. They had never openly discussed Mr Havelock's past transgressions. It was almost as though not talking about them meant they had never happened. They had ignored the master's vile actions – turned a blind eye – and pretended they knew nothing of what was going on in the house after he returned home from his stints of working overseas.

But now it would seem that their silence had given Mr Havelock even more power over them, for he had just told them very clearly and very calmly, and with a cruel smile slowly stretching across his lined face, how he was going to force them to do his bidding. If they refused, he would make sure that were the truth about him ever to come out, he would drag them both down with him. And if that meant lying about the roles they had played all those years ago, well so be it.

'I will make it quite clear that you were both procurers,' he'd told them just twenty minutes previously. 'I will make it clear that you both made sure the maids who were employed under this roof were – how would I put it – *to my liking.*' Another smile, this one pure evil. 'That they were young and blonde and blue-eyed.

'I might even elaborate a little,' Mr Havelock had added. 'Might feel compelled to get everything off my chest, and much as I would hate to be viewed as some sort of turncoat, I might have to confess to them that it wasn't just myself who liked to indulge in the forbidden fruits, but that you did too, Eddy.'

Eddy had felt sick to the very pit of his stomach. He had glanced at Agatha and they had exchanged looks. Deep down, they had always known their silence had made them culpable.

So, this is our punishment for keeping quiet. For our inactivity. Our passivity.

Mr Havelock had then given Agatha meticulous instructions on how to prepare the tincture, making her write them down so she got it exactly right.

'And don't even waste your time thinking of some way out of this,' he'd said, 'because there isn't one. I've got a full confession in my safe in the event of my death. It will stay there until this deed is done. Then it will be destroyed – you have my word. I will even give it to you to burn for yourselves.'

Only then had he left.

Since the master's departure, Agatha had barely taken her eyes off the pretty white flowers and lush green leaves of the plant laid out in front of her.

She looked up at Eddy.

'Let's not kid ourselves any more, eh? This is more than just a *misdemeanour.* Much more. This is murder, pure and simple,' she said.

Chapter Nine

'Mam!' Bobby shouted over to Gloria, who was leaving the canteen with the women welders. 'I've just got word from Gordon saying he's fine.' He headed over to her, waving his brother's letter in the air.

Gloria put her hand on her chest and let out a sigh of relief.

'Let's have a read,' she said, stretching out her hand.

Bobby slowed down as he reached the women. Seeing Dorothy, he smiled at her. She ignored him. It had been two weeks now since the punch-up with Toby, and Dorothy had not spoken a word to him. He knew to let well alone until Dorothy's temper had dissipated. He was happy to wait, though, as he'd learnt from his mam that it was all over with Toby. Now it was just a matter of playing his cards right. It would not be wise to charge in there like a bull in a china shop.

Handing over his brother's letter, Bobby laughed. 'Mind you, he sounds a bit cheesed off *Opportune* didn't get to see much action.' Gordon was stationed on HMS *Opportune*, a British destroyer whose job during the D-Day landings had been to keep the waters clear of any enemy ships or submarines.

'Well, that's good, isn't it? No action?' Hannah said.

'It *is* good,' said Gloria.

Bobby didn't say anything, just smiled and gave them his usual mock salute. They all watched as he turned and strode back over to his squad. It was hot and he had his overall top tied around his waist. It was hard not to admire his muscular body, tanned after weeks of blazing sun beating down on them all.

'Come on, let's find some shade,' Dorothy said, leading the way over to a part of the yard overcast by the shadow of one of the larger cranes.

They all sat down on some empty crates and a pile of stacked-up pallets to eat their lunch.

'Do yer think it's time yer talked to Bobby?' Angie asked, fiddling with the peaked cap she had taken to wearing to keep the sun off her fair skin. The weather had brought her freckles out in full force.

'Yes, just *talk* to him,' said Hannah, looking at Olly, who nodded his agreement.

Dorothy looked at Gloria, who didn't say anything. As Bobby's mam and Dorothy's friend, she had to tread carefully.

'I'm confused,' said Martha.

'You're always confused,' Dorothy jibed back.

'She's not the only one.' Polly defended her. 'I'm confused too. Now that you've called things off with Toby, why don't you just give it a go with Bobby? It's obvious the two of you have got the hots for each other.'

Dorothy tutted, but didn't deny it.

'Yes, and it's been two whole weeks since you told Toby, so I think that's a respectable amount of time before you start seeing someone else, don't you agree?' Polly looked around at her workmates and they all nodded.

'Just what I was sayin' last night, weren't it, Dor?' Angie said.

'*Wasn't it*,' Dorothy corrected. 'And yes, it was, Ange. That was, of course, after you'd been discussing the topic with Quentin for hours on the phone.'

'It wasn't hours. I just mentioned it briefly 'n he agreed. We've got better things to talk about than you, yer knar

'… Anyway, yer shouldn't have been earwigging in on our conversation.'

Dorothy was just about to bat back a reply when Rosie butted in.

'I think you're suffering from a bad bout of guilt, Dorothy.'

'And because she's feeling guilty, she's taking it out on Bobby,' Martha said.

'Exactly,' Rosie agreed, taking a sip of her tea.

'But it's *because* of Bobby that I'm feeling guilty,' said Dorothy. 'If he hadn't come along, I'd be fine and dandy and showing off a great big diamond ring to anyone who'd look.' The mention of the ring sent her mood plummeting.

'But it's not Bobby's fault that you like him,' said Hannah.

'Yeah, you can't be angry at Bobby because of how you feel about him,' Martha argued.

Dorothy was quiet. She looked over to where the riveters were having their lunch. Bobby wasn't there, which meant he must be getting his food from the canteen.

'I think what you've all said might be true,' she conceded. 'I think I might be angry with myself as much as with Bobby for spoiling what I had with Toby – for what I *could have* had with Toby.' She took a breath. 'And annoying though it is, I *do* like Bobby.' She thought about their passionate kiss and the goosebumps he gave her whenever he was near. She blew out air. 'But what if that's all it is? Physical attraction.' She looked at Gloria. 'He might think he wants me, but once he's got what he wants, he'll lose interest.'

'Blimey, Dor!' Gloria couldn't keep shtum any longer. 'Talk about having a low opinion of yerself. Yer probably the least boring person I know.'

They all chuckled their agreement.

'Have you thought any more about the ring?' Rosie asked.

Dorothy exhaled heavily.

'Lots,' she said.

'But we're still no further forward,' said Angie.

'It's like a poisoned chalice,' Dorothy added dramatically. 'Every time I look at it, I feel awful. Guilt-ridden. Horrible.'

Angie looked at the women and nodded. 'It's presently stuck behind the tea caddy in the back of the cupboard.'

'But someone keeps getting it out to check every five minutes,' Dorothy added, rolling her eyes in the direction of her flatmate.

'I can't help it,' said Angie. 'I've never seen a ring like it. Come to think of it, I dinnit think I've ever seen a real diamond before.'

'Well, you're making up for it now,' Dorothy said. She turned her attention away from Angie to the rest of her squad. 'She doesn't just look at it. She puts it on and waltzes around the kitchen with it, staring at it like she does Quentin, all love-struck and gooey-eyed.'

Angie thumped her on the arm.

'Ow, that hurt!' Dorothy stared at her best friend and rubbed her arm.

'Well, if it feels like a poisoned chalice – to Dorothy, at least,' Rosie said, 'then I think we should all have a good think and try to come up with a solution about what to do with it. See if we can't turn a negative into a positive. Perhaps sell it and do something with the money? Agreed?'

'Agreed,' everyone chorused.

As they walked back to the dry basin, Rosie dropped back to speak to Gloria.

'How's Jack?' Rosie asked. 'Is he any nearer getting his divorce?'

Gloria let out a bitter laugh. 'Oh God, don't mention the D-word. Miriam's been back nearly a month now 'n there's not been a squeak from her.'

'No divorce papers dropping on the mat?'

'No. Nothing.' Gloria sighed. 'I just don't understand why she's not getting it all sorted. When she was in Scotland, we put it down to the fact she'd want to wait until she was back home so she could use the family solicitor, but now I'm wondering.'

'Strange,' Rosie said. 'I mean, Jack must have ticked every box there is for the granting of a divorce.'

Gloria gave another exasperated sigh. 'I know. If living in sin with his mistress 'n illegitimate daughter doesn't have the divorce papers flying through the courts, I don't know what will.'

They reached the main gates and handed their clocking-off boards to Davey.

'I dunno,' Gloria mused. 'I have a bad feeling in my gut. Like this is the calm before the storm.'

Chapter Ten

Over the next week, work was busy. It didn't quite compare to the hectic pace of the months leading up to D-Day in June, but there was still a need for vessels of all kinds. The scales of war were tipping in the Allies' favour, however that didn't mean they could rest on their laurels. Doxford's had recently seen the cargo vessel *Registan* dispatched into the Wear. Today it was the Shipbuilding Corporation's turn to celebrate the launch of *Empire Cowdray*. As the yard was one of the smallest on the banks of the Wear, the town's bigwigs had decided it needed a show of gratitude and recognition, so the call had gone out to all the yards to send a representative to the launch.

As Harold, the main manager at Thompson's, rarely left his office these days, it had fallen to Helen to fulfil the role. She was just about to leave when she heard the main admin door swing shut and two familiar voices sound out their arrival. Looking up, Helen saw to her dismay that it was indeed her mother and her grandfather. She felt her jaws clench. *What were they doing here?* She had told them that she would see them there. She watched with a sinking heart as her personal assistant, Marie-Anne, showed them both into the office.

'I thought we agreed to meet at the Corporation?' Helen said.

Miriam ignored the question, instead walking around the office as though she owned the place, wiping her finger along the tops of the cabinets and wrinkling her nose.

'It was never this dirty when your father was in charge,' Miriam said.

Helen looked at her mother and then at her grandfather, who was easing himself into the chair at the side of the room. He had on his best Savile Row suit and looked well. Very well.

'Isn't it wonderful to have the whole family together?' Miriam brushed her hands clear of imaginary dust. 'Well, *almost* the whole family,' she said, casting a look through the partition glass towards the entrance to the main office.

'So, why are you both here?' Helen asked, making no attempt to keep the irritation from her voice.

'More like, what on earth is that flea-bitten thing doing in here?' Miriam replied, seeing Winston pad across the office and start winding himself around Helen's legs, purring loudly.

'That *flea-bitten thing*,' Helen said, 'is our resident rat-catcher and has as much right to be here as anyone.' In truth, Winston had not caught a mouse, never mind a rat, since Helen had brought him to the yard nearly two years ago, when his elderly owner had died during the Tatham Street bombing.

Hearing Marie-Anne's surprised voice welcoming yet another guest, Helen looked up to see her father arriving.

'It's Mr Crawford to see you,' Marie-Anne said. She was standing by the office door, her eyes darting between Helen, Miriam and Mr Havelock. This would be interesting. The gossip presently doing the rounds was that Miriam and Jack had split up and Jack was living with Gloria. And even more shockingly, little Hope, whom everyone thought adorable, *was actually Jack's love child*. Looking at Jack now as he pushed back his thick black hair, you could clearly see the resemblance. Hope and her half-sister Helen had inherited their father's dark good looks.

84

'Would you like a tea tray, Miss Crawford?' Marie-Anne asked. She glanced at Jack, who had clearly not expected to see his estranged wife or father-in-law here.

'No thank you, Marie-Anne. They're not staying long,' Helen said. She looked at her father and raised her eyebrows to show that this was a shock for her too.

'Come in, Dad, shut the door.' She waved him in before returning her attention to her mother. She still found it hard to look her grandfather in the eye after Pearl's revelations at Christmas.

'Well, Mama, you've obviously got us all here for a reason, so you might as well get on with it and spit it out.'

Helen and her mother had barely spoken a word to each other since her return from Scotland. They were ships passing in the night, with Helen coming home at around the same time her mother was going out.

Miriam smiled, pleased with herself for orchestrating the impromptu meeting, which hadn't been all that hard to organise. She'd guessed Helen would be in the office getting ready for the launch, but had rung Marie-Anne to double-check. This was followed by a quick phone call to Crown's to relay a message to Jack purporting to be from Helen and saying that she wanted to see him.

'If you're not going to offer us all the hospitality of a cup of tea, darling, I'll have to indulge in a glass of single malt.' Miriam walked over to one of the tall metal cabinets and pulled out a half-bottle of Scotch from the top drawer. Helen watched with disbelief as her mother helped herself, then poured another and handed it to her grandfather.

'Thank you, Miriam,' Mr Havelock said. He'd been happy to accompany his daughter to the yard, knowing she was up to something.

Helen looked at Jack. 'Would you like a drink, Dad, seeing as no one has had the courtesy to ask you?'

'Yer all right, Helen,' Jack said simply. He looked at his watch and then at Miriam. Just being in the same room as her made him feel ill. 'Yer've clearly got us all here for a reason, Miriam, so get on with what yer wanna say. You've got five minutes 'n then I'm out of here.'

'What? No "Lovely to see you, darling? How are you, Miriam?" Dearie me, how long is it since we've seen each other?'

'January 1942,' Jack retorted, quick as a flash. 'Two years 'n seven months. Every minute of which has been pure bliss. Now gerron with what yer've got to say.' He looked down at his watch. 'That's one minute gone already.'

Jack, like Helen, was ignoring his father-in-law – not to be rude, but simply because the very sight of the man repulsed him.

'Very well.' Miriam took a sip of her Scotch. It was not her preferred tipple, but any port in a storm. 'First of all, Jack, I'd like to remind you that we've been married twenty-five years and are still married. You are *still* my husband. Something you seem to have forgotten.'

'That's something I've most definitely not forgotten. Far, far from it,' Jack said, looking at the woman just yards away from him and hating himself more than ever for marrying her. Or rather, for having been duped into marrying her – conned by the oldest trick in the book.

'Good, because you're going to stay my husband whether you like it or not.' Miriam narrowed her eyes and smiled. Since Jack had been allowed back to live here, she had obsessed about the injustice of it all. Her fury grew every time she thought of him shacked up with his bit and their bastard, playing happy families. It was not just the public humiliation of being a spurned wife – abandoned for another woman, his childhood sweetheart no less, the woman from whom she had originally snatched him away. It was just as much about him winning – and her losing.

'Why don't you want a divorce, my dear?' Mr Havelock asked. He had hoped Miriam would change her mind. 'I'd have thought you'd want shot of the man.'

Helen was also giving her mother a look of total disbelief.

Miriam's attention, though, was focused on Jack, her look one of pure malice.

'She won't divorce me,' Jack said, 'because she knows that's what I want. She knows as soon as the ink is dry on the divorce papers, I'll be marrying Gloria. And she'll do anything to stop that happening – even to her own detriment.'

Miriam let out a tinkle of laughter. *Too right. If she couldn't have what she wanted, he damn well wasn't going to have what he wanted either.* 'Oh, Jack, you know me so well.' She kept her focus on her husband. 'I will *never* divorce you, and if you try and divorce me, I'll make sure I've got the best and most expensive lawyers fighting my corner, putting up insurmountable barriers every step of the way.'

Miriam glanced at her father. She fully intended to take him up on his promise of helping her in any way he could.

'Your child – ' she returned her attention to Jack ' – will continue to be a bastard in the true sense of the word. A child born out of wedlock. Illegitimate.' The corner of her mouth inched up into a snide smile. 'And I'll make sure everyone knows it. Every Tom, Dick and Harry in the east end.' She raised a manicured hand and moved it as though showing off a banner. 'Jack and Gloria – adulterers ... Their child – a bastard.'

'Enough, Mother!' Helen pushed back her chair and stood up.

Miriam ignored her daughter. 'I'm going to make it my mission to make your life an absolute misery.' Her tone dripped with spite.

Jack let out an angry laugh. 'I think you've already succeeded on that score.'

Miriam glowered at the man she had once set her heart on having, and had now set her heart on destroying. 'And don't think for one minute that I care two hoots about my reputation. Any hope of that disappeared on Christmas Day, when, I'm informed, you came racing back from the Clyde and set up home with your hussy.'

'I said, *enough*, Mother!' Helen started to move around her desk.

Miriam made a show of looking at her watch. 'Oh dear, look at the time! I believe my five minutes is up, dearest *Husband*.' She then turned her attention to Mr Havelock and Helen. 'And *we've* got a launch to attend, I do believe.'

Jack glared at Miriam. He opened his mouth to speak but stopped himself. He knew he'd end up saying something he'd regret. 'I'll see you later, Helen,' he said instead, before turning and marching out of the office.

Helen looked at her mother as she finished off her drink. Her grandfather had already finished his and was pushing himself out of the chair.

'Don't forget, Mother,' Helen hissed, 'that Hope is my sister.'

'Half-sister,' Miriam corrected.

'We share the same blood,' Helen countered. 'Hope's my sister. There are no half measures. Just as the man you have declared your intention of ruining is my father.'

Mr Havelock cleared his throat. 'Of course he is, Helen, my dear,' he interjected. 'But don't forget that *you* are also a Havelock just as much as you are a Crawford.'

Helen eyed her grandfather, feeling the return of her disgust and shame that they shared the same blood.

'And I hope you know just how much that sickens me to the very pit of my stomach,' she said.

Neither Mr Havelock nor Miriam was in any doubt that Helen meant every word she had just spoken.

*

When Mr Havelock and Miriam made it out of the admin building, the sound of the shipyard was overwhelming, as was the sun's shimmering heat. The summer this year seemed to be as hot as the winter had been cold. Mr Havelock raised his hand to shield himself from the blinding rays and stood surveying the concrete jungle of men, metal and machinery. He scanned the individual groups of workers, the squads of riveters with their heater boys and catchers, the platers with their helpers, the foreman with his whistle in his mouth, overseeing the lowering of a mammoth sheet of steel. The women welders, he knew, would not be hard to find. Women might well be a part of the workforce these days, but they were still very much outnumbered by the men. And they still stuck out like sore thumbs.

He continued searching the yard, glancing over the flat caps, trying to catch the glimpse of a headscarf. He spotted a group of women who were red-leaders, judging by the blood-like splatters on their denim dungarees, but he still couldn't see the women welders.

All of a sudden, he heard a piercing whistle. He looked up. *There they were.* Sitting on some scaffolding, their legs dangling over the edge, their faces just inches from the hull of the ship in the dry dock. They all had their welding masks down, apart from the one with light ginger hair poking out of her headscarf – the miner's daughter whose mother was having it off with a bloke half her age. She had her thumb and forefinger in her mouth and was whistling to someone below. He looked back down to see the dark-haired girl – the one whose mother was a bigamist. Watching as she smiled and waved back up to her friend, he wondered if she'd still be smiling when she was visiting her dear mama in jail.

Towering next to her was the daughter of the town's infamous child murderer. He smiled to himself. He could just imagine everyone's reaction when they found out the truth. She'd be shamed and shunned. Probably railroaded out of town.

A woman suddenly appeared at the top of the staging. Judging by her body language and the way the women all pushed up their masks and were looking at her, she must be their boss, Rosie Miller. He watched as she dropped down on her haunches and started talking to an older woman, Jack's bit. Miriam would make sure she got her comeuppance. Of that he was certain.

Ignoring his daughter's impatience as she started to shuffle about next to him, Mr Havelock continued to inspect them, imagining their reactions when he revealed their secrets to the world – when he destroyed their lives and the lives of everyone around them.

He'd like to see the state of the common one's mother after her brute of a husband finished with her. And then there was the pretty young brunette he'd just caught sight of. Polly. Bel Elliot's sister-in-law. My God, the Elliots wouldn't know what had hit them by the time he'd finished with them.

Feeling Miriam take hold of his arm, he turned to look at her. She was mouthing something to him, but it was too noisy to hear. She started stabbing her watch with a glossy red-painted nail. He nodded and allowed himself to be guided towards the waiting Jaguar, idling outside the giant gates of the shipyard.

He had much to look forward to. His plan was taking shape. He just wished he could move everything along that bit quicker.

Still. The waiting would, he was sure, be worth it.

Chapter Eleven

The launch at the Shipbuilding Corporation went off with a bang, or rather, with the smashing of a bottle of champagne. The crowd cheered and waved, the horns blared out and afterwards Mr Havelock and Miriam happily posed for pictures for the local paper. The photographer had wanted the entire Havelock family together and had been dismayed when he hadn't been able to locate the youngest and most attractive of the Havelock clan. He did, however, manage to catch her a little later in conversation with Doxford's manager, Matthew Royce Jnr. The pair made a striking couple. He had taken their photograph numerous times over the past year, usually at launches or the odd charity function, but each time he'd tentatively suggested they were a couple, he'd been told very firmly by Miss Crawford that this was certainly not the case.

The photographer was, nevertheless, glad to grab a shot of Mr Royce and his secretary, a rather sexy blonde called Dahlia, who was happy to tell him that she originally hailed from Sweden and that her parents had come over after the last war. He also managed to take a photograph of Helen with her secretary, a young woman called Marie-Anne McCarthy, who hadn't needed to tell him about her origins. Her ginger hair, pale complexion and scattering of light freckles, as well as the soft lilt in her accent, clearly told him she was Irish through and through. After he'd got the shots he knew would appease his editor, he struck up a conversation with her and was informed that she was not a 'secretary' but a 'personal assistant'. He'd liked her bite and crossed his fingers that he might well be leaving the do with a date to boot.

The general chatter at the launch was, as usual, about the continuing push to victory. Amphibious landings, like those used along the coast of Normandy, were now being used in southern France, and the Allies had reached the Gothic Line, Germany's last strategic position in northern Italy.

After an hour or so of schmoozing, the mayor said his farewells and left. Seeing him go, Mr Havelock gave Miriam the sign that they too were now ready to depart. Out of the corner of his eye, he caught the photographer watching them. He'd have noticed they hadn't bid farewell to Helen, which would undoubtedly add fuel to the rumours that there was dissent behind the closed doors of the town's richest and most revered family. Mr Havelock snorted through his nostrils, a habit he had when he was feeling full of fight. He'd have to have a chat with the paper's managing director. Remind him of the number of shares he had in the company. There was no way he wanted the *Echo* to print even a hint that the family might be at war.

Helen was chatting to Matthew, Dahlia and Marie-Anne when she saw her mother and grandfather leave. Dahlia was holding court. She irritated Helen a little, but she was pleased the attention wasn't focused on herself. She'd been thrown by her mother's declaration that she would not divorce her father – and her promise to make his life hell. As if her father and Gloria hadn't been through enough already.

Helen sighed. She'd go and see Gloria after work. She knew her father would be seething. She would take Hope out for a treat so as to give them a chance to talk about what had happened today. It was the least she could do – that and offer to finance the hiring of a decent lawyer. They were going to need it.

She watched as her grandfather made a show of allowing Miriam to get into the Jaguar first. He was clearly working hard to keep his daughter on board. And was succeeding. Shortly after her mother's return, when she had realised that Miriam was still on talking terms with her father, Helen had asked her, *'Why?'* Or rather, *How could she? How could she still be talking to that man when she knew what he'd done?* She'd been shocked when her mother had laughed. Laughed and then ridiculed her for believing a load of lies.

When Helen had pressed further, her mother had sniped at her and said that if she had deigned to speak to her grandfather about it all, she would have learnt that this all stemmed from Henrietta's sick, warped mind. That Henrietta had told Pearl the horrible untruths, and Pearl had used them to blackmail Helen's grandfather. Pearl, Miriam was sure, would have demanded money were it not for Little Miss Goody Two-Shoes, Bel, who had instead demanded that Jack be allowed back so that Hope could have a father. Something, Miriam had added bitchily, that Bel had never had herself and had clearly never got over.

Helen hadn't said anything, just listened. Perhaps her mother needed to believe the story spun by her grandfather. It was certainly more palatable than facing up to the truth. And perhaps if Helen had not become friends with Bel during her time working at the yard, or talked with Pearl that day in the Tatham about the rape, she might also have been taken in by her grandfather.

Either way, there was no doubting that he was a good liar, and an even better manipulator. He'd done a good job on her mother, that was for sure.

*

93

As the chauffeur-driven Jaguar rumbled across the cobbles, away from the main entrance of the Shipbuilding Corporation, Mr Havelock turned to address his daughter.

'I don't think that was the wisest decision you've ever made, Miriam,' he said, trying to keep his tone conciliatory.

Miriam shot her father an accusatory look.

'I do recall you saying on my return that you would support me in whatever way you could,' she snapped.

'Yes, by sorting you out with my chap from Gourley's – for a speedy, low-key divorce. What good is it going to do you having a husband who's shacked up with another woman? It's not good for the Havelock name.'

Miriam looked daggers at her father.

'Neither is having a wife in the local asylum.'

Mr Havelock forced back a scathing reply, reminding himself that he needed to keep his daughter sweet.

'Besides, you can keep it out of the press,' Miriam added, her tone more self-effacing. She knew she was skating on thin ice.

'I don't own *all* the local press, my dear, and I have no control over the gossipmongers, much as I'd like to,' Mr Havelock admitted reluctantly.

They were both quiet for a moment.

'Actually,' Mr Havelock said, turning his concentration back to his daughter, 'as you've brought up the subject of your dear mama, I was wondering if you were going to pay her a visit any time soon? You've been back a while now and as far as I know you've not been to see her.' *Unlike Helen, who seemed unable to keep away from the place.*

Miriam looked at her father. He had always liked to know when she was visiting her mother and had always wanted feedback afterwards.

'Soon,' she said. 'I'm going to see her soon.' The truth of the matter was she had been putting off seeing her mother since she'd come back. The place was depressing and at the moment she was having far too much fun with Amelia and the Admiralty at the Grand.

'Well, do tell me before you head over there next,' Mr Havelock said. 'I was thinking after our chat the other day how I shouldn't really bear Henrietta any ill will. It's not her fault she's the way she is. She's more to be pitied, really. And, you know, I'm not getting any younger.'

Miriam looked incredulously at her father. He had always acted as though he were immortal. 'Old' was not in his vocabulary when it came to describing himself.

'Do you ever take her any treats? Any presents?' Mr Havelock continued.

Miriam now looked at him as though he were mad. 'Of course not. She's got everything she needs there. If you visited yourself, you'd see the place has absolutely everything. It even has its own chapel.'

Mr Havelock looked thoughtful. 'Perhaps I will visit one day. One day in the not too distant future.' He paused. 'But in the meantime, my dear, it's up to you to hold the fort and make sure she doesn't get taken advantage of by any more gold-diggers.' The car came to a stop behind a tram. 'I was thinking about it – how that Pearl woman got away with visiting Henrietta and no one found out – and it really is beyond me.'

The tram lurched forward and the car trailed behind in second gear.

'It just shows you how vulnerable she is there.' He looked at Miriam. 'So, it's up to you to keep an eye on her. She is your mother, after all.'

Miriam pulled the glass partition down and tapped the driver on the shoulder to tell him to pull over. They had just crossed the Wearmouth Bridge and were starting down Bridge Street. The chauffeur didn't need to be told where to stop. He'd dropped Mr Havelock's daughter off here more times than he could remember.

'Yes, all right, Papa,' Miriam said, shuffling over as the driver jumped out and opened her door. 'I'll try and get there soon.'

*

After clocking off work at Crown's a little earlier than usual, Jack jogged up to the main road and caught a tram headed for town. Five minutes later, he was on the other side of the Wear and jumping off at the stop halfway down Fawcett Street. He had never had call to use a solicitor before, but he knew of a few well-established firms in the town. He'd try those first. He began with Gourley and Sons in John Street. Having got through the initial introductions with a friendly, portly chap who insisted on being called by his first name, Jack noticed the atmosphere change in an instant when he heard who it was that Jack wanted to divorce.

The same happened in the second place he tried.

At the third, Jack dismissed any formalities and said straight off that his wife was Miriam Crawford, née Havelock, and yes, she was Charles Havelock's daughter.

He was back out onto the street within minutes.

Of course, Jack berated himself. He should have known. Charles Havelock owned a good part of the town. He had a finger in a lot of pies. No one was prepared to go up against him – or his daughter.

Seeing the look of defeat on Jack's face, the secretary in the next place he tried scribbled down the name and address of a solicitor in the east end and pushed the piece of paper into his hand, saying that he might have more joy there.

Arriving at the address on Hendon Road, Jack thought that the legal firm seemed to be run from the front room of a residential property. Thankfully, though, Mr E.J. Emery Esq. didn't seem to have any objections about who it was that Jack intended to divorce.

It was a start.

Leaning forward in his worn leather chair, Mr Emery explained that it would be easier, less costly and quicker if 'the estranged Mrs Crawford' were 'the petitioner'. Seeing the confused look on Jack's face, the wiry, middle-aged lawyer explained that the 'petitioner' was the person doing the divorcing.

Jack explained that this was simply not going to happen – ever – but that he was more than willing to admit that it was he who had done wrong and had an affair. He couldn't deny it, even if he'd wanted to, as he was presently living with the woman in question, and if that were not proof enough, they had also had a child together.

'I'm afraid, Mr Crawford,' Mr Emery responded, 'that much as your honesty is honourable, you cannot petition for a divorce on the grounds of your *own* adultery. If you are the one who has committed adultery, your spouse will have to file the divorce petition. As you are the one to initiate the divorce, I'm afraid it is up to you to find the grounds for the divorce.' There was a brief pause. 'Although a change in legislation just before the start of the war offers up additional grounds, other than simple adultery.'

'And they are?' Jack asked.

'Cruelty, desertion and incurable insanity,' Mr Emery informed him.

Jack's face lit up. There was a flicker of hope. 'We have been living apart for more than two years.'

'Did your wife desert you?' Mr Emery asked.

'Not really. She stayed in the marital home while I was working on the Clyde.'

The solicitor's sallow face dropped.

'I'm afraid, once again the matrimonial laws of the land stipulate that it has to be the other way round.' Seeing Jack's dejected look, he added, 'But don't worry, we'll get there. It just might take a bit of time.'

Jack felt his heart sink even further. He'd waited long enough. This was going to be hard, much harder than he'd thought. *Damn Miriam.* They both knew that this was one battle she could not win. No one – not even a Havelock – could stop a divorce. What she could do, though, was make the battle as long and as drawn-out as possible. There was no doubt in Jack's mind that their fight would go the full twelve rounds.

'We could argue the case for cruelty?' Mr Emery said, thinking that if she was anything like her father that was a given.

Jack nodded. 'Well, she's certainly that.'

Mr Emery looked at Jack. 'I'm not going to beat about the bush. This is going to be difficult. But not impossible. Leave it with me and I will see what I can do.'

Jack thanked Mr Emery and handed over a small retainer. They agreed to meet in a week's time.

As Jack walked back home, he tried to console himself that at least he had found legal representation and Mr Emery had agreed to take on Jack's case, in spite of the Havelock name.

Chapter Twelve

The headlines over the following week seemed only to reinforce the belief that the war was not far from coming to an end. Romania broke with the Axis and joined the Allies after surrendering to the Soviet Union, and the Japanese were now in total retreat from India. Rosie in particular had been heartened to hear that Paris had been liberated by the Allies. Today, the papers were full of photographs showing de Gaulle and the Free French parading triumphantly down the Champs-Élysées.

Standing with her haversack slung over her shoulder, Rosie looked down at Dorothy and Angie. The klaxon had sounded out five minutes ago. Martha, Gloria and Polly had already started to walk over to the drawing office to pick up Hannah and Olly. The team's terrible two seemed to be taking ages packing up. They were usually the first off.

'Come on, slowcoaches,' Rosie cajoled. 'I need to have a quick word with Helen before I head home. And I promised Peter and Charlotte I'd be back in time to get changed and go and see the latest newsreels on France.'

'Bet yer Peter's dead chuffed,' Angie said.

'He is,' Rosie said. 'Very chuffed.'

'And yer dinnit mind him having to keep gannin away so soon after he just got back?' Angie asked. They all knew that Peter still worked for the organisation that had been nicknamed 'Churchill's Secret Army'.

'No, I don't mind,' Rosie smiled. 'As long as he's on this side of the Channel, I'm happy.'

Angie nodded her understanding. 'Yer gan ahead, miss,' she said. She still occasionally called Rosie 'miss'. It was a habit she hadn't quite managed to shake. 'Dor's got summat she's gorra dee.' Angie cocked her head over to Jimmy and his squad of riveters. Rosie spotted Bobby, his tall frame towering above his workmates.

'Oh,' Rosie said, looking down at Dorothy, who suddenly seemed to be concentrating very hard on tightening the laces on her boots. 'I'm guessing it's to do with a certain riveter?'

Dorothy's pale face looked up at her boss. 'Who else?'

Rosie looked surprised. Dorothy hadn't mentioned anything during the day.

'Dor didn't want to say owt in case she chickened out,' Angie said, reading her thoughts.

'Which I still might,' Dorothy said.

'Well, whatever it is, I hope it goes well,' said Rosie.

'We'll tell yer how it gans tomorrow,' Angie said, smiling. She had been desperate to tell everyone Dorothy's plans all day, but Dorothy had forbidden her from doing so, saying she wanted to 'just do it' without any kind of fuss.

Angie watched Rosie hurry off. She'd never known her boss so happy. She supposed that being told your husband was dead only to be informed there'd been a mistake would do that to a person.

'So, yer still up for it?' Angie asked, turning her attention back to Dorothy.

Dorothy nodded solemnly. 'I feel like I'm just about to walk the plank.'

Angie started scrabbling about in her bag for her compact. 'Here, do yer wanna smarten yerself up? Put a bit of lippy on?'

Dorothy shook her head. 'No, as discussed last night, Bobby's got to see me as I am. Warts and all.'

Angie didn't say anything. She'd never seen her friend like this. Last night when they'd been chatting through Dorothy's plan, she had taken a lot of what she'd said with a pinch of salt. She certainly didn't think Dorothy would approach her meeting with Bobby today without at least a smudge of her favourite Victory Red.

'Right, I'll leave yer to it,' Angie said, but didn't move.

'Yes, OK,' said Dorothy, glancing over at Bobby, who fortunately didn't look in any hurry to leave work. 'Wish me luck.'

'Wishing yer luck,' Angie said, reluctantly leaving her friend. 'Me 'n Mrs Kwiatkowski will have a nice cuppa waiting when yer ger back.'

'Thanks, Ange.' She hesitated. 'I don't know what I'd do without you.'

Angie smiled as she got up and slung her bag over her shoulder.

'And me you neither. Friends for ever.'

'Friends for ever.'

Angie thought she'd never seen her best mate look so pale.

'Rosie!' Helen waved her in. 'What's up? Please don't tell me there's any more problems with *Ganges*.'

Rosie smiled. 'No. None at all. Everything's going to plan, fingers crossed. Actually, I've come to have a quick chat to you about Gloria – and your dad.'

'Shut the door and come and sit down,' Helen said, delving into her handbag and getting out her cigarettes.

'It's about their divorce,' Rosie began.

Helen lit up her Pall Mall and sighed wearily.

'You don't mind me talking about it, do you?' Rosie asked. 'It must be difficult.'

Helen blew out a stream of smoke and shook her head.

'And you don't mind me talking about your mum?' Rosie could not envisage what it must be like to have a mother like Miriam.

Helen waved away her concerns with a flick of her hand. 'There's nothing anyone can say about my dear mama that I haven't said already myself.' She took a drag of her cigarette. 'So, no, I don't mind talking about her in the least. I just wish she'd see sense and get it all over and done with quickly and without all this awfulness and drama. It's so unnecessary.'

'Well,' Rosie said, 'I was just chatting to the women. Gloria's keeping us informed as to how the divorce is going – or rather, not going … It sounds as though your father was lucky to actually find a solicitor who would get involved with a case against a Havelock.' Rosie shook her head. 'I can't believe how much power that man has in this town.'

'His tentacles certainly stretch far and wide,' Helen said, blowing out smoke.

'Gloria said the problem is finding grounds for divorce – and then proving them.' Rosie stopped, unsure whether to continue.

'Go on,' said Helen. Her father had not talked much about the ins and outs of the divorce. She knew he didn't want to involve her. His belief being that it wasn't right for her, as their daughter, to be involved in their battle.

'Well, it seems this divorce is going to be problematic because, like I've said, your mother hasn't fulfilled one of the main "marital offences" – adultery, cruelty, separation … and what was the last one?' Rosie thought for a moment. 'That's it, "incurable insanity".'

Helen let out a bitter laugh. 'All sorted then.'

Rosie gave a sympathetic smile. 'The worst-case scenario,' she continued, 'is that they have to wait two to three years to show some kind of acceptable period of separation before the courts will sanction a divorce.'

'Which will make Hope five, going on six,' Helen said, blowing out smoke. 'Dear me, I do worry about the effect this will have on her.'

'I know,' Rosie agreed. 'Sounds like the name-calling has started already. Gloria said she tried to get Hope enrolled in some nursery that's just opened in the east end and the woman who was running the place took her aside and said she couldn't take "a child like Hope" and that she'd be a "bad influence".'

'How dare she!' Helen was shocked. 'That's outrageous. How can anyone in their right mind think being illegitimate equates to being *bad*?'

'I agree, but there's plenty who do,' Rosie said.

'What's the name of this nursery? I'll sort it!' Helen exclaimed.

'Don't,' Rosie pleaded. 'It's why Gloria's not told you. She doesn't want any unnecessary hassle. She says it'll just make it worse. Give the busybodies even more to chatter about.'

Helen crushed out her cigarette and immediately lit another. She was seething.

'The thing is,' Rosie said, 'the reason I wanted to chat to you about it, in private, was for you to know that, as Gloria's friends, we are all united in how we can help her. Even if it's just as a shoulder to cry on, or a sounding board if she wants to have a good rant.'

'Of course,' Helen said, taking another drag on her cigarette. 'If you think there's anything I can do to help, just say.' She paused. 'Even if that's nothing.'

Rosie smiled, reassured there would be no shenanigans at the offending nursery.

'Polly's going to have a word with Agnes and Beryl and suggest they start up a nursery.'

'I thought they already had one?' Helen asked. She knew that Polly's widowed mother and her neighbour Beryl ran a voluntary makeshift nursery. It had initially been run from the Elliots' house, but this past year had moved to Beryl's as she had more room and only her two daughters at home.

'It's been more of a childminding service, you know, to help the women around the doors who've had to go to work,' Rosie explained. 'But Polly reckons they'd be up for setting up an official nursery. Charge a nominal amount. Iris and Audrey could be involved with teaching the older ones to read – when they're not at work, of course.'

Helen nodded. She knew Beryl's two girls worked for the GPO. They'd babysat Hope and Lucille – Bel's daughter from her first husband, Teddy, who'd died out in North Africa – and they both adored baby Artie and the twins, Gabrielle and Stephen.

Rosie looked at Helen. 'And admittance will not depend on the marital status of the child's mother.'

'A brilliant solution,' Helen said. 'And you couldn't ask for better women to run it.' She smiled. 'Thanks, Rosie.'

'What for? I've not done anything.'

'For involving me,' said Helen.

'Of course – why wouldn't we?' said Rosie. 'You're one of us now – whether you like it or not.'

They both laughed.

Helen liked it a lot. Rosie's words had warmed her heart.

As well as dampened the anger she felt towards the owner of the nursery – although only a little.

*

'Hey, Bobby.' Dorothy tried to sound confident and carefree.

All the riveters turned around, all apart from Bobby, who hadn't heard. He was standing with his back to the brazier, looking at one of the newly launched ships from Austin's going out on her sea trials.

'Bobby!' Dorothy shouted out louder, now feeling incredibly self-conscious.

One of the young apprentices darted over to Bobby and pulled on his sleeve. As soon as he turned round and saw Dorothy, a wide smile spread across his face.

'Dorothy! To what do I owe this pleasure?'

Dorothy felt her heart thumping in her chest and beating in her ears. *God, why did he have this effect on her?* How could someone make you feel like kissing them and slapping them simultaneously? From the corner of her eye, she saw Jimmy and the rest of the squad quickly pack up and leave.

'See yer the morra, Bobby,' Jimmy shouted out as he tugged at the collar of one of the rivet burners who was standing staring at Dorothy.

'See you all in the morning!' Bobby said, before turning his attention back to Dorothy. As always, she took his breath away. Even more so when she was just in her vest and overalls like she was now.

'Been a scorcher today,' Bobby said, grabbing a green metal water container and offering it to her.

Realising that she was actually parched and had hardly drunk anything all day, or eaten anything for that matter, nerves always did that to her, she took it and had a drink.

'Thanks.' She handed it back.

Bobby laughed.

'What's so funny?' Dorothy asked, fighting her feelings of insecurity. Suddenly, she felt lost without Angie or her friends by her side.

'Us being civil to each other. Me offering you a drink and you taking it.'

'Well, I can soon remedy that,' Dorothy hit back.

'No, no, please don't,' Bobby said, his tone placatory. 'Why don't we sit over there.' He nodded to a sunny spot by the river. 'I'm in no rush to head home.'

'OK.' Dorothy forced herself to breathe normally. Talking to Bobby before they'd kissed had been much easier. Now, every time she looked at him, that was all she could think of.

When they reached the sunny spot of concrete, Dorothy turned towards Bobby.

'There's something I have to do first,' she said, matter-of-factly.

Bobby furrowed his brow.

'Oh yes, and what's that?' he asked.

Dumping her haversack on the ground, Dorothy stepped towards Bobby, went up on her tiptoes and kissed him.

As soon as her lips touched his, the whole world seemed to fade into the background and there was only her and Bobby standing, bodies pressed close together, kissing.

Bobby could not quite believe he had finally been granted his wish and was now kissing the woman he was crazy about – here in the yard. He put his hand to her face, gently touching her dirt-smeared cheeks, then kissing them, his lips finding her neck, wanting to go lower, to kiss every part of her. Not caring if anyone saw them.

Dorothy pulled away. Quickly looking around and checking that there was still no one in the vicinity.

'Right,' she said, her manner all officious. 'That's that done. Now let's sit down and talk.'

Bobby barked with laughter. His eyes were sparkling with a mix of passion and puzzlement.

'Dorothy, I can honestly say that I have never met a woman like you.'

'Mmm,' Dorothy said, sitting down by the quayside.

'What do you mean, "mmm"? I've never heard "mmm" sound so laden with meaning,' Bobby said.

'Ten out of ten for being perceptive.' Dorothy forced her voice to sound steady. She could have lost her resolve kissing Bobby just then. Could have lost herself in his kisses, his touch, his smell.

Again, Bobby looked perplexed.

'Because,' Dorothy said, 'that "mmm" *was* loaded with meaning.' She turned and crossed her legs so that the sun was on her back and she was facing Bobby. It also put a little space between them in case she felt the urge to kiss him again.

'Right.' She focused her mind on what she and Angie had planned last night over a pot of tea and a plate of biscuits.

'That kiss is to demonstrate that there is most definitely an attraction between the two of us. And that the kiss we shared at my flat was not just a one-off – and not simply a case of us both flying high because Rosie had got Peter back and you and Gloria had sorted out your differences.'

'Well, any time you need to be reassured,' Bobby said with a twinkle in his eye, 'just say and I'll be happy to prove the point.'

Dorothy felt herself flush.

'The "mmm",' she pressed on, 'also relates to you saying that you've never met a woman like me before.'

Bobby looked at Dorothy as she freed her thick dark brown hair from her turban and let it drop around her face and shoulders.

'You can say that again.'

'From my experiences of life, when a man says that about a woman it means that the woman is in reality just a novelty for the man – it's like when a piece of chewing gum has been chewed and lost its flavour, it's spat out.'

Bobby wanted to laugh but stopped himself. Dorothy clearly wanted to be taken seriously. He forced himself to concentrate.

'That's an interesting theory,' he said. 'And a very vivid way of explaining it.'

He offered Dorothy another drink from his water bottle. She took a mouthful and handed it back.

'So, you think that I view you as a new toy that once the shine has worn off, I'll cast aside in favour of a newer model. Is that right?'

Dorothy nodded. 'Exactly.'

'So, how do I go about proving that's not the case?'

'You can't,' Dorothy said. 'Because you yourself probably believe that you won't. That you won't get bored when the shine has worn off.' She paused. 'But you will.'

Bobby ran his hand over the top of his head.

'So, how can I prove that I won't? Because I know I won't.'

Dorothy inhaled the sea air.

'Ange and I have thought up a plan.'

A wide smile spread across Bobby's face.

'Go on,' he encouraged.

'The plan being that we go out with each other,' she said simply.

'Court as a proper couple?' Bobby couldn't believe what he was hearing.

'Yes.' Dorothy adopted her most schoolmarmish expression. 'But there's to be no hanky-panky – other than kissing.'

'OK,' Bobby said. 'That's fine by me.'

'And I think you should know from the off that I might seem a bit gobby and quite the freethinker, but there's a part of me which is still very conventional.'

Bobby laughed.

'I don't think you could be conventional if you tried,' Bobby chuckled. 'This conversation we're having now must be as far from conventional as you can get.'

'Well, that's where you're wrong,' Dorothy said, sitting up straight. 'Because this might come as a surprise to you, but I believe in saving myself for marriage.'

Bobby did look surprised.

Dorothy was quiet.

'Well, all that means,' Bobby said, his dark brown eyes finding Dorothy's and holding her stare, 'is that we'll have to get married sooner rather than later.'

Dorothy gasped in disbelief, dramatically rolling her eyes heavenwards.

Bobby's eyes were dancing, his smile broad.

'I have a feeling,' he said, 'that there's more you've got to tell me about our impending courtship.'

'Indeed, there is,' said Dorothy.

'If that's the case,' Bobby said, 'why don't we chat about it over a drink at the Admiral?'

'So,' Bobby said, taking a drink of his lemonade, 'we can go out as a couple. Go on dates?'

'Yes, but only kissing.'

'That's OK. I understand. Just kissing.'

'And there's to be no seeing any other women.'

Bobby looked affronted. 'Naturally.'

'Well, you never know, it's good to have these things spelled out. And agreed. One of my exes seemed to think courtship involved seeing at least one other woman.'

Bobby remembered the conversation he'd overheard at Pearl and Bill's wedding in the Tatham about some no-good riveter called Eddie, who had been seeing Angie behind Dorothy's back before the two women had become best buddies. Eddie, he'd surmised, must have been short of a few.

'Can I just add that goes both ways,' said Bobby. 'That you too have to be faithful to me. And not see any other blokes. Just for the sake of clarity.'

'Of course,' said Dorothy.

'And what about when you and Angie go off to the Ritz?' Bobby asked tentatively.

'What about when Ange and I go off to the Ritz?'

'Most blokes would also go to the Ritz with the woman they are dating,' Bobby added. The thought of Dorothy going drinking and dancing at the town's main hotspot was not a good one. Especially in that red dress of hers.

'Well, you're not most blokes, and as you've already pointed out, I'm not most women, so I shall continue to go to the Ritz with Angie every Friday.'

'Mmm,' Bobby said, finishing off his lemonade.

'Now it's you that's making a simple "mmm" sound loaded with meaning,' Dorothy said.

'Well, I don't think you can have everything your own way,' said Bobby. 'I think I should be allowed to come with you to the Ritz.'

Dorothy thought for a moment.

'No, that wouldn't be fair on Angie,' she said.

Another 'Mmm' from Bobby.

'How about you forsake the Ritz every fortnight to go out on a date with me?'

Dorothy had a drink of her lemonade.

'I shall ask Ange. If she agrees, you've got a deal.'

Bobby blew out air. 'Now that we've done our deal, can I walk you home and give you a goodnight kiss?'

'You may,' Dorothy said. She took a deep breath. 'But—'

'But only kissing,' Bobby said, beating her to it.

By the time they had reached the flat in Foyle Street, Bobby and Dorothy had already enjoyed several goodnight kisses.

When Dorothy got in, she found Angie supping tea with Mrs Kwiatkowski. They were both studying an article in the *Telegraph* that Dorothy knew to be about the recent announcement by the Russians that the Polish Committee of National Liberation was to be the new representative government of Poland. They'd torn it out of the paper during the lunch break to save for their neighbour.

They both looked up at Dorothy expectantly.

'Where have yer been?' Angie demanded. 'Yer've been gone ages. Me and Mrs Kwiatkowski have just about scoffed all the biscuits.'

'Well, we ended up going for a lemonade at the Admiral.'

Angie looked at Dorothy. Her pale, wan look had gone and had been replaced by rosy cheeks and a happiness she was trying to play down.

'By the looks of yer, it went well,' Angie said. 'Did yer stick to the plan?'

'Of course,' said Dorothy.

Angie looked at her friend as she sat down and poured herself a cup of tea.

'So, yer not still feeling guilt-ridden over Toby?' she asked.

Dorothy's face dropped. 'Don't, Angie. You know I feel terrible.'

'How many times did you think of Toby when you were with Bobby?' Angie asked.

Dorothy wasn't quick enough to lie, so instead she changed the subject. 'Actually, I've got a favour to ask you.'

Angie furrowed her brow. 'A favour?'

'Do you think we could go to the Ritz every other Friday, rather than every week?' Dorothy asked gingerly.

Angie felt like jumping off her chair and whooping loudly.

'Well, it'll be a wrench – but that's fine by me,' she said, forcing herself to rein in her delight, and giving Mrs Kwiatkowski a sidelong glance. She had confessed to her neighbour how she no longer had any interest whatsoever in going to the Ritz since getting it together with Quentin.

Relieved that Angie didn't seem too disappointed, Dorothy settled down to regale them with the events of the evening, bar the goodnight kisses. When she explained to Mrs Kwiatkowski about the rules of courtship she and Angie had drawn up and which, on the whole, Bobby had agreed to, Mrs Kwiatkowski shook her head, muttering that courting a suitor had never been so complicated in her day.

Chapter Thirteen

September

Mr Havelock was sitting at his desk, a glass of his favourite cognac in one hand, a thick Aroma de Cuba cigar smouldering in the ashtray. He had just been reading about the continuing repercussions for those involved in the failed plot to kill Hitler. He had been interested to see that the trial of the men involved was being presided over by the notorious judge Roland Freisler. The judge, he read, was rounding up the relatives of the principal plotters. All this went some way to lessening the frustration he'd felt on reading about the establishment of the new government of Free France.

He looked up at the clock. Miriam was late. As usual. Still, he had to count his blessings that she had finally decided to go and visit her mother at the asylum. He had gently tried to cajole her a number of times since her return, but hadn't wanted to push too much for fear of raising her suspicions that he might have an ulterior motive for wanting her to see Henrietta. Lately, though, he'd started to wonder if Miriam was *ever* going to be able to drag herself out of the Grand to make the trip to Ryhope. It was as though she was trying to make up for lost time – restocking the coffers depleted during her time in Scotland.

There was a knock on the door.

'Your daughter, sir,' Eddy announced, holding open the large oak door.

'Miriam! Lovely to see you!' Mr Havelock's smile and his enthusiastic welcome were genuine, although admittedly not for one of the reasons most fathers were glad of a visit from their offspring.

'Is having Thomas working out well?' Mr Havelock asked. It was a subtle reminder of his generosity in giving her full use of his driver, no matter the time of day or night. Thomas was on call to take Miriam wherever she wanted to go, which tended to be either from home to the Grand, or from the Grand back home. Now, hopefully, her chauffeur-driven excursions would extend to frequent visits to Ryhope.

'It is,' Miriam said, knowing she needed to show her gratitude. If her father ever gifted anything, he expected thanks. If he didn't get any, favours were withdrawn as quickly as they had been given. 'He really is quite the professional. And I am, of course, incredibly grateful. It really is such a luxury during these times.' Miriam hoped that would do it.

'Glad I can be of use in my dotage,' he said.

Miriam laughed. 'Father, I don't think you will ever be in your dotage.' *Or ever admit to it.* Walking quickly across the room, she sat down on a carved Biedermeier chair that had been shipped over before the start of the war. 'I'm afraid I haven't got long, Papa.'

'Don't worry, I won't keep you …' Mr Havelock took a puff on his cigar '… but there are a few things I need to go through with you.'

Seeing the look of impatience on his daughter's face as she got out her compact mirror and checked her reflection, he added, 'Something in particular that I believe will be to your advantage.' He knew Miriam was all about the self. She would suffer his company if there was something in it for her.

Mr Havelock took another puff on his cigar.

'I just wanted to thank you for agreeing to take Henrietta some presents,' he said. 'I know she won't take them if she thinks they're from me.'

Miriam waved her hand, dismissing the gratitude for what was a fairly innocuous favour.

'You see, my dear, after hearing what Henrietta said to that awful woman and her daughter, it's clear that she's still delusional. Still believes all those horrible, horrible imaginings of hers.'

'Don't worry, Father, I'll say they're from me. She'll be none the wiser.'

'And I'll know that I've been able to give her something,' Mr Havelock said with a smile. 'Something that might help with her suffering – ease the illness of her mind.' *For good.*

Hoping that was all her father had to say, Miriam picked up her handbag.

'Oh, one more thing before you go,' Mr Havelock said. 'It's a bit of a delicate matter.' He picked up his cigar, which had gone out, and relit it. 'I've been thinking about my age.' He laughed. 'Not getting any younger and all that.'

'I'd say you're looking well for your age, Father. Very well.' Miriam felt a wave of irritation. Her father had gone from never referring to his age to mentioning it twice in the space of a few minutes. Was he finally realising that he was, after all, not immortal?

'Perhaps so, but as the doctor told me during my last check-up, what's on the outside often belies what's going on in the inside. He's got me on these pills for my old ticker, but you never know. When your time's up – your time's up.' There was actually nothing wrong with Mr Havelock's 'ticker'. His personal physician had simply given him a lecture about cutting back on the brandy and given him some sort of vitamin pill.

'So,' he said, sensing his daughter's impatience, 'I've written a new will.'

'Really?' This surprised Miriam. And had her attention. Suddenly, she was not quite so eager to get away. 'And?'

'And,' Mr Havelock said, 'the long and short of it is …' He paused for effect. 'I'm leaving everything to you.'

Miriam's eyes lit up.

'What about Margaret – and Helen?' she asked, looking down at the document on top of the embossed-leather and mahogany desk.

'Well, Margaret's got Angus and he's loaded to the hilt. That estate of his in the back of beyond is worth a small fortune – and they've not got any dependants, have they?' He fought back a long-standing resentment. *Two daughters and neither of them had been capable of producing a male heir.*

'And Helen?' Miriam asked.

Mr Havelock almost spat out his reply.

'I wouldn't trust her not to give it away. She'd probably give it all to that child, Hope. Or her father and his mistress. No, no, no. Helen has made it clear what side of the fence she's standing on and it's not the Havelock side. And I'll be damned if a penny of my hard-earned cash is going to find its way into the pockets of people like that. Liars. Adulterers. Bastards. The lot of them.'

Miriam clasped her hands together. She had to stop herself clapping with joy. This was a turn-up for the books. That horrible Christmas Day last year was turning out to be worth enduring. She'd been convinced until then that Helen was his favourite. Her job at the yard made her the nearest he had to a son. A successor who would inherit the lot.

'Of course, there'll be the usual charitable donations,' Mr Havelock said, turning the will around so that Miriam could see it with her own eyes. 'But the rest, my dear, will be yours to do with as you will.'

Miriam stared at the words dancing in front of her. It was true. Apart from bequests to the usual charities and hospitals, the bulk of the Havelock fortune was to be hers.

'I don't know what to say, Father.' Miriam really was at a loss for words. 'Thank you. That's a wonderful thing to do. Thank you.'

Mr Havelock looked at his daughter. A normal mother would have wanted their only child to have at least a portion of his inheritance. The world was an unstable place at the moment. Who knew what was around the corner? Money meant security. Helen only had her wage at the yard. And it wasn't as if Jack would be able to help her out. He didn't have two pennies to rub together.

'Right, I will let you go and see your dear mother,' Mr Havelock said, standing up. 'And perhaps we can have a catch-up on Monday. There are two launches. Short's and Laing's. I think we'll go to Short's. There should be more press there.'

Miriam's mind was whirring. She'd go to both in one day and every day thereafter if that's what her father wanted. She got up and grabbed her handbag, sneaking another look at the will. She could clearly see her name in full with the words *main beneficiary* next to it.

'And you'll tell me how you got on with your mother?'

'Yes, of course,' Miriam said. She couldn't wait to get the visit over and done with so she could head straight to the Grand to celebrate her future windfall with Amelia.

And if her father's ticker was starting to slow down, well, her windfall might be landing sooner rather than later.

'There's just a few things in there,' Agatha said, handing Miriam the little wicker basket. 'Can you manage it all right? Or should I get Thomas to carry it?'

'Honestly, Agatha, stop fussing, it's as light as a feather,' Miriam said. She actually felt as though she could carry a cannonball. Her adrenaline was pumping.

As Agatha handed Miriam the basket, she held on to it for a moment.

'You all right, Agatha?' Miriam said, tugging the handle a little to force her father's housekeeper to relinquish her load. 'Your hand not glued on there, is it?' She laughed at her own joke.

Agatha remained stony-faced.

Miriam walked over to the front door, which was being held open by Eddy.

'Dear me, cheer up, the pair of you. You never know, it might never happen!' Miriam chuckled and made her way to the waiting Jaguar.

Agatha stole a look at Eddy.

If only it wouldn't.

'Henrietta's as mad as a hatter,' Eddy muttered to Agatha as he shut the front door. 'We're actually doing the woman a favour. Putting her out of her misery.'

They walked across the main hallway and back towards the servants' quarters. Both were glad that Mr Havelock had shut the door to his study and clearly didn't want to be disturbed.

'You keep telling yourself that, Edward,' said Agatha. 'And you might just end up really believing it.'

She, on the other hand, did not believe it.

Not one bit.

Mr Havelock watched at the window as the car drove off before he walked back over to his desk. He picked up the document that his daughter had believed to be his will and tore it up into small pieces, letting them drop into the fire. Striking a match, he tossed it onto the shredded paper. It

118

went up in a short sharp whoosh of orange flame, before quickly dying back, leaving just charred remains.

He then picked up the real will, which had been under the make-believe one, and folded it up before replacing it in his safe and turning the combination lock.

He sat back down at his desk and took a sip of his brandy.

The idea of the will had been a brilliant one, even if he said so himself. It was not only a huge carrot guaranteed to keep Miriam on side, but it also ensured that Miriam and Helen would remain at loggerheads with each other.

Everything was now in place and going according to plan.

With Henrietta out of the way, no one – not Pearl, nor her holier-than-thou daughter – *no one* would be able to prove what he'd done to the young girls who had come to work under his roof. It would be a case of their word against his, and any kind of blood test that might be used to claim paternity could easily be contested. He could even deny he had employed Pearl – or that girl who'd topped herself, or anyone else who might come out of the woodwork. Eddy and Agatha would back him up. They would have no choice. They would *have* to if they wanted to save their own skins.

And if anyone dared to suggest that it was his wife who had been at the asylum, they would be laughed out of court, for it would be 'Miss Girling' on the death certificate. Henrietta Havelock would remain his wife who had died out in India. Henrietta Girling would die at the asylum in obscurity. Those suggesting otherwise would be seen as a few slices short and might even end up in the nuthouse themselves.

Mr Havelock puffed on his cigar and smirked. *Now that was a thought.*

When Henrietta was out of the picture for good, he could finally regain control. And when he did, then the fun really could begin. He would take great joy in exposing the sordid secrets of the women welders one by one – the child-killing mother, the bigamist and the adulterer. Then he would take even greater pleasure in picking off the rest of them. He'd get the licence for the Tatham Arms recalled and the pub shut down. The new Mr and Mrs Lawson would find themselves on the street, along with the Elliots, once he'd spoken to their landlord. He just wished he could be there after he made the call to the local authorities and reported Bel Elliot and her crippled husband, Joe, as being unfit parents to their adopted twins. He would love to see their faces. Their anguish. Their heartbreak.

His joy would be unending.

Sighing as he rolled the end of his cigar in the ashtray, Mr Havelock's thin lips widened into a smile. So much to look forward to.

Now, it was just a matter of sitting back and waiting for the inevitable to happen.

He took a puff on his cigar.

Hopefully, the wait wouldn't be a long one.

Chapter Fourteen

'Well, this is a surprise.' Helen widened her eyes on seeing her mother walk into Henrietta's room at the Ryhope asylum.

'Miriam! My darling!' Henrietta jumped out of her chair and hurried over to her daughter.

'Where have you been? Oh ...' she put her hands to her cheeks '... how I've missed you. Haven't I, Helen?' Her head turned back to Helen.

'You have,' Helen agreed.

Miriam looked daggers at her daughter, before allowing herself to be embraced by her mother.

'And I have missed you too, Mama,' she lied.

Helen raised an eyebrow. 'So much so that you've been back nearly two months and are only now visiting? I'm surprised you managed to drag yourself off the bar stool at the Grand to come here.' Helen looked at her watch. 'Oh, mind you, this is a bit early, even for you.'

'I think I am to blame for your mother's love of the high life,' Henrietta said, sensing the barbed atmosphere and wanting to placate. 'Whereas you, dear Granddaughter, take after your father. Hard-working. Not an idle bone in your body.'

'I hope you're not suggesting that I am idle, Mama dear,' Miriam said, although she didn't really give a jot if her mother did believe that. She was on cloud nine. She was set to inherit a fortune. Miriam allowed herself a slight smirk.

It was a good job her daughter did work. There'd be no Havelock money coming her way. Not a penny.

Helen stood up. 'I'll leave you two to it. Seeing as it really is such a very long time since you've seen each other.' She grabbed her handbag. It was only then that she noticed the wicker basket her mother was holding by her side.

'You brought a picnic, Mother?' she joked.

'No,' Miriam sniped back. 'I have brought my dear mama some treats, seeing as I have been away for so long. And as you well know, the reason I have been away for so long is because I have been unwell. In a sanatorium. In Scotland.'

'Yes, Grandmother knows all about it,' Helen said. 'I've kept her informed.'

She looked again at the basket and was tempted to ask what Miriam had brought, but the need to get away from her mother outweighed her curiosity.

'Goodbye, Grandmother.' Helen gave Henrietta a kiss on the cheek. 'I'll see you early next week.'

'I shall look forward to it, as always,' Henrietta said, her smile showing just how much she adored her only grandchild.

As soon as Helen had left, Miriam walked over to the small round table in the middle of the room, on top of which was displayed a copy of *The Times*. 'Goodness me, Mother, since when do you read the papers?' She didn't wait for a reply, but instead roughly folded up the paper and jammed it into the little bin by the side of the sink. Henrietta opened her mouth to object but stopped herself. She watched as Miriam dumped the wicker basket on the tabletop in place of the paper. She flicked open one side of the lid.

'Now, what do we have here?' she said.

Henrietta's eyes widened with each item her daughter took out and displayed on the table.

'Oh, this is a treat,' she said, clapping her hands silently. Then her face dropped.

'But what about rationing?' she asked, picking up the little pot of Pond's face cream and some Bourjois baked powder rouge.

Miriam gave her mother a sceptical look. 'Since when have you been concerned about such trivialities?'

Henrietta didn't reply. She felt the question was rhetorical. She looked at her daughter, whom she hadn't seen since just before Christmas, more than eight months ago. Her prolonged stay at the sanatorium had done her well. She looked almost vibrant.

'Oh, and look what we have here.' Miriam's eyes widened in surprise. 'A little bottle of your favourite Russian vodka.' Her father must have got Eddy to go to the town's top wine and spirit merchants, J.W. Cameron & Co. on John Street. It was the only place that sold this particular brand. She noticed the seal had been broken. It looked like Eddy might have had a sneaky slug himself.

'Let me get a glass.' Miriam bustled over to the cabinet above the sink and retrieved two tumblers.

Henrietta sat down at the table and watched as her daughter poured her a drink.

'And,' Miriam said, going back over to the basket and retrieving another small bottle, 'a mixer.' She scrutinised the label. 'Elderflower.' She poured a little into the vodka.

'Aren't you having one?' Henrietta asked, taken aback by the presents.

'Oh, Mother, I hate vodka.' She wrinkled her nose. 'You know gin is *this* mother's ruin.' She smiled conspiratorially and pulled out a little engraved silver hip flask from her handbag. She unscrewed the top and poured out a good measure.

'Chin-chin, Mother.' She raised her drink, forcing Henrietta to do the same.

'To health and happiness,' Miriam said as they clinked glasses.

'And wealth, of course,' she added with a smile.

*

Helen looked at her watch. At least she'd had half an hour with her grandmother before her mother had turned up. She'd not totally spoiled her visit. Besides, she was glad for her grandmother's sake that her mother had finally deigned to visit. Before Miriam had run off to Scotland, Henrietta had said that she'd visited regularly. Helen had been a little concerned that her mother might stop, knowing that Helen was now visiting every week. She hadn't wanted her mother to think that she had taken on the mantle of care, not because she didn't want to shoulder that responsibility, but because Henrietta had missed Miriam – and had been concerned about her. Helen knew her grandmother loved her daughter, and that it was important to Henrietta that she saw her.

She turned down another corridor.

And in her own way, Helen believed, Miriam did genuinely love Henrietta, although her mother had seemed in a particularly good mood. Too good a mood simply because she was seeing her dear mama. Helen could only guess that she was meeting Amelia afterwards.

As she reached the main reception area, Helen saw Genevieve and waved to her.

'It's good to see your mother back,' the elderly receptionist said, closely observing Helen's response. She was pretty sure that Dr Eris had not let on that she was the one to have divulged Miss Girling's real identity, but still, she needed reassurance.

'Are you keeping well, Genevieve?' Helen asked, slowing her pace but not stopping.

The thin, grey-haired receptionist inwardly breathed a sigh of relief. 'I can't complain,' she replied cheerily. 'Every day's a blessing when you get to my time of life.'

As Helen walked through the main doors, her heart leapt.

'John!'

Dr Parker stopped in his tracks midway up the stone steps that led to the asylum's entrance.

'Helen!' His smile spoke of his joy at seeing the woman he still loved but whom he could have only as a friend. And not even that of late. 'How lovely to see you!' He turned. 'Come, let's have a walk.' He hesitated. 'That's unless you're in a rush?'

'No, no, not at all,' Helen said, walking down the steps with him and starting along the gravel pathway that hugged the perimeter of the main building.

'I'd almost forgotten what you look like, it's been that long since I've seen you,' Dr Parker joked.

'And me you,' Helen batted back.

Helen and Dr Parker had spoken a few times over the phone, but had not seen each other since that day in June when she'd been going to tell him her true feelings before being forced to do a U-turn by Dr Eris.

'I'm so glad we've bumped into each other,' Dr Parker said. He looked up to the sunny skies. 'What a lovely day. And lovelier still for seeing you.'

Helen looked at the man with whom she wanted to spend the rest of her life but couldn't. Not while Dr Eris had a hold over her, anyway.

'How's work? Any more new recruits?' Helen asked.

Dr Parker ran his fingers through his mop of sandy blond hair.

'Actually, yes, quite a few. So many casualties coming across from Europe.' He dropped his voice. 'From both sides.'

Helen raised an eyebrow. 'That must be difficult, having *friends and foe* together, under the same roof?' She was actually amazed there wasn't out and out rebellion.

'You would have thought so,' Dr Parker agreed. 'But when we get a new intake of soldiers onto the ward, it's standard practice for them to be stripped of their uniforms as they are usually filthy and lice-ridden.'

Helen wrinkled her nose.

'The uniforms are left in a pile outside. The men are brought in and bathed and put into bed to have their wounds dressed. The nursing staff and the other patients don't know what rank or nationality they are until they get to know them. And by that time, they've generally established a rapport. Amazingly, everyone tends to get on.'

'Sounds like once the uniforms are off, they just become normal men,' Helen ruminated.

'Many of them arrive in such a bad state it's hard to hate them,' Dr Parker mused. 'Hard not to pity the poor souls. Anyway, enough about my work.' He looked into Helen's emerald eyes. As always, he felt he could lose himself in them. 'How's work? Gloria? Hope? Your father? Gosh, there's always so much to ask you.' His face became serious. 'I'm guessing that's why you never get the chance to meet me for a cuppa in the canteen any more. Too busy. All these people in your life. And that's besides work.'

Helen could have let out a cry of exasperation. If only he knew.

'And Henrietta?' Dr Parker added. 'I'm guessing you've just been to see her? Although ...' he looked at his watch '... you've left early. It's only halfway through visiting hour.'

Helen's face dropped. 'Mother's finally decided to come. Armed with a basket of presents to assuage her guilt for not visiting. I left her to it.'

Dr Parker gave Helen a sidelong glance. 'You think your mother's capable of feeling guilty?'

Helen laughed. John had always had her mother down to a T.

'Oh, John it's so lovely to see you. To be with you.'

Dr Parker looked at Helen.

'There's not any other reason you've not been able to meet up, is there?' *There, he'd said it.*

Helen looked at Dr Parker. *He knows something's up.*

'No, of course not. I'd say if there was,' she lied.

'Well, if that's the case, I'm going to insist you join me for a proper catch-up next time you're visiting your grandmother.' He quickly checked no one was there. He knew how important it was that people believed Henrietta was Helen's great-aunt and not her grandmother. And certainly not Mr Havelock's wife. Even Claire didn't know.

Helen hesitated, not knowing what to say.

'Helen! Is that you?'

Helen and Dr Parker turned to see Dr Eris walking towards them.

Looking at Dr Eris in her perfectly tailored skirt suit, her hair styled in victory rolls, her make-up subtle, Helen could see why John found her attractive. She had that intelligent but feminine look. Very Katharine Hepburn.

'How lovely to see you,' Dr Eris said. The two women air-kissed.

Dr Parker looked down at his watch.

'Can I leave you two lovely ladies to it? I've got to pop to the Willows.' Helen knew that the Willows was an admissions and early-treatment block and a relatively new addition to the asylum. Her grandfather had donated a substantial amount of money when funds were being raised for the construction. At the time, she'd seen it as part of his philanthropic leanings; now she knew otherwise.

'Of course,' Dr Eris said. 'Be gone!'

Dr Parker turned to go.

'And I meant what I said about meeting up,' he said to Helen before hurrying off.

As soon as Dr Parker had gone, Dr Eris turned to Helen. 'What was all that about? What did I say about not seeing John?' she hissed.

Helen eyed her nemesis.

'That's exactly what I've been doing. Or rather, not doing. I haven't seen John once since we had our conversation,' she said. 'I've spoken to him a few times on the phone, but that's been it. And he's been the one to ring me.' That was a lie. Helen was hedging her bets that John hadn't mentioned their phone calls, or if he had, he hadn't stipulated who had rang whom.

The two women looked at each other.

'The thing is, Claire, I actually think John's a little suspicious as to why I seem to be avoiding him. I couldn't have made it any clearer to him that I see him just as a friend, but I think he might start to get suspicious if I continue to *not* see him. It's actually going to be easier convincing him that I only want him as a friend if that's the way I behave and I see him every now and again. As a friend. Like friends do.'

Dr Eris turned. Helen followed her lead and walked with her back to the asylum entrance.

Dr Eris thought of Dr Parker, of her plans to make him her husband, to show her cheating ex that he'd actually done her a favour when he'd jilted her at the altar – because she'd caught herself a bigger and better fish. She'd show him. She'd show the whole damn lot of them who had snickered behind their hands at her humiliation.

When they came to a stop at the bottom of the steps, Dr Eris turned to face Helen.

'Yes, I think you're right,' she agreed. 'You can meet up with John, but only now and again.' She turned to go, but then stopped and turned back to Helen. 'And if I pick up a sniff – a mere hint – that you are behaving in any way other than as a friend, well, you know the consequence, Helen, don't you?'

Helen looked at Dr Eris.

'I do, Claire.'

Walking back to her green sports car parked to the side of the entrance, Helen felt a spring in her step.

*

After Miriam left, Henrietta took her face cream and rouge and put them with the rest of her make-up on her dressing table.

She then washed up both glasses and returned them to the cabinet above the sink.

Bending down, she retrieved the newspaper Helen had brought, which was presently poking out of the top of her small bin. Walking back over to the table, she sat down and carefully smoothed out the creases before turning over each page until she found what she was looking for – a double-page spread on wartime fashion's victory over austerity.

Chapter Fifteen

Hitler's last throw of the dice were his new V-2 rockets, which were bigger, better and caused more destruction than the V-1s. But despite the flurry of V-2s being launched, there was a growing sense of impending victory as the Allies pushed into Europe. Canadian troops retook Dieppe and French and American troops liberated Lyon. Allied troops entered Belgium and soon afterwards Brussels was freed by the British Second Army. After overthrowing the national government, Bulgaria declared war on Germany, and a week later waves of paratroopers landed in the Netherlands with the aim of liberating Arnhem and turning the German flank.

As an invasion of British shores was now viewed as highly improbable, the blackout was reduced to a 'dim-out'. A crowd gathered and cheered in Fawcett Street when the new lights went on. And as many night-time guard duties in the town – along with most other parts of the country – were reduced, all daylight fire duties were abolished too. Civil Defence workers were also put on part-time rotas, and it was ruled that all pillboxes and roadblocks could be removed.

As there had not been any air raids for almost sixteen months, Martha, and others who had full-time jobs, were informed there was no longer any need for them to carry out their work as ARP wardens, news that was greeted with joy by her parents. Mr and Mrs Perkins were beyond relieved that their brave daughter was no longer putting her life on the line and pulling people out of bombed buildings.

The Sunderland shipyards, though, continued to work hard to get ships down the ways, with the launches of Laing's *Empire Chancellor* and Short's HMS *Dullisk Cove* hitting the Wear on the same day. Thompson's had just christened *Empire Ganges* and today the workforce had spent the first day laying down the keel of the yard's next commission.

As soon as the horn blasted out the end of the shift, Bobby helped to clear up the area where he and his squad of riveters were working, then he grabbed his haversack and hurried over to the women welders.

'Dorothy!'

Angie turned her head to see Bobby striding over to them. She nudged her friend.

'Dor, yer gone deaf? Bobby's calling yer.'

'I heard.' Dorothy spoke out the corner of her mouth. 'We're not supposed to fraternise at work.'

Angie looked at Gloria and Rosie and rolled her eyes to the heavens above.

'Dorothy,' Bobby repeated, a little out of breath, as he reached them.

'What?' Dorothy hissed.

Bobby looked affronted.

'You know we're not meant to see each other at work?' Dorothy railed.

Bobby laughed. 'Unless you master the art of becoming invisible or one of us goes blind, I don't think that's possible.'

'You know what I mean,' Dorothy said, her eyes searching the area around them to see if anyone had noticed they were chatting. Rosie and Gloria had returned to the task of putting away the work tools. Polly and Martha were grabbing their bags and waving their goodbyes.

'I believe our agreement was that we would not behave like a courting couple at work,' Bobby said, thinking how hard that had been for him since they had officially started to court. Every time he saw Dorothy, he just wanted to take her in his arms and kiss her to kingdom come – just like he wanted to now.

'What do you want?' Dorothy demanded.

'I thought we could go for a walk along the river – or up along the promenade. It's been such a lovely day, I thought we might enjoy the last of it.'

'OK,' Dorothy said, her tone still harsh. 'I'll meet you at the top of the embankment in five minutes.'

A wide smile spread across Bobby's face. Dorothy had been adamant that they would have one date a week, which meant in the three weeks they had been officially courting, they had only been out three times. Now, she had just broken one of the main rules of their courtship. It was a sign he was winning her over.

Turning to leave, Bobby caught his mam coming back from the shed where the welding equipment was stored.

'I might pop in for a quick cuppa later on, Mam.' He gave Dorothy a cheeky backward glance. 'That's if Dorothy doesn't keep me out late.'

Since the air between him and his mam had been cleared – when he'd confessed his resentments about the years she'd stayed with his nasty bastard of a father – he really enjoyed going round to the flat. He was amazed and heartened by how much his mam had changed. A change that had happened, he was sure, after she'd started work at the yard.

'A walk does not take up all of the evening,' Dorothy retorted. She looked at Gloria. 'He'll be there before *my god daughter's* bedtime.' Dorothy liked to take the opportunity to remind people of her special relationship with Hope whenever she could. All the women welders had helped deliver Hope that crazy day three years ago when Gloria had gone into labour in the middle of an air raid, but it had been Dorothy and Angie who had taken on the role of makeshift midwives.

Gloria suppressed a smile. 'Why don't yer 'n Bobby *both* pop in for a cuppa when yer've had yer walk?'

'I think that might be against the rules,' Bobby said, walking off chuckling.

As they reached the Bungalow Café and saw that it was still open, Bobby asked Dorothy if she wanted to go in for a cuppa and something to eat. She shook her head. She doubted she would ever go there with Bobby. It reminded her of Toby, when they'd been there on Valentine's Day, when he had told her he loved her – which, in turn, brought back her feelings of guilt. She was just glad Toby hadn't been returning to the front line, but simply going down south to his base. One of the women labourers at the yard who'd dumped her fiancé after meeting someone else had just heard that her ex had been killed during a skirmish in northern France. *How guilty must she be feeling?*

'Sounds like the riveters at Crown's went back to work today,' Bobby said. The strike at the yard next to Thompson's had been the talk of the town these past five days. The bone of contention being that it was not possible to earn as much on piecework rates as on time rates.

'Bet you Jack'll be pleased,' Dorothy said.

'That's why I'd hate being a manager,' Bobby said. 'All that negotiating.'

'Mmm,' Dorothy said, thinking of the punch-up with Toby. 'I can't imagine negotiating being your strong point.'

They walked in comfortable silence for a little while, the seagulls swooping and screeching above them.

133

'Do you miss being at sea?' Dorothy asked as they stopped by the stone barricade that ran along the promenade.

Bobby wrapped his arms around Dorothy and pulled her close.

'Not when I'm with you,' he told her, giving her a light kiss.

'Seriously, though,' Dorothy asked. 'Do you not miss it?'

'I missed it at first,' Bobby said.

Dorothy turned around and he slid his arms around her waist. They both looked out at the North Sea. The day had been sunny, but the waters looked choppy. The tide was coming in and waves were smashing into the pebbles on the beach.

'And I missed Gordon ... Still do,' Bobby said. He was quiet for a moment, thinking of how he had also been angry he had not been able to continue being part of the Battle of the Atlantic.

'But,' he said, kissing Dorothy's neck, 'and don't roll your eyes when I say this, you really have been quite a distraction.'

He kissed her neck again.

'Still are.'

Dorothy turned round and kissed him back.

But for how long would she be a distraction? Why did she feel so insecure when it came to Bobby? So fearful of being rejected by him? Was she worried he'd go off her when he really got to know her? Got to know all about her family? Would she still be a distraction – or would it turn into disappointment? How fast would the shine tarnish?

'Tell me,' Dorothy said, taking his hand and pushing away her negative thoughts of what might be, 'tell me about the most unusual country you've ever visited.' She loved to hear about the places he had been.

Bobby felt the warmth of Dorothy's hand.

'The most *unusual*,' he mused.

They continued their walk along the stretch of Roker Avenue, with its grand three-storey houses to the left and the grassy banks leading down to the cordoned-off beach, and Bobby described a place that was so hot it made you crave for the freezing cold of a north-east winter – a place where the colour grey did not exist, and where the natives wore paint on their bodies and not much else. Dorothy thought how wonderful it would be to see the world.

As they turned and walked back, they stopped at the bus shelter and kissed again.

'You know I'm serious about you, Dorothy, don't you?'

For the moment, Dorothy wanted to say, but held back. She didn't want to come across as one of those women who needed to be constantly reassured, which, if truth be told, she was. 'Mmm?' she asked, wondering where this was going. She had already allowed them two dates this week. *Give Bobby an inch and he was guaranteed to take a mile.*

'Well, I'd like to meet your parents,' Bobby said, aware that this was something that Toby had done not long before he had proposed. He didn't care, though; he saw no reason why he couldn't also present himself to Dorothy's family as her suitor. Her future husband.

Dorothy looked at Bobby's face and saw he was serious. Very serious. Her heart sank.

'Well ...' Dorothy hesitated, not knowing what to say.

'Well, what?'

Dorothy laughed nervously. 'I think that might be all a bit soon, don't you?'

Bobby wanted to say no, that in his opinion it *wasn't* at all a bit soon. But he didn't.

He was sure that Toby would have been welcomed with arms held wide open when he had gone to meet Mr and Mrs Williams. Toby was a lieutenant in the British Army and rich to boot. Bobby had heard about the diamond ring he had bought for Dorothy and that she was still dithering about what to do with it. Bobby had been an able seaman in the Royal Navy – not exactly comparable in rank. And now he was a riveter on a working man's basic wage. Far from rich. *Did Dorothy really think it was too soon – or was it because she didn't think him good enough?*

This week, while he had been considering asking Dorothy about meeting her parents, it had been the first time he'd really thought about the difference in their social standing. It hadn't been something he'd given too much thought to because of Dorothy's work in the yard. She wore overalls and hobnailed boots and welded ships for a living. It was a working-class occupation. But after hearing where her family lived and more about her life before Thompson's and her job in the china department at Binns, it was clear she was most definitely from the moneyed middle class.

Dorothy might like him, fancy him, enjoy spending time with him, but would she want to settle down with someone from the lower ranks with little by way of money or status?

Chapter Sixteen

'Looks like we can wave goodbye to an early end to this war,' Jack said, tapping the front page of the *Daily Mirror* as he put it down on the dining-room table to show Helen. He kissed Hope before bobbing his head through the kitchen doorway.

'I'm just gonna get cleaned up, Glor,' he said, going off to the bathroom.

Helen looked down at the headline: AIR TROOPS WITHDRAWN FROM ARNHEM. *2,000 Men Escape. 1,200 Wounded Left Behind.*

'Draw!' Hope demanded.

Helen turned her attention back to her little sister.

'Crayons at the ready?' she asked, keeping her voice light in spite of the depressing news. The whole nation had been rooting for an early victory. Hitler and his men might be down, but they were still not beaten.

'So, what shall we draw?' she asked.

'Ship!'

Helen smiled. *What else?* Last week, Hope had gone to see the launch of *Empire Ganges*, which, she had been told, her mam, brother and sister had helped to build. Ever since then, all she'd wanted to know about, talk about and draw had been ships, ships and more ships.

Helen had just sketched the outline of a hull when there was a loud knock on the door.

'I'll get it,' Gloria said, bustling out of the kitchen. Her face lit up as she opened the front door and saw that it was

Bobby. He was still in his overalls, having come straight from work.

'This is a surprise. I wasn't expecting yer,' she said, giving him a hug and ushering him into the flat.

'Are you all right?' Bobby looked at his mother, his face showing his concern.

'Of course I am. Why shouldn't I be?' she asked.

Bobby looked to see who else was there and saw Helen and Hope sitting at the dining-room table. They had crayons in their hands. Hope clambered off the chair and toddled towards him.

'Hello there, gorgeous!' Bobby picked her up and held her in the air, making her squeal with excitement.

Helen smiled as she watched Hope being returned to terra firma, her face lighting up as Bobby produced a comic from inside his dirty overalls.

'Hi, Helen, I didn't expect to see you here.'

'I just thought I'd pop in before going home.' Helen smiled. 'Also, I wanted to know how the "you-know-what" was going.' Bobby knew that was code for 'divorce'. Gloria and Jack had not wanted Hope repeating the word, especially as she seemed to be all ears at the moment and had a habit of repeating any new word she heard over and over.

'Good to see yer, Bobby. Everything all right?' Jack appeared from the bathroom, a towel still in his hands.

Bobby nodded, although his face was grave.

'Cuppa?' Gloria asked.

'Are you sure you're all right?' Bobby asked, looking at Gloria again with the same degree of concern.

'Course I am,' Gloria said, walking back into the kitchen.

Helen and Jack looked askance at Bobby.

'Why? Has something happened?' asked Jack.

Bobby was just about to speak when Gloria shouted through from the kitchen.

'It was nothing! Honestly, yer have to take what Dorothy says with a pinch of salt. She's such a drama queen.'

Now it was Jack and Helen's turn to look concerned.

'It wasn't just Dor,' Bobby said, 'but the rest of your squad as well. They all agreed it was nasty and upsetting.'

'What happened?' Jack demanded.

'Some woman at work went up to Mam and told her in no uncertain terms what she thought of someone who was living in sin with another woman's husband. And she also made no bones about what she thought of other aspects of Mam's life.' He cocked his head over at Hope, who was torn between reading her comic and looking at the adults, who had suddenly become very serious.

'I believe the language was offensive,' Bobby said, 'but worst of all – ' he looked at Jack and Helen and dropped his voice ' – the woman spat at Mam.'

'Oh my goodness, Gloria, that's awful!' Helen said.

'What did you do?' asked Jack, trying to mask his outrage for the sake of his younger daughter, who was now watching them all avidly.

'I did nothing,' Gloria said. 'I wasn't going to make a bad situation even worse.'

'Who was it?' Helen demanded, thinking she'd have the woman sacked the moment she got into work tomorrow.

'I have no idea,' Gloria said. 'I'm not even sure she works at Thompson's. I've certainly not seen her before.'

'This is just not on, Mam,' Bobby said, his voice a low rumble.

'I couldn't agree more,' Helen uttered through tight lips.

Jack didn't say anything, but his look spoke a thousand words.

'Yer right, it's not on,' Gloria said, her voice stern. 'But this is *my* problem. And no one else's. I'll sort it. I don't want anyone else getting involved.'

She glanced at Jack. She would talk to him when every-one was gone. She then fixed Helen and Bobby with a hard look. 'Understand?'

Helen and Bobby were silent.

'Understand?' Gloria demanded their acquiescence.

Bobby and Helen looked at each other before nodding, albeit reluctantly.

'Good,' Gloria said. 'Well, now that we've got that sorted, let's all have a nice cuppa tea.' She looked at Hope 'And I think it's time for Miss Flapper Lugs here to have her bed-time story.'

After reading Hope her new favourite story, a picture book about Noah's Ark, Bobby returned to the lounge.

'Henrietta doing all right?' he asked Helen. He now knew the truth, not just about Helen's grandmother, but about the rest of the women's secrets. All apart from Doro-thy's. She had told everyone that she wanted to tell Bobby in her own time.

'Yes, she's really well,' Helen said. 'I'm hoping to take her out soon for the afternoon – it'll be the first time in over twenty years.'

'That's quite some time to be shut away.' Bobby whis-tled. 'Fingers crossed it goes well.'

'It'll just be a little trip to Kate's to get measured up for some new clothes, so it won't be too much of a shock to the system.'

'Ease her back into the real world slowly,' Bobby said.

'Exactly,' said Helen, topping up everyone's tea and turning her attention to her father. 'So, your Mr Emery has finally got round to sorting out the divorce petition and getting it sent to Mother?'

'He has,' Jack said.

'So, what happens now?' Helen asked.

'Well,' Jack began, 'by law, Miriam has to acknowledge receipt of the petition, although obviously no one can force her to.'

'And if she doesn't?' Bobby asked.

'I have to wait a month and then the courts have to demand to be told whether or not Miriam's going to defend the divorce.'

No one said anything. They didn't have to. It was obvious Jack's divorce was going to take time. A long time.

*

As soon as Helen stepped through her front door, she heard her mother's voice.

'I told you, Jack Crawford!' Miriam's voice trilled out. 'I warned you!'

Helen walked across the hallway and pushed open the door to the lounge, which had been left ajar. Miriam was standing by the open fire, a gin and tonic in one hand and some official-looking papers in the other.

'Mother?' said Helen, walking into the room.

Miriam spun round and wobbled a little as she regained her footing.

'Helen, darling!' she said. 'Perfectly timed! I *so* wanted to share this moment with someone – and now I can!'

Helen looked at her mother. She was more than a few sheets to the wind.

'What are you doing, Mother?' She looked at the fire and could see a few burnt pieces of paper had fallen onto the hearth.

'I'm making good my promise, that's what I'm doing!' Miriam declared. She raised her right hand, in which she was holding the typed documentation, and waved it in the air. 'I told your father I would make this as hard as possible for him and that's exactly what I'm doing.'

The penny dropped. Helen took a step forward, automatically wanting to save the papers from being incinerated, but it was too late. Miriam turned and fed them to the flames, humming the Wedding March as she did so.

Helen stopped in her tracks as she watched her father's petition for divorce turn into a vibrant orange flame, before disintegrating into black ash.

'Why are you doing this, Mother?' asked Helen. 'It's not as if you can stop Dad divorcing you? He'll get it in the end.'

'True,' Miriam said, taking another sip of her drink, 'but the end will be a long time coming if I have my way. Especially when I get the town's top legal team to – what's the correct terminology? – "defend the divorce petition".' She looked at Helen. 'That's the joy of having plenty of money, you can get the best of everything.' She had a flash of her father's will. She was going to be rich. Very rich. There'd be nothing she couldn't have.

'Just this afternoon my solicitor has been informing me exactly what will happen.'

Miriam moved away from the fire and walked over to the drinks cabinet.

'In about a month's time, when the courts have not received an acknowledgement that I have received the divorce petition – ' Miriam threw her hand down at the fire ' – I will again be required by law to disclose whether or not I intend to defend the divorce. And that's when the fun and games start. There will have to be what is called '"defended divorce proceedings", which will result in a fully contested hearing. My solicitor knows how to drag things out and work the system – and is more than happy to do so as it means more of this.' Miriam rubbed her thumb and forefinger together. 'It'll cost a fortune, so it looks like Jack will be working all the overtime he can get. He won't have much time to play happy families. Come to think of it, he'll need Gloria to chip in as well, so she'll be spending every waking hour at that yard of yours.' A sly smile spread slowly across Miriam's face. 'Which means poor little illegitimate Hope will have to find a nursery to take her.'

Helen felt her temper, which had been simmering, come to the boil.

'It was you, wasn't it?'

'What was me?' asked Miriam, a knowing look on her face.

'It was you who got Hope rejected from that nursery in town?' she accused.

Miriam allowed another self-satisfied smile to creep across her face. 'You should know your mother by now, Helen, dear. I'm a woman of my word. I do what I say. I put my money where my mouth is – and I gave a promise that day in your office that I would make your father's life a misery, and that's exactly what I'm doing.'

Helen thought of what Bobby had told her earlier.

'And the name-calling? Were you behind that?' asked Helen.

'Of course, my dear. Nobody likes to hear of some harlot snatching another woman's husband – and then trapping him by the oldest trick in the book and getting pregnant.'

'Talk about the kettle calling the pot black, Mother. I believe that's exactly what *you* did to get Dad to walk you down the aisle.'

Miriam ignored her daughter.

'Although in Gloria's case,' she continued, 'that was quite some feat. I mean, she's hardly your typical femme fatale, is she? Not exactly Gloria Swanson. Not by any stretch. And getting pregnant at her age is actually quite embarrassing, don't you think?'

Helen struggled to find the words to articulate her disgust. She looked at her mother as she walked over to the phone and lifted the receiver. Putting her drink down, she shooed Helen away with her free hand.

As she left the room, Helen heard her mother asking to be connected to the Grand.

'It's Miriam. Miriam Havelock here. I want to reserve a table for four. And make sure you've got some Dom Pérignon on ice. I'm having a little celebration.'

Helen made her way up the stairs to her room.

With each step her resolve grew.

It was time to take the gloves off.

It was time to give the old Helen free rein.

Chapter Seventeen

October

The start of the new month was heralded by reports that the German garrison in Calais had surrendered to Canadian troops. At one time, it was feared the French port would be the focus of the cross-Channel invasion. Not any more.

For Helen, the beginning of October marked the start of her new resolve.

'Shut the door on your way out, Marie-Anne,' she ordered, taking a sip of the tea.

Marie-Anne did as she was told, wondering who it was her boss was going to call. Helen rarely made personal calls. In fact, she didn't seem to have much of a personal life at all. Rumours were still circulating that she and Matthew Royce were having a 'thing', but Marie-Anne was pretty sure she wasn't. Roger, the photographer from the *Echo* with whom Marie-Anne went out on occasional dates, kept quizzing her, but Dahlia had confirmed the two bosses were just friends – work colleagues who went to social functions together.

Helen waited until she saw Marie-Anne heading back to her desk. Her personal assistant was very good at her job, but she was nosy and had a tendency to loiter at the door to earwig in on conversations, especially if she thought they were not work-related.

Picking up the receiver, she dialled the operator.

'The *Sunderland Echo*,' she demanded. She was in no mood for niceties. She lit a cigarette. There was a click followed by the local newspaper's switchboard operator.

'Newsroom,' Helen said, blowing out smoke.

Another click. Another voice. This one male.

'I would like to speak to Georgina Pickering,' Helen said.

The voice on the other end of the line asked what it was about.

'None of your business,' Helen snapped. 'Now can you put me through to Miss Pickering or do I have to speak with your editor?'

There was silence. Another click.

'Hello, this is Miss Georgina Pickering. How can I help you?'

'Hi, Georgina, it's Helen, Helen Crawford, here.'

There was a moment's silence. This was the first time Georgina had spoken to Helen since she had handed her the report that had gone some way to proving that Charles Havelock was Bel's father.

'Hello, Miss Crawford,' Georgina said, the epitome of professionalism. 'How can I help you?'

Helen took another drag on her cigarette.

'I need you to come in and see me.' It wasn't a request. 'I'll pay you for your time and trouble. Call it a consultation fee.' Helen knew it was unlikely Georgina would come unless there was a financial incentive.

The two women agreed a time and a fee and rang off. The whole conversation had taken under a minute.

At five o'clock, Georgina turned up at the admin offices at Thompson's. She was surprised to see the office empty – apart from Helen, who immediately waved her in.

'Come sit down,' Helen commanded, shutting the door behind Georgina and checking that there was no one else about. She had allowed her staff to leave at half-past four, supposedly as a thank you for all the hard work they had been doing. In reality, she just wanted to keep her plans well under wraps and for there to be no chance of any leaks.

'Here you are.' Helen immediately handed Georgina a small brown envelope that contained the agreed 'consultation fee' in cash.

'You know I'm no longer in the business of private-eye work?' Georgina said as she pocketed the envelope.

'I know,' said Helen. That's what she liked about Georgina. Always straight to the point. Her fragile physique and unfashionable appearance belied a character that was steely and a mind that was progressive. Radical, even. 'I read the *Echo* every day. I thought the article you wrote on the inquest into the young apprentice who was killed at Doxford's was very well done.'

Georgina eyed Helen with a degree of suspicion. She knew of her closeness to Matthew Royce Jnr. They'd had a complaint that the article implied the yard might have played a part in the fifteen-year-old's demise, despite the coroner ruling 'accidental death'.

'I mean it,' Helen said, seeing Georgina's wariness. 'I thought the article printed next to it about the unions pushing for better safety standards was also well written – and well placed. It's something I'm all for here at Thompson's.' She smiled. 'A conversation for another time, perhaps. How about a cup of tea?'

Georgina shook her head and waited to hear what it was that Helen really wanted.

'OK, down to business,' said Helen. 'I know you are no longer a private investigator, but I want you to do one more job. One more job, for which I will pay handsomely.'

Georgina reached into her bag and pulled out her pen and book. She and her elderly father were having to live off the meagre wage she earned at the *Echo*. They needed the money.

Helen lit a cigarette and blew out a plume of smoke.

'It concerns my mother,' she began.

Georgina grimaced inwardly. Miriam was a cold, calculating woman and her father, Charles Havelock, was pure evil.

For the next quarter of an hour, Georgina scribbled down notes as Helen explained what she wanted her to do. It wasn't going to be the easiest of jobs. She had met Miriam Crawford before when she had employed Georgina's father to do some snooping on Rosie's squad of women welders. Thankfully, Miriam had thought Georgina was just her father's secretary and not the person actually digging up the dirt, but she would still have to be careful.

'So, is there anything else you need to know?' Helen asked when she had finished.

'No, I think I have everything,' Georgina said, knowing that this might be a lucrative job, but it was also a tricky one.

'Great,' Helen said, standing up, throwing on her coat and then grabbing her handbag. 'I'll leave it in your capable hands. Just keep me updated.'

Georgina stood up and the pair made their way out of the main office.

'Oh, I forgot,' said Helen. 'Can you also get me everything you can on that new nursery I mentioned that's just started up in the east end? As well as on the woman who runs it, please?'

'Yes, of course,' Georgina said. She knew why Helen wanted to know, but was curious as to what she might do with the information.

They made their way down the stairs.

'Miss Crawford ...' Georgina said a little hesitantly '... can I just reiterate what I have said previously?'

Helen looked at Georgina. 'About me not letting on to Rosie and the rest of the women what you do for a living – or rather, did?'

'Yes,' Georgina said simply.

Helen knew Georgina did not want Rosie and her squad to find out about her private-eye work – and even more that she had been the one to unearth all their secrets. Secrets that had then been used by Miriam to banish Jack to the Clyde. Georgina had become good friends with Rosie and her squad and Helen knew she did not want to jeopardise that friendship.

'Don't worry. If they find out, it won't be from me.'

Having parted from Georgina at the main gates, Helen jumped into her car. Firing up the engine and slowly driving up the embankment to the main road, her mind wandered to the work Georgina had done for her mother almost three years ago. Helen had often wondered if Georgina had held anything back about Rosie, especially after she'd found out that Rosie's and Georgina's mothers had once been good friends.

Indicating left and turning onto the Wearmouth Bridge, Helen told herself she'd just have to keep on wondering. Georgina would certainly never tell her. And she'd never have the nerve to ask Rosie outright.

Rosie, Gloria, Polly, Dorothy, Angie, Martha and Hannah all piled into Vera's café on High Street East. They had decided it was the perfect place to meet up as it was on their way home and the proprietor had no objections to allowing a group of women wearing dirty overalls to patronise the place, unlike some of the more salubrious eateries in the town centre.

They had just got themselves settled around a large table by the window when the bell above the café door tinkled and Helen walked in. Everyone in the cafeteria looked up, their attention lingering for a moment on the stunning young woman whose good looks and hourglass figure could not be disguised by the plain grey mackintosh she was wearing.

'Over here!' Gloria waved at her, smiling a welcome, knowing that meeting with the women en masse always made Helen a little nervous.

'Hi, everyone.' Helen tried to sound casual.

'Hi, Helen!' the women chorused.

Helen looked at everyone as she sat down in a spare chair between Rosie and Gloria, the two women she felt most at ease with.

'What are yer all having?' Vera suddenly appeared, arms akimbo, hands resting on her wide girth. She was eyeing the newcomer with suspicion. Helen had taken off her mac and the dress she was wearing made it very clear she was not from the east end.

'Tea all round, please, Vera,' Rosie said, taking charge and seeing the less than friendly look the old woman was giving Helen. 'And a selection of whatever you've got going.'

'I'll see what I've got left.' Vera made it sound as though she was doing them all a favour.

'How are you doing, Helen?' asked Hannah.

'Good, thanks,' she said, smiling at the group's 'little bird'. How could she complain about her own life when Hannah's parents were in the infamous Auschwitz concentration camp. 'Any news about your mother and father?'

Hannah shook her head and nodded over at a tall, dark-haired woman behind the counter.

'Aunty Rina keeps a ... how do you say it? ... she keeps a *close ear* to the ground ... but nothing. We've heard nothing.'

'We say *no news is good news*,' Martha said, 'don't we?'

Hannah smiled sadly. 'We do.'

'Mind yerselves!' Vera announced as she reappeared carrying a large tray weighed down with a big pot of tea and a mound of china cups and saucers. A few moments later, Rina followed with a tray of sandwiches and cakes. They all voiced their thanks and started to tuck in.

'How's Henrietta?' Rosie asked, pouring the tea.

'Oh, she's well,' Helen said. 'In really good spirits. Actually, I'm hoping she'll agree to a trip out.'

'From the asylum?' Angie asked, keeping her voice hushed.

Helen nodded. 'Probably just for a few hours to start with.'

'Won't someone recognise her?' Polly asked.

'Well, the plan is to take her straight to the Maison Nouvelle. Kate's going to shut up shop while she measures her up for a new outfit. A more modern look.'

The women had all heard about Henrietta's eccentric dress sense.

'It's unlikely she'll bump into anyone, let alone someone who knows her from back then.'

'I'm guessing,' Gloria chipped in, 'the plan is that when Henrietta is wearing normal clothes, it's unlikely she'll be recognised.'

'Exactly,' Helen said, taking a sip of her tea.

'Sounds like a good idea,' said Dorothy, fascinated.

'That way she'll be easier to pass off as some sort of distant, long-lost relative,' Helen explained.

'It would be lovely to meet her one day,' Hannah chirped up.

Everyone murmured their agreement.

'Hopefully, one day soon,' Helen said.

'It must be strange,' Angie mused, 'spending half yer life in a nuthouse.'

'I think what Angie meant to say,' Dorothy jumped in, 'is that it must change a person, living permanently in a mental institution.'

Helen smiled and nodded.

'And is that cow Claire still with Dr Parker?' Angie asked.

Dorothy looked at Angie and glared at her.

'Unfortunately, she is,' Helen laughed.

The women were all quiet for a moment as they tucked into sandwiches and cake and slurped back perfectly brewed tea. The sense of outrage and injustice they had initially felt when Gloria had told them about the hold Dr Eris had over Helen was still strong. And even though they had agreed that there was nothing to be done, they still railed against their sense of impotence. Helen had helped them all a lot over the past two years; they would have liked to have returned the favour.

'So,' Rosie said, after finishing a finger of melt-in-your-mouth shortbread, 'we have to decide what to do with Dorothy's diamond ring.'

Everyone looked at Dorothy, who flushed red. She'd be glad when she saw the back of the damned thing – unlike Angie, who would be gutted. She'd become quite attached to it. She might have stopped getting it out of the cupboard and dancing around the kitchen with it on, but Dorothy had caught her wearing it one night when she'd come back early from a date with Bobby. Angie had confessed to wearing it in the flat whenever Dorothy wasn't about.

'I believe,' Gloria said, 'that Helen might have a solution to the problem.'

Everyone stopped eating and drinking and looked at Helen.

Dorothy rummaged around in her handbag and produced the ring for everyone to see. The little red leather box was flipped open and handed around like pass the parcel. Having already agreed on swapping the ring for hard cash, it was just a matter of deciding what to do with the money.

'Well,' Helen began. 'When I was visiting Henrietta the other day, I got talking to John—'

'But I thought you weren't allowed to?' Martha asked.

'I've won myself a bit of a reprieve.' Helen smiled at Martha, with whom she shared a strange, unspoken bond since they'd both risked their lives to save Gloria and Hope.

'And?' Angie asked, taking a piece of cake. She'd been looking forward to a slice of Vera's carrot cake all day.

'Well,' Helen said, shuffling in her seat, 'John was telling me about a Christmas fund being set up at the Ryhope. They're trying to raise money to buy presents for all the wounded soldiers who'll be in hospital over the festive period. It might seem a long time to Christmas, but it's not long to raise the amount of money they'll need – so I wondered if it would be a good idea to put the money from the ring towards that?'

'*Oh. My. God*. Brilliant idea!' Dorothy exclaimed, clapping her hands in excitement.

'Couldn't be more perfect!' Polly said. They had all heard about the state of some of the men who had come back from war – men with missing limbs, or blind, or deaf, as well as those who'd had to be transferred to the asylum.

'It mightn't be as simple as just giving them the money, though,' Helen said. 'John was saying that they need volunteers to go out and buy the presents and wrap them up.' She paused. 'And they were hoping for volunteers who might feel able to sacrifice part of their Christmas Day to dole them out.'

Dorothy let out a squeal of excitement. Everyone in the café stared at her. Vera threw her a deathly look.

'Sorry,' Dorothy mouthed. Looking back at Helen and the women, she silently clapped her hands for a second time. 'This is just perfect!' she said. 'We can do it all! The buying, the wrapping, the doling out!'

Everyone nodded.

'Sounds like a plan,' Rosie said.

'And it would mean,' said Angie, nudging her best friend, 'that we dinnit have to gan home for Christmas. We'll have the perfect excuse.'

'Exactly!' said Dorothy.

Rosie ordered another pot of tea and for the next hour they chatted non-stop about the logistics of who would buy the presents, who would wrap, where the gifts could be kept and what kind of presents should be bought. There was also a more practical discussion as to whether the money they got for the ring would be enough, and if they would need to raise more funds.

Dorothy suddenly half jumped out of her chair – an idea having just sprung into her head.

'Why don't we go one step further,' she said, her voice high with excitement, 'and throw them a proper Christmas party?' She widened her eyes at her workmates. 'A Christmas Day they'll never forget.'

She took a deep, dramatic intake of breath.

'A Christmas Extravaganza!'

The women all looked at each other with tentative smiles on their faces.

'Why not?' said Rosie. 'If everyone's prepared to go that extra mile?'

'Yeah, why not?' Angie repeated, looking at Dorothy and smiling.

'I think that's a brilliant idea,' said Helen.

'Me too,' Gloria agreed.

'I'm in,' said Polly.

'And me,' said Hannah.

'And me,' said Martha through a mouthful of shortbread.

Dorothy looked like she was going to burst.

'Hurrah! Christmas is coming early this year!'

Chapter Eighteen

Over the ensuing weeks, events around the globe added to the feeling that Christmas was indeed coming early. Newsreels showed parties in the streets of Athens after the Germans lowered their swastika flag from the Acropolis and finally left the Greek capital. When American troops occupied Aachen it added to the sense of jubilation. It was the first major German city to be captured and it put the whole nation on a high.

Doxford's, Pickersgill's and Thompson's all enjoyed particularly well-attended launches, which seemed to involve more horn-blowing, cheering and joviality than normal. And POWs from the town, who'd been rescued when a Japanese ship was sunk, were given a hero's welcome. Caught up in it all, Dorothy declared that their 'Christmas Extravaganza' had to be 'the best ever'. 'We need to show those injured soldiers at Ryhope just how thankful we are to them. For helping beat Jerry – and the sacrifices they've made,' she said.

There was, of course, another reason why Dorothy was so keen to organise such an extravaganza: Christmas had never been a particularly joyous occasion for her. It was something that had to be endured rather than enjoyed. While her real father had still been at home, any festive cheer would sour by the time dinner was served and the air had invariably been filled with screaming and shouting, mixed with the smashing of plates and the slamming of doors. After Frank had married her mother, there was no drama, but not much fun or laughter either. And after her half-sisters had come along, Dorothy had found herself practically invisible. Frank had not treated Dorothy as one of his own, and her mother seemed more intent on keeping her new husband happy than making the day special for her eldest child.

Angie understood why Dorothy was so excited about the proposed extravaganza – as did the rest of the women. Dorothy might well have enjoyed a more affluent upbringing than most of them, but it had been slim pickings when it came to any kind of parental love. This was Dorothy's chance to have the kind of Christmas she had always wanted – with the people she loved. People who might not be her real family, but who were most definitely her family of friends.

And so, with Angie happy to take on the role of second in command, Dorothy set about organising with military precision what needed to be done. Hannah and Olly were tasked with liaising with Vera and Rina, who had agreed to do the catering. Vera had also come up with the idea of putting a tin by the till asking for donations for 'A Christmas Extravaganza', with a little placard next to it explaining the event in more detail.

It was decided the actual buying of presents would happen later, when, hopefully, there would be more in the shops – a possibility as there had been a slight easing in the rationing of some goods.

Marie-Anne also came up with an idea that Dorothy declared 'pure genius' when she suggested that the soldiers might also like some entertainment. They all thought long and hard of anyone who might fit the bill. Marie-Anne said she and Dahlia could sing, which was met with some scepticism. It was agreed they could do an audition.

Martha said Christmas wouldn't be Christmas without the Salvation Army and suggested seeing if they could go round the wards on the day. It was deemed another 'brilliant' idea and Martha was handed the responsibility for making it happen, along with instructions to tell the band leader that they would receive a generous donation for doing so.

Polly was asked if she could persuade Agnes and Beryl to put their knitting needles to work and make anything they thought an injured soldier might want in the middle of winter – hats, scarves, gloves, pullovers. Polly said that she was sure they'd jump at the chance. Both women would do anything to feel that they were helping those fighting for King and country. She didn't have to say why. Agnes had lost her husband, Harry, in the First War, and Beryl's husband was presently a POW in Burma.

'It might feel like it's a long time before Christmas,' Dorothy lectured, 'but it's not really.'

In her free time, when she wasn't organising the extravaganza, Dorothy continued to go out on dates with Bobby. One night, walking home after an evening at the flicks, having watched a rather melodramatic movie where one of the main female characters was a divorcee, Bobby tentatively asked Dorothy about her parents' divorce.

'It must have been quite a scandal at the time,' he said.

If they had been walking past one of the dimly lit street lamps, Bobby might have seen a flicker of angst cross his sweetheart's face.

'It was all done very quietly – with the least fuss possible,' Dorothy lied. *Suddenly, she was back in the past, with her mother just days before her wedding to Frank. She'd walked into her mother's bedroom and found her clutching some kind of official document, looking as white as a ghost.*

'Looks like we've got that in common as well,' Bobby said as they continued walking.

'What do you mean?' Dorothy asked, her mind still lost in the past. *Caught off guard, her mother had confided in her that her divorce had never been properly finalised. There had been a minor oversight, which was now causing a major problem.*

'That our parents are divorced,' Bobby said, putting his arm around Dorothy and squeezing her close. 'Not many couples can say that, can they?'

'It's not exactly something I'd be shouting about from the treetops,' Dorothy said.

Bobby laughed.

What Dorothy really wanted to say was that it wasn't true. *His* mam was a divorcee, whereas *her* mam was a bigamist. And worse still, her stepfather, Frank, was totally unaware that his wife was actually still married to someone else. It worried her that if Bobby got to know the truth about her seemingly respectable family, he might not think so much of her. He was forever saying that what he loved about her the most was her 'brutal honesty and forthrightness'. But she wasn't honest, was she? Or forthright? She was a liar. And her family was a fraud. Needing to change the subject, Dorothy started back on the subject of the Christmas Extravaganza.

Bobby looked at the woman he loved more than anything – but who also infuriated him more than anything or anyone. *Why was she so loath to chat about her family?* You could barely shut her up on almost any subject, but when it came to her home life, she clammed up good and proper.

His heart sank.

Was it because she didn't want him to meet them? Because he wasn't 'meeting the parents' material?

Chapter Nineteen

Lying in bed in her terraced cottage just off the West Wing in the asylum, Dr Eris looked across at the man she was now quite confident she was going to marry. He really was very handsome. What you might call very 'English-looking', with his mop of blond hair presently flopping over his forehead. As John shuffled onto his side, he kissed her gently. Claire thought how very considerate a lover he was. Just as he was careful. There were to be no little 'accidents'. Which was fine by her. She didn't need to take that particular route to get John down the aisle. After dealing with Helen, she felt everything was in hand.

It still puzzled her as to why Helen had been so set on John. He was an attractive man, but he wasn't really someone who had women swooning at his feet – not like the very dashing Matthew Royce. On looks alone, Helen and Matthew were a perfect match. Both dark-haired and drop-dead gorgeous. Never mind that they worked in the same industry and clearly had shipbuilding in their blood.

She sighed. Hopefully, Helen would bore of being single – she wasn't getting any younger, and with any luck she would turn her amour away from John and focus on a man who was not only available but very clearly keen on her.

As she sat up in the narrow bed and looked around the small bedroom of her rented digs, she looked forward to the day when they would have their own house. As soon as John proposed, she was going to start gently suggesting that they should move to London. Once the war was won, of course.

'How's your star patient doing?' Dr Parker asked. Helen had said Henrietta was doing really well, but it was always good to hear a professional opinion.

'Oh, she's good. *Very good*,' Dr Eris said, sliding out of bed and putting on a dressing gown. She couldn't let on to John that she knew who her 'star patient' really was – just as she knew John could not tell her that he too knew Henrietta's real identity. John would never betray Helen's confidence.

She went into her kitchenette to make a pot of tea.

'Thank goodness I got them to stop the electroconvulsive therapy that Dr Friedman was so keen on,' Dr Eris shouted through. She was even more thankful now that she knew there was nothing really wrong with the poor woman and the only reason she was there was because her husband had wanted shot of her.

She heard John's mumbled agreement. They were not huge fans of the various shock therapies that seemed to have grown in popularity over the past decade or so.

'I'm also rather pleased that I've just about weaned her off most of her medications,' she added. They had previously discussed her concern about the variety of drugs Henrietta was on. 'I wouldn't be surprised if in years to come they discover that some of the drugs she's been taking have actually been *making* her unwell – not curing her.'

She popped her head round the corner and smiled at John, who was now sitting up in bed, his hands clasped together on top of the sheets.

'Do you think there'll ever be a time when she can leave the asylum. Permanently?' he asked.

'Mmm.' Dr Eris hesitated. *Not likely. Not if Charles Havelock has his way.* 'That's a difficult one to call. I think, for

161

now, I'd like to see how she adapts to seeing life without the thick filter of medication.'

She turned back to finish the tea-making, suddenly feeling a little rankled by John's interest in Henrietta's welfare, which, she felt, was more to do with the fact that her 'star patient' was Helen's grandmother than because of Henrietta herself.

Chapter Twenty

'What does it feel like?' Helen turned her head to look at Henrietta. They had just gone through the main gates of the asylum and were now driving along Waterworks Road, past the Gothic red-brick Ryhope Pumping Station.

'Exhilarating!' Henrietta said, her expression a reflection of her words.

Helen's smile was wide. She too felt exhilarated. This was a huge step for her grandmother, and one Helen hadn't been entirely sure she would either want or be able to take. But Henrietta most certainly had wanted to. There had been no hesitation when Helen had arrived this morning to pick her up, her grandmother had very clearly been ready, willing and able. Helen did wonder, though, if her keenness was as much to do with getting a new outfit and visiting a boutique as it was about leaving the asylum for a few hours.

'And I can be myself?' Henrietta asked.

'You can in all ways,' Helen said. 'Kate knows that you are my grandmother.'

Henrietta smiled and squeezed Helen's hand, which was resting on the gearstick.

As they drove through Ryhope village and along the coastal road, they were both quiet. Henrietta's eyes were glued to the North Sea, only occasionally looking to her left at the surrounding countryside. Helen thought about her conversation with Dr Eris, how she had told the doctor that as Henrietta had been doing so well of late, she thought it would be a good idea to take her out. Dr Eris had shown her surprise and asked her if she thought that was wise, her tone indicating that it was not Henrietta's mental state which was the cause for concern, but the possibility of her being recognised. 'What would Mr Havelock have to say on the matter?' she'd whispered. Helen hadn't answered but had simply asked for the necessary paperwork and told her that she'd pick it up from Genevieve. She'd actually felt slightly empowered. It was now just as important to Dr Eris that Henrietta's identity be kept a secret as it was for Helen. If the real Henrietta Havelock was revealed to the world, then Claire would no longer have a hold over her.

As they reached the outskirts of the town, however, Helen started to feel a little apprehensive. She knew she was taking a risk bringing Henrietta out, although she had convinced herself and the women that the risk was minimal. It was a Sunday, after all. Kate was opening up the boutique purely for Henrietta. The 'Closed' sign, she had reassured her, would be on show and no one else would be allowed in, even if they came knocking at the door.

Driving down Holmeside, Helen thought it seemed busier than normal. Much busier. Then it occurred to her that it was the last Sunday of the month. The date the Shipbuilding Corporation was launching its latest cargo vessel, *Empire Mandalay*. Hordes of people – men, women and children – were all streaming down to the south docks.

'*Damn!*' Helen muttered under her breath.

She looked at Henrietta, who was staring out of the passenger window.

'How everything's changed,' she mused.

'It certainly has, Grandmama. Are you still feeling all right?' Helen asked gently. She had warned Kate that Henrietta might not feel able to go through with it all.

164

'Yes, yes, my dear. I've just seen a woman in the most amazing outfit. I feel quite inspired.'

Helen breathed a sigh of relief. Now she just had to get her grandmother into the shop without anyone seeing her. She knew she was being overcautious and a little paranoid, but there was a lot at stake. Sunderland was a relatively small town. People had long memories. And in her day, Henrietta had been a high-profile figure. The quicker Henrietta had a makeover, the better.

Parking up outside Maison Nouvelle, Helen silently cursed the fact she'd bought such a showy car. A group of children immediately surrounded it. Helen grabbed her handbag and pulled out her purse. Climbing out of the driver's seat, she opened her purse and emptied all the coins in it into her hand.

'Here, children,' Helen called out. 'To celebrate *Mandalay*!'

The lure of a handful of shiny coins did the trick and the children lined up to take one each before speeding off down the street.

As soon as they were gone, Helen hurried round the other side, smiling at an elderly gentleman who tipped his cap to her, his eyes, thankfully, fixed firmly on the car.

'Come on, Grandmama,' Helen said, helping Henrietta out of the low passenger seat. Putting her arm around her, she quickly ushered her into the boutique.

The bell rang out as soon as they opened the door and Helen breathed a sigh of relief that Kate had left it unlocked.

'You made it!' Kate called out as soon as she saw the pair enter the shop. She hurried over and shook hands with Henrietta. 'Lovely to meet you, Miss Girling.'

'Oh, my dear, please, call me Henrietta. I'm not one for standing on ceremony.'

Kate looked at the woman she had heard so much about. Her style was certainly different. Unique. Her red hair was piled high. Her taffeta skirt was amazing, but more like something you'd see on the stage or a film set at the turn of the century. Helen had been right in saying that her grandmother looked younger than her age. She could certainly pass as a woman in her late forties to early fifties.

'Well, Henrietta, it's an honour to have you here and for you to entrust me with creating you a new wardrobe.' And with that, Kate walked over to the front door, locked it and pulled down the blind. Ushering Henrietta into the boutique, she got to work with her tape measure while Helen made them each a cup of tea, which surprised Kate as she had only really known Helen as a client and had never imagined her as the type of person who made tea for others.

While double-checking Henrietta's measurements, Kate talked to her about the Utility Clothing Scheme, introduced by the government in response to the shortage of clothing materials and labour.

'The introduction of rationing, however,' Henrietta suddenly sparked up, 'has not made clothes any cheaper.'

Helen raised her eyebrows at her grandmother.

'I do read all those newspapers you leave for me, you know,' Henrietta said.

Kate chuckled. Helen and her grandmother were quite the pair. Seeing them together certainly shed a new light on Helen.

When the measuring was done, they all sat down and Kate got out a few magazines. Certain pages had been earmarked with examples of outfits she thought would suit Henrietta and bring her, as Helen had requested, into the modern world. 'What about this – not too showy, but a rather lovely blend of mature chic?'

'Oh, that's divine!' Henrietta said, clapping her hands at one particular outfit.

Helen breathed a sigh of relief. Kate had chosen well.

When Kate mentioned the Make Do and Mend campaign, Helen jumped up.

'I nearly forgot!'

Hurrying out of the boutique, she fetched some of Henrietta's old clothes from the boot of her car.

'Thank you,' Kate said, taking the clothes from Helen, her eyes scanning the quality of the fabric. 'I shall certainly put these to good use.'

After hanging up the donated clothes, Kate picked up a sample of fabric from her worktop and showed it to Henrietta.

'Oh, *my dear*,' Henrietta said suddenly, her face aghast as she gently took Kate's hands and turned them over in her own smooth, pale ones. 'You have not had an easy life, have you?' She traced one of the main scars across Kate's knuckles. There were scores of thin, pale lines where the skin had been repeatedly split open by Sister Bernadette's favourite birch stick.

Helen stared. In all the time she had known Kate, she had never noticed her scarred hands, or that her nails were bitten to the quick.

Kate gently pulled her hands away from Henrietta.

'Nor, I believe, have *you* had the easiest of lives,' she said.

'Oh, but I deserved mine,' Henrietta said, her eyes suddenly pooling with the start of tears. 'If I have any scars in here – ' she put a hand to her heart ' – or here –' she touched her head ' – then I deserve every one of them.'

Kate and Helen both stared at Henrietta.

'Really?' Kate asked. 'Is that what you honestly believe?'

Henrietta nodded.

'You know,' Kate said, 'the life I have led has made me a good reader of people, and I have to say I find it hard to believe that you deserve the scars you carry inside.'

'Oh, but I do,' Henrietta said with complete conviction. 'I *really do.*'

Helen threw Kate a look. 'I have to agree with Kate, Grandmama. You don't deserve to be punished for anything.'

'Like I've told you before, Helen, it is *my* fault all those poor girls suffered.' Henrietta put her hand to her chest. 'None more so than poor little Gracie ... I should have known ... Realised what that man was up to.'

It took a moment for Kate to remember what she had been told after the Christmas showdown – that Mr Havelock had raped a young girl who had given birth to his child and then taken her own life.

'Well, I think you're wrong, Henrietta. Completely and utterly wrong,' Kate said quite sharply.

Helen and Henrietta both looked at the diminutive seamstress.

'It makes me angry,' Kate said, her focus on Henrietta, 'that you believe you should bear the burden of another person's actions. You didn't do those horrendous acts. He did.'

Henrietta stared at Kate.

'Well, I couldn't have put it better myself,' Helen agreed.

There was a moment's quiet.

'Anyway, enough serious talk,' Kate said, her tone softening as she reached for her book of fabric samples. 'How about this for your first skirt suit? I could have it ready for Christmas.'

Helen looked at Henrietta. 'You will have an outfit for the Christmas Extravaganza.'

Henrietta's eyes lit up. 'Oh, that would be wonderful! Truly wonderful!'

'I'm guessing Dorothy has roped you in too?' Helen asked Kate.

'Oh yes,' Kate smiled. 'She seems to think that my seamstress skills somehow make me the perfect candidate to do the decorations.'

'Mmm, I'm not sure I see the connection.'

Kate chuckled. 'Me neither, but I don't mind – actually, I think I'll quite enjoy it.'

As they got up to leave, Helen touched Kate on the arm and said, 'Thank you.' The way she spoke, it was clear her gratitude was not just for her work but also for her words.

'So, I'll see you both again for the fitting, I'll call you with a date nearer the time?'

'Sounds perfect to me,' Helen said.

'Perfect,' agreed Henrietta.

Helen unlocked the door and quickly checked the street, which, thankfully, was now much quieter, before guiding Henrietta hastily back to the car.

Chapter Twenty-One

November

On the first Friday of November, Dorothy got out her calendar and informed everyone it was just seven weeks and three days to the big day.

'It's time to sell the ring!' she declared.

They all knew that Angie had become very attached to Dorothy's ring. It had been her idea to hold on to it that bit longer before selling it, telling the women that, according to Quentin, the price of both gold and precious stones was going up, in which case they might get more for it the longer they left it. Angie had been humoured, but the time had come for the ring to be forsaken for ready money.

It was agreed that having such a large amount of cash in the flat was not a good idea, and they might have to accept a cheque. They were also unsure how much the ring was worth. It was therefore decided that the best option was to open a bank account, which could also be used to add any more funds they might raise for the extravaganza. There was only one problem – a woman had to have the permission of her husband or a male relative to open an account.

Dorothy was apoplectic.

'So, we can weld ships, risk being blown to smithereens in a munitions factory or chop down trees like Angie's sister, *but we can't open a bank account without the say-so of some bloke!*'

'I'm surprised yer didn't know that already,' Gloria said.

Rosie, too, was surprised Dorothy didn't know. 'The powers that be,' she said, 'seem to think women are delicate creatures, incapable of understanding money and unable to handle anything financial.'

'But what about the comptometrists working in admin? They are nearly all women.' Martha was equally perplexed.

'Yes, exactly,' Dorothy argued.

'Tell that to the men who make the laws,' Rosie said.

'I might just do that!' Dorothy said.

'So, how's Dor gonna gerra bank account?' Angie asked.

'Well, I'm guessing she's going to have to ask Frank,' said Rosie.

'Frank!' Dorothy practically spat his name out.

'He's your mother's husband. That makes him a male relative,' Rosie said. 'I don't think you've got much choice.'

Dorothy let out a strangled sound of exasperation.

When Dorothy trudged round to her family home in The Cedars, one of the grandest streets in the town, Frank was quick to point out that if Dorothy had been married, like most young women her age, she wouldn't have had to come to him. He also took the opportunity to shake a copy of the *Sunderland Echo* in her face and jab a finger at a report on the inquest of a plater killed working at Bartram's shipyard after falling from staging. His argument being that it wasn't safe for women to work in the shipyards.

Dorothy knew, of course, that the real reason Frank didn't want her working in a shipyard was because he didn't like to admit to those in his circle that his wife's daughter was a welder at Thompson's. It was a truth she had to hold back from pointing out. It pained her to do so, but she needed his signature.

A few days later, Dorothy walked out of the Lloyds bank on Fawcett Street, linking arms with Angie, smiling like the Cheshire cat and brandishing a little blue bank book. As they passed a newsstand, they saw the main headlines about British forces distributing food in Athens, which was experiencing famine. Having watched Princess Marina, Duchess of Kent, take a cheque from the mayor last month for the Greek Red Cross, Dorothy and Angie agreed that it felt good to know the town had done its bit to help. It also spurred them on – even more than they were already – to give their wounded soldiers at the Ryhope hospital a Christmas to remember.

From the bank, they walked down a little way before cutting through Athenaeum Street and then crossing Waterloo Place and heading up Blandford Street. They were both drawing interested and admiring looks as they had dressed for the occasion and had put on their 'poshest' outfits.

Stopping outside one of the town's most expensive jeweller's, Dorothy took a deep breath. She looked at Angie, who was clearly very nervous. Dorothy was still amazed that Angie had never stepped foot in a jeweller's shop before. But then again, like Angie had said, why would she have? It wasn't as if she had ever *owned* a piece of jewellery in her life, never mind bought any. Knowing this, it went without saying that Dorothy would do the wheeling and dealing.

Walking into the quietness of the shop, Dorothy felt a little nervous. She hadn't liked to admit it to Angie, but she had only been in a jeweller's a few times herself. She'd always felt there was something a tad intimidating about the sombre atmosphere, the smell of polished wood and the sound of a pendulum clock.

'Good afternoon, ladies. How can I help you?' The man looked exactly like a jeweller should – wiry, with half-moon glasses, a waistcoat with a pocket watch – and dressed in such a way that he would not look out of place if he were suddenly to be transported back to the reign of Queen Victoria.

'Good afternoon, Mr ...' Dorothy looked at the man and raised one perfectly pencilled-in eyebrow.

'Mr Golding,' the man said, regarding the two women over his glasses. 'Proprietor.'

'Good to make your acquaintance,' Dorothy said as they reached the counter and she held out her hand.

Angie stared at her friend, who seemed to have morphed into royalty on stepping over the threshold.

'We're here to *sell*, not to buy,' Dorothy said, 'although I am sure once you see what we have, you will realise it will be to your benefit.' She looked at Angie, who fumbled around in her handbag before finally producing the little red leather box. She placed it on the glass counter and opened the lid.

'Put it on, Angela. Show Mr Golding how beautiful it looks.'

Angie nearly choked on hearing Dorothy call her 'Angela'. She didn't think her best friend had *ever* called her by her full name.

Angie did as she was told and took the ring out of the box and put it on the ring finger of her left hand, moving it around under the light that the jeweller had switched on and which was positioned on top of the counter. The movement under the bright white light beautifully showed off the sparkling diamond.

'Yes, it is very lovely,' the jeweller said. 'May I?' He put out his hand.

Angie gently eased off the ring and handed it over.

Taking a little round magnifier from his waistcoat pocket, he placed it in front of his right eye, squinting slightly so as to hold it in place.

'I do believe this may well be one of mine?'

'You might be right,' Dorothy said, thinking that Toby would have asked which was the best jeweller's in town and gone directly there.

'I also believe it was sold a good few months ago.' Mr Golding again looked at the two pretty women standing on the other side of his polished cherrywood counter. 'That being the case, I have to ask if it has been worn?'

Dorothy glanced at Angie and saw that she had gone bright red.

'No, never worn,' Dorothy said. She looked at the jeweller, who was giving her a sceptical look. 'I can reassure you it is in exactly the same condition as when it was given to me back in June this year – at the Palatine Hotel, if you must know.'

The old man's memory was returning. He recalled the buyer. An officer. He hoped the ring had been returned because the love affair had cooled and not because the woman's beau had been killed in action.

'Can I ask you why it has taken so long to return the ring, if you have not been wearing it?' he asked.

'The gentleman who bought the ring would not have it back after his proposal of marriage was turned down,' Dorothy answered truthfully. 'And it has been languishing in my bedside drawer at home.' Admitting it had been kept in the kitchen cupboard sounded a little odd.

Mr Golding nodded, relieved.

'And just so you know,' Dorothy said, 'I do not intend to benefit financially from the ring in any way – I am donating its worth to the Christmas Extravaganza appeal for the Ryhope Emergency Hospital.'

Dorothy looked at Angie, who presented one of the small leaflets that Marie-Anne had designed and reproduced.

'Oh,' the jeweller said, putting on his spectacles and taking the leaflet from the young woman who he had thought might be mute as she hadn't spoken a word since stepping into the shop.

'I see, I see,' he said, reading carefully. 'Well, that's very kind of you.'

'And that is why we are asking for the full price of the ring to be reimbursed.'

The jeweller smiled. 'Of course, my dear.' He got out a pencil and a notebook no bigger than the ones used by waitresses and scrawled a figure.

Dorothy inspected it.

'Add on another five pounds and you've got a deal,' she said.

She snuck a look at Angie and saw her eyes were practically out on stalks.

'You drive a hard bargain, my dear. A very hard bargain.'

'All for a good cause,' Dorothy said.

The jeweller took off his glasses. The price agreed was just a little less than the amount he'd sold it for. He was happy.

'Just wait there for a few minutes,' he said, before disappearing out the back.

'Blimey!' Angie whispered, looking at the ring.

She looked at Dorothy. 'I've never known anyone be so kind.'

Dorothy smiled. 'Go on – give it one last try.'

Angie slid the ring on and they both admired it.

Pulling a forlorn expression, Angie pulled the ring off her finger and carefully put it back in its leather box.

As they waited patiently for the jeweller to return with the money, an idea came to Dorothy.

When they got back to the flat, they went to see Mrs Kwiatkowski and await Quentin's call. As always, he rang on time and the old woman and Dorothy sat in the

175

hallway to give Angie her privacy. When Angie came out to announce she had ended the call, Dorothy made an excuse, saying that she had left something in their neighbour's flat and she'd see Angie up in their own place in a few minutes.

Angie declared she was shattered and trooped up the stairs, happy to put on her pyjamas and get ready for the nine o'clock news on the BBC Home Service.

Dorothy hadn't left anything in their neighbour's flat, but instead, as agreed with Mrs Kwiatkowski, she went straight to the phone, picked up the receiver and asked to be put through to the number that had just called.

A few moments later, Dorothy was connected.

'Hi, Quentin,' she said, keeping her voice low just in case Angie could hear from the flat above. 'Yes, yes, everything's fine.' Dorothy looked across to Mrs Kwiatkowski, who put her thumb up in excitement and muttered something in Polish.

'I just thought you might like to know something ...' Dorothy began.

A few minutes later, she hung up, a big smile on her face.

'Do you know, Mrs Kwiatkowski, I think I now know what it feels like to be Father Christmas.'

Chapter Twenty-Two

The following week the weather seemed to take a turn for the worse, which meant the canteen was even busier than usual. The women were settling down at their table. Angie was the last to arrive, having been waylaid by Muriel.

''Ere, listen to this,' she said, putting her tray down and taking the spare seat next to Dorothy. The women were all ears – happy to listen to the latest gossip while they ate. 'Yer knar that nursery that wouldn't take Hope?' She looked at Gloria, who nodded. 'Well, it was closed down this morning.'

'Really?' Rosie said, surprised.

'How come?' Gloria asked, equally surprised.

'Apparently, some official from the council was round there early doors 'n shut it down,' Angie said, blowing on a spoonful of steaming hot stew.

'I'm guessing this came from Muriel?' Polly asked.

Angie nodded.

'Well, I never,' Dorothy said. 'That's a turn-up for the books, isn't it?'

'Serves them right for being so horrible to Glor 'n not having Hope,' said Martha.

'I agree,' Hannah said. 'Sounds like that woman who said those awful things got her comeuppance.'

'What was the reason it was shut down?' Rosie asked.

'Muriel said summat about one of the bairns there not being looked after proper. And that there was some kind of "financial impropriety". Anyway, whatever it was, it was enough to close the place down.'

'Bet you Ma and Beryl have had their hands full this morning,' Polly said.

Martha pulled a puzzled expression.

'Because it means,' Dorothy informed her, 'that their little nursery they've just started up is going to get an awful lot bigger.'

'And will that be a good thing?' Hannah asked.

'Well, they've got the room, so I doubt they'll mind earning a bit of extra money,' said Polly.

'Good news all round then,' said Rosie.

'Yeah.' Angie nudged Gloria, who was sitting on her right. 'What goes around comes around, eh?'

'Looks that way, doesn't it?' Gloria said, glancing across at Rosie. 'You didn't tell Helen, did you?'

Rosie shook her head. 'No, of course not. You said not to.' She hated lying, but sometimes needs must.

Later on in the afternoon, Rosie went to see Helen in her office about some issues relating to safety measures and pay. As she was leaving, she turned just before she reached the door. 'Oh, I forgot to say ...' She looked at Helen. 'I heard at lunchtime that the nursery which wouldn't take Hope appears to have been closed down.'

'Really?' Helen did a good show of being surprised.

'Apparently, it had a couple of complaints. About different issues. Something about the neglect of one of the children in its care – the other about its finances.'

'Funny that,' Helen said. 'Just as well Hope didn't end up going there.'

'Yes, that's what I thought.' She looked at Helen and suppressed a smile. 'Oh, well, I'll let you get on.'

After Rosie had gone, Helen sat back in her chair and digested this latest news. She felt rather pleased with herself. Georgina had provided her with the necessary information within days of being asked, but she had sat on it for almost a month before she'd taken action and rung the council. She'd been rather surprised at herself for having the nerve to do what she'd done and the ability to sound like a proper east-ender – one benefit of working in a shipyard and being surrounded by strong north-east dialects day in, day out.

She just wished she'd also been able to track down the woman who had spat at Gloria and called her all those names. She'd asked Bobby if anyone else had been giving his mam any hassle, but he'd said not as far as he knew. The women had said the same. Helen wondered, though, whether Gloria would tell them if she had. She was pretty certain that Miriam would not have stopped at just the one verbal attack. She was sure there would have been more – and that there would be yet more planned.

Helen was right. Since that initial confrontation in the yard by the butch woman with a gob full of spittle, Gloria had continued to be harassed, name-called and spat at. Always when she was on her own. But Gloria wouldn't tell anyone. Not even Jack. She had resolved to put up with it for as long as it took. As long as no harm came to Hope, it didn't matter. She had a thick skin and broad shoulders. Sticks and stones and a bit of spit never hurt no one. That's what she told herself, anyway. Words were nothing after what she'd endured during her marriage to Vinnie. The physical abuse she'd suffered at his hands had hardened her up.

But sometimes she *didn't* feel so hard. These past few years she had been with Jack – and the love they had shared

179

during that time – had softened her up. Which was why, sometimes, it wasn't always so easy to shrug off the nasty comments as she wiped spit off her face.

Sometimes, just sometimes, she'd find herself a quiet spot where she could be on her own and have a quiet cry.

Chapter Twenty-Three

A few days later, on the second Friday of the month, the William Doxford & Sons shipyard in Pallion, on the south side of the River Wear, was abuzz with excitement, and for once, the atmosphere of joyful anticipation was not because of a launch.

'Helen! So glad you could make it!' Matthew kissed Helen on the cheek and had to hold back from gathering her in his arms and kissing her properly. *God, when was she going to give in to his charms?*

'Why, Matthew, you seem in a particularly good mood?' Helen said, taking a step back. For a moment there she'd thought he was going to kiss her full on the lips.

'Of course!' Matthew laughed. 'It's not every day you have Henry Hall and His Orchestra playing in the work canteen!'

Helen smiled. She had said the same herself when she had called Rosie to her office and told her that as a sign of appreciation for the work the women were doing in the yard, she was allowing all women shipyard workers to go to the show at Doxford's that was being recorded for the BBC's *Break for Music* show. If any of the men complained, she would tell them that it was to make up for the fact that the women were being paid less to do the same hours and work as the men.

Hearing a tap on the door, Helen turned round to see Dahlia standing in the office doorway.

'Can I get you anything else, Matthew?' she asked.

It always surprised Helen that Matthew allowed his secretary to address him by his first name. She looked at Dahlia. Her Swedish looks were always striking. Her long mane of corn-coloured hair was perfectly cut and came to rest on pert breasts. Helen thought she must be wearing one of the new Gossard bras she'd seen advertised.

'No, get yourself off, Dahlia – you'll miss all the action,' Matthew said, immediately turning his attention back to Helen.

'So, all well with you?' he asked, looking into Helen's emerald eyes. Eyes that bewitched him.

'Yes, yes, busy as always,' Helen said, aware that Dahlia was taking her time leaving the main office.

'Dahlia tells me you're now helping to organise some Christmas party up at the Ryhope?' Matthew asked.

'That's right,' Helen said, looking across as Dahlia finally departed. 'Your secretary and my personal assistant are going to do some kind of duet, I believe.'

Matthew laughed. 'Why is it Dahlia is a secretary and Marie-Anne a personal assistant?'

'Because,' Helen said, 'Marie-Anne's job far exceeds that of a mere secretary. As do her skills.' Helen realised she sounded a little bitchy but couldn't help it. Matthew's secretary had that effect on her.

Matthew chuckled and put out his arm. 'Let's go and enjoy the show.'

As she and Matthew made their way to the canteen, their hands occasionally brushed against each other.

'Just in time,' Matthew said as they walked into the crowded cafeteria.

A well-known presenter called Bryan Michie was warming up the crowd and doing the introductions. The place was heaving. It wasn't every day ENSA came to entertain the war workers in this neck of the woods. Matthew started trying to make his way to the front, but Helen put her hand on his arm and stopped him.

'Let's just watch from here,' she said.

Matthew smiled, took her hand from his arm and squeezed it gently.

'Good idea,' he said. 'Come in front of me, so you don't get jostled from behind.'

As the orchestra started playing its most popular song, 'The Teddy Bears' Picnic', the crowd clapped and cheered.

For the next half hour, Helen lost herself in the music and the atmosphere. She looked about the crowded canteen and spotted a few of the women shipyard workers from Thompson's, but she couldn't see Rosie and her squad. Her mind wandered to Henrietta. It bothered her that her grandmother seemed determined to blame herself for her husband's actions. Perhaps, in time, she could persuade her otherwise. Seeing a photographer from the *Echo* at the front of the makeshift stage, she wondered how Georgina was getting along with the job she'd assigned her to do.

It was only near the end of the show that Helen felt herself being pushed by a swell of over-enthusiastic workers who had started to dance. Matthew's hand gently went to her waist to steady her. He kept it there and was heartened when Helen didn't object, allowing him to hold her for a moment or two longer than necessary.

After the show ended, Helen hurried back to work. As soon as she walked through the door to her office, she headed for the phone. Whilst listening to the band, she'd come up with an idea. Dialling the four-digit number she knew by heart, it didn't take long before it was answered.

'Hi, Aunty Margaret. How are you and Uncle Angus?'

'Helen, darling, lovely to hear from you. We're just fine. Thank you for asking. How are *you*?' That's what Helen liked about her aunt – she was the complete opposite of her mother. She actually genuinely cared about her. Genuinely wanted to know about her life and how she was doing. It seemed so unfair that her aunt had not been able to have children while her mother, who did not possess a maternal bone in her body, had.

Helen told her aunt about work and the Henry Hall concert she'd just been to, and then the conversation drifted to the news that Sunderland had been named as one of the seven most badly bombed towns in the country due to Hitler's determination to destroy the shipyards and collieries. Margaret mentioned that more troops had been sent to bolster the battle for Metz in north-east France and they both agreed that the end of the war was near was justified.

Hearing the doorbell sound out in the background, Helen quickly told her aunt why she was calling.

'Actually, Aunty, I'm after the name of the sanatorium Mother was at.'

Helen listened as her aunt gave her the name and address. She wrote it all down and drew a line under it.

'Any particular reason?' Margaret asked.

Helen could hear voices in the background.

'Oh, I was after a copy of the bill. I'm just sorting out the accounts. I want Grandfather to pay for it. There's no reason why you and Uncle Angus should have shelled out for it.'

'We don't mind,' Margaret said. 'But if Father is going to pay for it, then that seems fair enough. I'm pretty sure he was the cause of Miriam ending up there. He might as well pay for some of the damage he's done in his life.' Helen heard her aunt's voice go unusually hard. And it was then that she realised Margaret knew about what had happened on Christmas Day – and that, unlike her sister, she believed her father guilty of everything he had been accused of.

'Actually, darling, we've got a report here from the sana-torium as well – from the doctor who treated Miriam. I can send that down to you – along with the bill?'

'Yes, please, Aunty, that would be great. Thanks.'

Hearing laughter in the background, Helen told her aunt to enjoy her company and rang off.

Resting the receiver back on its cradle, Helen looked down at Winston purring in his basket. She wondered if he'd picked up on her good mood. For this was good news. Very good news indeed.

Chapter Twenty-Four

Just under a fortnight later, on a Thursday afternoon, shipyard workers at Thompson's on the north side of the Wear crammed into their canteen. This time, though, it was a government minister rather than a big-band entertainer who was due to address the assembled crowd. The women welders, along with Hannah and Olly, were among the crush. Word had gone round that the joint parliamentary secretary to the Ministry of Labour and National Service, Mr Malcolm McCorquodale, was due to arrive in the next few minutes. He had been going round most of the Wearside shipyards giving speeches on behalf of the government.

'Will it ever stop raining?' Dorothy moaned, taking off her headscarf and shaking it out. Her dark hair fell free and she twisted it back to keep it out of her face. She caught Bobby's eye and scowled – not because she was in any way angry with him, but because it had become a habit; in fact, it could probably now be seen in the same way as a normal woman giving a loving smile to her sweetheart.

Bobby, who was chatting with his squad, smiled back.

'It's not stopped all week,' Hannah said, looking at the canteen windows, which were a blur of running water.

'The *Echo* said nearly four inches has fallen over the past month,' Olly chipped in.

'I've never understood how they measure that,' said Angie.

'Me neither,' Polly agreed.

'Here she is,' Martha said, turning and seeing Rosie making her way through the tightly packed throng of workers. She had just been to see Helen, who was waiting to greet Mr McCorquodale and bring him to the canteen.

The place was now crammed, and the women were all squashed together.

'Any more news on the divorce?' Rosie asked Gloria as they waited.

Gloria gave a weary sigh. 'It all appears to be very complicated. And, of course, Miriam being Miriam, she's using every trick in the book to make the whole process go at a snail's pace. She's already stalled by claiming not to have received the original papers, so another load had to be sent to her.'

'But couldn't she say the same again? That she didn't get them?' Polly asked.

'Yes,' said Gloria, 'which is why the second lot were handed to her personally. She's now got a week to either send them back signed or declare that she intends to defend the divorce.'

The women all looked at each other. Their 'mother hen' sounded downhearted and beaten.

'I dinnit understand how yer can defend a divorce,' Angie said.

Gloria gave a sad smile. 'You 'n me both, Ange.'

'So, if she does defend the divorce,' Hannah asked, 'what happens then?'

'A court case,' Gloria said simply.

The women all groaned.

'I'm guessing that won't happen until next year.'

'Exactly,' said Gloria. 'Jack's solicitor predicts she will use all the usual reasons to adjourn the case.'

'Like what?' Martha asked.

'Being unwell is the main one,' said Gloria. 'And I don't think there's any doubt Miriam will be able to pay the family doctor a decent wad to say she's suffering from some kind of illness that prevents her going to court.'

'Blimey,' said Angie, 'money gets yer owt.'

'It certainly does.'

'But I still don't get how a person can fight getting divorced,' Polly said, confused.

'Beats me too,' Gloria said, 'but it's like Angie says, if yer've got the money to get a top-notch lawyer, they'll find a way. They can argue black is white, by all accounts.'

All of a sudden, the noise of the canteen dropped and everyone looked over to the main counter, in front of which Muriel was placing a solid wooden box. They could see a dark grey suit appear through the doorway from the main kitchen. The whole cafeteria was now quiet, apart from the occasional cough. When Mr McCorquodale arrived from around the counter, the workers started to clap. Climbing up on the box, Mr McCorquodale waved his arm to show his audience that he did not want their applause.

'It is you,' his voice boomed out, 'that needs the applause!'

It was a good start and immediately caught everyone's interest.

'I could not leave Sunderland without speaking of the splendid record of the Sunderland shipyard workers,' he said loudly and clearly, 'as good as, *if not better than*, any group of workers in the country for production.'

Every shipyard worker in the canteen listened avidly as Mr McCorquodale told his audience that, once it was possible to relate the full story of the Wear shipbuilding production, they would have the satisfaction of knowing that their work would be hailed as second to none among the great shipbuilding centres in this country – and abroad.

'This town's record for the absence of industrial strife and industrial disputes,' he continued, 'is the finest in the country.'

Rosie nudged Gloria and whispered, 'Helen said he would bring that up. They're terrified of more strikes, by the sounds of it.'

'Do yer reckon that's why he's buttering us all up?' she whispered back.

Rosie raised her eyebrows.

Mr McCorquodale continued his impassioned oration, his voice getting louder as he approached the end of his speech. 'Mr Bevin asked me specifically to congratulate you, and say that there is no doubt, but for the fact that the women of this country were prepared to come forward in our hour of need – and do work which had always been supposedly too hard for them – we should not be in so good a position as we are today.'

The women all looked at each other and beamed. Other groups of women in the canteen were also looking as proud as Punch, smiling at each other. Some were blushing, having suddenly and unexpectedly found themselves the centre of attention.

'We men owe more than we can say to the magnificent way the women of this country, of this town, and of this firm, have come forward and done such good work.'

As the canteen erupted into applause, Dorothy looked over at Bobby and gave him a self-satisfied smile. His return smile was as wide as it was proud.

The women watched as Mr McCorquodale, whom they had not heard of before, but who was now a demigod in their eyes, stepped off his wooden box and was accompanied out of the canteen by Helen and Harold. Leaving by the main entrance, he shook hands with both the men and the women.

When Mr McCorquodale had gone, Rosie and her squad made their way to their usual table while Polly went to stand in the queue and get them all a pot of tea. She didn't mind as she knew once the chatter about what the MP had said ended, Dorothy would steer the conversation to the Christmas Extravaganza.

She was right. A few minutes after sitting down, Dorothy looked at Gloria.

'So, Glor, you won't forget to ask Helen to ask Dr Parker what he thinks the men would want for presents?'

'I won't,' Gloria said.

'Just that now we've got the money for the ring, we can start buying.'

'That's if there's anything to buy,' Martha said.

'I was reading the other day that steel can now be used in manufacturing items for domestic requirement,' said Hannah.

'Like wringers and kettles and stuff,' said Olly.

Angie laughed. 'Olly, I dinnit think one of our injured soldiers will be jumping up and down in excitement if he gets a kettle for Christmas.'

'Don't be cruel, Ange,' said Rosie. 'Olly's got a point. There might be a few of his men who might be going back home and want to take something back with them.'

'I thought we were saving our steel for the ships?' Martha asked.

'It would seem we can spare a little for other necessities now,' said Hannah.

'Which is another sign that we are well on our way to victory,' said Polly, catching the tail end of the conversation. She set the tea tray down in the middle of the table.

Angie put the cups and saucers out and Gloria started pouring.

They all supped in silence for a moment, enjoying the warmth of the tea. The rain might mean they had to work under cover, or in the bulkheads where it was dry, but it was still bitterly cold.

'Ask Joe what he thinks our injured soldiers might want – and the Major as well,' Dorothy said. 'They'll have a good idea.'

Polly nodded as she took a biscuit from a packet Martha was offering round. She was sure her brother and his Home Guard unit commander, Major Black, would come up with some good suggestions.

'Peter says he thinks the men will just be happy to have some female company,' Rosie said. She thought it was endearing that Dorothy and Angie had started to call the men 'our injured soldiers'.

'Well, they're gonna get an eyeful when Dahlia gets up and does her turn,' Dorothy said. She wished she'd never agreed to her doing a song. She'd forgotten how she'd been all over Bobby at Pearl and Bill's wedding reception. *Talk about putting it on a plate.*

'What about if any of the injured soldiers are Jewish?' Olly asked. They all knew he was learning about Judaism from Hannah's rabbi. Just as they all knew that if he wanted to ask for Hannah's hand in marriage, he would have to convert.

'They can still have fun, can't they?' Dorothy said. 'They don't have to agree to celebrate Christmas as such.' Hannah had explained to them that the Jews viewed Christ as a false prophet.

'Yeah, like they've just been invited to a party,' Angie chipped in.

'After what they've been through,' Gloria said, 'I think they'll just be celebrating still being alive.'

They all mumbled their agreement.

*

When the klaxon sounded out the end of the shift, Dorothy and Angie were the first to switch off their machines and put away their welding rods. They were clearly eager to leave on time.

'You two are in a hurry,' said Rosie.

'Double date,' Dorothy explained.

The women looked at Angie.

'Quentin's got a twenty-four-hour pass,' Angie elaborated, 'and Dor has insisted it be spent with her and Bobby as we've not all been out together.'

Polly raised her eyebrows. She knew that when she was dating Tommy, she'd never wanted to share him with anyone. She'd have been even worse if, like Angie, she'd only been able to see him very occasionally.

'Won't Quentin just want to be with you?' asked Martha. 'He doesn't get up here much these days, does he?'

'That might be true, Martha, but Quentin has to learn that he can't always have Ange all to himself,' Dorothy butted in.

Everyone looked at Angie, who had clearly had no say in the matter.

'But don't worry, I won't hog her all night,' Dorothy conceded, seeing her workmates' looks. 'Ange and Quentin just need to have a few drinks and a bit of a natter and then they can go back to the flat at around nine.'

'That's so kind of yer, Dor,' Gloria said, giving Angie a sympathetic look.

An hour and a half later, Dorothy and Angie, both done up to the nines, were hurrying up Fawcett Street to see Bobby and Quentin, whom they had arranged to meet in the Grand as a special treat. Dorothy had been worried that it

192

might be expensive for Bobby, so she and Angie had agreed they were just going to stay for one drink and then suggest going to a cosy – cheaper – bar round the corner in High Street West.

'My hair's gonna be ruined,' Angie complained as they crossed the road and continued onto Bridge Street. They were walking squashed together under an umbrella that Dorothy was holding. The wind was coming at them from all directions and forcing the rain underneath their partial cover.

'Here,' Dorothy said, giving her friend the *Sunderland Echo*. They had just bought it from a little newspaper boy who had been soaked through to the skin as he was keeping his wares dry under the overhang of the town hall at the expense of himself.

'Stick this over your head,' Dorothy ordered.

'But the article?' Angie objected. They had bought the late edition, having been told there would be a report about Mr McCorquodale's visit. Someone had said there had been a journalist tailing him on his shipyard visits.

'Sod the article!' Dorothy said. 'Your hair's more important.'

Angie had to laugh. She loved being with Dorothy. She was glad they were all going out together. It would be great if the men they were courting got on and if, like her and Dor, the difference in their class didn't get in the way of a friendship.

As they reached the huge five-storey building that was the Grand Hotel, they saw a familiar face sheltering under a stone archway next to the main entrance. The rain was pouring down in front of her, occasionally catching the wide-brimmed hat she was wearing.

'Georgina!' Dorothy called out.

'What are yer deeing here?' Angie asked, surprised Georgina didn't look at all wet.

'I'm just waiting for a friend,' Georgina lied. 'Didn't think it'd be this bad.' She looked up at the dark, wet skies.

'We're meeting Bobby and Quentin inside – why don't you come and join us? You can keep checking to see if your friend's arrived,' Dorothy suggested.

'No, honestly, I'm fine here,' said Georgina. 'I wouldn't want to miss her.'

'OK, but if you change your mind, come and find us,' said Dorothy.

'Thanks, I will,' said Georgina, although she had no intention whatsoever of taking one step into the hotel. She had the perfect vantage point where she was.

'Come to the flicks with us all next time, eh?' said Angie.

Georgina nodded.

'And you're still up for doing the photos for the Christmas Extravaganza?' Dorothy asked.

'Yes, of course!' said Georgina.

Angie tugged her away, rolling her eyes at Georgina and making her chuckle.

'Obsessed, she is,' she said as they waved their goodbyes and hurried towards the broad, canopied entrance, the weight of the collected rainwater now making the awning bow.

Georgina only had to wait another few minutes before the person she was really waiting for turned up. There was no wave of greeting, but rather a stealth-like move out of her hidey-hole as she pressed the button of her little Brownie, keeping her fingers crossed that the street lamp by the entrance and the light coming through the glass doors of the Grand would afford enough exposure to get her the snatched shot she needed. If her contact working in the laundry had given her good information, she would not have to return to the hotel until the early hours of the morning, when it would be much easier to get a clear image of a dishevelled Miriam leaving, having spent the night there.

Georgina continued to walk on with purpose. Reaching the end of Bridge Street, she turned right into West Wear Street. She was lucky she lived within spitting distance of the Grand. And luckier still that her work at the *Sunderland Echo* had enabled her to siphon off enough developer and fixer to allow her to set up her own little darkroom at home. Her father hadn't minded – had minded even less when she'd told him the exact nature of the job Helen had commissioned her to do.

As she turned right into Bedford Street, Georgina thought about the secrets that she herself had found out about Dorothy's mother and Angie's mam – and, of course, about Martha's monster of a mother. She had thought often about the consequences should those secrets ever be exposed. And every time she did, she felt a huge wave of guilt. A guilt that hadn't lessened with time but only grown. At first, when Miriam had asked for dirt on the women welders, Georgina had not cared too much – she and her father needed the money – but when she'd realised that one of those women was Rosie Thornton, the daughter of her mother's friend, someone she had met when she was young, before both their mothers had been taken from them, then it had not been so easy to be so distant – so detached. She had withheld what she had found out about Rosie's 'other' life, but had dished up the dirt on the rest of the women. What had made matters worse, though, was that it would now seem that it wasn't just Miriam who was privy to the information she had unearthed, but Charles Havelock too. And he was far more of a worry.

Having reached High Street West, Georgina crossed the road and hurried to the doorway of the building where she and her father lived. She took off her coat and shook it out with one arm, keeping her Brownie protected. Doing this one last job went some way to righting a wrong. At least she was snooping on a person who deserved everything she got – and it wasn't as if she would suffer much. The only real hardship she would have to endure would be knowing that Jack could marry the woman he loved, that Gloria would no longer have to endure any more vile comments, and that poor little Hope would never again be ostracised by any more nurseries.

Pushing her key into the door and stepping into the hallway, Georgina could hear the violin-playing of the music teacher, Mr Brown. She was glad he was playing and not one of his students. Walking towards her own front door, she again worried that her friends would find out that it had been she whom Miriam had hired. Whenever she was with the women, she felt like a wolf in sheep's clothing – a Judas. If they found out, would they spurn her? Blame her? They had become friends – *good* friends – since Rosie had introduced her to them. And now she was even part of their Christmas Extravaganza, which she was over the moon about, despite what Angie might think.

It would break her heart if they found out the truth and turned their backs on her.

Dorothy and Angie were sitting at their table for four in the Grand. Quentin and Bobby were at the bar, getting the drinks in.

'Bobby keeps mentioning meeting my parents,' Dorothy said with a glum expression.

'Well, if you want to put him off you,' Angie joked, 'that's the way to do it.'

Neither woman was in any doubt as to how Dorothy's parents would react to her going out with a shipyard worker. They had accepted Toby purely because he was a lieutenant in the British army. And for no other reason.

'I know,' Dorothy said. 'That's the irony of it all. At first, I wanted to put hurdles in the way of us courting – to test him.'

'Tests he's passed,' Angie said.

'He has …' Dorothy hesitated .'But now … well, now—'

'Now yer dinnit want any obstacles in yer path,' said Angie.

'Exactly,' said Dorothy. 'Now, I'm afraid he might decide he doesn't want me after all.'

'What? 'Cos of yer family? Yer really think he'll meet yer mam and Frank and then run a mile?' Angie gave her friend a look of pure incredulity. 'Honestly, Dor, I thought yer were meant to be the intelligent one, but yer can't half be thick as two short planks sometimes.' She took a deep breath. 'Bobby's crazy about you – 'n I really dinnit think anything's going to change that. He's gannin out with *you* – not with yer family.'

They both looked at their boyfriends chatting away at the crowded bar. Quentin was shouting into Bobby's right ear, aware of his lack of hearing in his left.

'Why don't yer just stomach it,' Angie said. 'Gerrit over with. Like me 'n Quentin are gonna dee.'

Dorothy looked surprised.

'We're just gonna gan round to my mam 'n dad's house, say hello, have a cup of tea 'n be done with it,' Angie explained.

'Really?' said Dorothy.

Angie nodded. 'We have both accepted that my mam 'n dad will dislike Quentin for been a stuck-up snob 'cos of the way he speaks, 'n his will be horrified their only son is seeing a coal miner's daughter – 'n one that works as a welder in the shipyards. But it doesn't matter, does it? It's what we think about each other that counts.'

Dorothy knew Angie was right. It was what she had told her a year ago when Angie had been fighting her feelings for Quentin – worried that the differences in their backgrounds and class would be fatal to any hopes of a proper courtship. It seemed the tables had turned.

But just as she knew Angie was right, Dorothy also knew taking Bobby to meet her own parents would be an outright disaster.

Chapter Twenty-Five

Miriam looked around her father's study and realised it hadn't changed at all since she was a small girl. The same dark wooden furniture, the same heavy damask drapes. It suddenly occurred to her that whenever she visited, she would always be shown through to her father's office – never to the comfort of the front reception room. She looked at her father and forced a smile as she sat down in the chair in front of his desk. It was almost as though she was being interviewed.

'So, how's your mother?' Mr Havelock asked, trying to sound as though he cared.

'She's well. Very well, actually, Father.' Miriam glanced around the room, suddenly needing to see something that had changed or was relatively new.

'That's good to hear,' he lied.

'In fact, she really doesn't look her age. She could easily pass as early fifties.' Miriam walked over to the mantel-piece and preened herself in the large gilt-framed mirror. 'Luckily, I seem to have inherited her youthful looks.'

Mr Havelock felt himself redden with anger. 'Well, at least she's come in handy for something, eh?'

Miriam didn't hear the bite in her father's voice, nor see the frustration on his own, wrinkled face; she was too busy inspecting her reflection.

'Right,' he said, looking at his watch, 'I'll get Thomas to give you a lift home.'

Miriam turned round sharply. She had expected to have to stay for a while longer and chat to her father. Her heart lifted. She'd get Thomas to drop her off at the Grand.

'Come on, I'll see you off,' Mr Havelock said, pushing himself out of his chair. 'Thomas will still be out there. I told him to give the old girl a bit of a buff and polish.'

Mr Havelock walked Miriam to the door. He watched her hurry down the stone steps and climb into the back passenger seat.

As soon as the car had turned right out of the driveway, he slammed the door shut with all his might.

'Eddy!' he bellowed. His voice resounded in the hall.

Within seconds, Eddy had appeared.

'Yes, sir?'

'You and Agatha. In my study. Now!'

He then stomped back into his domain. He had just enough time to pour himself a drink and have a few puffs on his cigar before Eddy and Agatha came bustling in.

They both looked white as a sheet and fearful.

'You've not been doing it right!' he barked at Agatha. 'Or you've not put enough in.' His nostrils flared in anger as he inhaled. 'According to my dear daughter, her mother is doing well – more than well. I'm told she's looking so well, she could pass as a bloody fifty-year-old!' Mr Havelock could feel spittle at the corners of his mouth. He took a large gulp of brandy.

'Perhaps she's not drinking it,' Agatha volunteered. She had only added half the amount stipulated by the master, but still, she'd have thought it would have been enough to make her poorly.

'She's got to be!' Mr Havelock said. 'Miriam's told me they both sit there drinking and chatting and listening to the ruddy wireless.'

'Well, that doesn't make sense,' Eddy said.

'No! It doesn't, does it!' Mr Havelock exclaimed. 'Bloody Henrietta. Looks as frail as a bloody bird but she's got the constitution of an ox.'

Eddy and Agatha stood in silence, unsure what to say.

There were a few moments of deathly quiet.

'Goddamnit!' Mr Havelock finally conceded.

He glared at Agatha.

'I think we have to work on the premise that she is indeed not drinking the damned vodka!'

He took another slug of brandy.

'And if that *is* the case, we need to find something else that she will most definitely consume.'

He took a puff on his cigar, giving the problem another few moments of intense thought.

Miriam had mentioned something about a Christmas Extravaganza happening at the military hospital in Ryhope. Christmas made him think of the huge affairs they used to have here – which Henrietta had loved to organise. She had always made a special effort to include dishes and delicacies from around the world. There had been the Italian Feast of the Seven Fishes on Christmas Eve, German stollen, the chocolate bûche de Noël from France … His mind continued to wander … *And then there were the various drinks peculiar to the festive period that she loved to concoct herself.*

Suddenly, his eyes lit up.

'I know just the thing!'

Agatha felt her heart sink. The man was not going to stop until Henrietta was six feet under.

'What one might call a two-pronged approach,' he said with gleeful eyes.

And with that he explained exactly what he wanted Agatha and Eddy to do.

He called it his 'Plan B'.

'And this one,' he said, '*will* work.'

Chapter Twenty-Six

Dr Parker was skimming the papers as he sat at a table in the hospital canteen, his mind only half on the latest developments across the globe. He checked his watch. Helen would be arriving any minute. He knew she was going to try and slip away early from the launch of *Weybank* at Doxford's. He thought of Matthew Royce. He couldn't believe he'd been convinced they were courting. Not that it would have made any difference. Helen wanted him only as a friend.

'A penny for your thoughts!'

Dr Parker jumped. 'Dear me, I was in my own world there.' He stood up and kissed Helen on the cheek before pulling out her chair.

'It's wonderful to see you,' he said, as he sat down and started to pour their tea.

'And you,' Helen said. *If only you knew how wonderful.*

'It feels ages.' Dr Parker pushed her cup towards her.

'I know,' she said, taking the cup and feeling their fingers touch briefly. 'Work just never seems to stop.' *If only he knew she'd come here to see him every day if she could, even if she was working twelve-hour shifts.* Still, she had to be content with being able to see him at all.

'First of all, how's Henrietta?' Dr Parker asked. Helen's grandmother, he knew, was bringing so much joy into Helen's life. It had been wonderful to see.

'Oh, she's doing incredibly well,' Helen enthused, her face lighting up. 'Kate's sorting her out with a new wardrobe – a new *up-to-date* wardrobe.'

Dr Parker knew about Henrietta's rather theatrical appearance.

'It'll be great to meet her one of these days,' Dr Parker said. 'It seems crazy she's literally just down the road and I've never met her.'

'I know,' Helen said a little guiltily. She had purposely kept the two from meeting each other for fear of complicating an already precarious situation, but most of all because she was sure her grandmother would have no qualms about telling John how her granddaughter really felt about him.

'Hopefully, you can meet her at the Christmas Extravaganza – when she's in her new outfit,' Helen suggested, thinking that would give her enough time to prime Henrietta on what she could and could not say.

'What if, by some remote chance, someone recognises her at the do?' Dr Parker asked.

'Then the line is that dear Miss Girling is always being mistaken for her poor long-dead relative, Mrs Havelock, which I'll say is hardly surprising as they are blood relatives. And then I'll subtly change the subject.'

'You sound as though you've got all your bases covered,' Dr Parker said.

'Let's hope so,' said Helen. 'And talking about the Christmas extravaganza …' she said, with a slightly weary sigh.

'Let me guess,' he said. 'Dorothy has given instructions.'

Helen laughed. 'She has – and I thought *I* was meant to be the boss.'

'Clearly not when it comes to Christmas,' Dr Parker chuckled.

Helen smiled, looking into John's sparkling brown eyes. She would actually like to thank Dorothy for being such a bossyboots and going totally over the top when it came to organising the soldiers' Christmas party, for it provided her with a convincing excuse to see a little more of John than she could have orchestrated otherwise – a legitimate excuse, should Dr Eris try and put a stop to it.

'So, tell me,' Dr Parker said. 'What part do I play in Dorothy's plans?'

'You, Dr Parker, get off scot-free, all in all,' Helen said. 'You just have to think up some ideas about what your "recruits" would like in the way of presents.'

'Deal. I shall endeavour to gently prise out of them what they'd like from Father Christmas this year.' Dr Parker was purposely making light of it when what he was really thinking was that he knew exactly what their answers would be: the return of their limbs, their minds, their former lives, the comrades-in-arms they'd seen die, friends they'd never see again.

'I'm guessing Tommy won't be back?' Dr Parker asked.

'He's told Polly he'll stay until the end of the war, even if he's allowed back earlier.'

'And Polly's all right with that?'

'Not really,' Helen gave a sad little laugh, 'but she understands. And more than anything, I think she's just eternally grateful he's survived the worst.'

Dr Parker nodded, remembering the heartache Polly had gone through when Tommy had been admitted to this very hospital at death's door, only for him to recover and then go back to his unit – back to removing limpet mines off the sides of Allied ships.

'And dare I ask about *the divorce*?' Dr Parker watched Helen's reaction. He smiled when he saw her face light up with a mix of mirth and mischievousness.

'Have we got time for another cup of tea?' Helen asked.

Dr Parker hooted with laughter.

'I knew you had something up your sleeve. Wait there, I'll get us another pot and you can tell me all about it.'

Helen watched Dr Parker as he headed over to the counter. She could stay here all day with him, chatting, drinking tea.

How she loved him.

If only she had realised it earlier.

Chapter Twenty-Seven

'Dr Eris,' Genevieve called out. She might have been out to dinner with the asylum's only woman doctor, and blabbed about Miss Girling's true identity, but that did not mean she could call her by her first name.

'Yes, Genevieve?' Dr Eris walked over to the main reception desk. She had a bounce in her step. She felt happy. And she had reason to be. Now that she had removed Helen as a contender for John's affections, she felt as though the path was clear. John, she was sure, was going to propose soon.

'Is everything all right?' Dr Eris asked Genevieve. She seemed anxious.

'Yes, yes, I've just been asked to tell you that the director would like a word.'

'What? Now?' Dr Eris asked, surprised. Any meetings with the head of the asylum were usually booked days, if not weeks, in advance.

'Yes,' Genevieve said. 'It seems it's a matter of urgency.'

Dr Eris looked at the elderly receptionist and wondered why she seemed so worried. She sensed she was holding something back.

'I'll head there now,' Dr Eris said. 'Feel free to ring through and tell him I'm en route.'

Walking along the many corridors to reach the director's office, which was situated towards the rear of the asylum, Dr Eris wondered why the urgency. She was doing well, her patients were doing well, very well, in fact. She started to feel more relaxed, having convinced herself that there was nothing for which she could be reprimanded. When she had started at the asylum over a year and a half ago, she had known she would have to work harder and prove herself more because of her gender. And she had done. Some of the patients had come on so well under her care that they had been discharged. Which was always welcome news as it meant it freed up beds.

Reaching the director's polished wooden door complete with nameplate, she took a deep breath and knocked.

'*Come in!*'

Dr Eris hesitated. The voice sounded unfamiliar. The director had a slightly high-pitched voice, which she had thought might be to do with some kind of hormone imbalance. This voice was low and sounded old.

Opening the door, she was proved right. The man sitting in the director's leather swivel chair was an old man. Dr Eris guessed him to be in his seventies – late seventies. She felt his hard, dark eyes lock on her the moment she stepped into the room.

'Oh,' Dr Eris said, not shielding her surprise. 'I thought I was to meet the director.'

'Come in! Come in!' Mr Havelock beckoned her. 'Don't fret yourself. You've come to the right room.'

Dr Eris immediately felt herself bristle. His words and tone were those of an adult talking to a child.

'Take a pew, my dear.' Mr Havelock waved a hand at the chair in front of the desk.

Dr Eris noticed it was not the usual chair, but a smaller, hard-backed wooden chair usually found in the corridor outside for those waiting to go in.

Dr Eris remained standing.

'I came here expecting to have a meeting with the director, so please don't think I'm rude if I ask who you are?'

Mr Havelock laughed and took out a cigar from his top pocket.

'I'm Charles Havelock.' He waited for her attitude to change. For the grovelling to begin.

Dr Eris worked hard to keep her face impassive. Of course, she'd thought his face was familiar. She should have recognised him. She'd seen his photograph in the *Sunderland Echo* enough times.

'Good to make your acquaintance, Mr Havelock.' Dr Eris stuck out her hand.

Mr Havelock eyed this upstart of a woman in front of him. He couldn't wait to take her down a peg or two. He kept her waiting, making a point of lighting his cigar before finally giving her his hand to shake. He did not stand up to do so.

'Good to make your acquaintance, Miss Eris.'

'*Doctor* Eris.'

Mr Havelock smiled. He'd succeeded in rattling her cage.

'Apologies, my dear. It still seems so strange to call a woman "Doctor".'

'Times are changing,' Dr Eris said. 'Thank goodness. Now, without wanting to seem rude, I have a busy afternoon ahead of me. How can I be of help?'

Mr Havelock gave her a hard stare, rested his cigar in the ashtray and put his elbows on the desktop. His hands were pressed together as though in prayer. It annoyed him that he was having to look up at this woman. 'Please, sit down. This might take some time.'

Dr Eris looked down at the low, hard wooden chair. *Like hell she would.*

'I'm comfortable standing, Mr Havelock. Now, if you wouldn't mind explaining why it is you wanted to meet with me? And why it is that you felt the need to get me here under false pretences?'

'Oh, always the psychologist, eh?'

Another put-down. Dr Eris's silence showed her ire.

'I'm sure you are aware that one of your patients, Miss Henrietta Girling, is distantly related to the Havelock family?' Mr Havelock asked.

'I believe she is your daughter's great-aunt,' Dr Eris lied.

Mr Havelock eyed the tall, attractive woman in front of him. He had wondered if she knew who Henrietta really was, but judging by her demeanour, he felt reassured that she was ignorant of the fact that her patient was in actuality his wife.

'That's correct. A relative by marriage rather than by blood. Thank God!' Mr Havelock laughed.

Dr Eris did not.

'She fell under my care many, *many* years ago, and every so often I like to hear how she's doing – from the horse's mouth.'

'By "the horse's mouth", I'm guessing you mean from the medical practitioner who is looking after your relative? Which, I'm assuming, is why I'm standing here now?'

'You assume right, my dear.' Mr Havelock picked up his cigar and relit it. He sucked on it, creating a cloud of smoke. Dr Eris stifled a cough. She hated smoking.

'She's doing well, very well.' Dr Eris looked at Mr Havelock, who was making a show of inspecting the room. 'It might be better for me to write you up a report,' she said. 'Perhaps you would be able to concentrate better if that were the case.'

Mr Havelock's dark eyes darted back to this insolent woman. *Didn't she realise who he was? What power he wielded?*

'That won't be necessary,' he said. 'All I want to know is what medication you have her on.'

For a brief moment, Dr Eris thought that she might have misread him and that underneath that rude, misogynistic exterior, he was a man who cared about the woman who was his wife.

'Well, I'm glad you've asked,' Dr Eris said, her tone sincere. 'Because Miss Girling is now just about weaned off most of the drugs she was on when she came under my care.' She proceeded to reel off the names of the drugs that Henrietta had been taking for many years. 'She really is so much more coherent, and her moods, I would say, are pretty stable. Probably as stable as most ordinary people. I can arrange for you to visit her if you want?'

'Definitely not!' Mr Havelock snapped.

The viciousness of his tone gave Dr Eris a shock.

'I'll just get straight to the point, Dr Eris.' Mr Havelock stubbed out his cigar. 'I want Miss Girling put back on the exact same drugs she was taking before you started meddling with her medication. The same ones the doctor – the highly regarded Dr William Friedman – had her on before your arrival.'

Dr Eris didn't attempt to hide her incredulity. Dr Friedman had left the hospital before his alcoholism and questionable treatments caused any more harm or cases of potential malpractice. She straightened her shoulders and made a point of looking down at Mr Havelock, who was leaning back in his chair and observing her with eyes that felt as though they were undressing her.

'No offence, Mr Havelock, but that's my call, as her doctor. Not yours.'

Mr Havelock sat up straight.

'No, my dear, that's where you're wrong. This *is* my call. And I'm telling you in no uncertain terms that you will put

Henrietta back on the drugs she was on before you tipped up here. If you don't,' he said, standing up, his hands splayed out on the desktop, 'then you will find yourself out of a job. And not only that, you will find it nigh on impossible to get a job anywhere else. And don't underestimate me – as the plaque at the entrance to this hospital proves, I practically built this place. And you should also be aware that I'm on the board of trustees – *and* have contacts that stretch far beyond the north-east.'

Dr Eris looked at this horrible man and knew he was not one to make idle threats.

'So, my dear, do we have an agreement?' He put out his hand.

Dr Eris looked at it.

'Same drugs. Same dosage,' he said.

Dr Eris hesitated. Her mind was spinning. It had not been easy getting a job here. Women doctors were few and far between and guaranteed to be way down the list when it came to employment. She looked at this man and knew he was not someone she could go up against. It would be a battle she had no chance of winning.

Tentatively, she put her hand out. It revolted her to have to touch the man, never mind agree with his demands.

They shook hands. As she tried to pull away, he held on to her hand with a surprisingly strong grip for someone so old.

'I need to hear you say it,' he said.

'Yes,' Dr Eris agreed. 'Same drugs. Same dose.'

Mr Havelock released his grasp.

'Good girl! So glad we've managed to sort all of that out.' He smiled, showing small, stained teeth.

Dr Eris turned to go.

'Oh, and just before you go,' he said.

Dr Eris turned back.

'Remember, I *will* be checking. I have eyes everywhere,' he said.

Dr Eris walked straight to her secretary's office and asked her to put back her next consultation until later in the day. She didn't give a reason. She went into her small office, which had a large window looking out onto the expansive grounds, sat in her leather chair and stared out at the dark abysmal day. If there was ever a case of nature reflecting reality, then this was it. The pewter grey clouds were emptying their wares onto the asylum and the surrounding landscape as far as the eye could see. It was a deluge. The rain was streaming down the window, causing the view of the outside world to become a mere blur.

Dr Eris sat there for the time she would have spent with her scheduled appointment. Then she stood up and walked out of her office and down two long corridors before reaching the pharmacy. She managed to make a show of normality as she wrote out a prescription for her patient, Miss Henrietta Girling.

The pharmacist widened his eyes on seeing the list of drugs he was being asked to dispense.

Dr Eris pulled her face into an expression she hoped conveyed a sad weariness that someone's mental health necessitated such a concoction of drugs.

'Well, I suppose if needs must,' the pharmacist said.

'Needs must,' Dr Eris said.

Two hours later, following a fifty-minute consultation and another spell of sitting in her chair and looking out at the continuing rainfall, Dr Eris got up and walked down another labyrinth of corridors before arriving at Henrietta's room.

Knocking, she opened the door to see Miriam sitting at the table with her mother – or rather, her 'great-aunty'. How could the woman keep her own mother in a lunatic asylum when it was unnecessary? Unless, of course, Miriam really did believe her mother to be mad.

'Ah, Mrs Crawford.'

'Dr Eris,' Miriam said.

Dr Eris thought she looked guilty. Looking down at the table, she saw there were two tumblers that appeared to contain water; the giveaway was the slight whiff of gin. If Miriam wanted to get plastered while she was visiting her mother, then so be it, but she hoped that Henrietta wasn't also drinking.

'I was just on my way out,' Miriam said, finishing off her drink and swilling her glass out in the little sink. She looked at her watch. She didn't want to keep Amelia waiting at the Grand. Glancing down at the small plastic medicine dispenser that her mother's doctor was holding and which was loaded with pills, she widened her eyes.

'Dear me, Mother, looks like it's time for your other cocktail!'

Dr Eris glowered at Miriam.

'Yes, your great-aunty is starting a new course of treatment.' She didn't say any more. She hoped, though, that she would report back to her abomination of a father that his wife's doctor was doing as she'd been told. Even if she was doing so under duress. She needed this job. Or rather, she did not need to have her career thwarted before it had really got off the ground. And she was under no illusion that Mr Havelock had the power not only to bring her career to a halt, but to end it for good.

For the first time, Dr Eris felt a sliver of sympathy for Helen. Imagine having a mother and grandfather like that.

When Miriam had gone, Dr Eris turned to Henrietta.

'So, how are you feeling today?'

'Doctor, I feel quite marvellous,' Henrietta said.

'And that's not because of any gin or alcoholic beverage you might have consumed during your great-niece's visit?'

'No, no, my dear,' Henrietta said.

She then took her glass of vodka mixed with elderflower cordial and poured it down the sink.

'It's all pretend. Make-believe, you know?'

Dr Eris was watching Henrietta closely.

'I'm very good at pretending. I sip the drink just so.' Henrietta mimed drinking from the now empty glass, pulling a slight grimace as she pretended to swallow. 'I used to do amateur dramatics when I was young.'

'Really?' Dr Eris said, although she was not surprised. Henrietta looked like she belonged on the stage, with her outrageous dress and made-up face.

'You see,' Henrietta continued, 'I don't like to hurt Miriam's feelings. She brought me all these lovely presents after her trip to Scotland. They were all so thoughtful. Make-up. Hair dye. And my favourite vodka from Cameron and Sons. It used to be my favourite tipple ...' Henrietta paused. She never liked to refer to her life before her incarceration. 'Back then.'

'I see,' Dr Eris said, putting the little cup of pills on the table.

'It's an upside-down world, isn't it, Doctor?' Henrietta said, seeing her medication and pouring herself a glass of water. 'When Miriam comes, I pretend to drink vodka, and when Helen comes, we drink water and pretend it's vodka. Perhaps I *am* as mad as a hatter.'

Dr Eris motioned for Henrietta to sit down. She was glad Henrietta was faking it. Having gone back over her notes from when she'd first taken her on as a patient, it had been clear she'd been drinking a lot before she'd been sectioned.

'That's very interesting,' Dr Eris said, handing Henrietta the plastic dispenser. 'Now, I just need to explain to you about your new medicine – and then I want you to take it. Is that all right?'

'Of course, Doctor, I trust you,' Henrietta said.

Dr Eris bit her lip. Taking a deep breath, she listed the various drugs.

Henrietta nodded her apparent understanding.

She then took each pill and swallowed them one by one.

Chapter Twenty-Eight

December

Dorothy was walking as fast as she was talking. She'd hardly drawn breath since Bobby had come to the flat to pick her up.

'Quite a momentous day, isn't it?' It was so cold she could see her breath.

'It is. The end of the Home Guard,' Bobby said, adjusting his tie nervously. *And that momentous day hadn't ended.*

'If anything says we're going to win this war, then this does.' Dorothy continued talking quickly. 'No invasion, no need for gas masks, no more blackout. And now no Home Guard.'

They overtook an elderly couple as they passed the front of the museum.

'Gloria said Helen's taking Hope to see the stand-down parade in Roker Park,' Dorothy continued.

'That's what I heard too,' Bobby said. He had a bottle of Scotch, loosely wrapped in tissue, in one hand, and a small posy of flowers in the other.

Dorothy looked at him. 'You sure you don't want me to take the flowers? Then you can hold my hand.'

Bobby relinquished the bouquet and took Dorothy's hand. They turned left and started the long walk up Burdon Road.

'It's so weird,' Dorothy said, enjoying the feel of his hand on hers, 'that Helen is your stepsister.'

'Will be when Mam and Jack actually marry,' Bobby said.

'Although that seems likely to be a while off,' Dorothy said. 'The solicitor Jack's got – what's his name, Mr Emery? Anyway, he's just had notice from the courts that Miriam's lawyers have declared their intention of contesting the divorce. I've never heard of anything so ridiculous.' Dorothy knew she was rambling. Her heart was racing, as were the thoughts in her head. *What happened if Angie was wrong and Bobby met her family and ran a mile? They were bound to be a nightmare. Why, oh why had she agreed to do this?*

They kept up their pace as they walked alongside the perimeter fence of Mowbray Park. A thin veil of sparkling white frost could be seen on the grass and on the bare branches of the trees.

'Are you sure you want to go for a walk in Backhouse Park afterwards?' Bobby asked. 'We might just freeze to death.'

'Yes,' Dorothy said, 'most definitely. Honestly, I go to sleep at night and all I can see is grey metal. I'm craving nature. Anything green. Actually, anything but grey.'

Bobby smiled. He wondered if Dorothy's craving to see a world other than metal and machinery was because of the tales she insisted he told her about his life at sea and the countries he had visited with the navy.

'And you're still up for a full Sunday lunch?' Dorothy asked, knowing it was too late for them to pull out now. Again, she berated herself for agreeing to go through with this ordeal at all, never mind *have a meal* with her parents and siblings.

'Oh, blast!' Bobby suddenly said. 'I forgot to get something for your sisters.'

'Oh, don't worry, they get enough. They're spoilt rotten.'

'No, sorry, Dor, I can't turn up empty-handed.' Bobby exhaled. 'I can't believe I forgot.' *Too damn nervous, that's why. Damn it!*

Seeing a tram, they jumped on. A few stops later, they disembarked and hurried to a little tobacconist at the top of Villette Road that also sold sweets and seemed to be open all hours.

When they arrived at the front door of Dorothy's grandiose family home, they were running quarter of an hour late. Dorothy knew this would not get the meeting off to a good start and when her stepfather opened the door, she was proved right.

Glancing down at his stepdaughter and her new bloke, he made a point of raising his arm and looking at his watch.

'Apologies for our late arrival,' Bobby said. He stretched out his hand, but it was too late; he found himself looking at Frank's back as he disappeared into the house.

'Come in! Come in!' Dorothy's mother appeared in her husband's place. 'You'll catch your death out there.'

They both stepped into the house.

'Oh, are they for me?' Mrs Williams said, looking at the flowers in her daughter's hand.

'Yes,' Dorothy said, looking at Bobby. 'They're from Bobby.' She offered her mother the small posy.

Mrs Williams forced a smile. In her day, the suitor carried his own presents and handed them over in person. She looked Bobby up and down. His coat looked worn and the suit he was wearing underneath told her what she and her husband had suspected – her daughter's new beau, unlike the last offering, was obviously not well off. Not by any stretch. She looked at the pitiful bouquet, then caught sight of the bottle of Scotch he'd brought. It wasn't even a single malt.

'Come through,' she said, not offering to take their coats.

Dorothy glared at her mother. 'I'll just hang our coats up.' She shook off her own and then took Bobby's old navy coat from him. She couldn't even look him in the eye, she

218

felt so embarrassed. Their welcome had been frostier than the weather outside.

When they walked into the living room, Mr Williams was already pouring himself a drink. Bobby walked across the room and handed him the bottle of whisky and once again put out his hand to shake.

'Bobby Armstrong,' he said.

Mr Williams had no choice but to take it. The handshake was unenthusiastic.

'Frank Williams,' he said.

All of a sudden, the door swung open and four young girls charged into the room, pushing each other aside to be the first to meet their big sister's new fella.

The eldest girl put out her hand.

Bobby took her small, white hand in his own giant one and shook it gently.

The sisters started to giggle.

'Present!' demanded the youngest one, whom Bobby knew to be around three years old.

Bobby laughed. 'Well, you're lucky,' he said, 'because I very nearly forgot.'

He put his hand into his inside pocket and produced four small bars of chocolate.

The sisters did not look impressed.

Dorothy silently cursed Toby. The presents he had brought them had been far superior and far more expensive.

'What do you say?' Dorothy demanded, throwing her mother a look. If her sisters had been this rude to one of their friends, they'd have been given a smack and sent up to their rooms.

'Thank you,' the sisters chorused, their tone full of cheek, their sentiment anything but one of gratitude.

'Would you like a cup of tea?' Mrs Williams said.

'Yes, please, Mrs Williams.'

'Milk? Sugar?'

'Yes, please.'

Bobby reached out and took the proffered china cup and saucer. As he did so, the arm of his suit, which no longer fitted him due to his work at the yard causing him to bulk out, slid up, revealing one of his tattoos.

'Oh my goodness!' Mrs Williams's hand went to her mouth in shock. 'You're a sailor boy!' she said, not even trying to hide her disdain.

'I was an able seaman with the Royal Navy before being medically discharged,' Bobby explained, glancing at Dorothy. She had gone red. *Was she embarrassed by him?*

Dorothy was just about to say something when her stepfather beat her to it.

'Well, old boy, I think we should just put our cards on the table now and be done with it – rather than endure lunch together.'

Everyone was staring at Mr Williams, who was standing, whisky glass in hand. He glared at Dorothy before turning his attention to Bobby.

'If you have come here today to ask for Dorothy's hand in marriage, well, you can think again.' He looked at Mrs Williams, who nodded her agreement. 'Dorothy will not be marrying below herself. We have allowed her to play around being a welder at that shipyard of hers, but that does not mean she can marry some shipyard worker.'

He looked at Dorothy and pointed his finger.

'And you, my girl, should have told us the truth about who it was you were bringing into our home. If you had, we could have avoided all of this.'

He waved his empty whisky glass in the air before turning back to the drinks cabinet for a refill. It was a clear sign that this was the end of the matter and they were now dismissed.

Bobby had never felt so angry. So mortified. So ridiculed. Why had he put himself in this situation? He should have known better. He looked at Dorothy, who was standing stock-still, glaring at her stepfather's back. He should have known. She was out of his league. They had enjoyed their time together, but now it was time for the real world. And people like Dorothy did not marry men like himself.

He stood up straight and turned to leave. As he did so, he saw Dorothy turn quickly. She grabbed his hand and held it tightly. For the first time since they had entered the house, she looked him in the eye. And as she did so, his heart soared as hope returned.

'We're not going just yet, Bobby,' she said. 'Frank's had his say, now I'm going to have mine.'

Mrs Williams opened her mouth to object, but it was too late.

'I'm not going to remind either of you – ' Dorothy swung her gaze from her mother to Frank '– that it's thanks to men like Bobby that we are now winning this war. Nor that that bottle of Scotch and those flowers and the chocolate have cost him a good part of his wages – hard-earned wages, I hasten to add. I'm not going to bother to try and make you understand why I work as a welder in a shipyard, because if you don't realise that now, then you never will.'

She kept hold of Bobby's hand.

'I don't know why I brought Bobby here. I knew it wasn't a good idea. Knew you would both be vile and snobby.'

'So why did you?' Frank asked.

'Because I was trying to do the right thing,' Dorothy said. 'I'd brought Toby here to meet you and it would seem like I was ashamed of Bobby if I didn't agree when he asked to meet you.' She looked at Bobby. 'And I'm most certainly *not* ashamed of him.'

Bobby squeezed her hand.

'Trying to do the right thing was actually the wrong thing to do,' she said.

She took a deep breath.

'I'm actually angry with myself for bringing Bobby here.' She looked at her stepfather. 'Frank, you have no right to make any kind of comment or judgement on my life – or really have anything to do with it, never mind think you have a say about who I should or should not marry – *or* where I work.'

Dorothy looked at her mother. Wanting her to come to her defence. To support her. She had, after all, kept her secret all these years.

'But you'll happily come here and beg a favour when you need to open a bank account,' Frank said.

Dorothy gasped with outrage. 'Only because of the stupid laws in this country! I had no choice.'

She drew breath. *Do it! Say it!*

'The funny thing is, Frank, the day I came here and asked you to sign that form for the bank – as a family member, as a male relative – well, we both broke the law.'

Frank looked puzzled. 'What are you talking about?'

Dorothy looked at her mother and then back at Frank. 'Because, Frank, legally you are not related to me.'

'What are you talking about?' he asked.

'Enough of this nonsense!' Mrs Williams suddenly butted in.

Bobby looked at Mrs Williams and thought she seemed anxious. Very anxious.

'It's not nonsense, though, is it, Mum?'

Bobby looked at his sweetheart. He had never seen her this angry.

'It's not nonsense because I'm not your stepdaughter, Frank!' Dorothy practically spat the words out.

Bobby saw a look of confusion on Frank's face, but increasing fear on his wife's.

Dorothy looked at her mother. 'Am I, Mother?'

'What's she on about?' Frank asked his panic-stricken wife.

'Would you like to explain, or should I?' Dorothy gave her mother another loaded look.

Mrs Williams was about to object when Dorothy spoke again.

'You see, Frank, you're not married to my mother.' She paused. 'I know, it's confusing, isn't it? I mean, you had a ceremony, didn't you? Quite a show, wasn't it? Must have cost a pretty penny. But the thing is, Frank, it was a complete waste of time and money, because ...' she paused '... because, you see, Frank, Mum was already married. Or should I say, was *still* married. To my real dad.'

She waited a beat.

'And as everyone knows, we don't hold with polygamy in this country, so that means you and Mum have been living in sin for ... how many years? Oh, and my lovely little sisters are all very much illegitimate.'

Dorothy looked at her mother, who had gone sickly pale.

'Your wife, Frank, is what they call a bigamist, which I'm sure you know, having had an education, is illegal and punishable by a not inconsiderable time in prison.'

Dorothy turned her attention to her mother. 'I just sincerely hope you don't get caught, Mum, for everyone's sake – especially the girls'.' She looked at her sisters, who had fallen silent and seemed quite mesmerised by the unexpected turn of events. 'Girls who, I have to add, are going to end up horrible spoilt brats if you're not careful.'

Her middle sister pushed her tongue out.

'And I do wonder whether Frank will have the balls to visit you if you do find yourself behind bars. To be honest, knowing what I know of Frank, I doubt wild horses would get him there.'

Dorothy turned to Bobby, who still had a tight grip on her hand.

'Well, we'd better get ourselves off.' She waited a beat, then fabricated a smile. 'I don't know about you, Bobby, but I'm starving.'

Dorothy and Bobby looked at Frank, who was staring in disbelief at the woman he'd just learnt was not actually his wife.

'Don't worry, Mum,' Dorothy said chirpily. 'I'll get our coats and we'll see ourselves out. Looks like you and Frank are going to have a lot to talk about.'

A few minutes later, Dorothy and Bobby were walking down the short driveway and out onto the main pathway.

Both had the beginnings of smiles on their faces.

Bobby looked at Dorothy and pulled her to a stop.

'I didn't think it was possible to love you more than I already did, but I do.' He looked into her eyes to show her the verity of his words. He had told Dorothy he loved her, but so far, she had never said it back to him.

He kissed her and she kissed him back. She had never felt so happy. So relieved. Bobby didn't give a toss about her family. He loved her regardless. Regardless of her family's incredibly snobbery. Regardless of her mother's bigamy. He didn't care. *Angie was right.* Bobby was crazy about her.

They started walking again, but after a few yards, Dorothy pulled Bobby to a halt.

'It pains me to have to say this,' she said, looking up and giving him a quick kiss on the lips. She then stood on her tiptoes so that her mouth was close to his good ear. 'But I think I've fallen in love with you too.'

Bobby laughed, elated by her words.

'Just *think* you have?' He grabbed her by her waist and pulled her close.

'OK,' she laughed. 'I have. Damn you, Bobby Armstrong. I know I have!'

Chapter Twenty-Nine

Agatha and Eddy were in the kitchen. The maid had gone for the day and Thomas the driver wasn't due in until later that afternoon.

'Have you put enough in?' Eddy asked, eyeing up the dried, powdered plant in the leather pouch that was lying half open on the kitchen table. He had just watched Agatha sprinkle some of the poison into the creamy mix she was pounding angrily with a wooden spoon in a large bowl.

Agatha didn't answer but instead gave him a dark look.

'Just seems funny she never got ill from the vodka.' Eddy eyed Agatha. He was sitting with his feet up on the edge of the table. He was drinking a cup of tea and smoking a hand-rolled cigarette.

'Get yer feet off the table,' she said, glowering at him.

'Sounds like the mad old cow's doing better than ever,' Eddy said, taking his time to move one foot and then the other back to the flagstone floor.

'She never got ill 'cos she wasn't drinking the damned vodka,' Agatha snapped. 'If she had, she'd have been ill.'

'And you think this'll do the trick?' Eddy asked, looking at the bowl of oatmeal mix. 'That and the eggnog?' He nodded over at the flask containing the chilled nutmeg and cinnamon milk drink at the far end of the kitchen table.

'Yes, I think it'll do the trick,' she lied. She had put only a small amount in the drink. Enough to make Henrietta unwell, but not poorly enough to kill her. She had been careful, very careful, with the measurement of the dried-out white snakeroot. She knew she was taking a risk, defying the master's orders, but she couldn't have Henrietta's death on her conscience. *She just couldn't.* Her reckoning was, if Henrietta fell ill, she'd be seen by a doctor, perhaps even hospitalised, and they'd treat her. Then the master would have to think of another way of getting shot of his wife. Another way that didn't involve her or Eddy.

Putting the wooden spoon on the edge of the bowl, she made her way over to the walk-in pantry.

'What you after?' Eddy asked, quickly putting his rollie in the ashtray and quietly standing up, making sure his chair didn't scrape on the stone floor.

'I'm sure I've got a few raisins somewhere ...' Her voice trailed off as she disappeared into the depths of the larder.

Quick as a flash, Eddy grabbed the pouch of poison, tiptoed around the table, unscrewed the top of the flask containing the eggnog and tapped in a good measure of the dried white powder. All the while, his heart pounded.

'Found them!' Agatha's voice sounded out from the pantry.

Carefully screwing the top back on and placing the pouch of poison where it had been lying on the table, Eddy scooted round to his chair and sat back down. He was just relighting his rollie when Agatha appeared, holding a small jar of raisins.

'Knew I had some somewhere,' she said, twisting the top off and sprinkling a small amount into the mix.

Eddy watched as Agatha then spooned out half a dozen creamy round blobs onto a tray lined with greaseproof paper.

'That's one bowl I won't be asking to lick out,' Eddy said with a chuckle.

Agatha gave him a stony look. She did not find anything even remotely amusing about what they were being forced to do.

As Eddy finished his cigarette, his heartbeat slowed down. He knew Agatha better than anyone and he knew exactly what she was doing. Well, he'd just made sure she'd done what she had been supposed to do. The sooner Henrietta was out of the way, the better.

Then, the so-called 'evidence' the master had fabricated against them, which was locked away in the master's safe, could be destroyed.

And they could all get on with their lives.

Chapter Thirty

Wearing a grey mackintosh and dark green headscarf, Helen had purposely dressed down for her visit to the offices of Mr Emery on the Hendon Road. This part of the east end was probably the poorest and she didn't want to draw attention to herself. It helped that it was now dark. She'd left the car parked in town and jumped on a tram that had brought her within a short walking distance of her father's solicitors. Mr Emery did not know the woman he had an appointment with was in any way connected to his client, Jack Crawford. Helen had not wanted to divulge anything over the phone and had made the appointment under the pseudonym of Mrs Parker. She knew there was something terribly sad about pretending to be John's wife, but she didn't care. It wasn't as if anyone would know who he was.

Arriving at a dark blue door with a plaque to the left telling her she had arrived at the right place, she pulled on an old-fashioned brass bell pull.

An elderly woman wearing a pinny, a duster in her hand and curlers peeking out of a tatty headscarf, opened the door. Were it not for the plaque, Helen might have thought she had the wrong address.

'Yer come for Mr Emery?' the woman asked, opening the door wide.

Helen nodded and the rotund little woman stepped aside.

'First door on yer left.'

She looked at Helen's feet.

'And if yer dinnit mind ...' She cast her eyes down at the doormat.

Helen wiped her feet and walked down the short hallway. The smell of polish was strong and the tiled floor had clearly just been scrubbed clean.

Helen knocked on the door, which was part varnished oak and part frosted glass. *Mr Emery, Solicitor* had been inscribed in gold lettering across the pane of glass.

'Come in!' a man's voice called out.

Helen opened the door and stepped into the office.

Mr Emery scratched his head.

'So, you're not Mrs Parker?' he asked.

'No, I'm Jack Crawford's daughter.'

'And you're here on his behalf?'

'I am indeed.'

'Although he doesn't know you are here – and you don't want him to know either?'

'Yes, that's right,' Helen said.

'And your purpose being to help your father, Mr Jack Crawford, divorce your mother, Mrs Miriam Crawford, née Havelock?'

'That's correct.'

Mr Emery smoothed back his thinning hair, momentarily resting his hand on the back of his neck.

'So, neither of your parents knows you are here?'

'They don't and that's the way I want to keep it,' Helen said.

Mr Emery put both hands together on his perfectly organised desk. Helen was impressed with how well ordered his office was.

'This might seem an odd question, but it is one I need an honest answer to.' He looked at the young woman sitting opposite him, her legs crossed, her green eyes intent.

'Yes?' Helen asked, intrigued.

'Does your grandfather, Charles Havelock, know any-thing about your visit here today – or will he be in any way involved in any work you wish me to carry out?' He needed to know what he was letting himself in for.

Helen looked at Mr Emery. His tone told her that he did not find her grandfather endearing.

'My grandfather does not know I am here, nor will he be involved with any work I wish you to carry out on my behalf. I am here purely to help my father.'

'Right,' Mr Emery said. 'If that's the case, you'd better tell me exactly what it is you would like me to do. And I shall tell you if I am able to do it.'

Ten minutes later, there was another pull on the front doorbell.

Helen heard the woman she'd presumed was Mr Emery's cleaner say, 'If yer dinnit mind ...'

There was the sound of feet being wiped on the mat, fol-lowed by the sound of light footsteps, then a gentle tap on the glass.

Mr Emery looked at Helen, who smiled.

'Come in, Georgina. We're expecting you.'

It took an hour and a half to complete what needed to be done, which was why Helen had booked a two-hour appointment. They had saved a little time thanks to Geor-gina's efficiency and the fact that she had typed up her reports, so it was just a case of Mr Emery writing them up on the appropriate headed paper to be witnessed and signed.

Georgina left first.

Helen paid the bill in full, in cash.

'Hopefully,' she said, getting up to leave, 'I shall see you soon.'

Walking her to the door, Mr Emery wished her luck.

Helen patted the file she'd just slipped inside her mackintosh.

'Hopefully, I won't need luck and this should suffice.'

After her departure, Mr Emery sat for a short while in his high-backed leather chair and did something he rarely did at this time of the day: he poured himself a small whisky from the decanter on his desk. He took a sip and savoured the burn.

Interesting. *Very interesting*.

Unlike all the other solicitors in the area, he'd had no qualms about taking on the Crawford v Crawford case. The other firms in town would never go up against anyone connected to Charles Havelock, never mind his daughter. They had too much to lose.

He didn't.

Mr Havelock had already seen to that many years ago.

Mr Emery had learnt over the years that having nothing to lose could be liberating. Silver linings and all that.

He had another sip.

There was a quick rat-a-tat-tat on the door.

'I'll be getting myself off then, Ethan.'

'Thanks, Mrs Evans. I'll see you on Friday.'

The housekeeper's ruddy face disappeared and a few moments later he heard the front door close.

He looked out of the window and watched the old woman hurry across the road.

He would have liked to be able to tell her about the case.

Finishing his whisky, he got up and prodded the fire.

What he'd heard today should really have shocked him – but it hadn't. Not really. This was the Havelock family, after all.

Nothing about that family could surprise him.

232

Chapter Thirty-One

When it was announced that this year all the shipyard workers in the town were to have Christmas Day and Boxing Day off as paid holiday, everyone was jubilant.

Angie was particularly cock-a-hoop as Quentin had just told her that he'd been allowed a forty-eight-hour pass over Christmas.

When Georgina informed Dorothy that she had persuaded her editor at the *Echo* to allow her to officially cover the extravaganza for the Boxing Day edition, with the expectation that it would make the front page, Dorothy became even more determined to make the event 'spectacular'. Georgina was pleased, as not only would she get her first front page with a byline, but she had been promised extra film and flashes, which were akin to gold dust in these times of rationing.

Sitting at their table in the canteen, Dorothy demanded updates from the women, even though mostly everything was in hand.

Polly relayed how the knitting of scarves, jumpers, gloves and hats was going, and how it now seemed that anyone Agnes and Beryl knew who could do a basic knit and purl had been roped into making winter woollies; if they couldn't knit, they had been tasked with finding old clothes and unpicking the wool to add to their dwindling supplies.

'And they're still managing to combine it with running the nursery?' Rosie asked.

Polly nodded. 'I think *combine* is the right word. They've even got some of the older children learning how to knit.'

Everyone chuckled.

'And Joe and Major Black?' Dorothy asked, looking down at her neatly penned agenda.

'Yes, they've come up with a list of practical presents the men would appreciate and which will come in handy when they're eventually discharged,' Polly said, handing over a piece of paper with what looked like a shopping list on it.

'Thank you.' Dorothy took the list and quickly scanned it before handing it to Angie.

'Oh, and Albert's said he'll give any produce from his allotment to Vera and Rina to use for the catering,' Polly added, taking a sip of her tea.

'Excellent,' Dorothy smiled. 'That means lots of leek, onion and potato pies – and carrot cake!'

'And Kate told me to tell you,' Rosie said, 'that she has roped Lily, George, Maisie and Vivian into helping her to "beg, borrow or buy" a load of Christmas decorations. She also told me to tell you the look she is aiming for is "Winter Wonderland".'

Dorothy clapped her hands in glee. 'Sounds amazing!'

'Vera and Rina are stockpiling ingredients,' Hannah reported.

'And Vera is apparently doing a great job of guilting customers into dropping any spare change they've got into the collection tin,' said Olly.

'Which is no longer a tin but a large clear glass jar,' Hannah said. 'So that customers can see there're notes in there as well as coins.'

'Typical Vera. She's a wily one,' Gloria chuckled.

'So, how much has been raised this week?' Dorothy asked when they'd all had their lunch and tidied away their trays.

Hannah got out her little notebook and handed it to Olly, who proceeded to tell them the amount collected by all the shops and cafés in town that had been willing to have a donation box on their counters – of which there had been quite a number.

'So, Rosie – is Charlotte still up for spending Saturday in town getting all the extra bits and bobs we need?'

Rosie nodded. 'She is. And naturally, she will be helped by Lily.' They all chuckled, knowing how much Lily and Charlotte adored each other.

'And will Peter be back for Christmas?'

'Definitely,' Rosie said with a smile. 'He wouldn't miss this for anything and has volunteered his services, so if you need him to do anything, just say.'

'Actually,' Dorothy looked at Angie, 'we wondered if Peter could act as interpreter for the French soldiers who can't speak English.'

'Of course,' Rosie said. 'He'd be over the moon. It'll probably make his Christmas Day.'

'I don't suppose he can speak any other languages?' Dorothy asked tentatively.

The mood sobered. Helen had relayed to the women that there was a possibility there would be soldiers from 'the other side' being cared for at the hospital over Christmas. Dr Parker knew of at least two from the Wehrmacht.

'No, I'm afraid not,' Rosie said.

The women all glanced at Hannah. They knew she spoke German. Most Czechs, she had told them, did.

'Oh, never mind,' Dorothy said, looking down at her list. 'Well, what else do I need to ask—'

'Actually,' Hannah interrupted. 'That's something *I* can do.'

Everyone was quiet.

'I'd like to volunteer my linguistic services along with Peter. I speak fluent German.'

'And she can speak a little Polish,' Olly added, proudly.

'Only a very little,' Hannah conceded. She smiled. 'I know how to say Merry Christmas and things like that, at least.'

'Well, that will be wonderful,' Rosie said. 'Just to hear someone speak their native tongue will be a Christmas present in itself, I'd have thought.'

The women all murmured their agreement.

They were quiet for a moment.

'But how will you feel about speaking German – to an *actual* German?' Martha asked what they had all been thinking.

Everyone stared at Hannah.

'I'll be fine,' she reassured them.

'Well, I think that's wonderful,' Polly said. 'Come here.'

She put her arms around Hannah, who felt so small and frail but was, she knew, so strong. So strong and so kind-hearted. And the most gentle and compassionate person she had ever known.

Chapter Thirty-Two

Kate watched Helen and Henrietta button up their coats and pull on their hats and gloves as they got ready to leave. Henrietta's fitting had gone well. A few nips and tucks were all that was needed.

Kate walked over to the front door and took off the safety latch. The Maison Nouvelle was as warm as toast, but outside it was bitterly cold. She guessed that snow was on the way, judging by the heavy, dark grey clouds that had loomed low all day. Her years on the street had made her quite a proficient weather forecaster. It was now just over two weeks until Christmas. Kate thought of Dorothy. She might get the white Christmas she was hoping for, after all.

Helen stepped out onto the street, quickly checking there was no one nearby.

'I shall see you both on Saturday for the final fitting,' Kate said to Henrietta, giving her a kiss on the cheek. 'When you will be walking out of here a new woman.'

Helen smiled as they waved their goodbyes and climbed into the car. Kate firmly believed that clothes were intrinsically interwoven with one's identity. A new look meant a new woman. Perhaps, Helen thought, she would get herself a new wardrobe in the New Year too.

As they drove along the coast road, the sun was just starting to drop and the evening was drawing in. Glancing across at Henrietta, she thought she seemed paler than usual. Perhaps she'd put on more powder than she would normally as she was having a trip out.

'Grandmama,' Helen asked tentatively, 'do you still feel like you should be punished for not realising what Grandfather was doing?'

Henrietta clasped and unclasped her hands.

'I don't know,' she said. 'I really don't know.'

Helen decided not to push the issue. The fact that her grandmother wasn't sure was a step forward. She was no longer adamant that she was to blame. Kate had planted the seed of doubt on the day they had come for the initial measuring up and it had clearly started to germinate. She would just need a little more time, and a little more coaxing, to convince her that she really was *not* to blame.

As they turned right into the road that led into Ryhope village, an image of her grandfather came to the fore and Helen was again awash with the now familiar sense of outrage that he had got off so lightly after everything he had done. All the lives he had ruined. He really did have an incredible capacity to glide through life without having to suffer any kind of punishment for the crimes he'd committed. He'd raped Pearl when she was fifteen, as well as that other poor girl who'd hanged herself, got them both pregnant and had fathered at least two illegitimate children. Those left behind had had to deal with the devastation. He'd got his wife incarcerated and drugged up to keep her quiet for fear she'd hang him out to dry. And yet he was still sitting pretty – totally unblemished – continuing to be fawned over by the people of this town. He hadn't suffered one iota. He'd not even had to part with any of his money. All he'd done was agree to allow her father to come back home. To be with Gloria and Hope.

'I remember when you were a little baby,' Henrietta said suddenly.

'Really?' Helen was surprised. Her grandmother never voluntarily brought up the past.

'You had a mop of thick black hair. I remember thinking you were the spit of your father. So dark. So handsome. And so unlike a Havelock. You were always destined to be your father's daughter. There was never any doubt of that.'

Helen felt the tears smart the backs of her eyes as she started down the narrow road that led back to the asylum.

'Thank you, Grandmama.' Helen blinked hard. 'You don't know how much that means to me.'

When Helen pulled up at the entrance of the asylum, she looked across at Henrietta. She seemed very subdued.

'You all right, Grandmama?'

'Just tired, my dear, just a little tired.'

As Helen helped Henrietta out of the car and up the stone steps to the asylum entrance, the outside light caught them in such a way that she saw her grandmother as a young woman. And it was then Helen realised that it wasn't just her father she looked like – but her grandmother too.

As they walked slowly down the corridor, Helen asked, 'If it were possible, would you like to leave the asylum and come and live at home with me? And Mother, of course.'

Henrietta stopped in her tracks and turned to her granddaughter.

'Oh, Helen.' Her dark eyes glistened as she searched her granddaughter's face. 'Would you really want me there?'

Helen laughed with joy. Her grandmother had not shown a flicker of indecision. It was clear she would be happy to leave the asylum in the blink of an eye.

'Of course I would, Grandmama,' Helen smiled. 'I'd absolutely love you to come and live with us.'

Henrietta squeezed Helen's arm as they walked on a little further. When they reached her room, she turned to her granddaughter.

'Do you think it would be possible?' she asked. She didn't need to voice the reasons why it might not be.

'I think it might,' Helen said. 'I have an idea. Something up my sleeve.' She gave her grandmother an artful smile. 'I just wanted to check that it would be something you'd want.'

'Oh, yes. Very much so, my dear,' Henrietta said. 'I shall have wonderful dreams tonight,' she added, a dreamy look on her face.

'Dreams that can – and will – come true,' Helen said, kissing Henrietta on the cheek and bidding her farewell.

Chapter Thirty-Three

Two days later, Kate's prediction was proved right and the snow came – in abundance.

As Miriam was driven down Burdon Road, which ran alongside the town's Mowbray Park, she watched as a mother and her two children, wrapped up from head to toe to keep warm, trudged through thick snow. A few minutes later, as they drove past the Grand on Bridge Street, she felt a little spark of excitement. Her meeting with Helen shouldn't take much more than an hour – maximum. Not long until she was sitting at the bar with Amelia enjoying a gin and tonic. She deserved it after the day she'd had. A day of family obligations. Her father had been on at her to visit her mother. *Again.* He was now insisting that she go and visit at least twice a week – armed with a flask of eggnog and a couple of Agatha's home-made oatmeal and raisin biscuits. He'd seemed even keener to spoil Henrietta after hearing she'd been a little under the weather this past week. Miriam had tentatively suggested that perhaps he go and visit his wife himself, especially as he seemed so eager to hear about her welfare. He had said he would, but not quite yet. Miriam had not laboured the point. She didn't want to upset the apple cart – not if she wanted to stay the main beneficiary in his will.

Crossing over the Wearmouth Bridge, Miriam mused how her father had seemed in a very good mood. He'd seemed quite jolly, in fact, as he stood in front of the huge

Christmas tree he'd just had delivered and which he'd had decorated and displayed in the hallway.

Miriam got out her compact and reapplied her lipstick. She always liked to look her best when seeing her daughter. There was nothing like being in the presence of a young woman in her bloom to make a middle-aged woman's spirits sag. She pinched her cheeks to give them a little colour. Still, she wasn't looking bad. Not bad at all. Her new Admiralty 'friend' certainly didn't think she looked her age. Miriam chuckled to herself. A little flattery could get you anywhere.

As they neared Thompson's, Miriam thought how much life had improved since she'd returned home. She was set to be one of the richest women in the north-east when her father finally popped his clogs, and the approach of Christmas meant she had an excuse to spend even more time than usual with Amelia in the Grand, enjoying the decadence of her new life. A life made all the better by knowing that Jack and Gloria were holed up in their little hovel on the Borough Road, frightened to go out for fear of being called names and spat on – shamed as the couple living in sin with their bastard child.

Long may it continue.

The end of the shift had sounded out, but, as always, there were still workers milling around – those doing overtime and those on the night shift. Helen was glad she'd asked her mother to the office after her staff had all gone for the day. The reason she'd not wanted to do this at home was out of fear of her mother becoming hysterical, which she still might, although here the chances were lessened. Helen knew her mother would not want people gossiping about her going doolally.

Hearing the main door to the admin office slam shut, Helen looked up to see her mother waltzing into her office.

'So glad you could drag yourself away from the Grand,' Helen said, looking at Miriam. She looked sober. Thank goodness.

'I've not come from the Grand!' Miriam snapped. She looked around, checking no one else was about. 'I hope this won't take long. Your little Irish girl not here?'

'Marie-Anne has gone home for the day, Mother, so you'll have to get your own tea if you fancy a cup.' Helen looked at her watch and laughed loudly. 'Silly me, it's far too late for tea. You must be feeling in need of a *proper* drink, Mother?'

Miriam scowled at her daughter and walked over to the metal cabinet.

'I'm afraid you won't find any Scotch there.' Helen sat back in her chair and took out a cigarette from her packet of Pall Malls. 'Like I said last time you were here with Grandfather – this is *my* office now. And I don't believe in sitting around and supping Scotch.' Helen lit her cigarette. She knew her mother disliked the smell.

Miriam waved her hand about in an attempt to dispel the swirls of grey smoke.

'Why don't you sit down, Mother?' Helen pointed to the chair in front of her desk. 'As I said, I won't take long and then you can get yourself back to the Grand.'

'I told you, I haven't come from the Grand,' Miriam said defensively. 'I've actually just come from seeing your darling grandmother.'

Helen didn't try to hold back her surprise. 'Really? My, my – twice in one week. Is this your guilty conscience finally kicking in?'

'I have nothing to feel guilty about,' Miriam said, outraged by the mere suggestion.

'Leaving your mother somewhere she should never have been for the past twenty-odd years might occasionally prick one's conscience,' Helen argued.

'On that point, we will have to agree to differ,' said Miriam.

'Of course, I keep forgetting,' said Helen. 'You have chosen to believe your father's lies.'

Miriam ignored her daughter's jibe, not wanting to discuss the subject with her. A subject that always, if she was honest, left her feeling uncomfortable.

'Your grandmother sends her love, by the way,' Miriam said, changing the subject.

'How's Grandmama feeling?' Helen asked, her tone now serious and sincere. 'She was still looking a bit peaky when I was there the other day.'

'Oh, she's fine.' Miriam waved away Helen's concern. 'Fit as a fiddle. Actually, I saw your doctor friend while I was there,' she said. 'I'm wondering how long it'll be before he proposes to the lovely Dr Eris.'

Seeing the look on Helen's face, Miriam let out a cruel laugh. 'So, you're still holding a candle for your handsome surgeon.'

Helen tried to appear indifferent.

'I can read you like a book, Helen. You are my daughter, after all.' Miriam settled back into the chair. 'It's a good job you never did become romantically involved with him, though, isn't it?' She gave Helen a knowing look. 'It would have been a bit embarrassing for him to have to tell you that you were not quite marriage material. What with him knowing all about your affair with the married Theodore and your pregnancy.' Miriam paused. 'I suppose it was a godsend you miscarried before it became obvious you were with child – if that had been the case, then *no one* would want to touch you with a bargepole. Even Royce Junior, love-struck though he might be.'

Helen wanted to scream at her mother that she was wrong. John *did* love her. Loved her regardless of her past.

And that the reason they were not together now had nothing to do with her mother's view that she was 'sullied' and 'second-hand goods'.

'It's all very sad,' Miriam said. 'You getting so involved in this Christmas Extravaganza, just so you can spend more time with the good doctor. It's almost pitiful.'

Her mother's words were hurtful but not off the mark.

'Almost as pitiful as this will be painful to you,' Helen said, pulling out her top drawer and dumping a file on her desk.

Miriam looked at the brown file. It had her name on it.

She stared at it. 'And?' Then pointed a manicured finger towards the offending file. 'What's that? Why does it have my name on it?'

'Because, Mother …' Helen took another drag of her cigarette and blew out a stream of smoke '… the file concerns you.'

Sitting up straight, she put her cigarette in the ashtray.

'These are the documents that you will be signing before you leave here.'

Helen handed Miriam the divorce forms, which stated the lesser matrimonial offence of desertion. There was also a document retracting her intention to defend the divorce.

Miriam snatched them from Helen and skimmed through them before flinging them back onto the desk.

'Well, this has been a wasted trip, Helen. I don't know why on earth you'd think I'd sign those.'

'You will sign …' Helen paused '… once you've seen the main contents of the file.'

Helen took her time taking out a stack of official-looking papers and two large brown envelopes.

Miriam watched as Helen carefully handed her a typed-up document with two signatures at the bottom.

'What's this?' Miriam demanded.

'Here, Mother, dear, we have a sworn affidavit which sets out how you banished your own husband to the Clyde for a period of two years.'

Helen pointed to the top paragraph of the first sheet of paper. 'You see here? It has the exact dates. Wednesday the seventh of January 1942.'

She pointed further down the page.

'And here you will see how you forced your husband from the marital home and his home town by means of blackmail.'

Miriam scanned the page. Her daughter had detailed everything she had heard that afternoon when she had stood and listened outside the living room as Miriam had threatened to ruin the lives of Gloria's workmates if Jack did not do as she wished.

Helen pulled out another document and laid it flat on the desk.

'And this affidavit has been sworn and signed by Miss Georgina Pickering, who was tasked with carrying out the private-eye work which gave you the information you needed to blackmail your husband into doing what you wanted.'

This had been something Helen had not asked Georgina to do, but which she herself had volunteered. Helen had been over the moon as it helped enormously to have her version of events backed up by a second party. She had asked Georgina if she was absolutely sure as she could not guarantee what her mother might do, but Georgina had insisted. Helen thought she knew why.

'And here we have another sworn statement detailing how the marriage was brought about through a deceit – how you also blackmailed my father into marriage, pretending you were pregnant in order to get him down the aisle.'

Helen looked at her mother's outraged face.

'But before you say it, I agree, it would be hard to prove, but the fact that your daughter is prepared to swear on the Bible and relate how her mother has boasted many times over the years of what she did to get the man she wanted … well –' Helen pursed her lips '– it will not look good. Plus, of course, if asked about your sleeping arrangements, I will have to tell the truth and relay to the court how before Dad was sent packing, you two had had your own bedrooms for a number of years. And that it was clear that the pair of you didn't like each other – never mind love each other.'

She continued to watch her mother.

'And, naturally, the local press will be given an anonymous tip about a very interesting high-society divorce case which will have them sprinting to the court, where they will undoubtedly sop up every last scandalous detail.' Helen widened her eyes as though she'd just been hit by a thought. 'You never know, the national newspapers might even get a hold of it. You know how they love a bit of tittle-tattle.'

'You wouldn't,' Miriam said, aghast.

'I will if I have to,' said Helen.

She flicked through the folder.

'Oh, and good old Aunty Margaret. She's so organised, isn't she?' Helen pulled out the bill for Miriam's stay in the sanatorium.

Miriam looked at it.

'Well, that doesn't mean anything. Just means I was a little under the weather.'

'Ah, but this does.' Helen pulled out a three-page doctor's report. 'I think it clearly spells out exactly why you were there.'

Miriam snatched it out of Helen's hand.

'Don't worry. That's just a duplicate copy. But the pièces de résistance,' Helen announced, 'are these ...'

She laid out two small black and white photographs. One showing Miriam going into the Grand, and one of Miriam coming out in the early hours of the morning, looking dishevelled. 'It will easily be proven that at no time have you ever taken out a room at the Grand. And if needs must, it won't take much to get a few more signed affidavits from staff at the hotel about your closeness to Mr Malcolm Price. A widower and one of the Admiralty billeted at the hotel.'

Miriam was staring at the photographs, more worried about how awful she looked as she left the Grand. Whoever had taken the photograph had caught her just under the street light.

'So, you see, Mother, if you do go ahead and contest the divorce in a court of law, Father's solicitor will air all your dirty laundry.' It was something Helen believed Mr Emery would enjoy doing. She was sure he had crossed the Havelocks at some time in the past – and something told her he had not come out of it well.

Miriam stopped looking at the photographs and threw Helen a piercing look.

'You are an abomination of a daughter!' she hissed.

'Perhaps,' Helen said. 'Or perhaps it's a case of you reap what you sow.'

Miriam pursed her lips. Her face was contorted with anger and frustration.

'Are you *really* going to blackmail your own mother?' she asked incredulously.

'I certainly am, Mother,' Helen said, a taut smile on her face. 'Just like you did Dad.' She looked into her mother's cold blue eyes. 'You taught me well.' Uncapping her fountain pen, she held it out.

Miriam stared at it as though it was contaminated.

'I'm afraid you really have no choice,' said Helen.

Miriam gave her daughter one last hateful stare and snatched the pen.

She looked down at the paper.

'I've marked where you need to sign,' Helen said.

Miriam paused, took a deep breath, cast her daughter one more disgusted look – and then she signed.

Helen watched and secretly cried out with joy. *She'd done it.*

Finally, her father could get his divorce. He and Gloria could marry. And at last Hope could be classed as legitimate, and thereby be freed from the burden of a childhood blighted by bullying and name-calling.

Miriam tossed the pen onto the document, causing a little blue ink to splatter.

Standing up, she looked down at Helen, who was dabbing the wet ink with a small sheet of blotting paper.

'Let him have his divorce. Let him have *boring Gloria* as his new wife,' she said, emitting a bitter laugh. 'I've had my fun, anyway.'

Helen looked at her mother and only then did she realise that Gloria had lied. The harassment *had* continued.

'I shall enjoy the reputation of a hard-done-by wife – divorced by an unfaithful husband. And then I shall make it known I'm back on the market and shall thoroughly enjoy wading through an army of suitors.'

'Well, judging by those photos,' Helen said, sliding them back into the envelope, 'it looks like you've already made a good start.'

'But what you don't realise, Helen, dear,' Miriam narrowed her eyes at her daughter, 'is that I will be one of the most eligible women in the whole of the north-east.'

Helen laughed. 'Mother, you really do have a rather overinflated sense of your self-worth.'

'I'm not just talking about my looks, Helen, but my wealth.' Miriam's face broke into a smug smile. 'I am going to be worth an absolute fortune in the not too distant future.'

'Really?' Helen's mind was now focused on getting shot of her mother and taking the signed documents to Mr Emery.

'Yes, really,' Miriam hissed. 'You see, Helen, your grandfather has decided to leave his entire estate to me. *To me and no one else.* Not Margaret. Not you. Just me.'

Helen stared at her mother – she looked like the cat that had got the cream. She took her time folding up the signed documents and putting them in her handbag.

'I think you might find that when Grandfather does finally shuffle off this mortal coil,' Helen said, choosing her words carefully, 'it will clear the pathway for it to be made known that Miss Henrietta Girling is actually Mrs Henrietta Havelock – that Charles Havelock's wife is not dead, as everyone was led to believe.'

Miriam laughed. 'I really don't think some mad spinster's claim to be the long-lost wife of the town's most revered philanthropist will hold much credence in court.'

Helen thought of the original creased and dog-eared admissions form that Dr Eris had shown her in June.

'Unless there is irrefutable proof,' she said.

Miriam's smile wavered.

'Well, even if there is "irrefutable proof", as you say, I do believe that the law states that those living in mental hospitals are not deemed to be of sound mind and therefore must forgo any inheritance.'

'Honestly, Mother, talk about sharp as a button.' Helen hesitated, amazed that her mother looked pleased with the compliment. 'But that would not be the case if the person concerned is no longer living in a mental institution, but is, in fact, certified sane and is happily living at home with her family.'

Miriam laughed at the mere notion. 'Not likely with the drugs she's taking.'

Helen stared at her mother.

'What do you mean?' she snapped.

'I mean that Dr Eris came in to see Mother the other week with a whole new regime of medications. A fishbowl full of drugs.'

Miriam turned to leave.

'See, my dear, you don't know everything.' Her face contorted into a grimace that was meant to be a smile.

'Well, I best get off.'

She looked at her watch.

'Now it really *is* time for the Grand.'

Chapter Thirty-Four

Shortly after Miriam left, Helen quickly gathered what she needed and made her way out of the admin building. She made a mental note to ask Henrietta about the 'fish-bowl full of drugs' she had apparently been given by Dr Eris. Her mother was either lying or exaggerating. She was pretty sure that Henrietta had been taken off most – if not all – of the medication she'd been prescribed by her old doctor.

Looking across the yard, she saw the light of the platers' shed and caught a glimpse of Bobby. If he wasn't on a date with Dorothy, he was working overtime, riveting, helping the platers, splicing ropes or doing general labouring. Gloria had confessed to Helen that she thought her son's need to work all hours was not just because he wanted to feel as though he was still part of the fight to beat Jerry, but because he was saving up to buy an engagement ring. Neither Helen nor Gloria needed to say what the other was thinking – there weren't enough hours in the day, or days in the week, for Bobby to afford to buy Dorothy a ring that might compare to the one Toby had bought her – and which was now funding a good part of the Christmas Extravaganza.

Walking through the gates and waving up at Davey the young timekeeper, she saw that Mickey the tea boy was with him. They were both reading a comic and sharing a cigarette. Helen hurried past and jumped into her green sports car. She put her handbag and her mother's file on the passenger seat. As she pulled away from the yard, she thought about John. Her mother's words had cut deep. She felt a dull ache in her chest as she thought of the prospect of John marrying Dr Eris. It was inevitable. They had been courting seriously for well over a year. Of course he would propose. It was just a matter of when. Soon, probably. Especially now the war was clearly nearing its end. It was the proper thing to do. And why not? They were perfectly matched.

As Helen drove across the river and into the east end, she could see the streets were full of life. Workers were making their way home or heading to their local drinking holes. Children were out on the snow-laden streets, building snowmen, tossing snowballs, their breath visible in the ice-cold weather.

Parking down a quiet, dark side street so as to avoid any attention, Helen hurried back onto the Hendon Road and walked for a short stretch before reaching the blue door with the polished brass plaque. She pulled on the bell and the door was again answered by the housekeeper. This time, though, she had on her coat over her pinny. Her work for the day was clearly done.

She opened the door wide.

'Thank you,' Helen said, making a show of wiping her feet. She walked down the short hallway and knocked on Mr Emery's office door. She turned to see the old woman's eyes on her as she slowly closed the front door behind her.

Having inspected the signed forms and added his own signature to the bottom, Mr Emery explained to Helen what would happen next. Listening intently, Helen hoped she would never have to call upon the knowledge she had garnered about the whole process of obtaining a divorce. Although, she thought rather self-pityingly, at the rate she was going, it was unlikely she'd ever get married, never mind divorced.

Mr Emery explained that the whole case had been much easier due to the fact that Jack had stated he did not want any money – not a penny – from Miriam, and that it would now be a matter of waiting for a call from himself to tell her that the signed forms had been dealt with by the judiciary and the decree nisi had been sanctioned. This did not mean the divorce was finalised, he stressed – that would take another six weeks. Only then would he receive the final decree – the decree absolute.

'For all intents and purposes, though, once we have the decree nisi, it's more or less a done deal,' Mr Emery explained.

'I can tell Jack and Gloria?' Helen asked hopefully.

'Yes, you can – but remember, they can't marry until the decree absolute. It is that which formally ends the marriage. If he marries before this comes through, he will be committing bigamy. And we don't want that.'

Helen thought of Dorothy's mother.

'No, we don't,' she agreed. 'Do you think we will get the decree nisi through before Christmas?'

'I will try and twist a few arms.' He smiled. 'Your Christmas present?'

Helen nodded. 'Fingers crossed.'

The next day Helen had been due to go and see Henrietta, but a problem at work prevented her. She rang Genevieve and asked her to tell Miss Girling that she wouldn't be able to visit as planned, but would be across on Saturday to take her for her final fitting.

'Do you want me to get Dr Eris to sign a day-release form in advance so it's all ready for you?' Genevieve asked.

'Yes, please. That would be helpful,' Helen replied curtly.

She had thought for a while that the elderly receptionist seemed very keen to please of late. Overly keen. With hind-sight, she had seemed particularly eager to please from around the time Dr Eris had told her she knew who Miss Girling really was. Helen had begun to suspect a guilty conscience. Then, the other day, while she had been chat-ting to her grandmother, she had learnt that Genevieve had been at the asylum longer than most of the patients and staff. And that she had been working at the asylum when Henrietta had been admitted. When Helen had quizzed her grandmother further, she'd learnt that Genevieve knew just about everything there was to know about the asylum – and those in it. Both the doctors and the patients.

'She knows everyone's secrets,' Henrietta had said conspiratorially.

It had cemented Helen's belief that it *had* been Gene-vieve who had told Claire about Henrietta.

Chapter Thirty-Five

As the countdown to Christmas continued, the town seemed to be whipping itself into a festive frenzy. This was largely due to the return of hundreds of excited children to homes they had been forced to leave at the start of the war when they had been evacuated to farms and villages far away from the reach of Hitler's bombs. Toys and sweets had also arrived from America to be distributed to the children of the poor, and the town's annual Christmas Fayre was opened with much aplomb. With posters advertising dances at the New Rink and the Seaburn Hall, there was no doubting that this Christmas was going to be one to remember.

Arriving at the asylum to take Henrietta to the Maison Nouvelle for her final fitting, Helen found her grandmother waiting in the foyer. She was wrapped up in her winter coat and was sitting in a chair next to the large reception desk. Genevieve was talking on the phone, her back ramrod straight as she scribbled on a notepad. As Helen hurried across the tiled flooring, the acoustics of the asylum's high-ceilinged entrance caused the sound of her heeled shoes to echo.

'Henrietta...' Helen was always careful to call her grandmother by her first name if there was a chance of anyone hearing her.

Genevieve placed the receiver back in its cradle.

'She's ready and raring to go,' she said, nodding over to Henrietta. 'Dr Eris has signed her day-release papers.'

Helen gave Genevieve a steely look as she took the form from her. She would have liked nothing more than to confront her about her indiscretions, but knew that would never be possible. Still, it didn't mean she had to be nice to her.

Helen glanced back at her grandmother. She thought Henrietta looked ready, but not exactly *raring*. Her anger towards Genevieve was replaced by concern for her grandmother.

'Are you all right?' she asked, sitting down on the chair next to Henrietta. 'You look a little pale.'

'Yes, yes, my dear, I'm fine. Just a little tired, that's all.'

'We can put this off until another day if you want?' Helen asked.

'No, no.' Henrietta smiled. 'I've been looking forward to this all week. Finally, I will have my new outfit ... And I can bring it back with me, can't I?'

'Yes, of course you can,' Helen said, touching her grandmother's hand. It felt stone cold. She caught her grandmother shivering.

'Dear me, I think we need to warm those hands up.' She took them both in her own and rubbed them. Her grandmother seemed subdued.

'Are you sure you're feeling up to this?' Helen asked again.

Henrietta pushed herself up out of her seat.

'Wild horses wouldn't stop me,' she declared determinedly.

'All right, but put my gloves on,' Helen said, digging around in her coat pockets and handing Henrietta her fur-lined leather gloves.

It only took them a few minutes to get to the car. A pathway through the snow had been cleared. Seeing her grandmother start to tremble a little, Helen started up the ignition and put the heater on full blast.

It took just over a quarter of an hour to drive to the Maison Nouvelle. Helping her grandmother out of the car, she saw that she was still shaking, in spite of the car feeling like a sauna.

As soon as they walked into the boutique, the little brass bell announced their arrival. Kate appeared from the back of the shop and hurried over to greet them.

'Oh, Henrietta, it's lovely to see you.' But the nearer she got to her client, the more she sensed that something was not right.

'Dear me …' She looked at Helen and then back to Henrietta. 'You look frozen to the bone.'

Henrietta smiled, but didn't reply. It was as though she hadn't heard Kate. Her eyes scanned the shop before she found what she was looking for. Her face lit up and she clapped her hands in excitement.

'Oh, Kate, it looks divine!'

Kate and Helen followed Henrietta's gaze to her new outfit – an elegant two-piece displayed on a padded coat hanger that had been hooked onto a dressmaker's dummy.

Henrietta took two steps towards the blue tailored skirt and jacket. She pulled off her gloves and reached out to touch the fine merino fabric. As she did so, she sighed and turned to Kate.

'Thank you. It's beautiful.'

As she looked back at her outfit, she swayed a little. She reached out to grab something to steady herself, but found only air.

Letting out a startled sound as her legs buckled, Henrietta sank to the floor in a small heap.

'Grandmama!' Helen rushed to her, dropping down on the ground and lifting Henrietta's head from the carpet. She had landed on her side and was curled up like a sleeping dormouse, snuggled up in her thick winter coat.

'I'll get some water ...' Kate hurried to the back room, returning seconds later with a tumbler of water.

Henrietta's eyes were fluttering open. She was still conscious.

'Try and take a sip,' Kate cajoled.

Henrietta did as she was told.

'She's shaking,' Helen said. 'I don't like this. Not one bit.'

Kate put the tumbler down by her side and took a hold of Henrietta's face. She gently pulled down Henrietta's lower eyelids.

Helen watched Kate's concerned face.

Grabbing a handkerchief from her cuff, Kate dabbed it in the glass of water and then started to wipe off Henrietta's foundation and powder.

Helen gasped in shock.

The hue of her grandmother's skin was a pale yellow.

'Does Henrietta drink?'

Helen looked confused.

'Spirits?' Kate said. 'Liquor? Any kind of alcohol?'

'No, no.' Helen shook her head vigorously. 'We just pretend.'

Kate gave her a puzzled look.

'She used to drink vodka – in the old days – before the asylum.' Helen shook her head again. 'We drink water. Pretend it's Russian vodka.'

Feeling her grandmother starting to tremble once more, Helen wrapped her arms around her.

'I think we need to get her to a hospital,' Kate said. 'I think she's suffering from liver failure.'

Helen looked at Kate, confused.

'I used to see it a lot on the street,' Kate explained. 'The jaundiced skin. The yellow tinge in the eyes.' She touched Henrietta's hand, which was still shaking. 'This shaking – we'd call it the "tremors".'

Kate touched Henrietta's cheek to focus her attention. 'Have you been drinking, Henrietta?'

Henrietta shook her head like a child. 'No, just our Russian water.' She looked up at Helen.

'That's right ...' Helen nodded, trying to give her grandmother a reassuring smile. She looked at her eyes. *Why hadn't she noticed the colour before?*

'Come on, let's see if we can get you on your feet,' Helen coaxed, moving Henrietta into a sitting position.

Helen and Kate positioned themselves on either side and gently lifted Henrietta to her feet. She was as light as a feather. Helen put her arm around Henrietta's waist. It was only then that she realised her grandmother had lost weight.

'I can manage her on my own,' Helen said. Henrietta was so light, she thought she could fling her over her shoulder if need be. 'Can you call Dr Parker at the Ryhope and Dr Eris at the asylum and get them to meet us at the Royal?'

Kate hurried to open the front door. 'I will.'

Helen turned just as Kate was shutting the door. 'Actually, Kate, call the asylum first. The receptionist there's called Genevieve. Tell her to find them both and get them over to the hospital immediately. Tell her, Helen says she knows what she did, so she better find them or there'll be hell to pay.'

Kate nodded, shut the door and hurried over to the wall phone behind the counter.

She got through to the asylum on the second ring. After telling Genevieve that Henrietta had fallen ill and been taken to the Royal, she repeated what Helen had told her to say. There was a second's silence before Genevieve assured her that she would get Dr Eris and Dr Parker to the hospital as quickly as humanly possible. She had just seen them both leave the asylum moments earlier. Not wanting to miss them, she banged the phone down and hurried out of the main entrance. It was dark, but she could clearly see them just as they were about to get into a taxi.

*

Henrietta looked at Helen's worried face as she sat in her lovely little sports car. She remembered being young and wanting to learn to drive herself, but Charles wasn't having any of it. He'd said it was ridiculous. A woman driving. She thought of Charles. Of his evil. *How had she been so blind?* Turning her head to the left, she looked out of the window at the shops along Holmeside, all decorated for Christmas. Nearly every single one of them had a Christmas tree on show. She remembered when she'd last walked down this street. For a moment, she was a young woman again, shopping, stopping for tea in one of the cafeterias. Henrietta felt herself leaning into the passenger door as the car took a sharp left. Looking out onto Stockton Street, she felt confused.

'Where am I?' she asked. She felt as though she was in a dream. Her eyelids seemed to have become so heavy. So very heavy.

'You're with me, Grandmama.' Helen's voice sounded strained. 'You're not well. I'm taking you to the hospital.'

Suddenly, Helen slammed on the brakes and they both lurched forward.

'Damn!' The road was closed off. It looked as though there was some kind of water leak. The street had turned into a gurgling stream.

Banging the car into reverse, she managed to do a three-point turn. A car behind her was doing the same, but more slowly. She cursed again.

'Get a move on!' She slammed the palm of her hand on the horn.

The car's brake lights went on and a hand appeared from the driver's side. The man's gesture left no doubt as to his feelings. Making her pay for her impatience, the car drove off at a snail's pace, aware that there was no way she could overtake.

Helen caught her grandmother's head drop to her chest. She was falling asleep.

'Grandmama! Stay awake!' she shouted.

Again, Helen thumped her hand on the horn and flashed her lights.

This time, the car in front of her stopped and she watched as a mountain of a man squeezed himself out of the driver's side.

Helen opened her door. 'You idiot! I've got a seriously ill woman here. I need to get her to the hospital!'

The man took a minute to digest what he had just heard before quickly turning around and cramming himself back into the driver's seat. He immediately started up the engine and manoeuvred his car onto the pavement, enabling Helen to pass.

Driving to the end of the street and turning left, Helen stamped her foot on the accelerator. She could see that Henrietta had started to shake again. As she returned her attention to the road, she saw an old man shuffling across. Again, she slammed on her brakes. Her heart was thumping. After driving around the old man, she kept her focus on the road, but continued talking to her grandmother. Instinct told her that she needed to keep her awake.

Driving down the Durham Road, she saw the entrance lights of the Royal Infirmary. She hated the place. The last time she'd been there was when she'd had her miscarriage. Tears sprang to her eyes. She couldn't lose someone else she loved. Pulling up at the entrance, she jumped out and ran round to the passenger side.

'Grandmama, stay awake! We're here. At the hospital!' She guided her up the steps.

'Help!' she shouted out as soon as she was through the front door. 'I need help!' she shouted again. Looking about her, the place seemed deserted. For an insane moment she thought there'd been an air raid and everyone had gone to shelter.

'Hello!' she bellowed. She caught movement out of the corner of her eye and saw the face of the receptionist appearing through a little hatch-like window.

'If you can just take a seat,' the young girl said, wiping crumbs from the side of her mouth. Helen caught the sound of distant laughter.

'No, I can't take a seat!' Helen practically screamed. 'I need a doctor now!'

As if on cue, Helen felt Henrietta's hand grip her arm as she suddenly bent over and threw up on the shiny lino-leum floor.

The young girl's face disappeared just as Helen heard the screech of car brakes, the thuds of two doors closing and two sets of footsteps hurrying up the stone entrance. Helen turned around just as Dr Parker and Dr Eris came rushing into the main foyer.

'Oh, thank God!'

'What's happened?' Dr Parker said, immediately taking charge. He looked down at the vomit on the floor, checking it quickly for any signs of blood, and was relieved to see none.

'I don't know,' Helen said, her voice shaking. She looked to see Dr Eris charging over to a wheelchair that had been parked further down the corridor. 'She seemed unwell when I picked her up.'

'How long ago?' Dr Parker demanded.

'About an hour or so,' Helen said, watching as he gently held Henrietta's head in both his hands and inspected her.

'Henrietta.' He spoke sternly and loudly. 'What have you had to drink today?' His eyes flickered down at the floor. The vomit was milky white, with what looked like small bits of dark grit.

'Eggnog,' Henrietta slurred.

'Here.' Dr Eris arrived with the wheelchair, avoiding the mess on the floor. 'Let's get you sat down, Henrietta.' Her voice was calm.

Helen stood back as Henrietta sank into the chair.

Dr Parker started firing questions.

'What have you eaten today, Henrietta?'

'Biscuit,' she said, her eyelids drooping. 'Oatmeal.'

'Anything else?'

She shook her head. 'Not hungry.'

'I think she's lost weight,' Helen chipped in. 'I hadn't really noticed until today.'

'Have you been drinking anything, Henrietta? Alcohol?' Dr Parker asked.

Again, Henrietta shook her head.

'Not even in the eggnog?'

'Mother's taken to bringing her eggnog,' Helen butted in, 'but there's no rum or anything in it.'

Dr Parker felt Henrietta's brow. She was burning up. He then felt her stomach. He looked at Dr Eris. 'What medication is she on?'

Dr Eris suddenly looked nervous.

'Can you remember? Or do you need to ring the asylum to access her file?' Dr Parker demanded.

Helen thought of her mother's words – 'a fishbowl full of drugs'.

'Mmm ...' Dr Eris hesitated.

'Claire!' Dr Parker's sharpness made both Dr Eris and Helen jump.

'Do you need to get her file? We've not got much time. I need to know what she's been taking.'

'No, no, I don't need her file. I know what she's been taking,' Dr Eris said.

Dr Parker stared at her.

'What, then?' Now he wasn't even trying to keep the sharpness out of his voice. *Why was she being so vague?*

'What is it?' Helen said, touching Dr Eris's arm. 'What is it you don't want to tell us?'

Dr Eris took a deep breath. 'Henrietta's not on anything.'

'What do you mean?' Dr Parker demanded.

'I've been giving her placebos. Sugar pills. That's all.'

Dr Parker nodded. There was no time to ask her why. 'That's good. That's going to go in her favour. Give her liver more of a chance.'

He turned back to Henrietta.

'Stay with us, Henrietta. We're going to get you some help. But I need you to try to stay awake.'

Hearing movement from further down the corridor, Helen looked up to see a doctor and a nurse jogging towards them.

Dr Parker took the handles of the wheelchair.

'You two stay here,' he said, as he started pushing Henrietta down the corridor at speed.

Helen and Dr Eris stood watching as Dr Parker stopped to speak to the doctor and the nurse. Seconds later, they all disappeared around the corner.

The two women stood in silence for a moment.

'Do you think she's going to be all right?' Helen asked.

'I don't know,' Dr Eris said. 'But I do know Henrietta's in good hands. The best.'

265

Helen looked at her and saw how much respect she had for the man she was set on marrying.

'Come on, let's sit down,' said Dr Eris.

Helen nodded. She suddenly felt exhausted, as though she had been drained of every ounce of energy.

As they both walked over to the seats by the front door, Dr Eris glanced at Helen. She looked terrible. Pale, with mascara smudges around her eyes.

They were both quiet as they sat down. Both immersed in their own thoughts, the only intrusion the sound of a wireless playing 'Jingle Bells' coming from the reception-ist's hatch.

Helen looked around the hospital waiting area. For the first time, she noticed that there was a Christmas tree in the corner, a few straggles of tinsel and paper chains dangling from pictures hanging on the wall. 'Jingle Bells' ended and the jolly strands of 'We Wish You a Merry Christmas' started up.

'Why were you giving Grandmother sugar pills?' Helen asked suddenly.

Dr Eris knew the cat was out of the bag. She sighed and looked at Helen.

'Your grandfather came to the asylum a while ago. He explained to me that Henrietta was a distant relative who had fallen under his care.' As soon as Dr Eris started to speak about Mr Havelock, her tone changed. It was clear to Helen that she did not like the man.

'Obviously, I didn't tell him I knew that wasn't the case.' Dr Eris regarded Helen. 'I told him that I had just about weaned her off most of her medication.' She let out a sharp laugh. 'I was feeling so positive about Henrietta's progress. She'd been on some pretty heavy drugs – and treatment.' She paused, thinking of the electric-shock therapy. 'For years.'

Helen was listening intently. For the first time since getting to know Dr Eris, she realised that she was totally dedicated to the job she did. Claire might be a total cow when it came to her personal life, but in her professional life she was clearly a caring person.

As if reading her thoughts, Dr Eris said, 'I love my job, you know. And my patients.' She smiled sadly. 'Probably more than I do normal people.'

Helen looked at her nemesis. She'd just caught a glimpse of humanity in the woman she despised, and it shocked her.

'So, why the sugar pills?' Helen asked.

Dr Eris arched a perfectly plucked eyebrow.

'Your grandfather made it absolutely clear he was not at all happy that Henrietta was off her medication. He said if I didn't comply with his demands, I'd find myself out of a job and unable to get another anywhere else.'

'So you lied,' said Helen.

'I did,' said Dr Eris. She gave Helen a bleak look.

'If it comes out that I've been giving Henrietta sugar pills, I'll be struck off. And if I'm not struck off, I'm sure your grandfather will make good his threats.'

Helen nodded. 'That's guaranteed.' She gave Dr Eris a look that she hoped conveyed her sincerity. 'Thanks, Claire. Thanks for doing that for Grandmama.'

'She's a lovely woman,' Dr Eris said, her eyes pooled with sadness. 'I really hope she pulls through.'

'Me too,' said Helen. 'Me too.'

Chapter Thirty-Six

Dr Parker walked down the corridor, back towards the main entrance. His face was strained and deadly serious. Passing the door to one of the staff toilets, he stopped and went in. Splashing his face with cold water, he then raked his hair away from his face and walked back out. As he approached the main foyer, where he knew Helen and Dr Eris would be anxiously awaiting news, he took a deep breath.

As soon as Helen saw Dr Parker's strained face, she burst out crying.

'No, no, no!' she cried out. Tears started to stream down her face.

Dr Parker saw an all too familiar devastation, one he had seen many times in his work. *Too* many times. He glanced at Dr Eris, who was staring at him, her hazel eyes trying to read his. Walking over to Helen's side, he sat down next to her and took her hand.

'She's still with us,' he said simply.

Helen gripped his hand.

'Really?' she asked, needing to hear the words again.

'Really,' Dr Parker reassured her. 'But,' he added, taking Helen's other hand, 'it's going to be touch and go over the next twenty-four hours.'

Helen took a shuddering breath and tried to calm herself. *There was hope.*

'What's wrong with her?' she asked.

Dr Parker took a breath. 'At first, I thought it might be some kind of alcohol-induced poisoning, but it's clear Henrietta hasn't been drinking.'

'But she's got liver damage?' Dr Eris asked.

'She has,' said Dr Parker. 'We're just not sure exactly what the underlying cause is. It seems to have come on relatively quickly – I'd guess weeks rather than months. Which is why I think she's ingested some kind of poison – something toxic – but we're not sure what.'

Dr Parker looked at Helen and then at Dr Eris.

'And until we know what it is, we're at a loss to know how to treat her.'

After Dr Parker went back to tend to Henrietta and to continue his discussions with the doctor in charge of admissions about what could possibly be causing her body to shut down, Dr Eris called a taxi to take her back to Ryhope.

'Why don't you go home and rest and come back later?' she suggested to Helen. 'You can always call the hospital and see how she's doing.'

Helen shook her head. It was clear she was adamant. She wasn't going anywhere.

'As your grandmother's doctor,' Dr Eris said, 'I have a duty to call Henrietta's next of kin.' She paused. 'Your mother.'

Helen shot her a look. 'Please, can you hold off?' Her mother was the last person on earth Helen wanted here at the hospital with her. 'At least wait until you've got back to the asylum.' Helen looked down at her watch. 'Perhaps have a cup of tea first, before you ring her.' Helen knew that by then her mother would have left for the Grand.

Dr Eris nodded her understanding. She'd probably want to be left on her own too if she had a mother like Miriam.

269

After Dr Eris left, Helen sat staring at the pale green walls of the reception area, thinking. Her mind went over the past couple of weeks. Henrietta had been a little under the weather, but everyone she knew seemed to have colds or sniffles. And no one had much colour to them. But Henrietta wasn't pale, was she? She was jaundiced. *Why hadn't she noticed it sooner?* She tried to argue with herself that it was because of all that damned make-up her grandmother wore. *But still, she should have noticed her eyes.* Then again, she hadn't seen Henrietta for a week. *God, why had she cancelled her last visit?* She might have noticed her grandmother was unwell if she had gone to see her as planned.

Helen wanted to scream. Her mind kept going round and round and round.

Then a terrible thought occurred to her.

Had Henrietta poisoned herself?

She had admitted feeling that she was to blame for what her husband had done to those poor girls in her employ. To Pearl and Gracie – and to God only knew how many other young girls with blonde hair and blue eyes who'd had the misfortune of finding a job in the Havelock household.

Had Henrietta tried to kill herself because she could not bear the guilt any more?

Suddenly, Helen remembered the documents that Dr Eris had shown her back in June – the original admissions forms. There had been two. One with Henrietta's real name inscribed on it, the other had been a replacement, with her new, unmarried name of 'Girling'. But they had both had the same date written in the top right-hand corner. Helen had remembered it because she'd always thought what an awful thing to have happened during what was meant to be such a happy time of year. The date had been 26 December. Boxing Day.

Twenty-three years ago – almost to the day – Henrietta's life had changed for ever.

Had she decided to change it again? Or rather, to end it? To pay the ultimate price for a wrongdoing she wasn't guilty of?

Tears started to drip down Helen's face.

Hearing the door swish open and feeling the blast of cold air, she automatically turned round to see who was coming into the hospital.

Through blurred vision she saw Gloria and Rosie, then Polly, followed by Martha and Hannah. The door was just swinging shut when it was pushed open again by Dorothy and Angie.

'Helen, are yer all right?' Gloria asked, hurrying over. She plonked herself down on the next chair, put her arms around her and gave her a big hug.

Helen tried to say she was fine, but the words were lost in the well of tears that instantaneously erupted. She sobbed and sobbed into Gloria's denim overalls. When she came up for air, she looked around to see a semicircle of seven worried faces looking at her. She quickly wiped away her tears with the back of her hand.

'Here,' Dorothy said, passing her a handkerchief and a small compact.

'Thanks,' said Helen. She dabbed her eyes and checked herself in the small mirror. She looked dreadful, but at least she'd managed to get rid of the the dark circles under her eyes. She took a deep, shuddering breath.

'Did Kate call you?' Helen asked, her voice still thick with tears. She looked at the women who were sitting around her.

'She rang work,' Rosie said. 'Marie-Anne came and told us.'

Helen looked at the women – all still in their work clothes.

'Do they know what's the matter with her?' Martha asked.

Helen shook her head. 'No, not really.'

'Kate told Marie-Anne that she thought there was something wrong with her liver?' said Polly.

Helen nodded. 'Yes, but they're not sure what it is that's causing her liver to fail.' She looked at the women's faces, so full of concern – for Helen herself as much as for her grandmother.

'Oh, it's been awful,' she blurted out. 'Grandmama was shaking, her whole body trembling, and then she just threw up everywhere.' She nodded over to the foyer. 'She was like a rag doll – it was as though all her strength had just left her.'

'Poor Henrietta,' Dorothy said. 'I know we've not met her yet, but I think we all feel like we know her.' She looked around for confirmation and the women nodded.

'And we all know how much she means to you,' said Gloria.

Helen blinked back more tears. 'Thanks for coming.'

They were quiet for a moment.

'When will they know more?' Rosie asked.

'I'm not sure,' Helen said, taking another juddering breath. 'Dr Parker said it's still pretty much touch and go. He thinks she's been poisoned.'

'Poisoned?' Dorothy gasped.

'Really?' Polly was wide-eyed.

'What? On purpose?' asked Hannah.

'I don't know.' Helen swallowed more tears, thinking of how frail Henrietta had looked as she'd been taken away in the wheelchair.

'I wondered whether she might have poisoned herself,' she said quietly.

'Oh, I don't think so. I'm surprised you'd think that,' said Rosie. 'I really wouldn't have thought so – not from what

Kate's told me. She seemed really happy – excited about her new clothes, and about the Christmas Extravaganza.'

Gloria took Helen's hand. 'I agree – from what yer've told me yerself, that seems really unlikely.'

They were quiet for a moment.

'You don't think someone's tried to poison her on purpose, do you?' Dorothy whispered, even though there was no one else about.

'Honestly, Dor!' Angie exclaimed. 'Yer read too many of them books by that woman writer – what's her name?'

'Agatha Christie,' said Dorothy.

'I think Angie might be right there,' Polly agreed.

'Yeah, who would want to hurt Henrietta?' said Martha.

Again, they were quiet.

They all knew of one person who would benefit from her demise.

His name hung heavy in the air.

'I hate the man, but even I doubt he'd try and poison his own wife,' said Helen.

Hearing footsteps coming down the corridor, they all turned to see Dr Parker heading towards them. He smiled on seeing the women. The troops had rallied. He knew how much that would mean to Helen.

'Just a quick update,' he said, looking at his small audience, all staring expectantly at him.

'Henrietta is stable – for now, that is,' he said, his focus on Helen. She was staring back at him with those emerald eyes – eyes that were bloodshot and desperate to hear good news. He hated this part of the job – being torn between telling the truth and offering words of comfort.

'Her heart rate is a little irregular and her breathing laboured, which is a worry.' He looked at the women, who had all turned their attention to Helen. He saw Gloria squeeze her hand. 'She's got round-the-clock care. A nurse is by her bedside. I'm staying put to monitor her progress and to see if we can work out what it is that has caused this to happen.'

'Could it be something she might have ingested at the asylum?' Hannah asked.

Dr Parker looked at Hannah. If she had been one of his students, he would have praised her for her logical thinking.

'Good question,' he said. 'Dr Eris has just called to say she's checked with all the other doctors and the ward heads, but so far no one else is showing any signs of being ill – and certainly no one is presenting with the kinds of symptoms Henrietta has suffered.'

'So, you need to find the cause?' said Rosie.

'Exactly,' said Dr Parker.

'And if you don't?' Helen's voice was croaky.

Dr Parker was quiet. What could he say? Comfort over truth or truth over comfort?

'I don't know. I really don't know, Helen.' If her friends weren't here, he would have liked to hold her. 'I'm sorry. I don't want to give you any false hope.' He looked at his watch. 'Why don't I come back in about half an hour and I can take you to see her.'

Helen's face lit up.

'But it'll just be for a few minutes,' he said with a sad smile.

A solitary tear ran down Helen's cheek as she mouthed 'Thank you.'

When Dr Parker had gone, Angie stood up. 'I reckon yer need a nice cuppa,' she declared.

Helen forced a smile. She looked at Angie, still wearing her orange headscarf.

'I reckon we *all* need a nice cuppa,' Helen said, looking around at the women, who looked tired and pale, their noses red. She knew they'd been out in the cold most of the day. And now they were here – with her – when they could be home, having their tea and sitting in front of a roaring fire.

'Why don't we see if the canteen's open?' she said, standing up. The women followed suit and they all trooped off down the corridor.

'But Dor's banned from talking about the Christmas Extravaganza,' said Angie, making everyone chuckle.

They did, of course, talk about the Christmas Extravaganza – anything to keep Helen's mind off Henrietta. Dorothy and Angie assumed their roles as court jesters, and Hannah regaled them with descriptions of some of the lovely Jewish delicacies her aunty Rina was intending to make, though she would have to be inventive with them as nuts and apples were in short supply.

When they finished their tea and returned to the reception area, they found Bobby pacing about. On seeing him, Dorothy's heart leapt, as it always did, and for once she offered him a smile rather than a scowl. Bobby gave her a worried look, before turning his attention to Helen.

'How's Henrietta?' he asked. He had never seen Helen look so rough.

'We don't really know,' she answered.

'Time will tell,' Gloria interrupted. She looked at Helen and then back at the women. 'I'm gonna wait here with Helen until she's been able to see Henrietta. Yer all get yerselves off home.'

'You sure you're OK to stay?' Helen asked Gloria.

'I'm sure,' she said. There was clearly no arguing the point.

Helen was relieved. She really didn't want to be left on her own but would never have admitted it. She looked at the women, who were hauling their haversacks over their shoulders. 'Thank you – thank you for coming. All of you.'

They took it in turns to give Helen a hug.

'Tell Henrietta that she's got to pull through,' said Dorothy.

'Tell her we're all rooting for her,' said Martha.

'And praying for her too,' Hannah added.

'Come on,' Rosie said to the women. 'Let's go.' She handed Helen a piece of paper with two telephone numbers on it. One was for Lily's, the other for Brookside Gardens. 'It doesn't matter what time, just call if you need anything – even if it's just to chat.'

Helen took the piece of paper.

'Thank you,' she said, fighting hard to choke back more tears.

Within minutes of the women going, Dr Parker appeared.

'Is she all right?' Helen asked, her eyes pleading with him to say yes.

'She's hanging in there,' he said.

'Can I still see her?'

'Of course,' Dr Parker smiled. 'She's conscious, although she is sounding a little muddled.' He looked at Gloria and smiled at her too. He was glad she was there. 'Are you OK to wait here?' he asked her.

'You don't have to stay, you know,' Helen said. 'I'll be fine. Honest.'

'I'm not budging,' Gloria said. 'I'm going to sit here 'n enjoy the peace 'n quiet.'

Just then a drunk with a bloody gash on his forehead staggered into the main foyer, offering up a loud and robust rendition of 'Good King Wenceslas'. He was followed by two male nurses who guided him down the corridor towards the Emergency Department.

'Spoke too soon,' Gloria said, shaking her head. 'Go on.' She shooed them away. 'Be as long as yer want.'

Dr Parker and Helen hurried down the corridor.

'You might get a shock when you see her,' Dr Parker said. 'She looks very frail, but she's not in any pain.'

Helen took a deep breath as they reached the admissions ward.

Dr Parker opened the door and Helen walked in.

Henrietta was in the first bed on the left.

As soon as she saw her grandmother, Helen nearly burst out crying. She looked like she was at death's door. Before, Henrietta had always looked younger than her age; now, she looked like an old woman, so tiny and frail.

Hurrying over to the side of her bed, Helen pulled up a chair.

'Grandmama,' she said, taking Henrietta's hand. It felt so small, so bony, her skin paper-thin.

Henrietta's eyes opened and she turned her head to look at Helen.

Seeing who it was, a smile spread across her jaundiced face. Her eyes widened.

'Helen,' she whispered. 'You must be careful.'

Helen was confused. 'About what, Grandmama?'

'Calling me –' she dropped her voice so that it was almost inaudible '– *Grandmama*.'

Helen looked about the ward. There were only three other beds that were occupied. The patient on her grand-mother's side was two beds down and snoring loudly. The other two were on the opposite side of the ward. Both looked like they, too, were sleeping.

'Don't worry, Grandmama, I don't think there's a risk of anyone hearing us.' Helen gently brushed a strand of Henrietta's hair away from her eyes. It felt dry and brittle.

277

'How are you feeling?' she asked.

'Tired,' said Henrietta. 'So very tired.'

Helen felt her heart constrict. 'We're going to get you better, Grandmama. But we need to find out what it is that is making you ill.'

Henrietta looked at her granddaughter with soulful eyes. 'Perhaps it is just my time ... You mustn't be sad.'

Helen shuffled forward on her seat. 'No, it is *not* your time. You've got a lot longer. *A lot longer.*' She looked at her grandmother. The nurses had washed off all her make-up. She looked different without her rouged cheeks and her favourite cobalt blue eyeshadow. 'We just need to find out what's making you ill.' Helen took a breath. 'Is there anything you have eaten or drunk that might not have agreed with you?'

Henrietta shook her head. As she did so, her eyes caught sight of a strand of tinsel that was hanging from the nurse's desk.

'How I used to love Christmas,' she said, her words slurring a little. Her eyes started to close.

Helen panicked and looked over to Dr Parker, who was bent over, reading a file that had been laid out on top of the nurse's desk. He caught her waving him over. Striding across, he saw Helen's face was fraught with worry.

'She seems terribly tired?' Her tone spoke of her concern. *Henrietta was dying.*

Dr Parker walked round to the other side of the bed and checked her grandmother's pulse, put his stethoscope to her bony chest and listened to her heartbeat. Then he took her temperature.

'She's fine,' he said.

'For now,' he added, putting a comforting hand on Helen's shoulder.

'Oh, John ...' Helen said, putting her hand on top of his.

Suddenly, Henrietta's eyes opened.

'Ah, so *this* is John.' Henrietta's words were slightly slurred. *'Your doctor.'* She looked from Dr Parker to her granddaughter. *'Your love.'* Her voice was barely a whisper as her eyes closed again.

'What did she say?' Dr Parker said.

'I'm not sure,' Helen lied.

Henrietta's eyes fluttered open. This time they were focused on Helen. *'Den Lille Pige med Svovlstikkerne.'*

Dr Parker looked at Helen.

'It's Danish. "The Little Match Girl",' Helen explained. 'She's talking about Pearl.'

'Tell her I'm sorry.' Henrietta's eyes fluttered, struggling to remain open. Suddenly, she grabbed Helen's hand with surprising strength. 'And my little Gracie. Poor little Gracie. Tell her mother and father that I'm sorry. Their gorgeous little girl ...' Her voice trailed off. She was quiet for a moment, her eyes fighting to stay open.

Then her grip tightened again, and she looked at Helen. 'Promise me you'll tell them.'

Helen felt the panic rise again. 'You can tell them yourself, Grandmama. When you're better.'

As she spoke, Henrietta's eyes closed. Her breathing was regular, but seemed shallow.

Helen's head snapped up to look at Dr Parker.

'It's OK,' he reassured. 'She's just tired. She needs to rest.'

Helen bent over Henrietta, so that her mouth was by the side of her grandmother's head. 'I *need* you, Grandmama. Please get better. For me.' Helen saw a tear fall onto Henrietta's cheek and realised she was crying.

Henrietta didn't move. She had already dropped into a deep sleep.

*

As Dr Parker walked Helen back to the main foyer, he slowed down and then stopped.

'I think you have to prepare yourself, Helen,' he said gently. 'It pains me to have to say it.' He looked at her, expecting to see more hurt, but he was wrong. Instead, he found himself staring into a pair of angry green eyes.

'I won't *prepare myself*,' Helen said. 'Henrietta is *not* going to die. *You're* going to save her. *You're going to find what it is that's made her so ill and then you're going to make her better.*'

*

As Henrietta slipped in and out of consciousness, she kept thinking about her life. She knew she was dying. She wasn't afraid, though. Had she ever really wanted to live after what she had found out all those years ago on that awful Christmas Day?

Henrietta felt her body tremble. These sudden sporadic bursts of shaking, which felt as though they were coming from her very core, seemed to be happening with greater frequency.

Were they perhaps shaking her free from life? Untangling her? Setting her free?

As the shaking subsided, her body started to relax again and as it did so, she returned to that afternoon on Christmas Day all those years ago. To her previous life.

All those poor young girls.

And Gracie. Poor Gracie. She would have happily swapped her life for that of her little maid. *Why hadn't she come to her and told her?* She had been close to all her maids. Why hadn't they confided in her?

It hadn't been until this past year, when she had started to emerge from the fugue caused by the drugs, that she had started to think with more clarity. It had been like doing a jigsaw puzzle. And not a particularly pleasant one. Piece by piece, she had realised the awful truth. And how she had helped bring the lambs to the slaughter.

How stupid she had been, getting maids that looked like her daughters. Blonde and blue-eyed. She hadn't realised at the time. Had not possessed the insight into her own psyche to realise that she was employing young girls who looked like her daughters because she missed her girls. They had been sent away to boarding school and their going had left a hole in her heart. The young maids she had employed, she had come to realise, were replacements. Surrogates.

Henrietta opened her eyes.

So like her daughters.

Thank God, Miriam and Margaret *had* been sent away and had had as little contact with their father as possible. At least until they were old enough not to warrant his interest.

Henrietta felt a nurse by her side. She was putting a damp cloth on her forehead, but she didn't feel hot. Quite the reverse. She felt chilled to the bone.

Henrietta let out a deep sigh. It was such a long time ago. How old would Gracie have been now? Of course, she'd be roughly the same age as Miriam and Margaret.

Oh, Gracie, you could have had all that life. I'm so sorry.

Perhaps, if there really is a life hereafter, I'll get to tell you myself. Soon. Very soon.

Chapter Thirty-Seven

Mr Havelock had his ear pressed to the phone's receiver. The person on the other end was speaking quietly for fear of being overheard.

He mightn't have caught everything, but Mr Havelock had heard enough.

Without saying a word to his informer, he hung up.

A smile spread across his face.

At last! At long bloody last! He was nearly free.

Slowly, slowly, catchy monkey.

It had certainly been slow – but he was on the verge of catching that monkey. And not only catching but killing the damn thing into the bargain.

He leant forward and flicked open his box of cigars.

'Eddy!' he bellowed.

He snipped the end of his cigar and slowly lit it. By the time he was turning it around and puffing on it gently, the door opened.

'Yes, Mr Havelock?'

'Have we still got a bottle or two of champagne in the cellar?'

Eddy nodded. 'We have indeed, sir.'

'Well, bring it up and get it chilled,' Mr Havelock said. 'We may well have something to celebrate soon. Very soon.'

Eddy was in no doubt as to what it was they might soon be celebrating. His eyes flickered to the safe behind Mr Havelock.

Catching the look, Mr Havelock laughed loudly. 'Yes, don't worry, Eddy. We'll have a little bonfire too.'

Eddy nodded, knowing his face would be evidence of his relief.

'Very good, sir. I shall go down to the cellar now.'

Agatha's hunched figure stood immobile by the little side table next to the sofa in the front reception room. She had the receiver of the black Bakelite phone pressed firmly against her ear and she was earwigging in on the conversation the master was having with an unknown man who clearly did not want to be overheard as he was speaking quietly and furtively. Judging by the information he was relaying, she guessed he worked at the hospital and was probably ringing from there.

The phone on which Agatha was listening in to the conversation was rarely used, rather like the room she was in. Mr Havelock seemed to prefer to have visitors in his study, which she had always put down to the fact that he needed to feel in charge and superior at all times, even with his family and friends.

Hearing the words of the whispering man, Agatha felt a wave of nausea rise up and, fearing she might actually throw up, she covered the receiver and swallowed hard.

No, no, no! How had this happened! Her mind whirred. *She'd made sure she had only added enough to cause a bad bout of sickness – not enough to kill her.*

Hearing the click of the phone as it was hung up, Agatha waited a moment to make sure the line had gone dead before she gently rested the receiver back in its hold. Her hand was shaking. She could feel the trickle of cold sweat under her arms. *This was her fault.* If Henrietta died, she would be a murderer. She had been the one to prepare the poison, to add it to the eggnog and biscuits, knowingly giving them to Miriam to transport to her mother.

Poor Henrietta. She had never hurt anyone. She did not deserve this.

Straightening herself up, Agatha tiptoed to the door, which she had pulled ajar. She heard Mr Havelock shouting for Eddy, followed by hurried footsteps along the corridor and across the hallway. Agatha strained to hear what was being said – something about champagne.

My God – he was going to celebrate! The man was going to dance on his wife's grave before they'd even had a chance to bury her.

Well, Henrietta wasn't dead yet.

Agatha watched through the crack in the door as Eddy hurried back out, no doubt going to the cellar to do as he was told. As he always did.

Checking the coast was clear, she quietly pulled open the door a fraction and slipped out into the hallway. Breathing a sigh of relief that Eddy had shut the door to the study, she hurried over to the tallboy and grabbed her winter coat and handbag. Tiptoeing the short distance to the front door, she carefully pulled the door handle down and as quietly as possible opened it just enough to squeeze through before shutting it without making a sound.

As she hurried down the stone steps, she was glad of the darkness and that all the curtains in the house had been drawn, in particular the ones in the study. She was sure no one would have seen her leave.

Turning right at the end of the gravelled driveway, Agatha pulled on her coat, hooked her handbag over her shoulder and hurried as fast as she could along The Cedars towards the Ryhope Road. She had no idea what she was going to do – only that she had to do *something*.

Chapter Thirty-Eight

Agatha didn't think she'd ever felt so desperate in her life. She'd believed she had dealt with the situation, had scuppered Mr Havelock's murderous intentions. Now, after hearing what she had over the phone, the bottom had fallen out of her world. Sucking in air as she hurried past Christ Church, she put her hand to her chest; the freezing cold was making her lungs feel on fire. Hurrying along the Ryhope Road, she berated herself over and over again. She gave up looking over her shoulder for a bus and resigned herself to half walking, half jogging all the way. She forced herself to stop obsessing about the prospect of Henrietta dying, and instead focus on what she could possibly do to save her former mistress.

It took her half an hour to reach her destination, by which time she had come up with an idea. It was a long shot, but it might – just might – work.

Walking up the Durham Road, she had her eyes peeled. Her heart leapt when she spotted a young lad kicking up snow and looking like he didn't have a home to go to, which, judging by his clothes, might have been true.

'Here!' Agatha called over to him. The boy looked up at her. His face was dirty and his eyes suspicious. 'Do you want to earn a few shillings?' she asked. The boy's suspicion was immediately replaced by shocked surprise and he ran over.

After explaining what he had to do, the unlikely pair waited at the bus stop across the road from the entrance to the Royal Infirmary for what felt like an age, but which, in reality, was only a few minutes. Agatha was frozen through to the bone – not that she cared. She looked down at her scruffy little street urchin jumping from one foot to the other to keep himself warm.

'Is that her?' he asked for the umpteenth time when a man and a woman walked out of the main entrance.

Agatha thanked her lucky stars that the blackout was now a dim-out and the street lights were affording a modicum of light – enough for her to see whether or not it was Helen coming out of the building.

'No,' Agatha said, looking behind the couple to see if anyone else was on their way out. If Helen didn't make an appearance soon, she was going to have to send the boy in there, but she preferred to get her note directly to Mr Havelock's granddaughter.

Agatha looked anxiously at her watch. When she looked up again, her heart leapt. There was a gaggle of women, all dressed in overalls, coming out. She'd heard about Helen's group of friends who were shipyard workers. Mr Havelock had mocked them enough and sneered that Helen couldn't find any friends of her own class and was having to slum it with the 'hoi polloi'.

Agatha scrutinised the women. *This had to be them.* Seeing a particularly large woman with a shorter girl who was speaking with a European accent convinced her. She'd heard talk that one of the women was a young Czechoslovakian refugee who worked as a draughtsman, while another was as tall and as strong as most of the men at the yard, if not more so. She watched as they said their goodbyes and hurried off in different directions – the piercing cold hastening their departure. Only one of the women was left chatting to her fella. They were both loitering on the steps, as though undecided as to what to do.

'Go!' Agatha grabbed the young boy's arm and pointed to the young couple. 'Give the note to that woman there.' Agatha pressed two shillings into his hand. She'd held back giving him the money for fear he might run off without doing what he was being paid to do.

Seeing the shiny coins, the young boy's face lit up.

'Now!' Agatha urged. She gave the young boy a slight push and he was off, half skidding, half sprinting across the road.

Bobby and Dorothy were standing on the top step of the entrance to the Royal. Angie and Polly had just jumped on a bus headed for the east end. Angie was to collect Hope from Agnes's. She would take her back home and tell Jack that Gloria was staying with Helen at the hospital. Hannah and Martha had trudged off up the road to catch a bus headed for Villette Road, and Rosie had already jogged off in the direction of Brookside Gardens. It was freezing cold, which gave Bobby the excuse to wrap his arms around Dorothy and hold her close.

'I hope Henrietta's going to be all right,' Dorothy said.

'Me too, but it doesn't look good,' said Bobby.

'Helen's going to be devastated if anything happens to her,' said Dorothy.

'I agree,' said Bobby. 'Whenever she's around the flat she's always chatting about her and telling Hope about her.'

Bobby kissed Dorothy quickly on the lips. 'Come on, let's go somewhere,' he said, breathing in the cold air, heavy with the smell of burning coal from the nearby houses.

'It doesn't feel right going out and enjoying ourselves while Henrietta's life is hanging in the balance,' Dorothy argued.

'Well, from what Helen's told me about Henrietta, she'd be all for us going out and enjoying ourselves. It beats going home and you and Angie moping about all evening,' Bobby countered.

'*When* she gets off the phone to Quentin, that is,' Dorothy added.

'Exactly,' said Bobby, 'so we might as well spend a few hours together, doing something nice – even if it's just going for a walk.'

Dorothy looked down at her dirty overalls. 'I think a walk might be the only possibility. I can't see me getting through the door anywhere half decent.'

Bobby laughed. 'Well, that'd be their loss.'

'It's a bit cold for a walk, though,' Dorothy pointed out. She was enjoying the feel of Bobby's arms around her – she always did – but at this moment in time it was the heat of his body she was relishing the most.

Just then, she felt someone tug at her sleeve.

'Sorry, miss!' The young boy looked up at Dorothy, his big blue eyes bloodshot with tiredness and cold.

'I've been told to give yer this,' he said, pulling the note from his trouser pocket and holding it aloft.

Dorothy glanced at Bobby, who returned her puzzled look.

'Who told you to do that?' Bobby asked.

The young boy turned around and looked across the road, but the old woman had gone.

'Some auld man.' He repeated what he'd been told to say. 'He was there – just a minute ago – honest.' He eyed the couple. 'He said yer might give us a tip for being a messenger boy?'

Bobby dug some coins out of his pocket. The boy beamed, took the money and sped off down the street before any more questions were asked.

'What does it say?' Bobby asked.

Dorothy looked at the scrappy piece of paper that had been folded over twice and opened it.

A sharp intake of breath followed.

'Oh my God!' she said. 'Look!' She handed the note to Bobby, who looked equally shocked.

'Shall we go and tell Helen?' Dorothy asked, panicked.

'No, it'll waste time – let's just go there,' Bobby said.

Seeing the lights of a tram heading into town, they both ran to catch it.

Jumping on board, they paid their fare and sat down on the leather seats. Dorothy unfolded the note and held it out in front of her.

'So, someone has *purposely* tried to poison Henrietta. It's not been some kind of mishap,' Bobby said.

'Definitely,' Dorothy concurred.

'"Look in the Winter Gardens for the reason Miss Girling is ill,"' she read. 'It looks like an old person's writing. Who do you think wrote it?'

Bobby shook his head. 'I've no idea, but let's worry about that later. What we've got to do now – and quickly – is work out what's in the Winter Gardens that is making Henrietta ill.'

'There's loads of plants there – it could be anything,' Dorothy said. She had been to the Winter Gardens many times over the years – when she was a child, then with Toby, and, more recently, with Bobby. She was quiet, her mind desperately trying to recall any of the plants she'd seen there.

Seeing they were almost at their stop, Bobby stood up. 'Let's just get there – we'll get more of an idea when we're able to have a good look around. We've got a bit of time before it shuts.'

Dorothy looked at Bobby. 'What if we can't find it?'

Her face suddenly hardened.

'Why didn't whoever wrote this note just put what it was?'

The bus came to a halt, the doors opened and they both jumped out.

'Perhaps the writer of the note was frightened it would give them away,' Bobby said, as they both ran across the Burdon Road and towards the museum. Taking the steps two at time, they hurried through the main entrance and into the grand hallway, where workers were decorating a tall, rather skinny-looking Christmas tree that had been positioned next to Wallace the lion, who was also joining in the festive spirit and wearing a garland of tinsel around his neck.

As they walked down the corridor and through the entrance to the Winter Gardens, they were immediately immersed in the clammy atmosphere and the smells of foreign lands. Dorothy stopped and turned to Bobby with a look of enlightenment on her face.

'Of course! Why didn't we think of it before? The *beautiful but deadly* section!' she said, wide-eyed. 'Beautiful but deadly' was their nickname for the part of the botanical gardens where the poisonous plants were kept.

'Of course!' Bobby said, taking her hand and marching down a small pathway that led them past a few palm trees and rubber plants to a section signposted 'The Toxic Plants Garden'.

Dorothy looked around at the array of pretty but potentially deadly vegetation.

'Just read the signs that tell you about the actual plant. Whoever gave us that note wanted us to find it – it must be something quite obvious,' Bobby said.

Dorothy started reading the first placard she came to. 'It's all in Latin,' she moaned, moving on to the next exhibit.

Bobby went down on his haunches to get to a brass plate that was just a few feet off the ground, moving aside a large shiny leaf in order to be able to read the information.

Seeing a plant they had noticed before when they'd visited previously, Dorothy went over to it. It had been in bloom when they had seen it and she had remembered saying to Bobby that she couldn't believe something so pretty could be so poisonous. Looking at it now, it just looked like a normal green shrub – gone were all its pretty white flowers. The placard, which before had been hidden by the large flowering heads, was now visible.

She started to read it:

'"*Ageratina altissima*. Also known as white snakeroot. Grows in the rich, moist soil of woods, thickets and woodland borders and is found throughout Kentucky, Indiana, Illinois and western Ohio."'

She suddenly took in a deep breath.

'Bobby! Come here!' She waved her arm behind her, keeping her eyes firmly on the information she was reading.

'Listen to this,' she said, feeling his presence next to her.

'"This is the plant that was responsible for the death of Nancy Lincoln – Abraham Lincoln's mother."'

'Really?' Bobby said. 'What, someone tried to poison her too?'

Dorothy turned back and continued to read, skimming through the descriptions of it being a shade-loving plant, its average height and when it came into bloom.

'Here we are!' Her voice went higher, and a couple nearby looked over in their direction.

'"In 1818, Lincoln's mother became desperately ill after caring for some neighbours who were sick. Two weeks later, Nancy Hanks Lincoln died of milk sickness."'

She continued reading as Bobby listened intently.

'"Milk sickness is poisoning by milk from cows that have eaten the white snakeroot plant ... Back then, cattle would wander off from poor pasturelands to wooded areas in search of food and end up eating the poisonous plant."'

Dorothy paused.

'"The illness has been called puking fever, sick stomach and the trembles because of how it affects an animal – *or a person*."'

She looked at Bobby with wide eyes.

'Those are exactly the symptoms Helen described Henrietta as having – she said the shaking and the body tremors were just awful.'

Bobby turned his head slightly and caught sight of a bronze plaque half hidden by some overhanging green foliage. He moved the leaves aside and read the engraved inscription.

'"Donated by North-East Shipping Co. Sales Negotiator & Philanthropist, Mr Charles Havelock, of Sunderland, County Durham."'

Dorothy stared at him. 'Oh. My. God!'

'Come on,' Bobby said, grabbing her hand. 'Let's go.'

Reaching the foyer, Bobby flung open the door.

As he did so, they were both hit by a blast of freezing cold air.

Seeing a taxi, they sprinted towards it.

'The Royal,' Dorothy told the driver breathlessly, 'as fast as you can, please.'

Bobby jumped in next to her.

'Go!' Dorothy tried to stop herself sounding hysterical, but did not succeed.

Chapter Thirty-Nine

Helen sat next to her grandmother's bed. She had forced Gloria to go home but had coaxed Dr Parker and the ward nurse into letting her stay. Henrietta had just had another unnatural tremor and Helen had taken hold of her hand to try and soothe her – to make it go away.

Make it all go away.

She felt angry. Desperate. She and her grandmother should be getting excited about her new outfit, about the Christmas Extravaganza – about her coming to live back home. She was on the cusp of so many good things – and now this had happened. Although what 'this' was, she didn't know. And more worryingly, neither did John, who was presently holed up in one of the consulting rooms with his head in a load of textbooks, desperately trying to find a possible answer. She felt awful for being so sharp with him earlier, but she couldn't give up – and she couldn't have him give up, either.

'Grandmama,' she whispered to Henrietta, 'I want you to know that I won't let you die. And I won't let you give up.' She moved nearer to the bed. 'Because something tells me you might … But I'm telling you now that you can't.' She looked around and checked no one could hear her words. They were for her grandmother's ears only. The three other patients in the ward were still sleeping.

'I know what you think,' she said. 'You think you're to blame for those poor girls and what happened to them. But you're not, Grandmama. You're not. Like Kate said that

293

day, there's only one person to blame for what happened back then and it's most certainly not you.' Helen could feel the anger rising. She took a deep breath and tried to calm herself. 'So, if you have a shadow of a doubt about that, I want you to shoo it away. And then I want you to use all your strength to beat whatever it is that has got a grip of you.'

Helen swallowed hard, forcing back the tears.

'I know it sounds selfish, Grandmama, but you've *got* to pull through. *For me.* You can't leave me now – not when I've just found you.' She reached over with her other hand and gently touched Henrietta's cheek. 'It's not on, you hear me – it's just not on.' As she spoke, tears started to trickle down her face. She thought of the last time she had been in this hospital. She had lost her unborn child. A baby that might have only been four months in the making, but whom she had loved more than anything else in the world. Now here she was in this damned hospital once again – and it was looking ever more likely that she was again going to lose someone she loved.

So immersed was Helen in her one-way conversation with Henrietta that she didn't hear the ward doors swing open, nor a soft muttering of voices. It was only when she caught sight of the nurse walking towards her that she looked up and saw an anxious-looking Dorothy and Bobby standing by the entrance. She wiped away the tears from her face.

'Miss Crawford,' the nurse said, 'there's a man and a woman here to see you. I can't have anyone else in the ward. Not outside of visiting times. I'm breaking the rules allowing you to be here.' Her words were spoken with empathy rather than as a reprimand.

Helen got up and walked over to them. All three went out into the corridor.

'Henrietta's been poisoned,' Dorothy said straight away. There was no time to lose. 'By a plant!'

'I don't understand,' said Helen, looking at Dorothy and Bobby. They were both out of breath and flushed. 'Why would Grandmama eat a plant?' she asked them. For a horrible moment, she had an image of Henrietta finding some poisonous plant and eating it to assuage her guilt. To punish herself.

Bobby shook his head. 'We don't think your grandmother knew she was being poisoned.'

Helen looked at them both. The penny finally dropping. 'You think someone else tried to poison her?'

Bobby and Dorothy nodded. Their faces grim.

'But what's really important,' Bobby continued, not wanting to distract Helen by pointing the finger of blame, 'is that we're pretty sure we know what it is that's causing Henrietta to be so ill.'

'A young boy gave us a note – a clue – saying to go to the Winter Gardens,' Dorothy blurted out. 'That whatever was making Henrietta ill was there.' Dorothy felt as if the words in her head were tripping over themselves to get out. 'We've just seen a plant in there – we were in the beautiful but deadly section. It's one that cows eat and it causes their milk to be poisonous.'

Helen looked from Dorothy to Bobby. 'A note?' she asked, confused. 'The Winter Gardens?'

'We can explain all that later,' Bobby said. *How could you tell someone that it looked highly likely that their grandfather had tried to kill their grandmother?* 'But what you need to know now is that we're pretty sure we know what's making your grandma so ill.' He looked around nervously to check that no one could overhear their conversation.

'Abraham Lincoln's wife – I mean, mum – died of it,' Dorothy butted in.

Helen looked at Dorothy. Now she was speaking gobble-degook. *What did Abraham Lincoln's mother have to do with all of this?*

'It causes the exact same symptoms Henrietta is suffering from,' Dorothy said.

Helen realised her grandmother was being offered a life-line. It might be tenuous, but she was going to grab it for all it was worth.

'Come on, talk to me as we walk. We're going to see John,' she said, as she started marching down the corridor.

Chapter Forty

'Tell John what you were telling me,' Helen said, her eyes darting from Bobby to Dorothy and then to the man she loved – the man who was her only hope for saving her grandmother.

Bobby briefly explained how they had been given a note by a young boy telling them to look in the Winter Gardens to find out what was causing Henrietta to be so ill.

'We think Henrietta has been poisoned by white snakeroot and that she has something called "milk poisoning",' Bobby said, his military training kicking in as he kept his emotions in check and relayed the necessary information as clearly and as succinctly as possible.

Dr Parker's eyes lit up. 'Yes, I've heard of it.' He put his fingers on his forehead and pressed hard. 'Dates way back to the early 1800s ... they think it was what killed Abraham Lincoln's mother.'

'That's the one!' Dorothy's voice was shrill. 'That's what the placard said.'

Dr Parker looked up, puzzled.

'The one in the Winter Gardens,' Bobby explained. 'It's called white snakeroot.'

'It has a Latin name,' Dorothy chipped in.

'The plant contains a natural toxic alcohol called tremetol,' Dr Parker said, starting to feel the beginnings of hope. 'It easily passes into the milk, which was how people at that time were exposed to it. Became quite an epidemic, if my memory serves me correctly.' Dr Parker could feel a surge of adrenaline. Everything was starting to click into place. Getting up, he began pulling out books from the shelves behind him. He dumped one the size of a Bible on his desk.

'Farmers used to notice their cattle becoming listless and unsteady on their feet,' he remembered as he ran his finger down the index and flicked the book open. 'The most noticeable sign was trembling,' he paraphrased as he read. 'And there was often an odour on the breath of the animals feeding on the plant.'

Helen's hand shot to her mouth. 'A chemical smell.'

Dr Parker looked up. 'Exactly. Like acetone. It's caused by the acids in the liver.'

He looked back down at the page and read: '"Weakness, vomiting, abdominal pains, muscle stiffness and eventually tremors, respiratory distress ... "' His voice trailed off. The paragraph he was reading went on to explain that death from milk sickness was agonising. If a surgeon had been able to do a post-mortem on Abraham Lincoln's mother, they would have likely noted inflammation of the gastrointestinal tract, enlarged liver and kidneys and swelling of her heart.

'Do you think you can save her?' Helen implored.

Dr Parker looked up at Helen, Dorothy and Bobby.

'I'm going to give it my damnedest,' he said, getting up. 'I need you to go and sit with Henrietta. Take it in turns. Just try and keep her awake.'

So focused was he on saving Henrietta, he never thought of how she might have come to ingest a plant presently growing in the town's botanical gardens. That would come later.

As soon as Helen, Dorothy and Bobby were out of the door, Dr Parker had his head back in the directory. It only took him a few minutes to find the doctor he wanted – a specialist in toxicology. He looked at his watch. Snatching up the phone, he called the number listed and left an urgent message asking for him to call back.

His next call was to Dr Eris. She had agreed to stay in her office at the asylum so that she could be instantly contactable.

'Claire, I need you to find out whatever you can about "milk sickness",' he said as soon as she picked up the receiver. 'It was prevalent in the early eighteen hundreds in North America. There must have been some research done on it at the time. Some attempt to find an antidote.'

'Leave it with me,' Dr Eris said, thankful to do something to help. 'I'll ring as soon as I've found something.' She was already on her feet as she hung up. Thankfully, the asylum had a library with an extensive medical section.

'I'm going straight back to sit with Henrietta,' Helen said as she hurried back towards the ward with Dorothy and Bobby.

'We'll go and get you a cuppa from the canteen,' Dorothy said. 'Then we can take it in turns to sit and talk to her. She'll never fall asleep with me gabbing in her ear.'

Helen turned to go into the ward, but stopped and turned back.

'Thank you. Both of you,' she said, her eyes glistening with hope.

Bobby and Dorothy watched as she disappeared through the ward's swing doors.

'I think "thank you" might be a little premature,' Bobby said as they walked on, turning right and heading towards the cafeteria.

'I know,' Dorothy agreed. 'I caught a glimpse of Henrietta when we turned up and she did not look in a good way.'

'Let's just hope,' Bobby said, opening the canteen door for Dorothy, 'that Dr Parker can find a cure.'

'O Come, All Ye Faithful' was playing when they entered the dining room.

'Goodness,' Dorothy said, putting her hand on her chest, 'I almost forgot it was Christmas.'

After Bobby had ordered two teas and a couple of mince pies, he looked at Dorothy.

'You know, this is serious stuff.' He dropped his voice. 'There's really only one culprit who could have done this to Helen's grandmother.'

'Do you really think it's him?' Dorothy whispered. 'That he's tried to poison Henrietta – *to kill her*?' Dorothy looked around to make sure no one was eavesdropping on their conversation.

'I can't see anyone else having any reason for wanting to get rid of Henrietta – can you?' Bobby speculated.

The old woman behind the counter put two cups of tea and two small plates each with a mince pie onto the counter. Dorothy put them onto the tray as Bobby paid.

'I agree,' Dorothy said as Bobby picked up the tray and they walked back out of the cafeteria.

Reaching the ward, Dorothy opened the door and Bobby carried the tea tray in.

'We thought you might also need a little pick-me-up,' Bobby said to the ward nurse.

Dorothy watched her face light up, which she thought had more to do with the good-looking bloke holding the tray, rather than the tepid tea and slightly stale mince pie he'd brought her.

'Thank you. That's kind. Just leave it here,' the nurse said, making room on her desk.

'Will you tell Miss Crawford that we're coming back in half an hour and my girlfriend here – ' he glanced back at

Dorothy still holding the door open ' – is going to sit with Miss Girling.'

Dorothy scowled at Bobby as they walked back to the canteen.

He let out a laugh. 'I love it when you're jealous.'

'Good job you made it plain I was your girlfriend,' Dorothy said.

Bobby mimed wiping his forehead. 'Close call. Disaster averted.'

They walked into the canteen and ordered a pot of tea and sandwiches.

'On a more serious note, though,' Dorothy said as they sat down. 'If it's proved that it is "milk sickness" that's caused Henrietta to fall ill, Helen's grandfather is going to look a likely suspect. Like you said, who else would want to see Henrietta dead?'

'I know,' Bobby said. 'And he *is* the one to have brought the plant into the country. I can't see anyone else having travelled to North America, never mind growing and cultivating a poisonous plant.'

'And who was it that got the note to us?' Dorothy mused.

'Someone involved who didn't want to be involved?' Bobby speculated.

'Someone who doesn't want Henrietta's death on their conscience,' Dorothy said.

'Someone close to Mr Havelock,' Bobby added.

They were quiet for a moment.

'Why doesn't it surprise me,' Dorothy mused, 'that such a poisonous man liked to bring poisonous plants back to England to flourish. And I reckon he didn't give all the plants to the Winter Gardens. I'll bet my bottom dollar he saved a few for himself.'

'That would make sense,' Bobby agreed. 'The Winter Gardens is really just a huge greenhouse. There's no reason he couldn't cultivate them himself – or get a gardener to do it.'

They were quiet while the woman from behind the counter brought them their tea and sandwiches. They both thanked her. Dorothy poured. She felt parched. And starving. She hadn't had anything to eat or drink since lunchtime. She was sure Bobby hadn't either.

Bobby took his cup, blew on it and took a big slurp. 'I guess it would be proving it.' He put his teacup back on the saucer. 'Just because he brought a few seedlings back to England years ago and donated them to the Winter Gardens, it doesn't mean he's responsible. It could be argued that someone might have taken some. You saw there's no real barrier there – just a length of rope.

'But the main problem,' Bobby said, picking up a sandwich, 'is that Charles Havelock is a very rich, very well-connected man. There's no way, even if all the evidence pointed to it being him, that he would get his collar pulled. No way.'

Chapter Forty-One

Half an hour later, the phone rang. Dr Parker snatched the receiver from the cradle.

'Hi, John, it's me,' Dr Eris said, her tone deathly serious.

'Hi, Claire.' Dr Parker grabbed his notebook and pen, jamming the receiver between his ear and shoulder. 'Give me everything you've got.'

'Well, you were right about the symptoms, but I have to add that the article I came across mentioned the possibility of the patient falling into a coma.'

'That was my fear – go on,' he urged.

'The best – and only – treatment, it would appear, is something called Ringer's lactate solution,' Dr Eris said. 'Also known as sodium lactate solution – a mixture of sodium chloride, sodium lactate, potassium chloride and calcium chloride in water.'

'Of course,' Dr Parker said, slapping his head. 'It makes sense.' He drew breath. 'It's used to treat metabolic acidosis.'

'A disruption of the body's acid balance,' Dr Eris summarised. Although she was a psychologist, she still had a basic understanding of medicine and human biology.

'Exactly. Let's hope the pharmacy holds some.' Dr Parker was already scrabbling around for the internal phone directory.

'If not, call me straight back and I can ring round all the nearby hospitals,' Dr Eris said. 'You're going to have to act quickly, though. It says here that milk sickness, if left untreated, can cause death within two to ten days of the onset of symptoms.'

'When did you first notice Henrietta becoming unwell?' Dr Parker asked.

'It's hard to say ... I've been thinking.' Dr Eris paused. 'To be honest, she's seemed tired for a little while now.'

Dr Parker could hear pages being flipped over.

'I'm just looking at my diary. I saw her on ...' There was a pause. 'It was exactly a week ago. That's when I thought she wasn't quite herself. I just put it down to a cold. The weather. Not getting enough fresh air. That kind of thing.'

Dr Parker could hear the guilt in her voice.

'This isn't your fault, Claire. I'll ring you back if I need anything else. Is that OK? You don't mind staying there?'

'Of course I'll be here. I'm not going anywhere.'

'Thanks, Claire,' Dr Parker said, relieved.

Dr Eris was just about to tell him 'I love you' but he hung up before the words were out. As she listened to dead air, she realised that telling John she loved him might not have been a first, but it would have been the first time she'd said it and really meant it.

Dr Parker pressed the hook and then let it go, immediately ringing down to the pharmacy in the basement. His heart was hammering. *Please let them have what he needed.* If Claire *did* have to ring round all the local hospitals, it was going to take time – time they didn't have. Time Henrietta certainly didn't have.

The line rang three times. Then, finally:

'Hello, Pharmacy. Mrs Boyle speaking.' The voice sounded middle-aged and middle class.

'Hello, Dr Parker speaking. I need you to see if you've got any Ringer's lactate solution in stock.'

'Sorry, did you say "Dr Parker"?' There was a snootiness to her voice.

'Yes.'

'I don't believe,' the pharmacist said, pausing as she flicked open her file and scanned the list of medical staff employed by the hospital, 'I have you down here as one of the hospital doctors.'

'That's because I'm not.' Dr Parker was curt. 'I'm from the Ryhope.' A quick intake of breath. 'I'm sorry, Mrs Boyle, but this is a matter of life and death. I really need to know if you have that solution now. Can you check for me, please? As in *now*. This very minute.' It wasn't often Dr Parker pulled rank, but this was one of those times.

'Yes,' the pharmacist said, quickly climbing off her high horse, 'I'll have a look and call you back. What extension are you on?'

'No, you won't. I'll wait.'

Dr Parker heard the clunk of the receiver as it was put down. He could hear footsteps quickly walking away from the phone. It seemed like an age before he heard the footsteps returning.

He crossed his fingers.

'You're in luck, Dr Parker.'

That was all he needed to hear. He immediately hung up and sped out of the office.

It took Dr Parker five minutes to run down to the pharmacy. He was greeted by a sour-faced Mrs Boyle, who handed him a pen to sign for the Ringer's solution. He grabbed the plastic container and sped back up to the ward.

As soon as he saw Helen's face and the back of the nurse as she tended to Henrietta, he knew something was wrong. Seriously wrong.

He strode over.

'What's happened?'

'She's unresponsive,' the nurse said, giving Dr Parker a worried look.

'She was fine,' Helen said. 'Then she just seemed to nod off and I couldn't wake her up.'

'Let me just check her vitals,' Dr Parker said, handing the bottle to the nurse and manoeuvring himself around the bed.

Helen watched as Dr Parker carried out all the usual checks. During it all, Henrietta didn't move a muscle.

Dr Parker stood up straight and looked at the nurse. 'We're going to give Miss Girling intravenous therapy.'

Helen caught the look on the nurse's face.

'I … I …' the nurse stuttered.

'I know,' Dr Parker reassured her, 'it's unlikely you've done this before. Don't worry – I have. I just need you to get me the necessary equipment …' his gaze dropped down to her name tag '… Nurse Rodgers.'

He turned to Helen.

'I'm sorry, I'm going to have to ask you to leave, Helen. I'll come and give you an update as soon as I can.' He wanted to add that everything would be all right, but couldn't. It wouldn't be fair.

Helen leant across Henrietta and kissed her quickly on the cheek.

'Hang in there, Grandmama. I love you.'

Choking back a well of tears, she took one last look at Henrietta and left.

Helen had been pacing around the waiting area for over half an hour. She had just persuaded Dorothy and Bobby to go home. Hearing footsteps down the corridor, she looked up to see Dr Parker hurrying towards her.

'How is she?' Helen asked, wringing her hands.

306

'It's hard to tell,' Dr Parker said, taking her hands and holding them. He sat down on one of the cushioned chairs, forcing Helen to do likewise.

'The toxins in Henrietta's system have built up to such an extent that her body has started to shut down.'

Helen felt the sting of tears.

'Is she going to wake up?' she asked.

'I'll be honest with you, Helen, I really don't know … Only time will tell,' Dr Parker said, still holding her hands. 'She's having what is known medically as intravenous therapy. This basically means that the solution which could possibly even out the imbalance caused by the poison in your grandmother's body is being administered straight into Henrietta's veins.'

Helen nodded. 'I understand. *Intra* meaning "in", and *venous* meaning "veins".'

'Precisely,' Dr Parker said.

Helen was listening intently.

'It might be too late; it might not,' he said. 'But I think you have to brace yourself for the worst.'

'Can I sit with her?' Helen asked.

'Yes, of course you can,' Dr Parker said. 'But when you get tired, go home. I'll ring you if there's any change.'

Helen smiled sadly at Dr Parker. 'Thanks, but that won't be necessary. I won't be going home. I'm staying with her.'

Dr Parker looked at Helen and knew there'd be no changing her mind.

Chapter Forty-Two

The next morning, Helen woke to find Dr Parker's jacket draped over her. For the briefest of moments, she thought he was there, lying next to her, for she could smell his scent, so distinct, *so John*. And then she opened her eyes and reality hit her hard. She turned her head and saw Henrietta lying in her bed. She looked so peaceful. *Too peaceful.*

Panic set in.

'Grandmama! Grandmama!' She reached over and touched her cheek. It felt cold.

She turned to the nurse, who was hurrying over, having seen her wake and become distressed.

Helen's eyes pooled with tears.

'I think she's dead!' She started to cry.

The nurse immediately reached for Henrietta's wrist to feel for a pulse, her head bobbing down to her patient's chest to listen for a heartbeat.

Tears were now trickling down Helen's face.

'Please, no, no, no, don't die on me,' she whispered through the tears.

The nurse lifted her head from Henrietta's chest.

'Miss Girling, can you hear me?' she said, her voice loud in the quietness of the early morning.

Helen could barely see through the tears.

The worst was happening.

Her grandmother had given up. *No, she'd been killed.* A slow death from the moment that evil man had had her sectioned – until a final sudden, sharp push at the end. Anger

suddenly burst through Helen's grief. *He had poisoned Hen-*
rietta. She was sure of it. She'd had plenty of time to think
whilst sitting there, keeping a vigil at her grandmother's
bedside. Bobby and Dorothy had tried to remain impassive
when they had mentioned that the plant had been donated
to the Winter Gardens by her grandfather, but it was glar-
ingly obvious that he was the culprit. *This was his doing.*

Helen watched as the nurse straightened up, took out
her pocket torch and again bent over Henrietta. Gently
pulling her lids down, she shone a beam of light into Henrietta's eyes.

Helen took her grandmother's cold, porcelain-white
hand, raised it to her mouth and kissed it.

'Oh, Grandmama.' She kissed it again. This time she
could feel salty tears on her lips as they dribbled down her
face.

And then she felt Henrietta's hand move.

Or was it her imagination?

Helen looked at her grandmother's still face and gently
squeezed her hand again.

And then she felt it again – only this time it was stronger.

'Grandmama!' Helen called out, looking at Henrietta
and then up to the nurse.

'Is she conscious?'

The nurse smiled. 'I believe she is ... Henrietta?' she said
loudly. 'Can you hear me?'

Helen felt another squeeze of her hand.

'She just squeezed my hand!' Helen said, joy bubbling
up inside her.

'I'm going to get the doctor,' the nurse said, hurrying
away.

'Grandmama,' Helen said, her hand reaching out and
touching the side of her grandmother's face. It felt cold,
but for the first time, Helen realised, it did not look yellow.

'It's me, Helen. Your granddaughter.' As Helen spoke, she saw the slight flickering of movement underneath Henrietta's eyelids.

'Grandmama,' Helen said softly.

And with that word, Helen saw Henrietta's eyes slowly open. Blinking, she turned her head to the side to look at her granddaughter.

'Helen, my dearest, dearest granddaughter,' she said, her voice croaky and weak. 'Why are you so sad?' She swallowed. Her lips were dry. 'And you've been crying.'

Helen let out a splutter of laughter.

'Oh, I'm not sad, Grandmama. Not sad at all.' She leant over and gave Henrietta a gentle kiss on her cheek.

'I couldn't be happier,' she said.

Dr Parker arrived just moments after Henrietta had opened her eyes. He glanced at Helen, who met his look. Her emerald eyes sparkled with a mix of sheer relief and overwhelming joy. Reaching the side of the bed, he focused on Henrietta, who was turning her head slightly to look at him.

'Good morning, Henrietta,' Dr Parker said, taking his thermometer from the top pocket of his crumpled white coat. He had spent the night drifting in and out of sleep in a chair in the consultation room he had temporarily commandeered.

'How are you feeling today?'

Henrietta looked up at him and smiled.

'I just want you to open your mouth,' he said, holding out the thermometer so Henrietta could see. She did as he said. 'Now, just close your mouth ... perfect.' He then took hold of his stethoscope and listened to her chest. Out of the corner of his eye, he could see Helen holding her grandmother's hand. Her eyes were concentrating on him. Awaiting his verdict. When he finished listening, he looked at Helen and gave her an encouraging smile.

'Well, Henrietta,' he said, looking down at his watch as he took her wrist and felt for her pulse. 'Looks like that long sleep has done you the world of good.'

Helen choked back the tears.

'Is she going to be OK?' she asked.

'I think she is,' he said, smiling down at Henrietta.

He turned his attention back to Helen. 'Her heart rate and blood pressure are good. And ...' He leant down and took the thermometer from Henrietta's mouth. He squinted. 'And her temperature is also back to normal.'

He looked back at Henrietta.

'It's good to have you back, Henrietta. Very good indeed.'

Over the next hour, the nurse helped Henrietta to sit up and take a few sips of water. She explained that it was now important that she got as much fluid down her as possible – and then a little later they could bring her something to eat. Henrietta nodded, showing her compliance. Helen was by her side all the time, encouraging her grandmother to do what the nurse told her.

'We need to get you better,' Helen told her. 'So you have to do what the nurse tells you – and Dr Parker.'

Every time she mentioned John's name, Henrietta's face lit up and she would point a bony finger at Helen. 'Your doctor friend. *Your love.*'

And each time, Helen would smile sadly and say, 'Yes, my doctor friend, but not my love, I'm afraid, Grandmama.'

When she asked Henrietta what she could recall of the past couple of days, she was met by a blank look.

'What's the last thing you can remember?' Helen asked. She had been told by John to see if her grandmother had any memories of falling ill – and of anything about the week or so leading up to her collapse.

Helen watched as her grandmother supped on her beaker of water and squinted, showing that she was thinking. Suddenly, her expression came to life. A smile spread across her face.

'Going to the Maison Nouvelle,' she said. Her voice was still raspy. She gave a little cough.

'That's right. We went to see Kate, didn't we? For your final fitting.'

Henrietta nodded.

They were quiet for a moment.

'Can you remember if you had eaten or had anything to drink? Anything different?'

Henrietta took another sip of her water. Once again, her eyes lit up.

'Eggnog,' she said.

'Of course, the eggnog,' Helen said, more to herself than to her grandmother. 'The eggnog and oatmeal biscuits Mother was bringing you as a treat.'

Helen leant forward.

'Did Mother tell you who gave her the eggnog and biscuits, Grandmama?'

Henrietta suddenly became distracted by someone coming into the ward.

Helen heard her mother's voice before she saw her.

'I've come to see one of your patients. Miss Henrietta Girling. My great-aunty.' Miriam's voice seemed to echo around the room as she spoke to the nurse.

Helen watched as her mother turned around and scanned the ward.

The nurse, who had just taken over from the night nurse, looked down at her list and then up again. 'She's just over in the end bed.'

Miriam manufactured a smile before clip-clopping her way over to them in her high heels. The way she was dressed and made-up, Helen thought, she looked as though she was on her way out for a night out – not rushing to her mother's bedside. Helen wondered how much Dr Eris had told her.

'What on earth has happened?' she asked as she sat down in the chair by the side of the bed. She looked around to make sure no one could hear. 'What have you been up to, Mother?'

'She's not been *up to* anything,' Helen snapped back. 'Grandmother is lucky to be alive. She's been seriously ill.'

Miriam furrowed her brow and looked at Henrietta. 'Well, she looks fine to me.' She raised a sceptical eyebrow at Helen.

Helen thought she might burst.

'She's been poisoned! And whatever she had nearly killed her. If you'd seen her last night, she looked as yellow as that scarf you're wearing.'

Miriam looked down at her canary yellow Jaeger neck scarf. She let out a light laugh. 'Honestly, Helen, you've become such a drama queen lately.' She looked at Henrietta. 'She never used to be like this, you know. She's changed a lot lately. And let's just say it's not for the better.'

Helen could feel her face redden with anger. She had to use all her willpower not to reach over and wring her mother's neck with her expensive silk scarf.

'Now, now, no arguing, you two.' Henrietta patted Miriam's jewelled hand.

Helen took a deep breath. 'Grandmama was just—'

'Just be careful, my dear,' Miriam said, putting her finger to her lips and looking around.

Helen closed her eyes for a moment, trying to keep herself from exploding.

'*Grandmama*,' she said, 'was just telling me that she's been drinking eggnog.'

'Ah,' Miriam smiled. 'She has been.' She looked at her mother and smiled again, as one would to a child. 'Apparently, she used to love it back in the day.'

'And where did you get the eggnog from?' Helen asked.

'Agatha made it, along with some of ...' she dropped her voice '... *Mother's* favourite oatmeal biscuits.'

'Really?' Helen asked. 'And when did she start giving you eggnog and biscuits to take to Grandmama?'

'Oh, I don't know ... a couple of weeks ago.'

'And how often have you been taking Grandmama the eggnog and biscuits?'

Miriam pulled a face and sat up straight. 'Dear me, Helen, why the Spanish Inquisition?'

'Just answer the question, Mother,' Helen said sternly.

'Oh, I don't know. Every time I've visited.'

Helen recalled thinking that her mother seemed to have been visiting more frequently of late.

'What? Twice a week?'

'I'd say so,' Miriam said disinterestedly.

She inspected Helen.

'Darling, I have to say, you look dreadful.' She looked at Henrietta and gave her a cheeky smile. 'You look worse than Mother here – who you *claim* to have been at death's door.'

'She *has* been at death's door,' Helen hissed. 'Whose idea was it to give Grandmama the eggnog and biscuits?'

'What makes you think it wasn't my idea?' Miriam asked, affronted.

'Because you're too selfish to think about anyone but yourself, and as far as I know, you've never taken Grandmama anything before now.'

Helen felt Henrietta's hand on her own. 'Oh, but she has, my dear. She brought me some of my favourite Russian vodka and some elderflower cordial, didn't you, dear?'

Miriam threw her daughter a triumphant look. 'I did indeed, Mother. And all that make-up and hair dye.'

Helen's mind was working overtime.

'Really?' She looked at Henrietta. 'And did you drink it, Grandmama?'

Henrietta looked guiltily at Miriam. 'I'm afraid I didn't. Sorry, my dear, I didn't like to hurt your feelings. It was such a kind thought.'

'A kind thought which I'm guessing didn't come from you, Mother. Whose idea was it to give her the vodka?'

'Honestly, Helen, you make it sound like I can't do a single kind thing.'

Helen bit back a reply.

'Who?' she asked simply.

Miriam sighed. 'Your grandfather thought it would be a good idea. He really wanted to give your grandmother something. A present. A treat.'

Helen stared in disbelief at her mother. 'Really? You really believe that?'

Miriam looked puzzled. 'Of course, I do, Helen. Why wouldn't I?'

Helen laughed and looked at her mother. 'Oh, I forgot. You still believe everything you're told, don't you?'

Standing up, Helen gave her grandmother a kiss on the cheek. 'Do everything the nurse tells you to do, OK?'

Henrietta nodded.

'I've just got to go and do an errand. I won't be long. If you feel unwell, you must tell the nurse.'

'I'm fine, Helen. I feel so much better. Really, I do,' Henrietta reassured her.

Helen walked around the bed and looked down at her mother's handbag.

'You've not brought any more *treats*, have you?'

'As if I've had time,' Miriam said, defensively. 'I rushed here as soon as I got the phone call that Mother was unwell.' She sighed. 'Although I have to say, I think that Dr Eris was a little over the top about it all. I came here expecting the worst.' She looked at Henrietta. 'She looks full of the joys to me.'

Helen took one more look at her grandmother. Thank goodness, she was going to be all right. She couldn't wait to see John and tell him how thankful she was to him. And Dorothy and Bobby. There was no doubt in her mind that they'd all saved her grandmother's life. Her words of gratitude would have to wait, though. There was something more pressing she wanted to do. Something that simply couldn't wait.

Helen had just reached the main foyer of the hospital when she saw a familiar figure striding towards her.

'Are you all right?' Matthew Royce's face was full of genuine concern.

'Matthew – what are you doing here?' Helen asked. He was the last person she'd expect to bump into.

'Marie-Anne told Dahlia that you hadn't come in this morning – that someone you were close to was seriously ill in hospital ...'

Having reached her, he put his hands on her shoulders.

'Gosh, you look terrible,' he said, inspecting her face. Her make-up had worn off, and she had dark circles under her eyes. '

'Thanks, Matthew,' Helen laughed.

'No, honestly, you look as white as a sheet. Let me take you for a cuppa?'

Helen shook her head. 'I'm all right, honestly.'

316

Matthew desperately wanted to put his arms around her and kiss her. She had a vulnerability about her that made her seem even more ravishing. *God, he wanted her.*

'Honestly?' he asked.

'Yes, honestly, Matthew, I'm fine. I'm just off home to get myself cleaned up and then I need to do an errand. Come on, walk me to my car.'

Matthew shrugged off his coat and wrapped it around Helen.

'That I can do,' he said, putting his arm around her and giving her a gentle squeeze.

Dr Parker was hurrying to catch Helen before she left. He'd popped his head into the ward and seen that Miriam was visiting. The ward nurse had told him that Helen had just left. He broke into a jog. He wanted to be with her, revel in the good news, rejoice in her grandmother's close call. *Very* close call. Henrietta was stronger than she looked.

Turning the corner, his heart lifted on seeing Helen heading towards the main foyer.

He was just about to shout out her name when he saw Matthew Royce striding into the hospital, exuding confidence and charm.

God! Just looking at the man riled him.

Slowing his pace, Dr Parker watched as Matthew put his hands on Helen's shoulders as they talked. He noted that Helen didn't seem to mind.

Stop it! Dr Parker reprimanded himself. *Stop it! Stop it! Stop it!* Helen was his friend. She had made it more than clear to him during their brutally honest talk back in June. It had broken his heart, but at least he knew the truth. So, why was he still struggling to accept it and let go of his feelings for Helen? To be content with her friendship and nothing more?

317

He stopped walking and watched as Matthew put his coat around Helen's shoulders and then put his arm around her.

Damn the man!

As Dr Parker turned and made his way back to the ward, he thought about Matthew and Helen. She had claimed that Matthew was purely a friend – she'd actually told John off for even suggesting she would be interested in someone like that. But now he was thinking about it, perhaps she had objected too vehemently. Perhaps she had been embarrassed about liking Matthew. From what he had just seen, they looked very close and very cosy with each other.

Again, he castigated himself. *Whoever Helen dates is her choice. Just because I can't stand the man, doesn't mean Helen shouldn't go out with him.*

Or was it because, deep down, he couldn't abide to see Helen with *any* man?

Because the only man he wanted to see Helen with was himself?

Chapter Forty-Three

As soon as she arrived back home, Helen was met by the cook, Mrs Westley, who had also taken on the role of house-keeper since the beginning of the war. Mrs Westley knew Helen had been at the hospital all night as the mistress of the house, Mrs Crawford, had told her.

Taking one look at Helen, Mrs Westley ushered her upstairs to get herself cleaned up and changed and told her to come back down to the kitchen when she was ready. Helen didn't mind being bossed about by Mrs Westley. She'd been part of the family since Helen was a child and had ended up being more of a mother to her than her own ever had.

'You're not leaving this house until you've put some-thing in your stomach,' the portly cook nagged.

Helen acquiesced to Mrs Westley's command, realising that she hadn't eaten since yesterday afternoon. Besides which, she knew she needed to have some kind of susten-ance to fortify her for her next port of call.

When she was sitting at the kitchen table, blowing on a bowl of home-made soup, Helen asked how Mrs Westley might feel about increasing her hours and looking after her great-aunty when she was discharged from hospital. Mrs Westley didn't need to think about it. More hours meant more money.

Half an hour later, Helen arrived at the asylum. Hurrying past Genevieve and throwing her a look that was far from affable, she hurried to her grandmother's room. When she got there, she found two cleaners leaving. One was carrying a bucket and mop, the other a box overflowing with cleaning implements. Stepping into the room, she was accosted by the smell of polish and floor cleaner. Every surface shined. Every inch of the place had been scrubbed and sterilised.

Her grandfather had covered his tracks.

Leaving the room, she walked back along the corridor, turning right at the top. When she arrived at Dr Eris's office, she stopped.

Taking a deep breath, she knocked.

'Come in!'

Helen was glad Claire was there and she didn't have to hunt around the asylum to find her.

'Helen!' Dr Eris seemed genuine in her welcome when she saw who it was, but also a little surprised. 'John told me the good news.' She looked at the phone by way of an explanation. She, too, had barely slept since Henrietta had fallen ill, considering herself 'on call' should John need her help.

'I've just been to Henrietta's room and the cleaners were coming out. Looks like they've done a thorough job,' Helen said, looking at Dr Eris.

Dr Eris shook her head. 'Why doesn't that surprise me.' She had just spoken to John and they had agreed it was clear who was responsible for Henrietta's illness, just as it was equally clear it could never be proven.

She fixed her attention on Helen. 'I *am* surprised that you're here, though?' She continued to inspect Helen, who sat down on the chair in front of the desk. 'I'm guessing you've been home, but have come here before going back to see your grandmother, who is doing really well by all accounts?'

Helen smiled. 'She is … And I have to say, it's thanks to John – and Dorothy and Bobby.' She paused. 'And you too.'

Dr Eris raised her eyebrows in surprise.

'*You* found the antidote,' Helen said. 'And if you hadn't been giving Grandmama the sugar pills, I'm pretty sure she wouldn't be here now, but lying on a slab in the morgue.'

Dr Eris knew that to be the truth. Henrietta's liver would have given up the ghost had it also had to cope with the calibre and dosage of drugs she was purported to be taking. Unsure of what to say, Dr Eris shuffled a little uncomfortably in her chair. The basis of her relationship with Helen had shifted these past twenty-four hours and she was uncertain of her footing.

'I appreciate your gratitude,' Dr Eris said, tentatively. 'I genuinely care for Henrietta. I really am incredibly happy and relieved that she is going to be all right.'

The two women looked at each other.

'I sense, though,' Dr Eris said, narrowing her eyes, 'that there is another reason you have come here – other than to thank me?'

Helen let out a light laugh. 'Something tells me that you're good at your job, Claire … Yes, you're right. I *have* come here for another reason.'

'You want something from me?' Dr Eris guessed.

'You're right. I do,' said Helen.

Dr Eris looked puzzled.

'You know when we talked that afternoon you caught me coming to see John?' Helen said. 'When you gave me a choice – or rather, an ultimatum?'

Dr Eris nodded.

'And you produced two documents that proved "Miss Girling" was my grandmother? The original admissions form and the forgery?'

'Yes?'

'Well,' Helen said, 'I have a proposition for you. And one I think you will like.'

'Go on,' Dr Eris encouraged.

After leaving Dr Eris, it took Helen longer than usual to drive across to her grandfather's house due to the snow and ice on the roads. Pulling up in the gravelled driveway, which thankfully had been shovelled clear, she stepped out of the car and took a deep breath. She stood still. She could smell burning. A bonfire. She looked around to see where the smoke was coming from. It didn't appear to be from the neighbours. She walked up the steps to the front door. Pulling the brass lever, she heard the bell ringing inside the house. She stamped her feet on the ground, not just because it was freezing, but because of the adrenaline coursing around her body.

A few moments later, Eddy answered. He opened the door and moved aside to allow her to enter the house. Helen glared at him as she stepped over the threshold. She knew he was no innocent in what had happened to her grandmother. The same went for Agatha. The question in Helen's mind now, though, was whether or not either of them had got the little boy to give the note to Dorothy and Bobby.

Helen walked into the large, square hall and was immediately taken aback by the huge, beautifully decorated Christmas tree that was standing sparkling in the foyer. She put down her handbag on the polished tiled floor and turned her back to Eddy, showing him that he was to help her out of her coat.

'Gosh, someone's getting into the Christmas spirit this year,' she said over her shoulder. 'Grandfather must feel like he has a lot to celebrate, don't you think, Eddy?' Helen shrugged off her woollen winter coat and turned to face him.

She felt nothing but contempt for both her grandfather's servants. She was one hundred per cent sure they were involved in his attempts at poisoning her grandmother. Just as they had known exactly what her grandfather had been up to all those years ago and had done nothing to stop him. They hadn't even warned the poor girls who looked likely to fall prey to his perversions.

Helen watched as Eddy walked over to the stand on the other side of the hallway and hung up her coat.

'I'm guessing you're here to see Mr Havelock,' Eddy said, his voice not betraying any emotion.

'Who else would I be here to see?' Helen said, turning and walking towards the study. The large oak door was open, but there was no one there.

'Where is he?' she demanded.

'I'm afraid the master is indisposed at the moment,' Eddy said.

'*Indisposed*, my foot,' Helen said, walking towards the door that led to the servants' quarters and the kitchen.

'Where are you going?' Eddy hurried after her, wanting to give his master a warning.

'Don't worry, Eddy,' Helen said. 'I can take it from here. I don't need to be announced. I am family, after all.' She continued walking down the narrow corridor. 'As I could smell smoke when I arrived, I'm going to take a stab in the dark and say that Grandfather is in the garden having a bonfire.'

Helen reached the kitchen.

'Ah, Agatha,' she said, seeing the housekeeper appear from the depths of the large pantry. 'Don't mind me, I'm just cutting through to the garden. Carry on with whatever you're doing.'

'Oh, Miss Crawford, is something wrong? Is there bad news?' Agatha couldn't stop herself from asking. They weren't supposed to know that Henrietta was unwell. Out of the corner of her eye, she saw Eddy throw her a dark look.

Helen surveyed Agatha. 'No, quite the reverse. Good news. Very good news. Grandmother has been ill – very ill – these past twenty-four hours, but has pulled through.'

Thank God! Agatha tried to keep the relief from showing on her face. 'That *is* good news,' she said.

Suddenly feeling sapped of energy, she pulled out a chair next to the kitchen table and plonked herself down.

Helen looked at Agatha, trying to read her. *Had she been behind the note?*

'Yes, it is,' Helen said, before turning and making her way to the back door.

'Oh, you don't want to go out there,' Eddy panicked.

Helen stopped by the back door.

'Why ever not, Eddy?' Helen stared at him and saw the guilt in his eyes.

'Perhaps you'd like a cup of tea or something?' he asked, stepping towards her.

For a moment, Helen thought he was going to grab her and stop her from going out. Ignoring him, she opened the door and stepped into the garden.

Sure enough, there was her grandfather, standing by a small bonfire that was crackling and hissing. Smoke was billowing up and over the house due to a slight westerly breeze.

'Hello, Grandfather, I thought I'd surprise you,' Helen said, walking down the snowy pathway. She looked over at the greenhouse and saw the door was open.

'Well, you've certainly done that,' Mr Havelock said, from behind a large white handkerchief he was holding over his mouth. He turned away from the fire and walked towards Helen.

'I'm guessing if I had a look around your greenhouse, I would most likely find a patch of earth which has recently been dug over,' Helen said, cutting straight to the chase.

'My, my, Helen, since when have you been interested in horticulture?'

Helen gave a loud burst of mirthless laughter. 'I am when it comes to the cultivation of poisonous plants,' she goaded.

Mr Havelock's eyes were dancing. 'And why on earth would you be interested in such a strange pastime?'

'I'm not – but I believe you are,' she sniped, walking over to the greenhouse. 'There you are – I was right. There's a section over there which has obviously just been cleared.'

'How observant. Sinclair has been having a good clear-out. Hence the fire …' Mr Havelock took one last look at the bonfire, which had served its purpose. It could dwindle and die out now.

'Well, I don't know about you, Helen, but this old man needs to get himself indoors before he freezes to death.'

He walked past Helen, forcing her to follow. She looked about the garden. The white snakeroot plant could be right under her nose, but she wouldn't know as she had no idea what it looked like. Judging by her grandfather's cool, self-satisfied demeanour, though, she would guess that there was not even a leaf of the poisonous plant left any-where on the property.

When they were back indoors, Mr Havelock demanded that Eddy bring him a hot toddy in his study. This time it was Agatha who asked if Helen would like something. Helen shook her head.

'Although,' she added cryptically, 'I'm tempted to have a glass of eggnog.'

The colour immediately drained from Agatha's face.

'I've heard it's rather delicious,' Helen said, putting her finger to her mouth as though considering whether to indulge or not. 'No – no, I'd better not. I'll leave it this time.'

Helen threw Agatha one last questioning look, before turning and walking out of the kitchen.

'So, to what do I owe this visit from my only grand-daughter?' Mr Havelock asked as he entered his warm but slightly stuffy and smoky study.

Helen followed and stopped in the middle of the Tur-key-red carpet. She watched as her grandfather headed straight over to the fire and added another log.

'I just wanted to come and tell you personally, Grand-father, that your wife – who you have seemed keen to ingratiate yourself with of late with presents and the like – is doing well. *Very well*. The doctors have predicted she will be up and about and back to her old self in no time. No time at all.'

Helen scrutinised her grandfather's face through his reflection in the mirror. Unaware that she could see him, he silently cursed, his face creasing up in frustration. Helen watched as he slowly turned around.

'Really? I had no idea she was unwell,' he said, walking over to his desk. He sat down in his chair.

Helen smiled. 'Oh, but I think you did, Grandfather.'

She watched as Mr Havelock picked up a half-smoked cigar from the ashtray, lit it and sat up in his chair. He eyed his granddaughter. His gaze did not leave her as she remained standing on the other side of his desk.

'Grandmama's made of strong stuff, though. The doc-tors were amazed her body managed to keep function-ing – especially with the amount of drugs she's been on.' She stared at her grandfather. 'They believe that she was poisoned by a plant – coincidentally, one brought over by yourself from North America, called white snakeroot. It apparently has quite deadly properties.'

Eddy arrived with the hot toddy, put it down on the desk and left without a word.

'Well, isn't that a coincidence,' Mr Havelock said. 'I do believe I may have donated some seedlings many years back.'

He took a sip of his drink.

'That's the only problem with being a resident in a lunatic asylum,' he mused. 'God only knows to what extremes those who are mentally afflicted will go to hurt themselves or others.'

Helen looked at her grandfather. He had it all worked out. It would be a good argument in court. It would be nigh on impossible to prove that he was the culprit. She looked into her grandfather's dark eyes. They were almost black. As she did so, she swore she saw the Devil himself in them.

'It horrifies me,' she said, her mouth tight and her eyes narrowed, 'that a person can be so evil, so dark, so murderous. That a human being can be wholly without any kind of goodness is truly quite terrifying.'

Helen stepped forward so that she was standing in front of his desk. She put her hands on the top and leaned towards her grandfather as though needing to see what true evil looked like up close.

'You have a black hole where your heart should be. It's you who should have been locked up in an asylum. You are the one who really is insane.' She paused. 'Inhuman.'

Mr Havelock didn't move a muscle, despite her proximity. A sickening smile, though, spread slowly across his face.

327

'I know what you did,' Helen continued. 'Or rather, I should say, what you *tried* to do. Because, of course, you failed. And I know how much you must be hating that.

'Grandmama is going to be just fine,' she went on, rubbing salt into the wound. She straightened herself up. 'Actually, she's going to be more than fine. In a funny kind of way, what you tried to do has ended up working in her favour – and mine.'

Mr Havelock leant forward. His gnarled hands came together in a knot.

'You see,' Helen said, 'you were right in what you just said – about the dangers of living in a mental institution.'

Mr Havelock looked surprised, as well as a little suspicious.

'You know,' Helen explained, 'about how you don't know to what extremes those who are mentally afflicted will go to hurt themselves or others.' She paused. 'So I've come to the conclusion that Grandmama is not safe there. Not safe from the actions of those who are insane. Inhuman.'

She took a deep breath.

'I've decided Grandmama is *not* going back to the asylum,' she said, holding her grandfather's stare. 'When she's deemed well enough to be discharged from the Royal, she's going to come back to live with me – and Mother, of course. The house is big enough.'

Helen opened her handbag and started rummaging around.

'I thought she could have Father's old room,' she added, a little distracted as she pulled out a piece of folded-up paper. 'Mrs Westley had agreed and is going to keep an eye on her.'

Helen gave her grandfather a piercing look.

'She'll make sure she gets all the right food and drink.'

Mr Havelock returned his granddaughter's stare. 'Over my dead body!'

'If only!' Helen quipped.

'Who the hell do you think you are?' he spat. *How dare she talk to him in such a way.* 'There's no way Henrietta's going to be let out into the real world. That's not your decision to make.'

'I think you'll find it is,' Helen said. She held up the document so that her grandfather could read it. 'This just happened to fall into my lap very recently.'

Mr Havelock made to grab it, but Helen was too quick and snatched it away.

'Where the hell did you get that from?' Mr Havelock demanded.

Helen ignored his question.

'As you can clearly see, it's the original document showing Mrs Henrietta Havelock's admittance to the asylum. A document, I'm guessing by your reaction, you thought was no longer in existence.'

Mr Havelock's eyes were glued to the admissions report. *Why had it not been destroyed?* He could feel his heart pounding in his ears. If it ever got to see the light of day, he'd be finished. Ruined. His secret would be out. His mind was spinning. He could still make out Henrietta was as mad as a hatter – that he'd had her sectioned for her own good – but he'd still be hauled over the coals for lying about her death. He could be done for fraud. Twice over – for falsifying her death *and* her identity. If Henrietta started to sing his sins from the treetops like she had originally threatened, there was a good chance she might be believed. Henrietta's Little Match Girl and the parents of little Gracie would undoubtedly make an appearance. And worse still, more former employees might well come out of the woodwork.

'This,' Helen added victoriously, 'is evidence you can't burn.'

Folding up the document, she put it back into her bag. She stepped away from her grandfather. Suddenly, she couldn't wait to get out of there.

'Don't worry,' said Helen, making to leave. 'Grandmother will still be known as Miss Girling. That secret is safe – as are all your others.'

Mr Havelock felt his body sag with relief.

Helen stopped and looked him straight in the eye.

'For now, anyway.'

And then she turned her back and left.

Chapter Forty-Four

The next day, Helen caught Rosie and the rest of the women as they were leaving work. No one needed persuading when she suggested a drink at the Admiral.

'You and Bobby were right,' she said to Dorothy. 'It *was* my grandfather.'

Even though it had seemed obvious to them all that Charles Havelock was indeed the one behind the poisoning of Henrietta, it was still shocking.

Between sips of their drinks, Helen told them how she'd arrived at her grandfather's house just as he was burning the evidence. And that judging by the panicked and guilt-stricken looks on Eddy's and Agatha's faces, they had been instrumental in lacing her grandfather's so-called 'treats' for his wife with poison – treats that had then been transported to the asylum and given to Henrietta by Miriam on her now more frequent visits. Helen said she still wasn't sure who was responsible for the note, although she was determined to find out.

'Do yer think yer mam knew about it?' Angie asked rather bluntly.

It was a question they'd all wanted to ask, but had held back. Miriam might not have a decent bone in her body, but she was still Helen's mother.

'No,' Helen said, looking at the faces of the women, 'I'm pretty sure she didn't. My grandfather's done a good job on her. She's still choosing not to see him for the man he is – helped by the fact that he's told her he's leaving everything to her in his will.'

'Really?' Gloria was shocked. 'When did she tell yer this?' She was surprised Helen hadn't told her – and even more that she hadn't told her father.

'Oh, the other week,' Helen said, not wanting to make an issue of it.

'Won't that mean you'll end up with nothing?' Rosie asked. Out of all the women, she was the most astute when it came to financial matters.

Helen nodded.

'Well, what will you do?' asked Polly. She had always had the protection of her family around her – both financially and emotionally – and couldn't imagine not having either.

'Well, I won't starve.' Helen laughed lightly. 'I have a job. I take home a decent wage.'

The women didn't say anything, but thought all the more. Dorothy, in particular, related to what was in store for Helen. She had not heard hide nor hair from her parents. The tenuous link she had maintained with her family had been broken. She was on her own. Not that she minded.

She had learnt so much of late. About herself and her family. And about Bobby. She had come to realise that her initial insecurities about him had really been about her fear of being rejected – because that was what she had come to expect from life: rejection. Her real father had rejected her; her mother had rejected her after meeting Frank and having more children. And Frank had quite simply never accepted her or anything about her or her life. Bobby, though, was not going to reject her. Quite the opposite. He knew everything about her and still loved her for the person she was.

'Anyway,' Helen said, changing the subject back to Henrietta, 'I made it clear to Grandfather that I knew exactly what he'd done.'

'I hope you also told him exactly what you thought of him,' Martha said. She had not been able to think about anything else since hearing that Helen's poor grandmother had been purposely poisoned. She kept thinking how her own mother had done the same to her children.

'Oh, I most certainly did,' Helen said. 'And better still, I have managed to secure Henrietta's release from the asylum.' A wide smile spread across her face. 'When she's discharged from the hospital, she's coming to live back home with me.'

'That's brilliant!' Hannah said. 'How did you manage that?'

Helen pulled out the admissions report from her handbag and showed the women.

'Where did yer get that from?' Gloria asked.

'Let me guess,' Dorothy said. '*Dr Eris.*'

Helen nodded.

'The one she had over yer – the one stopping yer from telling Dr Parker how yer felt?' Angie asked.

'The very one,' Helen said.

'Does that mean you can tell Dr Parker how you really feel?' Dorothy asked, her eyes wide.

'I'm afraid it's not as straightforward as that,' Helen said. 'But the most important thing at the moment is that it's forced Grandfather's hand. Henrietta is coming home.'

Seeing that more questions were forthcoming, Helen put paid to them by raising her glass.

'So, a toast to Henrietta – to her recovery, and to her release back into the real world.'

'To her recovery and her return,' Gloria said as everyone clinked their glasses.

Over the next few days, Helen split her time between work and visits to the hospital. Henrietta was making huge progress and was now sitting up in her bed, chatting to the other patients on the ward and winning over the changing shifts of nurses and doctors to become their star patient. Dr Parker had returned to the Ryhope but was keeping tabs on Henrietta's progress with regular calls to the ward. In turn, he passed on those updates to Dr Eris, with whom he was spending any free time he had. They had worked as a team to save Henrietta. And it had been thanks to Claire that an antidote had been found. If he had waited for the expert in London to call back, Henrietta would now be dead. Something, he felt, had changed between himself and Claire. It had been an almost imperceptible change, one he couldn't quite put his finger on, but a change all the same.

As Dr Parker tended to a growing number of wounded soldiers arriving at the hospital, he kept thinking of the conversation he'd had with Claire when he had arrived back from the Royal and asked her why she had given Henrietta sugar pills. He had initially presumed it was as a placebo – part of Henrietta's treatment. But it soon became clear there was more to it. Much more. He had listened and his blood had started to boil as Claire had told him how Mr Havelock had orchestrated the meeting with her a few weeks earlier to demand that Henrietta be put back on her previous heavy medication or, one way or another, Claire would lose her career. Perhaps it was then the change had happened. Claire had risked her job and her future for her patient.

They had both talked about the evil of a man who could try to poison his wife. They had both agreed, however, that it would be impossible to prove. It was a relief that Claire now knew about Charles Havelock's real relationship with Henrietta. And that she supported Helen in her need to keep Henrietta's true identity a secret, although he was fairly sure that Helen had not told her of the wider implications should it become public knowledge.

Henrietta's near death had brought their love to life in a way they had not experienced before. He had loved Claire, was attracted to her, but something had been missing. Something that had caused him to hold off doing what he now knew he was going to do. He just had to pick the right moment – and he had a good idea exactly when that right moment would be.

Chapter Forty-Five

Dorothy and Bobby had just left Gloria's flat, having spent an hour playing with Hope and spoiling her rotten. She was in a particularly excitable mood as, so she had told them several times, it was just *three* days before Santa visited.

'So,' Bobby said, taking hold of Dorothy's hand as they walked along Borough Road, 'Helen's still not sure who it was that gave us the note?'

'I think she's pretty convinced it has to be someone working for her grandfather,' Dorothy said. 'Perhaps Thomas, the driver, or one of the maids who might have overheard something or worked out what Mr Havelock was up to. It's proving it, though, isn't it? Whoever it was, they're sure to deny it until they're blue in the face if they're ever asked. Who would dare get on the bad side of Mr Havelock – a man who's prepared to poison his wife?'

They crossed the road and made their way to the museum.

'She doesn't think it could be Eddy or Agatha?' Bobby asked. 'She seems pretty convinced they were a part of it all – which would suggest they might have wanted to put a stop to it.'

'Perhaps,' Dorothy said. 'Although Helen said the look of guilt on both their faces when she went round there made her think otherwise.'

'So, it looks like it will remain a mystery,' Bobby mused as they walked up the steps.

'One which Helen is determined to solve, no matter how long it takes.' Dorothy laughed. 'And no one is in any doubt that she will.'

Bobby smiled, thinking that his soon-to-be stepsister was one very determined woman when she put her mind to something.

He pulled open the heavy door to the entrance of the museum.

'Oh, it's lovely and warm in here,' Dorothy said as she walked into the foyer. Her last few words, though, were obliterated by the ear-splitting sound of a toddler who was refusing to get off Wallace, the museum's stuffed lion. The more his mother tried to get him off, the more he screamed.

Dorothy pointed to the main art gallery and hurried past the exasperated mother and red-faced child, who was gripping poor Wallace's mane as if his life depended on it. The lion's Christmas hat had been knocked off and was lying next to his front paw.

As soon as the door to the gallery closed behind them, Dorothy exhaled dramatically.

'Oh. My. God. What a racket!'

Bobby laughed. 'Nothing like the sound of a screaming infant.'

'You can say that again,' Dorothy said, looking around the high-ceilinged room, which was filled with the largest oil paintings she had ever seen. 'Thank goodness there's no toddlers having tantrums here.'

'No one at all, in fact,' Bobby said, glancing round.

They started to walk towards a magnificent gilt-framed oil painting of a ship riding high on turbulent waters.

'You know,' Dorothy said suddenly, 'I've been thinking a lot lately.'

'About?' Bobby asked.

'About lots of things really. Life … The way society is …' Dorothy's voice trailed off.

'Sounds very serious?' Bobby asked.

'I guess it is.' Dorothy let out a short laugh. 'I have my moments.'

'Go on,' Bobby encouraged. 'This sounds intriguing.'

'Mmm, I don't know if *intriguing* is the word you'll use when you hear what's been going through my mind.'

Just then, the curator opened the door and the sound of the toddler's crying once again pierced the air.

Dorothy laughed. 'Simply put, I don't think I want all that.'

'What's "all that"?' Bobby asked as they ambled towards the next work of art.

'Screaming children,' Dorothy said. She gave Bobby a sideways glance. 'The whole family thing.' She paused. 'Marriage.'

'Really?' Bobby asked, shocked.

Dorothy was quiet. She'd shocked *herself* lately with how she was thinking, never mind Bobby.

Bobby looked at Dorothy and forced a smile, not wanting her to see his disappointment at her sudden confession. 'Not all children are like that one out there,' he argued. They had now reached another huge oil painting, this one showing an armada of British ships setting sail.

'I don't think that came out right,' Dorothy said. 'It's not just the children, it's everything that goes alongside them.'

'Is that why you turned Toby down? Because you don't really want to get married?'

'No,' Dorothy said without hesitation.

Bobby's face showed his relief.

'I turned Toby down because of you,' she said, laughing.

Bobby smiled.

'So, you're adamant you really don't want to get married?' Bobby said, his focus on Dorothy. Watching her expression.

'I don't think it's just about not wanting to get married,' Dorothy said. 'I think it's more about me not wanting to live a traditional life.'

Dorothy turned her attention to a beautiful painting of Venice.

'You've seen so much of the world,' she said. 'You've had all that excitement. So, I'm guessing you're happy to settle down.'

Bobby laughed, causing the curator, who had settled in the leather chair by the door, to scowl over at them.

'I don't know if I'm ready for my slippers and pipe yet.' Bobby dropped his voice to a whisper as he guided Dorothy back out into the main hallway. The mother and child had now gone. The quietness of the museum had resumed.

Seeing the sign to the 'Foreign Exhibits', Bobby took Dorothy's hand. 'Come on, let's go and pretend we're somewhere else. In some faraway land, batting off the mosquitoes and getting burned by the midday sun.'

'Sounds lovely – the midday sun, not getting bit or burned,' Dorothy said, raising her face to the ceiling lights and pretending to revel in the sun's rays.

As they entered the small exhibition room, Bobby turned to Dorothy.

'I was just thinking,' he said, with a playful smile. 'If you're not sure about marriage and keeping to tradition, then does that mean you're having second thoughts … about *other things*?'

Dorothy looked at him, puzzled.

Bobby raised his eyebrows.

'Oh, Bobby.' She laughed loudly and batted him on the arm. 'You never give up, do you!'

He chuckled. 'It's your fault for being so irresistible.'

As they sauntered along, looking at bows and arrows and hand-made jewellery brought back from faraway places, Bobby put his arm around Dorothy and kissed her ear.

'So, when we run off to live in sin, where would you like to go first?' he asked.

They walked past a mannequin dressed in a straw skirt.

'How about Hawaii?' Dorothy suggested.

'Hawaii it is,' Bobby said, noting that Dorothy had not objected to the suggestion that they live in sin.

Seeing a bench, Bobby guided Dorothy towards it and they sat down. 'Do you think what happened with your mam is making you feel the way you do about getting married?' he asked. 'I mean, her first marriage was violent and her second isn't exactly ... well ... one that I think you'd want.'

'Too right,' Dorothy said.

'Do you think that might have made you change your mind?' Bobby tried to sound casual. Dorothy's comments on marriage had floored him, though he was trying his hardest not to let it show.

'I don't know if it's made me change my mind,' Dorothy said, her tone now serious. 'I think what happened that day at the house, it just got me thinking – and, well, I kept on thinking. Thinking about everything ... all those other marriages, and the way women are, or are expected to be ... and I'm not sure if that's what I want – what is expected. I think I want more.' She looked at Bobby. 'Doesn't what happened with your mam and dad make you think?'

Bobby let out a slightly bitter-sounding laugh. 'It made me think that what they had was the complete opposite of what I'd want out of a marriage.'

They sat for a moment. Both pensive.

'Come on,' Dorothy said finally, standing up. 'Let's go and treat ourselves to a hot chocolate at Meng's.'

'Sounds like a plan,' said Bobby. 'And you can tell me more about any other thoughts you might have been having lately.'

As they made their way out, Bobby put his arm around Dorothy's waist and pulled her close. The woman he loved clearly wanted to venture down the road less travelled.

Well, there was no way she was going to do it on her own.

He would be with her every step of the way.

Chapter Forty-Six

The next day, Helen had decided to give her father and Gloria their Christmas present early. It was something she knew all the women would want to be a part of and help celebrate, which was why she had organised a little party and had let her staff leave early.

Rosie, Dorothy and Angie were the first to arrive.

'Do you want us to do anything?' Rosie asked, looking around the office.

'I just thought we could move these tables together,' Helen said, walking over to the main sorting desk.

Polly came banging through the main door, carrying a wooden box. Seeing them manoeuvring the table, she laughed.

'Oh, I've just had a feeling of déjà vu!' she said.

They all looked up and knew she was talking about the day they had moved this very table in order for her to give birth to Artie, who had decided to come early.

'Ugh,' said Angie, looking down at the wooden top. 'And we're gonna eat off this?'

'Who says there's going to be food?' Martha said, coming in behind Polly and carrying another box.

'Yer can't have a party without some nosh,' said Angie.

'And Angie would be right,' Helen said, walking into her office and coming back out with a tray of sandwiches and sausage rolls.

Polly put the box down and started to take out bottles of lemonade and dandelion and burdock, which she had got from the Admiral. Martha followed and unpacked her box, which contained bottles of beer, as well as a bottle of port and a half-bottle of whisky.

'Blimey, there's only gonna be …' Angie did the addition in her head '… eleven of us.'

'Any leftovers can be divided up and taken home,' Helen said, walking over to Marie-Anne's desk, where she had left a tray of clean and polished glasses.

'The lovebirds have arrived!' Dorothy shouted out on seeing Hannah and Olly walk through the door.

Hannah blushed as Olly took her hand and they sat down at the table.

'Where's Gloria?'

'She's gone to wait for Jack at the main gates,' Martha informed them. They all knew that Jack was coming straight to the yard from Crown's.

Polly had just started to pour the drinks when Bobby walked in, stopping to hold the door open. A second later, Georgina appeared, her handbag and her little boxed-up Brownie slung over her shoulder as she had just come from a rather boring cheque presentation.

'Georgina!' Helen exclaimed. She had been unsure if she would turn up. 'So glad you could make it.'

Bobby followed her in.

The door was just closing when it was once again pulled open.

'Yeah!' Dorothy called out. 'Last but not least!'

Gloria and Jack walked into the open-plan office, both with big smiles on their faces.

They all knew that Gloria was particularly happy today as she had got a Christmas card from Gordon. Bobby had reassured her that *Opportune*'s role in the war was now mainly escorting convoys and minelaying, but it still didn't stop her worrying. She'd told them it was the best

343

Christmas present she could ever have received, and they knew she meant every word.

'This looks like a proper party,' Gloria said, looking at Helen. 'I thought yer said it was just a little get-together?'

Jack chuckled as he looked around at the office, which had been decorated a week ago for the run-up to Christmas. Every day, another paper chain had been added, or a string of tinsel. Christmas cards were also dotted around the room.

'Ah,' Helen explained, 'Marie-Anne and her cohorts asked me if they could go to town on the decorations this year.'

'No guessing what your answer was,' Jack laughed. He caught Bobby taking a seat next to Dorothy and nodded over at him. 'All right, Bobby?'

'Couldn't be better,' came the reply. Jack knew this to be true. He had never seen Gloria's son so happy.

As everyone settled at the table, Polly continued to pour the drinks and Martha handed out plates. Helen told everyone to tuck in. Looking across at Georgina, she thought she looked a little nervous, or was there something worrying her?

'Is your father all right?' she asked.

Georgina nodded. 'Yes, he's fine.'

'And work's going well?' This question was from Gloria, who had also noticed that Georgina looked a little pale. Anxious, even.

'Oh, yes, yes,' she tapped the top of her camera. 'All well there.'

'And the *Echo*'s still up for you doing the photos on Christmas Day?' Dorothy asked.

There was a communal sigh from the women.

Angie let out a ribald laugh. 'We can't complain. We've been here more than five minutes and she's only just mentioned the extravaganza.'

'Yes,' Martha laughed. 'Must be a record.'

Dorothy rolled her eyes.

Georgina let out a nervous cough and started to shuffle uncomfortably on her chair. She hadn't touched her drink or her sandwich.

Picking up that something was amiss, Rosie looked at her friend and furrowed her brow.

'Actually,' Georgina said, 'there's something I need to tell you all.' Her tone was deadly serious, causing everyone at the table to stop chattering and concentrate on their friend.

Rosie looked at Helen and back to Georgina, wondering if she knew what this was all about. Helen's expression told her she didn't.

'What is it you need to tell us?' Dorothy said, flashing Bobby a concerned look. They had all welcomed Georgina into the fold and thought the world of her. She had also been a good friend to Rosie and had helped her by spending time with Charlotte when she'd gone through a stage of not wanting to be on her own.

Suddenly, Georgina took a huge gulp of her port and lemon and declared:

'*It was me.*'

Everyone looked at her and waited for further clarification.

'It was me that did Miriam's dirty work for her.' Georgina looked at Helen, a little guiltily. She was aware this was probably not the topic of conversation Helen had anticipated for her little Christmas soirée.

'*You* were the private eye that found out our secrets for Miriam?' Dorothy asked.

Georgina nodded solemnly. 'I was ... Well, Miriam didn't know it was *me* doing the work. She thought it was my father. I think she was under the misapprehension that I was Dad's secretary.'

'So, it was you who found out about my real mother?' Martha asked.

A nod and a guilt-ridden look from Georgina.

'And about both our mams?' Angie said, cocking her head in Dorothy's direction.

Another nod and another equally guilt-ridden look.

'And about my aunty being in debt?' Hannah asked.

Georgina looked shamefaced. As if Hannah and her aunty hadn't had enough worries on their shoulders, without her actions having the potential to add to them.

'I'm sorry,' Georgina said. 'Really, *so* sorry. There isn't any excuse, other than I would never have done it if I had known you all back then ... Never ... I promise you.'

Everyone was quiet for a moment. Bobby looked at Dorothy, who didn't appear angry, and at his mam and Jack, who also didn't seem in any way outraged – just shocked.

'I feel terrible,' Georgina said, trying her hardest to keep her feelings in check. She did not want to cry and for them to feel sorry for her, for that to detract from the fury that they would – should – feel towards her. 'I should have told you all from the start, but I didn't. I could pretend I didn't because of "client confidentiality", but that would be a lie too.'

She took a deep breath. She had come this far; she needed to get it all out, like excising a boil.

'I didn't tell you because I was ashamed of the work I had done. And of the consequences of that work.' She looked at Gloria and Jack for the first time. 'I wouldn't blame you one bit for hating me and never wanting to see me again.'

Her eyes flickered to Rosie. She was the person she was most concerned about, but her friend's attention seemed to be on the rest of the women's faces, gauging their reactions.

Bobby sat back in his chair. *So, this was the person who had provided the ammunition for Miriam to banish Jack to the Clyde?*

346

The air was still. No one was eating or drinking. Everyone looked totally gobsmacked, which was not so surprising. Never in a million years would he have thought this book-ish, very strait-laced young woman had worked as a private eye.

'So, that's why I agreed to come today,' she said, casting a look at Helen. 'I couldn't carry this guilt around with me any more.'

She stood up.

'So, I just want you to know. All of you ...' She scanned the faces around the table. 'I'm so sorry for all the heart-ache my actions have caused.'

Helen looked at everyone and then back at Georgina. She was one of the proudest and most stoic people she knew. As well as probably one of the most intelligent.

'Georgina, sit down ... please,' she implored. 'Because that's not quite the whole picture, is it?'

'There's more?' Angie asked, agog.

'More, but in a good way,' Helen said, her eyes survey-ing the women's faces. 'You see, Georgina was also respon-sible for helping me to find out about Bel's true paternity, and for providing me with the report.'

'The report that helped bring Jack home?' Polly said.

Helen nodded. They all knew how Helen had given the report to Bel, who had used it as leverage when she and Pearl had gone to confront Mr Havelock last Christmas.

Georgina looked at Helen and then at the rest of the women. They didn't look as though they were going to lynch her.

Martha gave Georgina a gap-toothed smile. 'Well, I'd say that easily evens the score.' She looked at her workmates. 'The way I see it, Georgina helped to get Jack banished but she also helped to get him back.'

'And,' Hannah was quick to agree, 'in a funny kind of a way, it worked to Aunty Rina's advantage … Miriam finding out that the business was in a load of debt led to Rosie and Gloria getting her a job with Vera – and we all know how that worked out.'

Everyone chuckled thinking of the two women, chalk and cheese, one always grumbling about the other and loving it.

Georgina couldn't believe it. *They were laughing. They didn't hate her. They were forgiving her.*

'And it's not as if *we've* suffered, is it, Dor?' Angie said. 'My mam's gonna get caught out eventually. It's just a matter of time.'

'That's true,' Dorothy agreed, looking at Bobby, so glad he knew the truth about her mother's bigamy. 'Both our mothers have been walking a fine line for ages.'

Rosie leant forward and put her hand over Georgina's.

'I can't help thinking that you've been too harsh on yourself,' she said, looking at her friend directly. 'Because when you did your work for Miriam, I believe you found out something about me, but you held it back, knowing how potentially devastating it could be.'

Georgina forced herself to return her friend's look. She could feel tears forming in her eyes and she blinked hard to keep them at bay.

'You found out about Lily's, didn't you?' Rosie asked. 'You found out that I used to work there before my accident.' She touched the light smattering of scars on her face self-consciously. 'But you never let on, did you? And you never let on to Helen either?'

Helen was suddenly aware of everyone looking at her. She tried to keep her shock from showing. *So, Rosie had been a working girl!*

'That's right,' she said. 'Georgina never breathed a word.'

The room was charged. Rosie's 'other life' was never openly talked about.

'Well, in my opinion,' Gloria said, breaking the silence and drawing the conversation away from Rosie and back to Georgina, 'I really don't think there's anything to forgive.' She looked at Jack, who nodded his agreement.

'There's nothing to feel guilty about, Georgina,' he said. 'Yer were just doing your job. Looking after yer 'n yer father, keeping food on the table 'n a roof over yer heads. If Miriam hadn't employed yer, she'd have paid someone else to find out everyone's secrets, and they certainly wouldn't have held back what they found out about Rosie here.'

The women all mumbled their agreement.

Georgina felt her chest constrict as she desperately held back the tears and the myriad emotions welling up inside of her, bursting to come out.

'Well, I think this deserves a toast!' Hannah said, smiling at Georgina and looking around the table. 'A toast to friendship!'

'Hear! Hear!' everyone chorused. 'To friendship!'

Georgina tentatively lifted her glass.

'To friendship,' she said. It was what she had always wanted – and been terrified of losing.

Everyone clinked glasses, making sure that theirs touched Georgina's – their eyes showing her that there were no unspoken resentments.

They all took a sip of their drinks.

'And the best Christmas Extravaganza ever!' Dorothy chipped in.

Everyone groaned and rolled their eyes, but they still made the toast.

'To the best Christmas Extravaganza ever!'

'Time to tuck in, everyone,' Helen ordered, getting up and putting on the wireless. She was pleased to hear the early-evening programme was playing festive songs. Walking back to her seat, she smiled as she saw that Dorothy and Angie had already started quizzing Georgina about her past life as a private eye. They were clearly captivated. Everyone else was listening, equally curious.

Over the next twenty minutes, Georgina continued to be grilled about all aspects of the job. *What was the strangest job she'd had to do? The most exciting? Dangerous? Where did she get her information from? Did she have to pay people?* When the conversation turned to Georgina's work at the *Echo*, Helen leant towards Rosie, who was sitting to her right.

'You know, I always suspected Georgina was holding something back – that for some reason she was protecting you.' It had always puzzled Helen how Rosie had been able to afford to send her sister, Charlotte, to boarding school and then, more recently, to the Sunderland Church High School. Now she knew. 'When I heard about Maisie and her work at Lily's, well, I started to wonder.' She looked at Rosie and gave her a half smile. 'I'm guessing that was why you didn't want Charlotte to come back here to live?'

Rosie took a sip of her drink and nodded.

'So Charlotte knows?' Helen asked hesitantly.

Rosie nodded.

'Must have been difficult – telling her?' Helen couldn't stop herself. She had been so curious for so long.

Rosie let out a bitter laugh. 'Just a little.'

'But you obviously worked it out,' Helen said.

'We did,' said Rosie.

Helen desperately wanted to ask about Peter and how he had reacted to Rosie's past, especially as he'd been a detective for the Borough Police, but she knew this was a step too far. 'You know I would never judge, don't you?' she said instead.

Rosie looked at Helen. 'I appreciate you saying that.'

They were both quiet for a moment, looking at everyone as they chatted away, the noise getting louder, the Christmas songs adding to an atmosphere that seemed to have become even more festive since Georgina's confession and absolution.

Helen decided this was the perfect moment to go ahead with what she had planned to do – the reason she had organised this intimate Christmas party. She took a deep breath and tapped her glass with a teaspoon.

The noise quietened down.

'I have a confession to make too,' Helen said, suppressing a chuckle on seeing Dorothy nudge Angie and nearly knock her off her chair.

'But it's nothing salacious, I'm afraid. Nothing as juicy as working as a private eye.' Helen smiled at Georgina, whose cheeks were now rosy and who looked happier than she had ever seen her before.

'I really organised this party so that I could get you all together and we could all enjoy a Christmas present I've managed to get – thanks in part to Georgina.'

Everyone turned to look at Georgina.

'A rather unusual Christmas present I've managed to get for Gloria and my father,' Helen said.

Everyone's attention now swung to Gloria and Jack, who were sitting next to each other, looking relaxed.

Helen pulled out an envelope from her handbag.

'Can you pass this to my father and his wife-to-be, please?'

Helen handed the brown, very unfestive-looking present to Georgina, who passed it to Gloria.

Narrowing her eyes suspiciously at the envelope, Gloria turned to Jack and gave him a puzzled look.

'Go on, open it,' he encouraged. He, too, seemed perplexed.

'Do yer know what's inside?' Gloria asked him.

He laughed and shook his head. 'I've no idea what my daughter's been up to.'

Everyone fell silent as Gloria gently tore open the envelope.

Pulling out the document, she turned it the right way up and started to read. Jack sat forward and read it with her.

Everyone looked at Helen.

'Cor, the suspense is killing us,' Angie said. 'What is it?'

Helen laughed. 'It's Dad's official divorce document. It's what's known as a decree nisi, which means the divorce is not quite there – but nearly.'

Everyone was puzzled.

'It means,' Gloria said, looking at Helen and showing her how thankful she was, 'that we just have to wait six weeks before it becomes official.'

'That's when Dad will get the decree absolute,' Helen explained. 'Provided there are no last-minute challenges, which there won't be. There's no way Mother's going to object.' Helen looked at Georgina. 'Is there?'

Georgina shook her head. 'I doubt it very much.'

'How come?' Martha asked.

'I thought there was no way Miriam was going to agree to it?' Polly asked.

'It was a bit of a team effort, wasn't it, Georgina?' Helen said.

They were all looking from one woman to the other.

Jack and Gloria looked up. Both had tears in their eyes.

'Well, let's just say someone pointed out to Miriam what would come out in a court case if she went ahead and continued to defend the divorce,' Helen explained.

'And I'm guessing you had to have the evidence to bring up in court?' Dorothy said. Suddenly, she sat up straight and looked at Angie. They stared at each other, wide-eyed.

'The Grand!' they shouted in excitement, before turning their focus to Georgina.

'That's why you were waiting in the rain outside the Grand!' Dorothy exclaimed.

Georgina looked at Helen.

'That's right,' Helen said. 'Although I think Mother's concern about the photos taken of her staggering out of the hotel in the early hours was more to do with the state she looked, rather than what she might have been up to.' She glanced over to her father, who was still looking shocked but happy. Very happy.

'Georgina also gave sworn statements to be used in any legal proceedings. They outlined the work she did for Miriam that enabled her to banish Dad to the Clyde. The solicitor – a very nice chap called Mr Emery – seemed confident that a judge would see this as tantamount to desertion. An enforced separation as well as cruelty. Of which there was more evidence. But let's just say, when Mother read the folder full of statements and saw the photographs, she signed on the dotted line. And hey presto, Mr Emery did his stuff and we are now just weeks away from a full and proper divorce.' She looked at Gloria, who was wiping away a stray tear, and then at her father, who had his arm around his future wife's shoulders, holding her close. No one needed to say it, but the divorce and subsequent marriage would be a blessing for Hope too.

'Oh. My. God!' Dorothy said. 'I've just thought – you'll be divorced in time to get married on Valentine's Day. That would be *sooo* romantic!'

'This is brilliant news!' said Polly.

'It is,' Gloria said, looking at Helen. 'I don't know what to say.' She turned to Jack.

'I think we'd like to say "Thank you",' Jack said, regarding his daughter, who, he thought, had changed so much since he had been away. 'You're the best daughter a father could wish for.'

'And the best friend – 'n soon-to-be best stepdaughter – *I* could wish for,' Gloria added.

They all raised their glasses again.

'A toast!' Polly said.

'To love!' Hannah said, taking hold of Olly's hand.

'To a happy marriage!' Bobby said, looking at his mam. She certainly deserved it.

'I'll second that,' Helen said, looking at her father and thinking that he certainly did too.

Chapter Forty-Seven

Christmas Eve

When Dorothy woke the next morning, she said a quick prayer of thanks that Christmas Eve had fallen on a Sunday this year. She reiterated that thanks to a bleary-eyed Angie as she sat down at the kitchen table.

'Just think, if this was last year, or next year, we'd have to go into work,' Dorothy said, handing Angie a cup of tea before turning back to the hob and stirring a pan of porridge.

'Ta, Dor,' Angie said. She was particularly grateful as she was feeling a tad tender, having drunk a little too much port at yesterday's party.

Dorothy was also feeling fragile, but was determined not to give in to it. There was too much to do today.

'Get that down you,' she said, ladling out a bowl of hot oats and putting it on the table. 'You're going to need it for what we've got to do today.'

Angie groaned.

'And don't forget that later you've got to make yourself look gorgeous for Quentin's arrival.'

Angie's face brightened up.

'This is going to be *the best Christmas ever*,' Dorothy declared.

'And the most *exhausting ever*,' Angie said, eyeing the list of last-minute chores they had to do for the Christmas Extravaganza.

Having eaten breakfast, they both went to get changed, Angie mumbling that she thought she would have had an easier time of it if they had, in fact, had to go to work.

'Then we'd just have had twice as much to do,' Dorothy argued back.

'Yer weren't meant to hear that!' Angie shouted through from her room, pulling a jumper over her head and then pulling on a pair of trousers. Anything to keep warm. It was wonderful that the snow showed no sign of abating, but not that the temperature was below freezing.

'Never miss a trick, me,' Dorothy joshed back. She had also opted to wear the warmest clothes she could find in her wardrobe. They had a lot of walking and toing and fro-ing to do today.

'Actually,' she added, 'I'm thinking of going into pri-vate-investigation work when they chuck us out of the yard.'

'They're not gonna chuck us out of the yard, are they?' Angie came out of her room and was standing in Dorothy's bedroom doorway. Her friend was wearing practically identical clothes to the ones she had on. A cream-coloured jumper with high-waisted flared navy blue trousers.

'Of course, they are,' Dorothy said, turning round. When she saw Angie was wearing the same outfit, she burst out laughing. 'Two peas in a pod, eh?'

Angie turned and headed for the front door, where she pulled on her ankle boots.

'Why're they gonna chuck us out?' she asked again, slid-ing her arms into her three-quarter-length winter coat.

'Because,' Dorothy said, bobbing into the kitchen to retrieve her list from the table, '*the men* will be home and they'll want their jobs back.'

'But that's not fair – it'll mean *we'll* be out of a job,' Angie said, berating herself for not having thought about this before. 'What are we meant to do? We've got this flat to pay rent on. We'll have to find another job.'

Dorothy pulled on her boots and, in keeping with their identical outfits, chose her woollen coat instead of her mackintosh.

'Exactly why I'm thinking of going into private-eye work,' Dorothy said. 'It sounds so exciting.'

Angie tutted as she opened the front door to their flat and they both stepped out onto the landing. 'Seriously, though, Dor, what we gonna dee? Everyone's saying the war will be over by spring at the latest.'

Dorothy shut the door and they made their way down the stairs.

'I think us *little women* are expected to go back to the way we were before – hurry back to the kitchen sink and get on with baking and breeding.'

Angie laughed. 'Eee, Dor, yer dee have a way with words.'

A blast of icy air hit them as they walked out onto the pavement. They both automatically buttoned up their coats and pulled out their headscarves and gloves from their handbags.

'But what if us *little women* dinnit want to gan back to *baking and breeding*?' Angie said mournfully.

'Well, no one can force us, can they?' Dorothy said, grabbing her friend's arm as they headed to Tatham Street. 'We'll just have to work out what we do "wanna dee".'

Dorothy was a little concerned, though, by her friend's reaction to becoming a wife and mother. As she was sure Quentin would be if he had been privy to the conversation. The walk to the Elliots' might have taken only a few minutes, but by the time they'd reached the front door, their teeth were chattering. Yet more snow had started to fall, which Dorothy was pleased about. A white Christmas was now a guarantee.

Bobby answered the door, knowing that Dorothy and Angie would be arriving just after breakfast. He grabbed hold of Dorothy and gave her a kiss on the lips. Angie swatted him on the arm. 'Move ower, yer git big heffalump. I'm gonna turn to ice if I stand out here much longer.'

Bobby laughed. 'Sorry, Angie, your friend here is just too irresistible.'

Angie pushed past them and into the warmth of the Elliot household, where she was greeted by an excited Tramp and Pup, whose tails were wagging nineteen to the dozen.

'Yer might wanna try living with her,' she said, bending down to pat the dogs. 'Yer might think differently then.'

Bobby looked down at Dorothy and raised his eyebrows. 'Now, that's a thought.'

Dorothy rolled her eyes and followed her friend into the kitchen.

For the next hour or so they sat around the table, drinking tea and chatting about what had to be done by whom. Much as everyone was enjoying calling Dorothy a slave-driver, it was clear that they too were very excited about having such an unusual Christmas Day. Agnes showed everyone the bags of woollens that had been knitted by herself, Beryl and anyone else they had been able to rope in. Those who only had basic knitting skills had been tasked with making scarfs and patchwork blankets. The more experienced had made jumpers, which, they'd all agreed, were a necessity in this northern winter weather.

As Dorothy watched Agnes show them the fruits of their labour, she thought she seemed a little different. Very well and happy. She'd always thought Polly's ma was a handsome woman but a little worn out and jaded. That could not be said of her today. She had dyed her hair a deep chestnut brown and losing the grey had taken years off her.

Beryl bustled in just as they were getting ready to leave and triumphantly told them that the problem of the wrapping paper had been sorted. As paper was still rationed, it had been looking as though they would have to wrap the presents in newspapers, which Dorothy had found abhorrent – she'd said it would be like they were 'handing out fish lots'. Luckily, Beryl announced proudly, her two girls, Iris and Audrey, had been inventive and had managed to get their hands on quite a substantial amount of brown paper that was apparently 'going spare' at the GPO, where they worked. These past two days, Beryl declared, the nursery had been like Santa's factory, with the children taking on the role of little elves and putting their artistic talents to use by decorating the coarse brown paper with crayon drawings of anything that signified Christmas. Most of the drawings had been of Santa, snowmen, Christmas trees, baubles or even the odd reindeer, although one of the older children had done a very artistic drawing of the Nativity that Beryl and her daughters had agreed was too good to be used as wrapping paper and was going to be given as a gift.

After leaving the Elliots' and walking back towards town, Dorothy asked if Angie had really meant what she'd said about not wanting to be a homemaker.

'You're not really against marriage, are you?' Dorothy asked, worried her own change of heart might be influencing her friend.

'Wouldn't you be,' Angie shot back, 'if yer'd been brought up in a madhouse with a mam 'n dad who hated each other but kept spilling out bairns with barely two pennies to rub together?'

'I know, but that's not to say that would be the case with you,' Dorothy argued back. 'You could do it differently.'

'I suppose so,' Angie ruminated. 'Which reminds me, yer dee realise we're ganna have to pop in 'n see my mam 'n dad later?'

Dorothy had indeed realised a home visit was inevitable, but had decided not to think about it until they were there. 'At least we've got an excuse not to stay long.'

'Exactly,' Angie agreed, suddenly thankful that she was spending Christmas Eve helping Dorothy with her chores.

Walking into Vera's café, their senses were assailed by just about every kind of Christmas culinary delight.

'Mmm,' Angie said, closing her eyes and smelling all the wonderful aromas drifting from the kitchen into the main cafeteria.

Dorothy chuckled. 'You look like one of the Bisto Kids!'

Seeing Vera bustle out the back having heard the jangle of the brass doorbell, Dorothy and Angie made their way over to the counter.

'Before yer ask,' Vera said, 'we're all set. Well, just about, anyway.'

Seeing a family come into the café, Vera looked at Dorothy and Angie and pointed to a quiet table in the corner. 'Sit yerselves down. Me 'n Rina'll be over in a minute.'

Hearing the kerfuffle out front, Rina appeared, waved her hello and disappeared again before returning with a tea tray that not only had a big pot of tea on it, but a couple of sausage rolls as well. The two friends were joined a few minutes later by Vera, who had seen to the family and had turned the 'Open' sign to 'Closed'.

As Dorothy and Angie savoured the sausage rolls, which they later agreed were the best they'd ever tasted, Vera and Rina went through the list of sweets and savouries they'd be bringing to the do. Answering a question about transportation, Vera turned to Rina and said, 'Yer have this one to thank fer that. Some bloke's got the glad eye fer her. Said he'd be *honoured* to offer the use of his van 'n of himself as driver.'

Dorothy kicked Angie under the table as Rina, who had the beginnings of a blush creeping across her face, threw her boss the darkest of looks.

Leaving the café with a smattering of crumbs on their jumpers and warm, full bellies, Dorothy and Angie jumped on a tram that took them over the water to Monkwearmouth, known locally as the Barbary Coast. It was where Angie had been born and brought up. They'd decided to get the family visit done now to 'get it out of the way'.

As usual, Dorothy was immediately bowled over by a feral band of screaming children, who, thankfully, were distracted a few minutes later by Angie putting the family's Christmas present on the table: a load of pastries she had bought from the local bakery. Forcing down the obligatory cup of tea, they both listened as Angie's mam and dad made no bones of the fact they were unhappy that their daughter was not coming round on Christmas Day, especially as Liz, the eldest child, was away working as a Lumberjill and had not been given leave. Dorothy knew Angie's sister's no-show was because of a farmer's son she'd met, rather than her not being granted a Christmas pass. Just as she knew that Angie's mam and dad's unhappiness at not having either of their two oldest children back home for Christmas Day was because they wouldn't have anyone to help cook the dinner and look after the children. Angie's mam was particularly riled as it meant she would not be able to slip off to see her fancy man while her husband fell asleep in front of the fire at teatime.

Angie's parents were appeased, however, when their daughter produced a ten-shilling note and they only half listened when Angie told them to make the most of it because, she said with undisguised bitterness, she had just realised that she would be booted out of the yard once the war ended.

'When are you going to tell them about Quentin?' Dorothy asked as they left the madness and mayhem of Angie's childhood home and walked along Victor Street.

'I keep putting it off,' Angie said. 'Besides, I dinnit want to spend the little time I get to see Quentin with them.'

They walked in silence for a short while.

'Nothing to do with the fact Quentin's "posh"?' Dorothy asked tentatively.

They turned the corner and started along Dundas Street.

'Might be,' Angie conceded. 'I knar they'll say he's just "after one thing", and don't expect someone who "speaks like that to make an honest woman of yer".'

Dorothy thought her friend was spot on when it came to her family. Angie, she had learnt, saw life and people for what they were – even if the picture wasn't a particularly pleasant one.

When they arrived at Marie-Anne's house, they heard her and Dahlia before they saw them. They were singing Bing Crosby's hit 'Swinging on a Star', taking it in turns to sing alternate lines. It sounded remarkably good and their voices incredibly harmonious.

'How's that gorgeous hunk of a man of yours, Dorothy?' Dahlia asked as they sat down at the kitchen table to go over the programme. Matthew's secretary knew how much Dorothy hated the fact that she had been out on a date with Bobby before Dorothy had started to court him. Bobby had reassured Dorothy that 'nothing much' had gone on between the two of them, but Dorothy knew that first off, Bobby wouldn't admit it if it had, and secondly, Dahlia had not earned her nickname 'the Swedish seductress' for nothing.

Marie-Anne went through the order of entertainment, which also included Mick, a friend of the family who, she reassured Dorothy, was a very good magician. When Dahlia disappeared only to return with two crimson dresses with plunging necklines, Dorothy resolved to wear her black dress with an even deeper neckline.

After Dorothy and Angie had used the outside lavatory, they said their goodbyes and Dorothy stressed the time they were to arrive at the hospital and that they couldn't be late as everything had been planned down to the last minute.

'Don't worry. We won't be late,' Dahlia said. 'Not with all those brave wounded soldiers needing to be entertained and shown how much we appreciate them. It's just a shame there won't be any Yanks there.'

Angie had to suffer Dorothy muttering on about Dahlia for a good part of the journey back over to the other side of the river.

'I hope she doesn't bring the tone down,' Dorothy bitched.

Angie laughed. 'I hate to say it, Dor, but I think it'll be Dahlia that brings a smile to the men's faces tomorrow more than anything else we've got planned.'

Dorothy huffed, but didn't say anything.

Their final stop was at the Maison Nouvelle, where they slumped down in the back room and begged Kate not to offer them a pot of tea. It was the best part of the day as their work was almost done and they loved going to Kate's boutique and looking at her latest creations and trailing their hands across her rolls of fabric.

Kate showed them the decorations she had made and those she'd been given by some of her more well-off patrons who had been eager to contribute. Some of them had even gifted old suits they said their husbands wouldn't be wearing again, either because they were not as svelte as they used to be or because they'd passed on.

Dorothy and Angie were amazed at both the amount and the quality of the decorations Kate had managed to acquire, or make, on top of doing her normal seamstress work, which was busy at the best of times, never mind before Christmas.

Before they left, Kate brought out Angie's dress, which Dorothy had paid to be jazzed up as her Christmas present for her friend, and to thank her for helping with the extravaganza and putting up with her 'being a right old bossyboots'.

'Yer right there!' Angie laughed, but secretly she was really touched by what Dorothy had done.

'Try it on,' Kate insisted. 'I've made a few alterations, so I need to check it's OK.'

Angie's eyes were out on stalks looking at the dress, which now bore no resemblance to the one she'd had hanging in her wardrobe. Kate had created a stylish sweetheart neckline, which she had trimmed with lace. She had also shortened the hemline and added another lace trim.

When Angie came out of the dressing room and gave them a twirl, Kate and Dorothy agreed it looked even better on.

'A classy, Christmassy look,' Dorothy declared.

Kate insisted on adding a little make-up and quickly styled Angie's hair into victory rolls.

'Perfect,' Kate said, standing back and surveying her handiwork.

Angie caught herself in the mirror and was taken aback.

'Thanks, Kate.'

She looked at her best friend.

'And thanks, Dor – this really is *the best Christmas present ever*.'

Dorothy chuckled, pleased with her friend's reaction.

When they arrived back at the flat, they caught sight of Quentin as he hurried round the corner, trudging through fresh snow. As soon as he saw Angie standing at the bottom of the steps, his face lit up.

'You look sensational!' he said. When he reached the woman he'd fallen for the first time he'd seen her at this very spot two years ago, he held her for a moment.

'Sensational!' he repeated, before giving her a gentle kiss on the lips.

Not for the first time, Dorothy thought how similar the pair looked. They were around the same height – Quentin was just a smidgen taller – and they had the same strawberry-blond hair. Personality-wise, though, and in terms of class, they were at opposite ends of the spectrum.

'I thought you normally got dropped off at the door?' Angie asked, taking Quentin's hand and walking up the steps to their front door.

'Oh, I had a few errands to run,' he said. 'I'm parched. Cup of tea?'

Angie groaned. 'I'll make you a nice cuppa, but Dor and I have had enough to sink a ship.'

Leaving the lovebirds to spend the rest of Christmas Eve on their own, Dorothy popped her head in to check on Mrs Kwiatkowski before making her way up to the flat. She was exhausted. For once, she was glad she was in on her own and having an early night. She needed all the energy she could muster for the extravaganza. And she needed all the beauty sleep she could get, for she was determined to look stunning tomorrow. There was no way she was going to be outshone by the likes of Dahlia.

Chapter Forty-Eight

Christmas Day

For Helen, Christmas Day began with an early-morning call to the Royal Infirmary. It was a call she made every day to check on her grandmother's progress. As soon as she was put through to the ward, she was surprised to hear a broad North Yorkshire accent rather than the familiar local dialect of Annette, the day nurse.

Helen checked her watch. It had just gone eight o'clock. She knew the night and day shifts swapped at half seven. It was one of the reasons she always rang at this time as the new shift would have just been given an update on their patients. Helen also liked to make herself known to whoever was on duty and ensure they were aware that Henrietta was a family member, a relation of the Havelocks. It pained her to admit to anyone that she had Havelock blood coursing through her veins, but it guaranteed her grandmother first-class treatment.

'Good morning,' Helen said, keeping her tone soft and friendly. She had learnt over the years, especially during the time her father had been in this very hospital, that it paid to be pleasant and polite to the nursing staff; they were the ones who wielded the true power.

'This is Helen Crawford calling … I'm sorry, but I'm afraid I don't know your name. I normally speak to Annette at this time.'

'Annette was called away on a bit of an emergency,' the Yorkshire voice said. 'You're speaking to Nurse Taylor. I've been called in to cover.'

'Oh, I hope it's nothing serious?' Helen asked, genuinely concerned. She liked Annette. She had been brilliant with her grandmother, not just with her physical welfare, but she had spent time talking to her, checking on her emotional well-being, knowing that she was a long-term patient from the asylum.

'Actually,' Nurse Taylor said, pausing momentarily, unsure how much to disclose, 'she's gone to Oldham. One of them blasted doodlebugs landed on the street where her aunty lives. Annette's mother is beside herself. They've not been able to make any contact with her, so Annette's gone there to find out what she can.'

'Oh, that's terrible,' said Helen. She had caught the news last night about a load of buzz bombs being dropped on Manchester and the surrounding area. She'd heard there'd been casualties. 'What a terrible thing to happen – never mind at Christmas. Poor Annette. Please tell her I was asking after her if you do speak to her.'

'I will.' Nurse Taylor could hear that the Havelock girl was sincere. 'I'm guessing you're calling about Miss Girling?' she asked. She'd been told to expect a call from Charles Havelock's granddaughter.

'I am,' Helen said.

'Yes, she's had a good night,' Nurse Taylor said. Helen could hear the shuffling of paper. 'It says here there's been a request for her to go out for a few hours today. It being Christmas Day.'

Helen held her breath. The nurse had the authority to refuse the request if she felt Henrietta wasn't up to it.

'Well,' Nurse Taylor said, 'I've had a chat with her and given her a check-over and she seems very determined to go to this party at the Ryhope. I have to stress, though, that she is still very weak physically – her body is still recovering. In herself, though, she seems well. *Very well.* I'm looking at her now and she's sat up in her bed, chatting to the old lady in the bed next to her.' Helen heard a light chuckle down the phone. 'I think I need to inform your great-aunty that her neighbour is as deaf as a post.'

'I'm sure Aunty Henrietta won't mind one bit!' Helen joked, relieved she'd been given the green light. It had only been just over a week since she'd been at death's door, and although she'd amazed doctors with the speed of her recovery, she was still quite fragile. 'I'll be there around midday, if that's all right?'

'Yes, of course,' Nurse Taylor said. 'We'll see you then.'

'Thank you,' Helen said. 'And Happy Christmas!'

As she put the phone down, Helen really did feel that it *was* going to be a happy Christmas. Her heart still hurt when she thought of John, but she couldn't let that override her joy that her grandmother had lived. And after hearing what poor Annette's Christmas Day looked likely to entail, she knew she had much to be thankful for.

As she hurried back upstairs to get ready for the day of festivities, Helen heard the church bells start to ring out, calling parishioners to the early-morning Christmas service. Suddenly, she felt the joy of Yuletide wash over her. As she started to get ready for the day, her mind again wandered to John and she realised she was still holding on to a thread of hope that the barriers keeping her from the man she loved – from the man she now knew loved her back – were not insurmountable.

*

It had been decided that number 34 would be the meeting point for those involved in the Christmas Extravaganza. While Agnes and Beryl bustled about indoors getting the presents sorted, Lucille and Hope tore around the house with their new toys, still in a state of adrenaline-fuelled glee at the presents Santa had brought them.

Tramp and Pup would normally have been racing around with them, but Agnes had procured them each a big marrow bone from the local butcher. By midday, the Elliot household was bursting at the seams and spilling out onto Tatham Street. Not that anyone minded waiting out in the cold as it had turned out to be a picture-perfect Christmas Day. The snow was thick on the ground and crisp, but the sun was out and the air refreshing, if icy. The atmosphere was buzzing with excitement, the festive feel added to by the children who lived around the doors getting up to high jinks, skidding about in the snow, throwing snowballs and building snowmen. The lack of traffic on the road meant that the entire street had become their playground.

Dorothy, Angie, Gloria, Polly, Martha and Hannah stood in a gaggle, chatting away. They cut a comic picture as they were all dressed up to the nines, wearing their best dresses, which could be seen peeking out from under the hems of their woollen winter coats, but on their feet they were wearing their hobnailed leather work boots. Their best shoes were in cloth bags hanging off their shoulders.

Dorothy was also holding a clipboard and looking very serious and official as she ticked off everyone's names. She had organised this extravaganza with military precision and there were to be no hiccups as they approached the final furlong.

Bobby, wearing his navy uniform, and Joe, in his army attire, were standing chatting to Quentin and Olly. Bobby kept breaking off to chuck a few snowballs at the children, who screeched with excitement at the tall ex-seaman who lodged at the Elliot house joining in with their play.

When they all saw the army truck making its way down Tatham Street, there was a spontaneous shout of joy from everyone – the delight of the children further exacerbated by now having a moving target.

Jack was at the wheel of the khaki-coloured military truck and the Major was in the front passenger seat, sitting bolt upright in his regimental outfit, looking not unlike Father Christmas, with his grey-white beard and ruddy complexion. And like Santa Claus, he might already have indulged in a glass of brandy and a mince pie or two, which had given his cheeks their rosy glow.

'Merry Christmas!' he shouted out of the window. 'Your sleigh has arrived!'

His jolly welcome was met with an equally festive cheer of 'Merry Christmas!'

Jumping out of the driver's side, Jack hurried round to the back of Santa's metal sleigh and opened it up.

'It's cleaner than it looks,' he said, turning to the women crowding around him, all dressed in their best outfits, stamping their feet in the cold. 'And there's plenty of blankets in the corner there to keep you all warm.'

Dorothy baulked on seeing the distance from the ground to the floor of the truck. Normally, it would not have proved a problem for the women, who spent their days climbing scaffolding and going up and down ladders, but that was with their overalls on, not tight, tailored dresses. Positioning herself at the side of their transport with her clipboard in front of her, she looked at Martha.

'Can you help everyone in, please?'

'I think I can do the honours,' Bobby butted in, moving to the front of the women and putting his arm out to Martha to help her climb in.

'Thanks, Bobby,' Martha said with a chuckle. 'But I can manage.' Proving the point, she climbed into the back with no difficulty, her wide skirt not impeding her movement. She stayed standing so as to help the rest of the women up.

'I'll go and get the cargo,' Jack said, grabbing a couple of old sacks from the floor of the truck.

'And I'll go and say bye to Artie,' Polly panicked. She had been torn about leaving her son, now fifteen months old, but had convinced herself that he wouldn't miss his mammy, not with the twins, a house full of children and a mound of toys to play with.

Quentin and Olly climbed on board, followed by Gloria, Hannah and Angie.

Shifting along the bench to allow Angie to sit next to him, Quentin checked his pocket. It was something he'd been doing all morning.

When everyone had been ticked off Dorothy's list, Bobby took great pleasure in taking her clipboard off her, handing it to Martha, then sweeping her up in his arms and lifting her into the back of the truck, as though carrying her over the threshold.

Dorothy scowled at him as she stood up and straightened her clothes, although she was secretly glad as she could hardly move in her skin-tight black dress, never mind clamber into the back of a truck.

Seeing the front door of the Tatham Arms open, Dorothy spotted Pearl waving over to them, fag in mouth.

'Holdyer horses!' she shouted across, taking the cigarette out of her mouth and blowing out a plume of smoke. 'The best is yet to come!' Her cackle morphed into a hacking cough.

For a mad moment, Dorothy thought that Pearl had decided to invite herself and Bill to the do. A feeling of relief immediately followed when she saw Bill walk out of the pub with a heavy crate in his arms.

'Our Christmas box for your extravaganza,' he said breathlessly as he trudged across the road, taking care not to slip in the snow.

Pearl stayed in the doorway, her cardigan wrapped around her skinny frame, puffing on her cigarette.

'Tell them it's compliments of the Tatham 'n they're to patronise us when they're back on their feet!' she shouted over.

'Will do! Thanks, Pearl!' Dorothy shouted back.

Bobby took the crate off Bill and dumped it in the truck.

When Dorothy viewed the contents, her eyes nearly popped out. There were bottles of whisky, port, brandy and rum, along with some lemonade and ginger beer.

Dorothy looked up to thank Pearl again but just caught her disappearing back into the pub in a cloud of cigarette smoke.

'Thanks, Bill!' Bobby said. The two men shook hands.

'Have yourselves a good time.' Bill looked at everyone seated on the benches running along the inside of the truck. 'And Happy Christmas!'

His words were punctuated by a snowball hitting him on the side of the head.

Everyone chuckled as he bent down, scooped up a handful of snow and went in search of his attackers, bellowing 'Fee-fi-fo-fum' as he did so. The shrieks of the children as they scattered pierced the air.

'Now, you two, behave yourselves!' Beryl shouted out from her front doorstep, slippers on her feet, curlers in her hair and a pinny tied around her substantial girth.

'Yes, Mam!' Iris and Audrey called back. They were each carrying a sack of presents.

'You keep an eye on them!' she commanded Dorothy. 'I know what these young soldiers are like.'

'Of course I will, Beryl!' Dorothy replied, keeping a straight face. 'Like a hawk!'

Martha took the two sacks off Iris and Audrey and put them in the truck as Bobby helped them both clamber in.

Dorothy gave them the once-over. 'Angie's got the make-up,' she mumbled out of the corner of her mouth.

Polly hurried out of her front door, also carrying a sack. As she was climbing into the back, Maud and Mavis Goode from the sweet shop came hurrying over.

'Stocking fillers!' they announced. They were each holding a small box filled with little paper bags stuffed with an assortment of sweets. They handed them to Polly, for whom they had a soft spot, having watched her grow up.

'Thank you,' Polly said, taking the boxes. Seeing how much was there, she gasped. 'Oh my goodness, your shelves are going to be empty!'

The two women looked at each other. 'You just tell them young men thank you from us.'

'I will,' Polly promised, seeing how much their words were meant.

Dorothy looked down at her clipboard.

'Now, we're just waiting for—'

Before her words were out, they all saw Georgina hurrying around the corner of Hudson Road.

'Sorry!' she shouted out. 'Sorry I'm late!'

She stopped on reaching the truck.

'I managed to get some extra film!' She held up a small cylinder in her hand with a gleeful look in her eye.

373

'Well done, Georgina!' Dorothy put her hand out and helped her on board.

Jack appeared round the side of the truck.

'We ready for the off?' he asked.

Bobby jumped in.

'We are now,' he said, putting his arm around Dorothy and giving her a quick kiss.

Jack pulled the wooden doors shut, smiling as he did so at the happy, chattering faces lining either side of the truck.

Hobbling over to give Bel a kiss goodbye, Joe ruffled Lucille's hair and kissed the foreheads of the twins, who were nestled in their mammy's arms. Using his stick to navigate the snow, he walked to the passenger door, where Jack gave him a hand up.

Hurrying round the front, Jack jumped into the driver's seat and slowly pulled away. As he beeped the horn, the snowball-throwing children rearmed themselves and gave Santa's sleigh a good send-off.

*

Meanwhile, Rosie, Peter and Charlotte were being chauffeur-driven to the Ryhope by Lily's fiancé, George, in his red MG, which he insisted was his Christmas treat as he rarely got to drive 'the old gal'. When he'd got up that morning and had seen the street outside and the cricket ground opposite the house covered in a fresh thick white blanket of glistening snow, he had been even more enthused about his chauffeuring duties. He loved driving in challenging conditions. Lily, Maisie and Vivian had waved them off from the front door, after it had been arranged that George would pick them up later on and then bring them back home, along with Kate, for their own little Christmas soirée and swapping of presents.

'I want the whole family together!' Lily had demanded.

*

Matthew was also driving to the extravaganza in an MG, although his was a more up-to-date model and was glossy black. He had been invited due to the fact that he had persuaded the owners of Doxford's and Thompson's to pool their resources and organise the delivery of a huge Christmas tree, complete with decorations and fairy lights.

As Matthew's secretary and Helen's personal assistant were also playing such a large part in the extravaganza, he had offered to transport them both to the do. 'We can't have the two stars slumming it on public transport, can we? Or in the back of a truck,' he'd said.

The women all knew, though, that Matthew's eagerness to spend Christmas Day at the Ryhope Emergency Hospital was not so much driven by his need to be charitable as by the chance of romance. For, of course, Helen Crawford would be there.

The women had wondered amongst themselves if Helen would ever succumb to Matthew Royce's charms, or if she would continue to pine for her doctor – for a man, it was clear to them all, she could never have.

*

As the truck started along the long stretch of coastal road to Ryhope village, Dorothy checked her watch. Rina's 'admirer' should be turning up at the café around now. She had worked out that would give them plenty of time to load up his van, drive there and unload at the other end. Feeling that everything was in order, she turned her attention to her workmates.

375

'So, Polly—'

They all jerked forward as the truck hit another pothole.

'—was your ma really not put out you're not spending Christmas Day at home?'

'Yeah,' Gloria said. 'Agnes told me she wasn't, but I couldn't tell whether she might be, deep down.'

'No,' said Polly, speaking loudly to be heard over the noise of the engine. 'I really don't think she was.' She raised her eyebrows. 'She's invited Dr Billingham over.'

They all knew that Dr Billingham had become friendly with Agnes after he had helped Polly with a troublesome pregnancy. But not *that* friendly.

'Really?' Dorothy's voice rose several octaves.

'What's that?' Angie asked. She had been chatting to Quentin, who seemed a little ill at ease.

'Agnes is having Dr Billingham over for Christmas dinner!' Dorothy said, wide-eyed.

'Really?' Angie said. 'Do yer think they might get it together?'

Polly laughed. 'I don't know about that, but they've certainly become good friends this past year. Anyway, what about everyone else's mams and dads?' She looked around at everyone in the truck. 'Are they all right with you all going AWOL most of Christmas Day?'

'Mine still aren't talking to me,' Dorothy said, glancing at Bobby, who gave her a sympathetic look. 'Nor me them.'

'Mine are keeping me a plate warm for when I get back,' said Martha.

'Mine are happy because I gave them a ten-shilling note in compensation,' Angie said.

Everyone looked at Hannah. They were quiet for a moment. Not knowing what to say.

Gloria leant forward and squeezed her hand.

*

In the front of the truck, Jack, Joe and the Major chatted about the latest news reports. The Belgian transport ship SS *Léopoldville* had been sunk off the coast of France on Christmas Eve, with more than eight hundred lives lost. Closer to home, a stray V-1, having been launched by German bombers flying over the North Sea, had landed in the mining village of Tudhoe. Thankfully, there'd been no casualties, unlike in the north-west, where buzz bombs had caused the deaths of at least twenty-one civilians and obliterated hundreds of homes.

The main topic of conversation, though, was what was happening in the Ardennes, where Allied troops were fighting a major counter-offensive launched by Hitler just nine days previously.

'The papers are calling it the "'Battle of the Bulge",' the Major said, puffing on his cigar and blowing the smoke out of the open window.

'Why "bulge"?' Jack asked, driving carefully along the long coastal road, which was thick with snow, making it hard to avoid the dips and pits.

'The bulge is the wedge that Jerry has driven into the Allied lines,' the Major explained. 'It's put back our plans for a final offensive on the Western Front – although it's also going to exhaust Jerry's resources. We're still heading for victory, but it's going to cost more lives.' The sadness in his voice was clear.

*

When Helen went to pick up her grandmother from the hospital, she found her sitting in the chair by the side of her made-up bed.

Seeing her granddaughter appear through the swing doors of the ward, Henrietta's face lit up. She waved excitedly.

Helen smiled. Her grandmother's joie de vivre was infectious. It never ceased to amaze her that after all she had been through, Henrietta could still love life. All the badness that she had been subjected to had not corroded some kind of inherent innocence that seemed to form the bedrock of her personality.

Henrietta watched with bright eyes as Helen had a quick word with the brusque but friendly ward nurse, who, she had learnt, was from the town of Skipton on the edge of the Yorkshire Dales.

'Merry Christmas, Aunty.' Helen gave her grandmother a little wink. They were both keen to keep her real identity under wraps – Helen for fear of what her grandfather would do should he find out, Henrietta because she preferred the make-believe to reality.

'And a very Merry Christmas to you too, my dear.' Henrietta put her arms out and kissed her granddaughter lightly on both cheeks. 'You look quite stunning.' She looked at Helen in her figure-hugging, vibrant green dress. 'Quite beautiful.'

Helen smiled her thanks. She might not be able to tell John she loved him, but she could still spread out her tail feathers. Her deal with Dr Eris had not included walking around with a bag over her head.

Nurse Taylor brought the wheelchair to the bed.

'Doesn't she look the belle of the ball?' Henrietta said as she reluctantly allowed the nurse to help her into what she was calling her 'getaway transport'. She had to concede – even if it was just to herself – that her spirit felt strong, but her body was still lagging behind somewhat.

'She most certainly does,' Nurse Taylor agreed, turning the wheelchair around so that it was facing the main entrance. She moved to the side to allow Helen to take over.

'Your aunt's still a little weak, so be careful she doesn't overdo it,' she said directly to Helen.

'*I am here,*' Henrietta said, affronted. 'My legs might be a little shaky, but my ears are working perfectly well, thank you very much.'

Helen and Nurse Taylor exchanged looks.

'Cinderella is going to the ball!' Henrietta declared.

Nurse Taylor chuckled. 'She might well be, but this Cinders has to be back by four o'clock – and not a minute later.' She put a blanket over Henrietta's lap and tucked her in.

'Of course. I'll have her back safe and sound before her carriage turns into a pumpkin,' Helen reassured, looking at the nurse and showing her she understood that her grandmother was still recovering. If it had not been Christmas, she doubted the day trip would have been sanctioned.

Nurse Taylor watched as Helen wheeled Miss Girling off. She couldn't help but smile. What an odd couple.

Having reached the main foyer, Helen helped Henrietta out of the wheelchair. They walked slowly out of the main doors and down the steps to where Helen had parked her car. Helen opened the passenger door, wondering if her grandmother would be thinking about the last time she had been in it. If she was, she didn't say. And she didn't need reminding. This was Christmas. A day for happy thoughts and remembrances.

'What a shame your mother couldn't come too,' Henrietta said. 'I would have thought Miriam would have enjoyed going to such an "extravaganza". She did love to go to parties as a child. She would talk endlessly about what she would wear and who would be there.'

Helen had to bite her tongue. Her grandmother could not – or perhaps would not – see any bad in her daughter. If

379

Miriam turned up, she'd be shown the door. She'd caused too much grief to too many people.

'I don't think wild horses would keep Mother away from the Grand – especially on Christmas Day,' Helen said.

A few minutes later, they had pulled up outside the Maison Nouvelle.

Kate was waiting, looking out of the window, watching as couples and families walked past. She was indulging in her favourite pastime – people-watching, or rather, looking at what people were wearing.

As soon as Helen and Henrietta got out of the car, she opened the door.

'Come in!' She ushered them inside.

Stepping into the boutique, Helen was hit by the warmth, which was a relief. The hospital had been warm, but as soon as they'd stepped outside, the icy air had hit them like a slap in the face. She didn't want her grandmother catching a cold.

'I do love it here,' Henrietta said, looking around at all the fabrics. 'I feel like a child in a sweetie shop.'

'Can you remember what your new outfit looks like, Grandmother?' Helen asked tentatively. John had warned her that as Henrietta had been unconscious for several hours, she might have suffered some neurological damage, memory loss being his main concern.

'Of course I can,' Henrietta said, her eyes looking around and finding her stylish navy blue skirt suit, which had been laid out on the front counter. 'How could I forget.' She looked at Kate. 'You are such a talent, my dear. Although I'm sure you don't need me to tell you that.'

'Come on then, Grandmother,' Helen said, sensing Kate's discomfort at being praised. 'Cinders needs to get changed.' She led her to the back room, enjoying playing the part of fairy godmother.

Twenty minutes later, having changed into her elegant skirt and jacket ensemble and allowed Kate to do her make-up, Henrietta was ready to go to the ball. It took another ten minutes for Helen and Kate to pack up the car with the Christmas decorations and a huge pile of second-hand suits, and then they were off. Helen was driving, with Henrietta in the passenger seat and Kate in the back, her pale face and bobbed dark brown hair just about visible amongst the piles of second-hand clothes and mounds of tinsel.

Chapter Forty-Nine

There was a great sense of anticipation at the Ryhope Emergency Hospital. The patients had been given their Christmas dinner, which, it had to be said, did not resemble anything the men remembered from before the war – and wasn't helped by being barely warm, served up on trays and eaten while they sat up in bed. But no one complained. Why would they? Most of them were just glad to be alive and back in Blighty. On top of which, word had gone round that their Christmas Extravaganza also included some sort of a buffet.

Dr Parker and a few of the other doctors who were on call, as well as a group of nurses who were either on their break or had managed to leave their posts for a few minutes, were standing at the top of the steps to the hospital entrance, ready to greet the new arrivals. It was not just the patients who were excited by the prospect of the extravaganza.

Seeing the olive green truck turning into the long driveway, they all started waving frantically, as though welcoming back long-lost friends. As the truck crunched to a halt on the driveway, they all shouted out in unison, 'Hurrah!'

Dr Parker smiled as he watched Dorothy, Angie, Gloria, Polly, Hannah and Martha spill out of the back while the nurses hurried down to greet them and wish them a Merry Christmas. He looked on as Dorothy introduced them to Bobby, Quentin and Olly, who were hauling out sacks of presents, the nurses telling them all how much everyone was looking forward to the day's events.

Having been forewarned that there would be an amputee, there was a wheelchair at the ready and two of the porters helped the Major out of the passenger side and into his own tinsel-clad mobile throne.

'You know,' one of the young nurses said, looking at Major Black in his uniform, his medals proudly on display, 'we were just saying how we wished we had a Father Christmas – how it would be the icing on the cake.' She chuckled, her blue eyes twinkling. 'Now it would appear my Christmas wish has been granted! We just need to find you a Santa hat.'

Major Black let out a bark of laughter. 'Well, my dear, we had better go and find one!' As he was whisked away, his voice boomed out, 'Now why didn't they have nurses like you in my day? Eh?'

Dr Parker had specifically asked Helen to invite the Major, so full of life and laughter, knowing he'd be the perfect tonic for some of his less fortunate new recruits whose lives he'd saved, but not their limbs. It was also why he'd asked Helen to invite Joe, now hobbling over to greet one of the doctors. As a married man with a young family, he was proof that having a disability did not stop you leading a normal life.

Seeing Helen's father appear from the back of the truck carrying a sack of presents, Dr Parker strode over to greet him.

'Good to see you, Jack! You look well! Very well!' Dr Parker had been Jack's doctor when he'd nearly drowned after his ship had been bombed.

The two men shook hands.

'You too!' Jack said, slapping Dr Parker on the back.

Walking round to the rear of the truck, Dr Parker spotted Bobby, his muscular arms straining through his naval uniform as he lugged the crate of booze out of the back.

Dr Parker looked at Dorothy, who was presently bossing everyone about. He caught her eye and tilted his head in the direction of Bobby, whose rolling gait was indicative of the weight of the contraband Christmas spirit. Guilt immediately washed over Dorothy's face. Dr Parker had told her it was hospital policy not to have any alcohol on the premises.

'It's all Pearl and Bill's fault,' Dorothy said, grimacing. 'I couldn't exactly tell them to take it back – that the extravaganza was meant to be a teetotal affair.' Though she knew as she said this that the thought had never once entered her head. 'Besides, it's not as if anyone's going to overindulge,' Dorothy continued arguing the case. 'There's probably just enough there for a toast after the King's speech.'

Dr Parker laughed. The hospital might have a no-alcohol policy, but it had been hard to enforce, what with visitors smuggling in hip flasks and quarter-bottles of spirits to their loved ones.

'As long as the doctors and nurses get a tipple as well, I think I can turn a blind eye,' he said.

Dorothy beamed. 'That goes without saying.'

'Come on, let's go in,' he said, looking down at Dorothy's clipboard. 'I have a feeling you have instructions to impart.'

Once inside, Dorothy's jaw dropped on seeing the rather grand Christmas tree, which had a large plaque at the bottom wishing all the brave men at the Ryhope Emergency Hospital a Merry Christmas from Doxford & Sons and J.L. Thompson & Sons.

Dorothy felt Bobby behind her as he slid his arms around her waist and whispered in her ear, 'Amazing, isn't it?'

'It is,' she agreed, enjoying the feel of his body pressing against hers. She had only seen him in his navy uniform a few times and she thought he looked even more dashing than normal.

'Almost as amazing as my girl,' he added.

Dorothy turned round, reluctantly breaking free from his hold.

'Woman,' she corrected. 'Not *girl*. Your *woman*.'

Bobby stood back and looked at Dorothy in a dress that showed off every wonderful curve. 'And you're certainly that. All woman.' He beamed. 'And all mine.'

Dorothy shook her head and turned her attention back to her clipboard.

Clearing her throat, she looked at the Christmas Extravaganza volunteers, now all gathered around the huge glittering Christmas tree, which had been decorated in just about every colour of the rainbow. It had also been lit up with an array of coloured Christmas lights, an extravagance rarely seen during these times of austerity.

'If I can have everyone's attention,' she said, not needing to raise her voice too much as the high ceiling of the foyer afforded good acoustics.

Everyone stopped chattering and listened to Dorothy as she took them through the timetable of events.

As he looked out of the main door, Dr Parker saw a green sports car pull up. His heart started to beat fast and he admonished himself. By the time he'd made it down the stone steps, Helen was climbing out of the car. Seeing her in her vibrant green velvet dress took his breath away. She looked incredible.

'Helen!' He slowed down when he reached her. 'Merry Christmas. And I have to say, you look amazing.'

'Thank you, John,' Helen said, stepping towards him. 'Merry Christmas to you too.' She gently put her hand on his arm and kissed him lightly on his cheek.

Feeling his body shiver involuntarily, a shiver that had nothing to do with the cold, Dr Parker went to return the kiss. As he did so, his eyes flickered momentarily to her lips.

'Merry Christmas, Helen,' he said, his mouth touching her cheek. He could smell a mixture of make-up and perfume.

They both stood looking at each other. He mesmerised as he always was by her emerald eyes. She still feeling the touch of his lips on her skin.

Hearing the passenger door open, Helen turned to see Henrietta stepping unsteadily out of the car. 'Grandmama, you have to be careful.'

'I told her to wait,' Kate said, having seen that Helen and Dr Parker were having a moment and not wanting to spoil it. 'But I think Henrietta is afraid they'll start without her,' she joked as she too clambered out of the car.

'Kate! Miss Girling!' Dr Parker said. 'How lovely to see you both.'

Henrietta's eyes fixed on Dr Parker as Helen took hold of her arm.

'Go,' Helen told Kate, knowing she would be itching to get started on the decorations. 'I'll leave the car open so that people can come and get what they need.'

Dr Parker looked at the back passenger seat as Kate pulled out a bag overflowing with tinsel. 'Looks like the Christmas Extravaganza is even going to have Santa's grotto.'

'More of a Winter Wonderland, I hope,' Kate said, hurrying off.

Dr Parker looked at Helen as he cocked his head at Henrietta and smiled. 'She looks well. Very well.'

Henrietta sighed. 'Why have people started talking over me?'

Dr Parker laughed. 'Apologies, Miss Girling. Occupational hazard.' He offered her his arm. 'You look well – very well.'

Henrietta took his arm. 'You are a gentleman.' She looked at Helen and smiled. 'My granddaughter here could do with a Prince Charming to take her to the ball – are you available?'

'Grandmother!' Helen reprimanded. They'd had a chat about John and how it was imperative he did not know how she really felt about him. Reluctantly, Henrietta had told her she would 'behave'.

'Miss Girling, I'm sure your granddaughter is going to have an army of Prince Charmings falling over themselves to take her to the ball,' Dr Parker said.

'Besides which,' Helen said, flashing her grandmother a *don't-dare-say-another word* look, 'this Prince Charming is already taken.'

'Shame,' Henrietta said. 'I think you'd make a perfect couple.'

Helen threw her grandmother another warning glare, which Henrietta ignored.

As they reached the hospital entrance, Bobby, Quentin and Olly passed them on the way out to collect the rest of the decorations and the second-hand suits.

'Happy Christmas!' they shouted.

'Merry Christmas!' Henrietta, Helen and Dr Parker called back.

'Look, your chariot awaits, Grandmama!' Helen said, seeing through the open doors a large, old-fashioned wooden wheelchair with a high back.

Henrietta narrowed her eyes and viewed it suspiciously. 'I'm not staying in it for the duration. I'll only be using it for when I need a rest.'

'As you wish, Grandmama.' Helen looked at Dr Parker and raised her eyes skywards. They smiled at one another.

Walking into the foyer, they saw everyone milling around in front of the huge Christmas tree.

'Oh, what a beautiful sight,' Henrietta said a little breathlessly as she sat herself in the wheelchair. Relinquishing Dr Parker's arm, she patted his hand. 'Thank you, young man.'

Keeping hold of his hand, her voice became serious. 'And I must also thank you for saving my life. Helen has told me what you did. I do believe it is due to you that I am here today.'

'You are more than welcome,' Dr Parker said. 'But I can't take all the credit. It was most definitely a team effort.' He thought of Dorothy and Bobby. If it hadn't been for them, he would never have guessed in a million years that Henrietta had been poisoned by a plant indigenous to a country on the other side of the world. And had it not been for Claire, he would not have known what antidote to use.

'They still haven't told me what exactly was wrong with me – what it was that poisoned me,' Henrietta probed.

Helen threw John a look that told him she had not yet disclosed to her grandmother the real cause of her near-death experience – nor the perpetrator.

'Oh, look who's here,' Helen said, seeing Dr Eris walk into the foyer. She was glad of the distraction, but not that it was Claire – especially as she looked quite stunning in a pair of cream silk slacks and a matching blouse, her auburn hair piled high, accentuating her cheekbones. Her make-up was minimal, but done so as to show off her hazel eyes. The only splash of colour was her red lipstick.

'Miss Girling, aren't you looking splendid?' Dr Eris said. 'And very well. Very well indeed. Quite the turnaround.' She looked at Helen and Dr Parker, who nodded their agreement.

Henrietta smiled up at Dr Eris. 'See, she doesn't talk about me as if I'm not here.'

Helen and Dr Parker laughed, making Dr Eris bristle. She felt an outsider, not privy to the 'in' joke.

'I'll catch you both later,' Helen said, moving to the back of the wheelchair and taking hold of the handles. She didn't want to be around them for too long for fear her grandmother would work out that it was Dr Eris who was courting Dr Parker – that it was her own doctor who had something over Helen, preventing her from being with the man she loved. She didn't trust Henrietta not to say anything – certainly not after hearing her Prince Charming comment. She would have to tell her at some point. But not today.

Swivelling Henrietta's wheelchair around so that her grandmother was facing away from Dr Parker and Dr Eris, Helen took a step back. 'Oh, Claire,' she said, dropping her voice. 'Do you mind if I have a quiet word with you a little later?'

Dr Eris smiled. 'No, of course not. Just come and get me.'

Helen glanced at John and then Claire. They made a nice-looking couple. She tried to anaesthetise the pain in her heart but didn't succeed. Pushing the wheelchair forward, she headed over to see Dorothy and the rest of the women.

On seeing Henrietta, there was great excitement.

'We've all been wanting to meet you for a long time!' Dorothy said, trying to keep her enthusiasm under control.

'Let me introduce you to the gang …'

*

'Claire, you look gorgeous – as always,' Dr Parker said, kissing her on the cheek.

'Thank you, John.' She gave him a cheeky smile. 'As do you.'

Dr Parker laughed, looking down at his white doctor's coat. 'I try my best.'

When he had seen Claire, his heart had skipped a beat, not because of the way she looked, although she did look lovely, but because today was going to be a special day in more ways than one. Finally, he felt as though he had sorted out his muddled thoughts. Helen was his friend – probably his best friend – but that was all. He had thought a lot about the conversation they'd had back in June at this very hospital. Helen had spelled out quite clearly that she loved him – but only as a friend. At the time, something hadn't sat quite right about what Helen had said, or perhaps it had been the way she'd said it, but lately he'd realised that this was just his subconscious hanging on to the hope that Helen wanted him. But it was a fantasy. Comprehending this had made him realise it was time to move on.

As had the fact that Helen and Claire seemed to be getting on much better lately. They had clearly bonded over Henrietta's illness and put their differences aside, whatever those differences might have been.

Giving him a peck on the cheek, Dr Eris told him she wanted to check on a patient who was due to be referred to her and that she would catch up with him later.

As she left, Dr Parker saw that Rosie, Peter and Charlotte had arrived. He waved them over. He was keen to take them to what had been nicknamed the 'Normandy ward', as most of the men there were French and had been injured on D-Day. As no one on his staff or on the other wards could speak more than a few words of basic French, the men were pretty much in the dark about what was happening.

Catching sight of Matthew walking through the door with Dahlia and Marie-Anne, Dr Parker quickly wished Peter, Rosie and Charlotte a Merry Christmas and ushered them off down the corridor. Halfway there, he suddenly realised he had forgotten to get Hannah and Olly, who were to speak to a few of the German soldiers on the main ward. Thankfully, Charlotte immediately volunteered to go back and get them. She too had seen the dishy Matthew Royce arrive and was keen to get another look.

*

Looking at her watch, Martha headed outside and was pleased to see the Salvation Army truck trundling down the driveway. Bang on time. She waved a welcome and heaved a sigh of relief that everything was going to plan. She would not want to be subjected to the wrath of Dorothy should it not. All Martha had to do now was give the band leader the donation that had been promised and which was in an envelope in her pocket, and then get them to follow her into the hospital. Once there, they could tune up their instruments by the Christmas tree before going onto the main ward and playing their first song, which would herald the start of the extravaganza.

Watching the band members climb out of the back of the truck, Martha was entranced by the array of glinting brass instruments being hauled out: French horns, trumpets, a bugle, all matching the red tunics and gold braids of the Salvation Army uniform. The last band member to appear was a young man who stood head and shoulders above the rest. He had the largest instrument – a huge tuba that seemed to wrap itself around him like a mammoth golden python. Martha couldn't stop herself staring – there weren't many men who were actually taller than she was. Feeling her attention on him, the tuba-playing giant turned and saw Martha. He responded to her stare with a wave and a smile. Martha thought it was the widest, kindest smile she had ever seen on a man. Certainly, on one of his size.

As the band followed Martha into the main foyer, a small olive green van came down the long driveway. The buffet had arrived. Angie, Polly and Gloria hurried out to help carry the food in, and to show Vera, Rina and Rina's admirer, who they learnt was called Harvey, to the canteen.

Twenty minutes later, Dorothy gave the signal to the band to start their first Christmas song. She had written an order of play, which she and Angie had spent many hours agonising over, ensuring that every slow song was followed by one that was bright and cheerful. She had given the list to the band leader, who'd seemed a little put out by the fact he was being told what they should play and when. Seeing that he was about to object, Dorothy had asked him in her sweetest, politest voice if he had received the donation from Martha. The band leader swallowed back his irritation. They would have to play a dozen Christmas Days from morning until night to collect the amount now safely tucked away in the top pocket of his tunic.

As the band positioned themselves at the top of the main ward, just past the nurse's desk, they were greeted by over a hundred expectant faces. Most of the men were either sitting up in their beds, a good majority with arms or legs held up in pulleys, or in chairs next to their beds. A number had put on their old army jackets, which had been cleaned up and returned to them. Joe was now seated with a small group of men. His photograph of Bel was doing the rounds, while the chatter was of the battles in which they had all fought, in Europe and in parts of the world they had never even heard of before this war.

As the band struck up and started playing 'We Wish You a Merry Christmas', the sound of the brass instruments infused the air, transforming the atmosphere in the ward from quiet, uncertain expectation to one of joy and excitement. Midway through the song, Major Black appeared in his wheelchair, which now had even more tinsel wrapped around it. A large, floppy Santa's hat had been found and placed on his head and his medals had been given a polish. The pretty young nurse, wearing a garland of paper chains around her neck and the Major's cap on her head, pushed Father Christmas slowly onto the ward. A huge round of applause was accompanied by a swell of voices shouting out a welcome fit for a king. A moment later, Dahlia and Marie-Anne came through the swing doors, pushing a trolley loaded up with sacks overflowing with presents. With the arrival of Santa's incredibly gorgeous helpers, both in vibrant red dresses and high-heeled shoes, the sound of the brass band was nearly drowned out by cheers and whistles.

'I think I should have told Dahlia and Marie-Anne to wear elf costumes,' Dorothy muttered to Angie.

'I think everyone's glad yer didn't,' said Angie.

As the Major was wheeled to the first beds and his 'helpers' started to hand out presents, along with a kiss on the cheek, the band struck up 'Santa Claus is Comin' to Town'.

Georgina followed, taking photographs and making notes of the men's names and regiments.

Dorothy, Angie, Gloria, Polly and Martha enjoyed watching the fruits of their labour. Dr Parker was standing to one side of the entrance with Helen and Henrietta, who had decided she was content to remain in her wheelchair for the time being. They all had smiles on their faces. The men's happiness was infectious.

For the next hour, the band played back-to-back festive songs and carols. The wrapping paper was admired – many of the men carefully folding the children's artwork and putting it aside, and many no doubt thinking of their own children. Presents were opened and held in the air to show everyone what gift they had received.

Helen wheeled Henrietta around and handed out the bags of sweets from Maud and Mavis. The men enjoyed chatting with a woman they suspected might be famous, as she was so stunning, and her elderly aunty, who looked like she might also have been a starlet in her heyday.

When the band played 'Silent Night', there were a few glassy eyes – the men as well as the women. The carol was too unbearable for Helen to listen to. Grief for the baby she had lost suddenly resurfaced, as it was wont to do every now and again. Making her excuses, she asked one of the older doctors, who had introduced himself simply as Dr Bernard, to keep an eye on Henrietta.

When it was time to move to the next ward, Dr Bernard, twirling the ends of his impressive handlebar moustache, asked if Henrietta would like to accompany him in fetching the men's Christmas Day visitors.

'Only if I can leave my chariot behind,' Henrietta declared, standing up gingerly and straightening her new tailored skirt.

'Only if you'll take my arm,' Dr Bernard replied, holding his arm out and showing there was to be no argument.

Helen returned to find Dr Bernard helping her grand-mother back into her wheelchair, having shown the guests onto the ward. The three of them quietly remained there, enjoying watching the men's faces light up as they greeted their families.

*

Meanwhile, the canteen was being decorated – or rather, transformed into the promised Winter Wonderland. Bobby, Quentin and Olly were up and down ladders, hanging streamers and star-shaped cut-outs, silver tinsel and bau-bles from the ceilings and walls, or wherever they were told to by Kate. A large bundle of mistletoe had already taken centre stage in the middle of the room, hanging just above head height, and a huge banner reading MERRY CHRISTMAS stretched across the canteen.

Audrey and Iris had been tasked with covering all the tables with white paper tablecloths and putting out small festive displays made up of thick church candles surrounded by holly. When they'd finished, Kate told them to go and help with the giving out of presents as it would be much more fun – for them and the soldiers. They didn't need telling twice.

Vera and Rina had taken over the kitchen and were busy putting out sandwiches, pies, vol-au-vent and sausage rolls onto large silver trays they had found in one of the cupboards. Harvey had also been roped into helping, not that he minded. This was turning out to be the best Christmas he'd had in a long time.

Chapter Fifty

When the Salvation Army played their final carol, 'God Rest Ye Merry, Gentlemen', which Dorothy and Angie had chosen as they felt it would end the gift-giving part of the day on a high, hopeful note, they announced to each ward that it was time for everyone to head to the canteen for the King's message to the Commonwealth. 'Which,' Dorothy announced loudly, 'will be followed by entertainment and a buffet.'

Seeing that some of the men needed a little cajoling as many had already started to play games of cards or dominoes, Angie added equally loudly that there might also be 'a little nip of something to toast King 'n country'. It was an enticement that led to the putting down of cards and a more concerted effort to obey Dorothy's instructions.

As they crowded into the canteen, there were gasps of amazement from every person who walked or was wheeled through the main entrance, for the place really had been transformed. The main overhead lights had been switched off and replaced by fairy lights, whilst candles had been lit on all the tables, the flickering flames highlighting the sparkling silver tinsel. The whole effect was magical.

Polly and Gloria took trays of drinks around the tables for toasting King and country. Martha took soft drinks to the Salvation Army, who had accepted the offer to stay and enjoy the rest of the day. And the tuba player took the opportunity of introducing himself properly to Martha, quickly telling her his name was Adam and he worked at the local colliery.

Dorothy and Angie noticed that Helen and Dr Eris seemed to be deep in conversation.

'I wonder what they're chatting about,' Dorothy mused. 'They don't seem as frosty with each other.'

'Maybe because Dr Eris helped save Henrietta,' Angie suggested. 'And she gave her those admissions forms.'

'Could be,' Dorothy ruminated. 'But it looks as though she's still stopping Helen from having her man.'

Looking up at the clock on the wall, Dorothy threw Angie a nervous look. 'It's time.'

She stepped forward and announced in her most sombre voice:

'And now for the King's Christmas Day message.'

A hush fell as Angie switched on the wireless and it crackled to life. She turned the volume up high.

Everyone fell silent as King George VI's faltering voice came through the airways.

'Once more, on Christmas Day, I speak to millions of you scattered far and near across the world. I count it a high privilege to be able to use these moments to send a Christmas message of goodwill to men and women of whatever creed and colour who may be listening to me throughout our Commonwealth and Empire – on the battlefields, on the high seas or in foreign lands. At this Christmas time we think proudly and gratefully of our fighting men wherever they may be. May God bless and protect them and bring them victory.'

Dorothy looked at Bobby, knowing he would be thinking of Gordon. He might claim his brother was a born survivor and could swim the Channel if he had to, but she knew that was for his mam's benefit.

'Our message goes to all who are wounded or sick in hospital and to the doctors and nurses in their labour of mercy.'

Dorothy looked around at the faces of everyone in the canteen – the wounded soldiers, the doctors and the nurses. It was the first time she felt emotional. She grabbed Angie's hand and squeezed it. She didn't need to look at her best friend to know she was feeling the same.

'And our thoughts and prayers are also with our men who are prisoners of war, and with their relatives in their loneliness and anxiety. Among the deepest sorrows we have felt in these years of strife, the one we feel most is the grief of separation. Families rent apart by the call of service.'

Dorothy and Angie looked at Polly, Gloria and Hannah. Their eyes were glistening with tears.

'We have rejoiced in the victories of this year, not least because they have broken down some of the barriers between us and our friends and brought us nearer to the time when we can all be together again with those we love. For the moment, we have a foretaste of that joy and we enter into the fellowship of Christmas Day. At this great festival, more perhaps than at any other season of the year, we long for a new birth of freedom and order among all nations, so that happiness and concord may prevail, and the scourge of war may be banished from our midst.'

It was so quiet you could hear a pin drop.

'We do not know what awaits us when we open the door of 1945, but if we look back to those earlier Christmas days of the war, we can surely say that the darkness daily grows less and less. The lamps which the Germans put out all over Europe, first in 1914 and then in 1939, are being slowly rekindled. Already, we can see some of them beginning to shine through the fog of war that still shrouds so many lands. Anxiety is giving way to confidence, and let us hope that before next Christmas Day, God willing, the story of liberation and triumph will be complete.

'Throughout the Empire, men and women and boys and girls, through hard work and much self-sacrifice, have all helped to bring victory nearer.'

The women automatically looked at each other – it was a look of pride.

'*In the meantime, in the old words that never lose their force, I wish you from my heart a happy Christmas and for the coming year a full measure of that courage and faith in God which alone enables us to bear old sorrows and face new trials until the day when the Christmas message – Peace on earth and goodwill toward men – finally comes true.*'

At this point, the quietness was broken by a murmuring of 'Hear! Hear!'

When the King's speech finished, those who were able stood for the National Anthem. The atmosphere was still and serious. As the first chords sounded out, everyone started to sing. After the final words of 'God Save the King', there was a moment's pause before Major Black raised his glass and boomed out, 'Hip hip hooray!'

'Hip hip hooray!' The whole canteen was filled with the sound of deep voices.

'Hip hip hooray!' The cheers rang louder still.

And then everyone took a slug of their drinks.

As they all sat back down, the cafeteria was filled with the noise of scraping chairs and the beginnings of chatter. Dorothy positioned herself at the front and waited for everyone to settle. As she did so, she had another quick sip of her port and lemon. Normally, she liked to be the centre of attention, but this was different. This was not holding court with her workmates in the middle of the shipyard. This was altogether very different and rather nerve-racking.

She tapped her glass with a teaspoon and cleared her throat as loudly as she could. She looked nervously at Bobby, who gave her a reassuring smile and a thumbs up.

'Next on today's Christmas Extravaganza agenda – ' she raised her voice as loud as she could without having to shout ' – is some live entertainment by Dahlia and

Marie-Anne, who you may all know as Santa's "not-so-little helpers".' There was a smatter of chuckling from the audience, which gave Dorothy some confidence. 'They are going to perform some Christmas songs for you.' She took in a gulp of air, realising that she actually needed to breathe. 'And afterwards Mick the Magician is going to amaze you with his wizardry.'

She put her hands together to applaud. Everyone followed her lead.

There – she'd done it!

Dorothy went over to Bobby, who slid his arm around her waist and whispered in her ear, 'I'm so incredibly proud of you.'

Watching Dahlia and Marie-Anne walk to the front, smiling at their audience, for once Dorothy felt not a flicker of envy. She would not want to swap places with either of them for all the tea in China. As they started singing 'Swinging on a Star', neither showed even a smidgen of nerves. They were both naturals, playing to the camera when Georgina stepped forward to take a shot. They had their audience captivated. Spotting one of the soldiers with a harmonica and his friend who was holding a flute, they waved them to the front to join in. After a raucous round of applause, they continued their set, ending with 'Winter Wonderland'. The men were up on their feet, whistling and cheering. Even Dorothy had to admit they were pretty good.

Chapter Fifty-One

Mick the Magician took over the entertainment as Vera, Rina, Harvey and Olly started to bring out the buffet. Bobby and Quentin carried out the big bowl of punch, putting it down on a long table before returning to the kitchen and fetching tumblers and glasses. Once everything had been laid out and the last trick performed, Polly and Gloria were put in charge of the gramophone and told by Dorothy to 'keep the music going'.

It didn't take long for everyone – the wounded soldiers, their families, the doctors and nurses and, of course, the organisers themselves, to fill their plates and return to their tables, after which Rina and Vera went to take over the music.

'Yer must be starving? Bet yer've not had owt to eat since this morning,' Vera said, pushing them towards the buffet.

Polly and Gloria smiled. It was true, they hadn't. The sausage rolls and pies had been heated up in the kitchen and the smell was making their mouths water.

'Yer missing Tommy?' Gloria asked as they put food onto their plates. 'Silly question, really.'

Polly smiled. 'I am, but I keep thinking that next year he'll be here – and we'll all be together for Christmas. And every time I think of him back home, I feel excited.'

'I feel the same about Gordon,' Gloria said, as they made their way over to the women's table. 'It feels possible now.'

'More so than ever,' said Polly.

'Good selection of songs,' Angie complimented them both as they sat down.

Martha, Hannah, Rosie and Georgina agreed. They all looked at Dorothy, but she was oblivious to Polly and Gloria's arrival and was staring over at Dahlia, who was standing at the punch table, chatting to Bobby.

'Can't that woman get her own bloke?' she said, her eyes still glued to her boyfriend and the Swedish seductress.

'Perhaps that's Dahlia's thing,' Polly said. 'She likes the ones she can't have.'

'Well, I wish she'd go and pick on someone else,' Dorothy huffed.

Rosie thought that Bobby wasn't the real focus of Dahlia's attention. She had noticed how Matthew's secretary kept glancing over to the table where her boss was.

'At least you know that Bobby only has eyes for you,' Rosie reassured her.

As if on cue, Bobby looked over at Dorothy and gave her what appeared to be an apologetic smile.

'Well,' Gloria said, changing the subject, 'I think yer deserve a huge pat on the back, Dor – 'n yer, too, Ange.'

'Thanks, Glor,' Dorothy said, finally bringing her attention back to her workmates. 'But it really was a team effort.' She took a bite of her sandwich. 'I'm just glad I don't have to do any more compèring.'

They were quiet for a moment while they tucked into their food.

Rosie looked over to check on Charlotte, who was sitting with Peter, both chatting away to a couple of soldiers, one of whom was in a wheelchair and was wearing one of Agnes's knitted jumpers on his top half and hospital regulation pyjamas on his bottom half.

Following Rosie's line of vision, Georgina picked up her camera and left the table. She returned a minute later, having got just the shot she was after.

'So, Hannah,' Dorothy said tentatively, 'was it all right – talking to the Germans?'

Everyone was quiet.

Hannah smiled a little sadly. 'Yes, it was.' She paused. 'Funnily enough, it probably helped me more than it did them.'

'How so?' Martha asked.

'I think it's easy to see people – situations – in a two-dimensional way,' she tried to explain. 'But it's never that simple, is it?'

Angie frowned, showing she was still unclear as to her friend's meaning.

'Well, it's easy to say they're the enemy and therefore they are bad … evil … but when Olly and I were chatting to them, they were just normal people. One of them was even telling us he wanted to stay here. That he didn't want to go back to Germany.'

'Really?' Polly said, surprised.

'Olly thinks he might have a soft spot for one of the nurses – and she for him.' Hannah looked over at Olly by the punch table, subtly trying to add a slug of spirits to each cup pushed in his direction.

'Blimey,' Angie said, incredulously. 'And there's me and Quentin putting off meeting the parents 'cos of their reaction – imagine taking a Jerry home?'

Seeing Quentin leave his post as bartender and start walking over to the toilets at the far end of the canteen, Angie announced: 'Quentin's off to the lav *again*. If he were a woman, I'd say he was preggers.'

'Why's that?' Martha asked.

''Cos every time my mam's up the duff, she's never off the loo.' Angie watched as he disappeared into the men's washroom.

'I suppose nerves can do that to a person,' Dorothy said without thinking.

'What's Quentin got to be nervous about?' Angie asked.

Dorothy didn't answer, pretending not to have heard.

'So, when do you think you'll be getting married, Glor?' Polly asked.

Gloria chuckled. 'If it's up to Jack, he'll be dragging me down to the registry office as soon as the divorce-absolute document drops on the doormat.'

Dorothy looked horrified. 'You can't get married on your own. You have to invite all of us, you know? And Georgina will have to take the photographs.'

Georgina smiled as she ate her sandwich. The relief she felt at finally having told the truth was great. Their acceptance and forgiveness had made this Christmas for her.

Gloria smiled. 'Don't worry, Dor, I think I'll make sure we pop in 'n tell yer en route.'

'No, Glor, you have to do it properly. Make sure we've all got warning so we can sort out a party and get new outfits. You can't just do it on the spur of the moment. I'll get Bobby to have a word with Jack.'

'I thought you'd be telling Gloria not to bother,' Polly laughed.

'Why's that?' Dorothy said, confused.

'Lately, you don't seem to be the biggest fan of marriage,' Rosie said.

'Yeah,' said Angie, 'yer knar, it being all about "baking and breeding".'

The women hooted with laughter.

Dorothy looked at Gloria, then back at Angie. 'I think marriage is perfect for certain people.' She kept her focus on her best friend. 'For some, it's the *best thing ever* – but I'm not sure I'm one of those.'

Gloria glanced at Dorothy and then over to Bobby. She wondered what her son thought of his sweetheart's recent change of heart.

Martha got up. 'I'm just going up for some more – anyone want anything?'

The women shook their heads.

'Talking of marriage,' Polly asked, turning her attention to Rosie. 'Have Lily and George decided on a date yet?' It was now two years since they had gifted their wedding to Polly and Tommy before he went back to Gibraltar.

'Still on the back burner,' Rosie said. '"Too much happening at the moment to organise the wedding of the decade" is all I'm ever told.' They chatted on for a while about Lily's plans to go legit, how she'd bought a few properties in town, which Rosie was managing, and how Rosie believed it was Lily's closeness to Charlotte that had her wanting to turn the West Lawn house into a proper home.

'Oh. My. God!' Dorothy suddenly said. 'Look at Martha! Chatting away to that tuba player!'

Everyone looked. Martha was indeed chatting to the Salvation Army soldier, who had joined their workmate at the buffet.

'She's allowed to chat to the opposite sex,' Hannah defended her. Martha had confided in her that the tuba player had introduced himself.

'I can't believe it, *Martha* – with a *bloke*!' Dorothy exclaimed.

'She's not exactly *with* him,' Polly said.

'Yeah, Dor, they're only *talking*,' said Angie.

'They actually look a bit like each other,' Dorothy said, still stunned.

'Well, they do say like attracts like,' said Rosie.

'Yeah, like yer 'n Bobby,' said Gloria.

'Yes, now that you point it out,' said Hannah, 'you are both quite tall, and dark, and very good-looking.'

'Thank you, Hannah!' Dorothy said, preening herself.

'Although they do *also* say opposites attract,' Angie said, nodding over in the direction of Dahlia, who was still chatting to Bobby.

'Don't goad her,' Polly said, 'otherwise there'll be handbags at dawn.'

Hearing a loud burst of laughter, their attention went to Matthew Royce, who was sitting with Helen, Dr Parker, Dr Eris, Henrietta and the elderly doctor with the outrageous moustache.

The women caught Helen watching Dr Parker, unaware that anyone else could see.

They all looked at each other. They had seen the love etched on Helen's face. Their hearts went out to her. Helen had made such a huge sacrifice for them all. She'd given up her love for their sakes and the sakes of their families. A love that could have been, were it not for Dr Claire Eris.

They would not forget what Helen had done for them all.

Chapter Fifty-Two

Helen looked at her watch. The time had come for Henrietta to return to the hospital. She turned to her grandmother, who had been chatting for quite some time to Dr Bernard. They seemed to be getting on very well and were clearly in the middle of an in-depth discussion.

'I'm awfully sorry,' Helen said, 'but I'm going to have to drag my aunty away from you. I promised I'd have her back by four. And not a minute later.'

'What a shame,' he lamented. 'We were just having the most interesting discussion about *A Tree Grows in Brooklyn*. So few people seem to read these days. And it's such a relief to chat to someone who doesn't want me to diagnose some ailment or other they might have.'

Helen laughed. John had told her it was one of the downsides of working in the medical profession. As soon as someone knew you were a doctor, you could wave goodbye to a normal evening of socialising.

'Well, it's been a joy chatting to you, Dr Bernard. You've made my Christmas Day even more enjoyable – if that was at all possible,' Henrietta said.

Was her grandmother flirting?

Helen watched as Dr Bernard took hold of Henrietta's pale hand and kissed it.

'My sentiments exactly!' he said, standing up.

Was the doctor flirting with her grandmother?

Helen put out her arm for Henrietta to hold so as to aid her walk back to the corridor, where she had insisted on putting her wheelchair.

'So sorry,' Helen said to Dr Bernard, sensing his disappointment, 'but I have to get Cinders back or the spell will be broken. Her carriage will be turned back into a pumpkin and then I'll never get her to the Royal.'

'Surely that wouldn't be such a catastrophe?' Dr Bernard said, smiling at Henrietta. 'Your aunty would just have to bed down here for the night instead of at the Infirmary. There'd even be a doctor to hand.'

He *was* flirting.

'I'm sure we'll meet again – as the song goes,' Henrietta said. And with that she turned and walked with her granddaughter across the canteen-turned-Winter Wonderland to the exit. As she did so, one of her gloves, which she had just pulled from her handbag, fell to the ground.

Dr Bernard smiled. He twisted his light grey moustache, walked over and picked it up. He had his glass slipper. They *would* meet again.

As Helen helped Henrietta back into her wheelchair, she shook her head. 'Well, Grandmother, I do believe you have an admirer.'

Henrietta looked wide-eyed at her granddaughter. 'And would that be such a surprise?'

Helen laughed as she started pushing the wheelchair down the corridor.

'No, not at all, Grandmother. Nothing surprises me about you. Absolutely nothing.'

*

Helen glanced at her watch as they neared the Royal. She could see that her grandmother was tiring. She pulled up in the parking area at the front of the hospital.

'Helen ...' Henrietta gave her granddaughter a serious look as the car came to a halt '... I have a request to make.'

'That sounds a tad ominous, Grandmama,' Helen said. 'What is it?'

'When I'm back on my feet properly,' she said, 'I want to go and see Gracie's parents. It's something I've been thinking about a lot these past few days.' She paused. 'Would you help me to find them? Arrange for me to meet them?'

'Yes, of course, Grandmama.' Helen hesitated. 'But let's take one step at a time, eh? Let's get you one hundred per cent fit and healthy first.'

Henrietta nodded. 'All right, my dear. But when I'm ready, will you do it? Will you find them and take me to them?'

'Of course I will,' she said.

Helen knew that her grandmother wanted to make amends, even though, in her opinion, Henrietta had done nothing wrong and was blameless, but she knew that her grandmother was not of the same mind.

Aware that Pearl visited Gracie's parents occasionally, Helen knew that there would be no problem locating them. She was unsure, though, how keen Gracie's mother and father would be to meet Henrietta. Gracie's parents hated Charles Havelock with as much intensity as Pearl did, and had made it clear that they would tell the world of the crimes committed against their daughter if needs be.

'On a lighter note,' Helen said, 'I have another Christmas present to give you, but it's not something I can hand to you at this moment in time.'

Henrietta looked at her granddaughter. Sometimes she caught her younger self in Helen. Not that she would ever tell her. Helen might love her dearly, but she doubted very much she wanted to be like her.

'But, Helen, you have already given me more than enough – this wonderful day, and this wonderful outfit.'

She looked down and smoothed her skirt. 'That and so much more. More than you will ever realise.'

Helen felt the prick of tears. She wanted to tell her grandmother that she had given her so much too. Much more than *she* would ever realise. But she didn't. She didn't trust herself.

Henrietta clasped her hands. 'It sounds very mysterious.' She looked at Helen. 'What is it?'

'I've got it all organised – and agreed officially. You're coming to live with me and Mother as soon as you're discharged from hospital.' After her chat with Dr Eris, she now had everything in place.

'Oh, my dearest Helen!' Henrietta was taken aback. 'Are you sure? Is that what you *really* want? And your mother? To have me come and live with you both?'

Helen smiled.

'Yes, Grandmother, it's what we want. What we *really* want,' she reassured. It was certainly what Helen wanted. She doubted her mother would be so keen, but she had no say in the matter. If she didn't like it, she could always go and live at the Grand permanently, which, come to think of it, might not be such a bad idea.

As Helen helped Henrietta out of the car, she could see her grandmother's face was alive with excitement, despite the fact she was clearly exhausted after the day's jollities. As they walked to the entrance, though, her mood suddenly changed and her face clouded over.

'But ...' she hesitated '... are you're sure I'll be *allowed* to?'

'Yes, you're *allowed* to,' Helen said, her voice steely. 'No one can or will stop you.'

She'd made damn sure of that.

*

As Helen drove back to the Christmas Extravaganza, her mind wandered to thoughts of her grandfather. It angered her that her grandmother still felt the pull of his leash. Her concerns about being 'allowed' were evidence of that.

Helen knew she had won a minor victory over her grandfather in forcing his hand over Henrietta's release from the asylum – and how much he would hate this, even though Henrietta was to continue living under a false identity.

She also knew, though, that a good part of her grandfather's ire would be because his failure to get rid of Henrietta meant it would not be possible for him to do what he really wanted to do – wreak revenge on all those he perceived had done him an injustice. And Helen knew it would not be just Pearl and Bel who would be the focus of his vitriol, but all those they loved and cared for.

Helen also realised that there was another reason for her grandfather's desire for revenge – a far more worrying and perverse reason – and that was because he loved nothing more than to inflict pain on others. He had been doing it all his life – and he was not going to stop now simply because he was old. He was a sadist in the true meaning of the word.

Helen may well have trounced her grandfather on this occasion, and his hands might be tied – for now – but he would not take this defeat lying down. As well as being a cold-hearted, evil man, Charles Havelock lived for the thrill of a good fight. And he didn't give a fig if that fight was with his own flesh and blood. Her grandfather was not one to be beaten. He would be plotting and planning – of that she was sure.

She would have to be vigilant.

*

Back at the Christmas Extravaganza, the tables had been moved aside to create a makeshift dance hall. Seeing her father and Gloria, Helen headed over. She saw John and waved, but he didn't see her. He was looking rather preoccupied and was making his way over to Dr Eris.

'Everything all right?' Gloria asked.

'Yes, yes,' Helen said, sitting down. 'Really good, actually. I've just told Grandmama I've got the green light for her to come and live with me – and Mother, too, of course.'

'That's great news.' Gloria turned to Jack, who nodded.

'Aye, that's brilliant. And I'd have thought a lot safer for Henrietta,' he added sagely.

'Definitely,' Helen agreed. It had been one of her primary concerns. Who knew what else her grandfather might try?

'Dr Eris has agreed to sign the discharge papers. She said she'd have them all ready for me tomorrow and I just need to add the date when Grandmama's well enough to leave the Royal and ready to come home.'

'I'm pleased for yer,' Gloria said, taking her hand and squeezing it.

They were quiet for a moment. Helen watched as Dr Parker and Dr Eris walked out of the canteen together.

'It seems like yer 'n Dr Eris are getting on better?' Gloria asked.

'We are,' Helen agreed. 'We had a good chat the other day. I told her how thankful I was to her for going against Grandfather's orders. She was risking her job. Her career.' Helen laughed. 'She actually wanted to make sure I wouldn't let on what she'd done. Honestly, as if I'd drop her in it after she helped save Grandmother's life.'

Gloria shook her head. 'She obviously doesn't know yer.'

'I also told her that I had a proposition to make,' Helen said.

Gloria looked at her. 'A proposition?'

'I said that if she gave me Henrietta's original admissions form,' Helen explained, 'then I could get Henrietta discharged from the asylum for good and then Dr Eris wouldn't have to keep feeding her sugar pills and risk being found out and having her career cut short. Grandfather would be removed from her life.'

'She obviously agreed,' Gloria said, 'which surprises me as surely that means she's handed over the document she's been using to blackmail yer with – to keep yer away from John. That document was her bargaining chip, wasn't it? Proof of Henrietta's true identity?'

Helen laughed again. A little bitterly. 'She might have done right by Grandmama, but she's still on a mission to get John down the aisle by hook or by crook. There's no way she'll ever risk letting me get in the way.' Helen raised her eyebrows. 'I had to promise to give the form back to her.'

'And have yer?' Gloria asked.

'Of course, I am a woman of my word.'

Gloria looked at Helen. She could see her heartache.

Feeling the need for a cigarette, Helen looked in her handbag, but there weren't any.

'I won't be a minute,' she said, standing up. 'I've left my cigarettes in the car. I'll be back.'

Manoeuvring herself around the table and across the dance floor, Helen left the party.

Taking her time as she walked down the various corridors to the main entrance, her mind wandered to John and all the times she had walked this way to meet him in the canteen, to drink tea and eat iced buns. It still surprised her how much she simply enjoyed being in his company. She never got bored. Never got fidgety. Never wanted to leave.

She sighed. Perhaps there was still hope. John might end his relationship with Claire. It wasn't beyond the realms

413

of possibility. They had been courting for some time now and there had not been the whisper of an engagement, even though it must be clear to John that there was nothing Claire would like more.

When she reached the reception area, Helen looked over at the new receptionist. Even her predecessor, Denise, had managed to bag herself a husband, by all accounts. John had told her she'd gone out with one of the younger doctors from the Royal and ended up falling for his widowed father. Sometimes, she mused, it seemed that life liked to throw the occasional curve ball. The odds might be against her and John at the moment, but you never knew – that could change in the blink of an eye.

Helen opened the main door and stepped out into the dark, cold, but also very beautiful evening. The snow had continued to fall and the vast grounds of the hospital were now covered in a sheer white blanket of virgin snow. The sight of it caught her breath and she stood for a moment, enjoying the view and the stillness.

She was just about to make her way down the stone steps to her car when in her peripheral vision she caught movement. She looked to her right, where she knew there was a bench. One on which in warmer weather she had often sat with John and chatted.

She could just about make out two figures in the dark. A man and a woman. At first, she thought it must be a courting couple. Perhaps a wounded soldier and one of the pretty young nurses. But as her eyes adjusted to the darkness, she realised there was something familiar about the two figures.

Standing as still as a statue, she continued to look. Suddenly feeling a little voyeuristic, she forced herself to look away. But before she did so, the man stood up. And as he did, her heart sank.

It was John.

He was standing up and doing that thing with his hair – raking it back with his fingers to keep it from flopping forward.

Unsure whether to continue down the steps to the car or turn and go back into the foyer, she ended up staying glued to the spot.

She watched, her eyes fixed on John as he went down on one knee.

At first, Helen thought he'd dropped something.

But of course, he hadn't.

He was proposing to Claire.

Helen couldn't help but look. After a few moments, Claire, who was still seated on the bench, leant forward and kissed him

There was no need to second-guess her answer.

Finally, Helen managed to break the spell of inertia.

Turning, she stepped back on tiptoes, suddenly terrified of being seen, of feeling that she was snooping on them. *Of them seeing the devastation on her face.*

Quietly, she pushed open the door and slipped back into the main hall.

From there she made her way straight to the Ladies, where she stayed for a while, allowing herself to give free rein to her heartbreak.

Chapter Fifty-Three

'Claire Anna Eris ...' Dr Parker was looking up at the woman he had decided was going to be his wife. His life-long partner. The mother of his children, God willing. He felt a strange feeling of euphoria mixed with fear – followed by a flash of doubt.

Was he doing the right thing?

He pushed the thought from his mind. He was on his knee now, goddamnit. A bit late to be having second thoughts. It was last-minute jitters. *Ignore.*

'Would you do me the honour of becoming my wife?' *There, he had said the words. No going back.*

He caught movement to his right. He turned his head a fraction. *Was that Helen?*

'Oh, John Anthony Parker ...'

Dr Parker heard the words, saw the look on Dr Eris's face.

'... I'd be *honoured* to be your wife.'

Dr Parker took a quick look to his right. *Whoever it was had gone.*

Suddenly, he felt Dr Eris's hands on his face and then her lips on his mouth.

He'd done it. His fate was sealed. He was going to marry Claire.

*

Looking at John as he brushed his hair back, something he did when he was nervous, Dr Eris held her breath. *This was it. This was the moment she had been waiting for.*

Watching the man she loved – the man she now truly did love – drop down to his knee, Dr Eris felt overwhelmed with happiness.

Finally, John was proposing.

Finally, she was going to be married – a 'Mrs', not doomed to be a 'Miss' her whole life, a spinster, an old maid.

Finally, she was being taken off the shelf.

Finally, she would be able to show her ex that he'd done her a favour. She had risen up from the embarrassment of being jilted. And what's more, she had done better. Much better.

She had worked hard for this moment. Very hard indeed. All that plotting and planning at the beginning when she had first started working at the asylum and had met John. It hadn't been love at first sight – more a case of *This is the man I am going to marry*. John was perfect. Ticked all the boxes. Good-looking, well off, a professional man, unmarried, unattached. She should have guessed, though, that there would be someone else on the sidelines wanting to take what she wanted.

Well, Helen hadn't succeeded.

She'd put paid to that.

*

It was only later that Dr Parker realised the word 'love' had not once been uttered during his proposal to Claire – nor when she had accepted him as her future husband.

Chapter Fifty-Four

Helen stayed in the toilets for a good ten minutes before she felt able to face the world. The flicker of hope she had felt earlier – that her love for John might somehow be possible – had been well and truly snuffed out. John would never be hers. She had to accept it and move on with her life. She was in her mid-twenties. Most women of her age and 'standing', as her dear mother would put it, were married. Most of them had already started having their families.

She walked back down the corridor. It seemed as if the frustration she felt, knowing that John loved her and that she could never tell him she loved him too, might send her mad.

As she walked back into the hall, she seemed to see couples everywhere. Happy couples. Carefree. In love. Dorothy and Bobby were dancing close together, their chemistry plain to see. Then there was Angie and Quentin, complete opposites yet perfectly matched, enjoying the slow waltz. Hannah and Olly could be mistaken for professional ballroom dancers, Rina was with her 'admirer', Harvey, Martha was with the Salvation Army tuba player, and Iris and Audrey were with two of the French freedom fighters. A nurse, dancing with a tall soldier who had a bandaged head and was wearing what looked like one of the suits Kate had brought, was smiling up at her patient. Helen could see the love in her look – and that her love was very much reciprocated.

Walking over to Jack and Gloria, Helen saw they were chatting to a couple of younger soldiers. John had told her that some of his 'new recruits' were very young, but these lads seemed more like boys than men. She dodged a couple of soldiers dancing together, laughing and acting the clown, and another soldier who was being spun around by his mate in his wheelchair, a glass of punch spilling onto his dressing gown as his more able-bodied partner got a little carried away.

She was just a few yards from reaching her father and Gloria when she heard her name being called. She looked round to see Matthew. Dahlia was behind him, raising her hand to tap him on the shoulder, but it was too late, he had spotted Helen and had started striding towards her. Dahlia looked crestfallen.

'Thank goodness for that!' Matthew exclaimed on reaching Helen. 'I was starting to panic that you'd left without saying goodbye.'

Helen forced a smile as he stood looking at her.

'May I have the pleasure of a dance, Miss Crawford?' He bowed slightly, his eyes sparkling with a hint of roguishness, as they always did.

'You may,' Helen said, resignedly.

She stepped towards him.

They waited a moment for the next song to start.

There was a crackle as the needle was placed on the new record. Then came the resonant voice of Judy Garland as she started singing 'Have Yourself a Merry Little Christmas'. The song had been a smash hit, but every time Helen heard it played, it made her feel sad. She felt Matthew's hands go around her waist as he gently pulled her close. She rested her hand on his shoulder and held his hand with her other one. His touch, she thought, was surprisingly gentle.

As the song played, they danced slowly. A meandering waltz. Helen could feel Matthew pull her closer as they turned. She closed her eyes and saw John's face. She didn't push the image away, but allowed herself to be deceived. Allowed herself to believe that it was John holding her – John's breath on her neck. She lifted her head slightly and could feel warm lips brush her own. They were John's lips. And so, she allowed herself to be kissed. Just briefly. Gently. Because it was John. *It really was John.*

Helen rested her head on Matthew's shoulder.

She listened to the lyrics.

And as she listened and danced, she thought of John and a solitary tear escaped from the corner of her eye and slowly trickled down the side of her face.

Chapter Fifty-Five

There was a break of a few seconds as the record was changed and then the unmistakable sound of Bing Crosby singing 'White Christmas' rang out, bringing even more people onto the floor. The back-to-back slow songs were a sign that the Christmas Extravaganza was drawing to a close. Quentin continued to hold Angie tight as they danced. The song was one of Angie's favourites.

The time had come.

'It's been the best Christmas Day ever, hasn't it?' Angie's voice was low and a little tired, but she sounded happy and contented. The extravaganza had been a huge success. Much more than she or Dorothy or any of the women could have wished for or imagined.

'It will be,' Quentin said.

'What do you mean, "It will be"?' Angie looked at him with a puzzled expression.

'I want to ask you something,' Quentin said. 'And then it will be. Or I hope it will be.'

He slowly stopped dancing and looked at Angie. Taking hold of her hand, he pulled her to a quieter, darker area of the dance floor.

Putting his hand in his pocket, he panicked. *Damn it! He'd been checking it was there obsessively all day.* He had purposely taken the ring out of the little red leather box as he wanted to put it on Angie's finger himself. He breathed a huge sigh of relief when he felt the slightly jagged edge of the diamond.

Angie was looking at Quentin, thinking he had gone quite white.

'Are you all right?' she asked.

'I'm fine,' Quentin said. 'I don't think I've ever felt better in my entire life.' His beaming smile showed the veracity of his words.

'Although I'm a little nervous,' he added.

As he went to pull the ring out of his pocket, he did so a little too quickly – at the exact moment the nurse and the soldier with the bandaged head, who had been chatting as they danced and not watching where they were going, bumped into him.

The slight collision caused Quentin to stumble forward.

As he did so, his arm went out to steady himself and he accidentally tossed the ring up into the air.

Angie put her arms out to save Quentin from toppling over, but she was looking up in the air, mesmerised by the glint of the ring.

Of the *diamond* ring.

Quentin was going to propose!

Of course he was. Why hadn't she cottoned on earlier? All those trips to the toilets. And he'd seemed uncomfortable in his jacket. Had kept fidgeting. Checking his breast pocket.

For the ring.

The diamond *ring.*

The diamond ring now flying up into the air.

All these thoughts raced through Angie's head as she watched the ring drop down, giving in to gravity and hitting the dance floor.

Fear and panic struck.

Someone might stand on it.

'Where's it gone?' Angie asked, alarmed.

She stood with Quentin, staring at the ground, desperately looking for it.

'There!' Angie shouted out as she spotted the ring on the floor.

Before Quentin had a chance to get it, Angie leapt forward. Seeing a couple about to waltz right over it, she splayed her arms out to stop them going near it, then ducked down and snatched it up.

'Oh, thank goodness for that!' She held the ring out and beamed at Quentin. 'I thought it was gonna get crushed.'

Quentin looked at Angie, standing there holding the ring out to him.

'Don't worry,' he reassured her, 'diamonds are pretty sturdy.'

This proposal was not going the way it should.

He looked at the diamond, unsure what to do next. Should he take the ring off her? Or just drop down on one knee? *God, he wished he'd planned this better.*

Suddenly, he became aware that people had stopped dancing and were looking at them both. Angie, though, seemed oblivious. Her attention focused on the ring.

'Angie, I wanted to tell you how much I love you,' Quentin said.

Angie was still staring at the ring. *It couldn't be? Could it? It looked like the ring, but, no, really, it couldn't be. They had sold it to the jeweller's on Blandford Street.*

She looked up at Quentin.

'I think this is the same ring that Dor sold,' she said, incredulous.

'It is,' Quentin said. 'It *is* the same ring.'

Angie looked at Quentin, then to the ring and then back to Quentin.

'Oh. My. God,' Angie said, realising she sounded like Dorothy and not caring.

'Did yer buy it for me?' she asked, still incredulous.

'I did,' Quentin said.

'I *love* this ring,' she said. 'How did yer knar I loved it so much?'

Quentin raised his eyebrows.

'Of course! *Dorothy!*' Angie exclaimed.

'White Christmas' had now ended and 'Only Forever' had started to play.

'Are yer giving it to me?' Angie said, holding out the ring.

Quentin nodded.

'Really?'

'Really,' Quentin said. He hesitated. 'But there's a condition attached.'

Angie made a puzzled expression.

'What's that?'

Now was the time.

The whole dance floor had come to a standstill. Everyone was quiet. Only Bing Crosby's velvet voice filled the air.

'The condition being …' Quentin said '… that you agree to be my wife.'

What had happened to dropping down on his knee and asking her properly? This was not how he'd envisaged his proposal. Not in the slightest.

He watched as his words sank in and Angie's face was illuminated by a wide smile.

She flung her arms around him and hugged him.

'Ah, Quentin! I'd love to be your wife. Love. Love. *Love* to be your wife.' She kissed him full on the lips.

As soon as she did so, the canteen erupted into cheers and whistles and shouts.

Quentin kissed her back, feeling like the happiest man on the planet. *Now this really was the best Christmas ever.* It might have ended up the most disastrous proposal of marriage ever, but he couldn't have asked for a more perfect response. The woman he loved more than anyone else in the world loved him back with equal fervour. Angie was as excited about being his wife as he was about being her husband.

He'd found his perfect match. His own rough diamond. And like the song that was playing said, he knew their love was for ever.

'Oh. My. God!' Dorothy declared as soon as everyone had stopped clapping and congratulating Angie and Quentin.

Dorothy was ecstatic. She had been watching and waiting intently, knowing that the moment was imminent. Seeing them on the dance floor, she had taken over the music and was pleased as punch that she had managed to put on 'Only Forever' just as Quentin had finally decided to propose.

'You're going to get married!' She grabbed her best friend and hugged her hard.

Angie hugged her back equally hard.

'Eee, Dor, look at the ring!' She held her hand out. 'Yer dinnit mind, do yer?'

Dorothy laughed. 'Of course I *dinnit mind*!'

'It was actually Dorothy's idea,' Quentin admitted. 'She rang me the day you'd been to the jeweller's and sold it.'

'Really?' Angie said. 'Did yer really, Dor?'

'I did. Really,' Dorothy laughed. 'Quentin rang Mr Golding the next day and told him that he wanted to buy the ring and to keep it for him.'

'Ahh, Dor, thank you!' Angie hugged her friend again.

'I'm just glad you said yes.' Dorothy threw a guilty look at Quentin, who had just been handed a cigar by one of the soldiers. 'I thought I might have gone on too much about marriage being all about—'

'*Baking and breeding,*' Angie and Quentin said in unison, chuckling.

Dorothy laughed. Of course, she should have guessed Angie would have told Quentin. They told each other everything.

Feeling herself being gently nudged to the side, she looked to see the rest of the women waiting to congratulate their friend.

'Move over, Dor, yer can't hog her all to yerself,' Gloria said, opening her arms and embracing her workmate.

Rosie, Polly, Martha, Hannah and Georgina followed suit.

'Congratulations, Angie!' They all beamed.

Dorothy looked over their heads to see Olly and Adam, the tuba player, waiting a few yards away. 'All this proposing malarkey might be contagious.'

Martha shook her head in exasperation. It was not the first time this evening that Dorothy had jibed her about her new friend.

Hannah laughed. 'Olly has to complete a full cycle of the Jewish calendar before he can convert.'

Everyone looked at Gloria.

'Looks like you'll be next on the list, then,' said Dorothy. '*Congratulations!*'

They all looked around, having recognised Helen's voice.

'Wishing you both all the happiness and love in the world!' Helen put her arms out and gave Angie a kiss on the cheek. She then shook Quentin's hand.

'Ah, thanks, Helen,' Angie said. Her face was a picture of pure joy. 'That's lovely.'

'Happiness and love!' Dorothy said.

'*Happiness and love!*' the women chorused, all beaming.

*

Quentin's proposal brought the Christmas Extravaganza to a natural and very happy end – an ending made all the more special when one of the wounded soldiers hobbled to the front of the makeshift dance hall on crutches and shouted out for quiet. His tone was commanding. Everyone obeyed.

'Bet you he was a sergeant major,' Dorothy whispered to Bobby.

Everyone's attention was focused on the smartly dressed army officer. Even the left trouser leg, which was now redundant, had been neatly pinned back.

Bobby stood behind Dorothy and put his arms around her waist as they waited to listen to what the officer had to say.

'On behalf of all the soldiers in the Ryhope Emergency Hospital, I want to convey a huge "Thank you" to the organisers of this Christmas Extravaganza. I don't know the names of all those who have made this happen, and I wouldn't want to name anyone, in case I left someone out – but I do know that the idea and most of the hard work and fundraising has been done by a group of women welders from Thompson's shipyard in town.'

There was some muttering.

He grinned.

'Yes, you heard right. A group of *women* welders!'

Dorothy, Angie, Rosie, Gloria, Polly, Hannah and Martha all looked at each other and beamed with pride.

'I can say hand on heart that there isn't a soldier here that has not been taken aback by the time and effort that has gone into making this day so special. You have all sacrificed most of your own Christmas Day to be with us. I can't say how much that alone means to us, never mind all the presents, food – *and entertainment*.'

There were a few whistles at this point.

Dorothy looked over at Dahlia and Marie-Anne, who were smiling and lapping up the last bit of attention.

'So, thank you!' the sergeant major said, resting his elbows on the top of his crutches and putting his hands together. 'Thank you! And wishing you all a Merry Christmas and a very Happy New Year!'

The canteen was filled with the sound of shouts and whistles and clapping.

The women looked at each other. They were all beaming from ear to ear. Their eyes shining with emotion.

This Christmas really had been the *best ever*.

Chapter Fifty-Six

As everyone headed to the truck, which was waiting at the front of the hospital, ready to take everyone back home, Bobby pulled Dorothy aside when they reached the huge Christmas tree in the foyer.

'I never got to kiss you under the mistletoe,' he said.

Dorothy laughed. 'Not many people know this, but mistletoe is poisonous.'

Now it was Bobby's turn to chuckle. 'Only if you eat it and I have no intention of doing that.'

They both automatically thought of Henrietta.

'I'm so glad she's all right,' Dorothy said, suddenly feeling a little overwhelmed.

'I am too,' Bobby said.

Bobby gave Dorothy a slightly mischievous look and put his hand in the trouser pocket of his blue naval trousers.

Dorothy held her breath, unsure what Bobby was about to do.

She watched as he pulled out a little branch of mistletoe, which she could only presume he had pinched off the bundle hanging in the middle of the canteen.

She exhaled and smiled.

'There's only thing I want to do with mistletoe,' Bobby said, pulling her close. 'And that's use it as an excuse to kiss you.'

He looked at the woman he was sure he was going to love for the rest of his life.

'Well, you don't need an excuse for that,' Dorothy said, taking the mistletoe, turning slightly and laying it carefully on a branch of the Christmas tree.

'You can kiss me wherever and whenever you want,' she whispered into his good ear.

And so they kissed. And then kissed some more.

When they stopped, Bobby looked at Dorothy.

'What you did was amazing. You know that, don't you?'

Unusually, Dorothy was at a loss for words.

Bobby laughed. 'For someone who craves attention, you can also be very uncomfortable with it.'

Dorothy smiled.

'And to think it all came about because of Toby's ring.' Bobby eyed Dorothy, watching her reaction. 'If it hadn't been for his ring, this would never have happened.'

Dorothy nodded. 'You're right. I wouldn't have been stressing over what to do with it and then Helen wouldn't have come up with the idea.'

Bobby paused. There was something he wanted to ask her that had been on his mind.

'So, you didn't mind Quentin buying Toby's engagement ring? I'd have thought you wouldn't want reminding of him.'

Dorothy laughed. 'I don't *want* reminding of him, but I don't mind being reminded of him either. It's not as if Toby was awful in any way. He just wasn't "The One".'

Bobby took a deep breath.

'I want to ask you a question,' he said in earnest.

He could feel Dorothy stiffen a little in his embrace.

'Much as I'd like to –' Bobby was watching Dorothy's expression intently '– I'm *not* going to ask you to marry me.'

He could see the relief on her face and feel her body relax in his arms.

'And much as I'd love to ask you to live in sin with me, I won't.' He gave Dorothy a cheeky look. 'Not yet anyway.'

Dorothy raised an eyebrow, signalling that perhaps she might be open to such a request.

'But I do want to ask you one question. A question I think is equally important,' he said.

Dorothy looked at Bobby. He had gone unusually serious.

'You know I love you, don't you?' he asked.

Dorothy nodded. He had told her many times and each time she had known the words had been spoken from his heart.

'And I believe you also love me?'

'I do,' Dorothy said. She, too, had told him that she loved him in a way that left no room for doubt.

'I want to ask you ...'

He hesitated. Then took a deep breath.

'Do you believe that I am "The One" for you?' he asked, looking into Dorothy's blue eyes.

He saw the answer before she said the words.

'I do,' Dorothy said, her eyes glistening with love and passion.

'I really do.'

The women welders waited in the truck and looked as Dorothy and Bobby made their way down the main steps and sauntered towards them with their arms wrapped around each other.

No one needed to say anything, but they smiled at each other. Dorothy had finally found the man who was right for her and organised a Christmas she'd always dreamed of.

Their friend had finally got her own happy ending.

Welcome to

Penny Street

where your favourite authors and stories live.

Meet casts of characters you'll never forget,
create memories you'll treasure forever,
and discover places that will stay with
you long after the last page.

Turn the page to step into the home of

Nancy Revell

and discover more about

The Shipyard Girls...

Dear Reader,

When I finished writing *Shipyard Girls under the Mistletoe* I realised how much of the drama and plot are driven by different types of love. There's the romantic love of Dorothy and Bobby, the caring love Helen feels for her grandmother and, indeed, which Henrietta also has for her granddaughter, and the friendship which all the women have for one another, and which is particularly prominent whenever one of them finds themselves in difficult times.

So this Christmas, dear Reader, I wish you, above all else – love, love and more love.

Surely that's something impossible to overindulge in!

Merry Christmas!

With Love,

Nancy x

Historical notes

I love this image, which was published in the *Sunderland Echo* and was taken during the Second World War, of a group of real women shipyard workers enjoying their packed lunches – just like Rosie, Gloria, Polly, Dorothy, Angie, Martha and Hannah. I love the smiles on their faces!

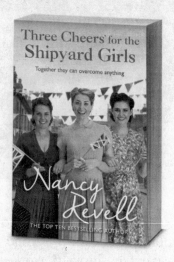

Shipyard Girls
Under the Mistletoe

Nancy Revell is the author of the Shipyard Girls series, which is set in the north-east of England during World War II.

She is a former journalist who worked for all the national newspapers, providing them with hard-hitting news stories and in-depth features. Nancy also wrote amazing and inspirational true life stories for just about every woman's magazine in the country.

When she first started writing the Shipyard Girls series, Nancy relocated back to her hometown of Sunderland, Tyne and Wear, along with her husband, Paul, and their English bull mastiff, Rosie. They lived just a short walk away from the beautiful award-winning beaches of Roker and Seaburn, within a mile of where the books are set.

The subject is particularly close to Nancy's heart as she comes from a long line of shipbuilders, who were well known in the area.

Why YOU love Nancy Revell

'Nancy, your books are so good. I could cry when I finish them. I read a bit each night to savour it like a box of chocolates. I can't wait for the next one!'

'I absolutely love these books, I feel like all the wonderful characters are like family'

'Once again an astounding follow-on book in the Shipyard Girls series'

'Nancy Revell brings the characters to life and you get totally engrossed in their lives and hope things turn out well for them. Have read all of the books now and can't wait for the next one. Please keep them coming'

'The Shipyard Girls is one of my favourite series of all time'

'How wonderful to read about everyday women, young, middle-aged, married or single, all coming to work in a man's world. The pride and courage they all showed in taking over from the men who had gone to war – a debt of gratitude is very much owed'

'Yet again another brilliant book in the Shipyard Girls series – I could not put down! This is another triumph for Nancy Revell and a recommended five star read'

'It's a gripping, heart-breaking and poignant storyline. I couldn't put it down and yet didn't want it to end'

'This series of books just gets better and better; a fantastic group of girls who could be any one of us if we were alive in the war. Could only give 5 STARS but worth many more'

'What a brilliant read – the story is so good it keeps you wanting more . . . I fell in love with the girls; their stories, laughter, tears and so much more'

'When you thought it couldn't get any better, it does. An amazing read, I couldn't put this book down.'

'I absolutely love these books . . . Nancy Revell manages to pull you in from the first page and you can't wait to finish each book but at the same time don't want it to end. I can't wait to see what all these lovely people are up to next'